Award-winning author **Jennifer Faye** pens fun, heart-warming, contemporary romances, filled with rugged cowboys, sexy billionaires and enchanting royalty. Internationally published, with books translated into nine languages, she is a two-times winner of the *RT Book Reviews Reviewers'* Choice Award. She has also won the CataRomance Reviewers' Choice Award, been named a TOP PICK author, and has been nominated for numerous other awards.

Joanna Sims is proud to pen contemporary romance for Mills & Boon. Joanna's series, The Brands of Montana, features hardworking characters with hometown values. You are cordially invited to join the Brands of Montana as they wrangle their own happily-ever-afters. And, as always, Joanna welcomes you to visit her at her website, joannasimsromance.com

Discover more at millsandboon.co.uk

WEARING THE GREEK MILLIONAIRE'S RING

JENNIFER FAYE

THE MAVERICK'S WEDDING WAGER

JOANNA SIMS

MILLS & BOON

First Published in Great Britain 2019
by Mills & Boon, an imprint of HarperCollinsPublishers,
1 London Bridge Street, London, SE1 9GF

Wearing the Greek Millionaire's Ring © 2019 Jennifer F. Stroka
The Maverick's Wedding Wager © 2019 Harlequin Books S.A.

Special thanks and acknowledgement are given
to Joanna Sims for her contribution to the
Montana Mavericks: Six Brides for Six Brothers continuity.

ISBN: 978-0-263-27259-8

0919

MIX
Paper from
responsible sources
FSC® C007454

This book is produced from independently certified FSC™
paper to ensure responsible forest management.

For more information visit: www.harpercollins.co.uk/green

Printed and bound in Spain
by CPI, Barcelona

WEARING THE GREEK MILLIONAIRE'S RING

JENNIFER FAYE

PROLOGUE

May... Infinity Island, Greece

SOMETIMES SHE FELT as though there was nowhere she truly belonged.

And sometimes she enjoyed the freedom that allowed her.

Other times, like now, Stasia Marinakos wanted a clear path in life.

She'd had one not so long ago. Suddenly, that life had been brutally wrenched from her grasp. Though with each passing day, she was learning to live with the loss, allowing herself to smile again and forcing herself to remember that she was still living and breathing.

For the almost two years since her husband passed, Stasia had been focused on fulfilling his last wishes, tending to his estate and piecing together the broken pieces of her heart. But now that was complete. All of his wishes had been fulfilled, except one.

As she sat at one of the tables at the Hideaway Café, her gaze moved across the table to her brother. She knew if she opened up to him he wouldn't understand. He would try to tell her what to do with her life and she didn't want that. She needed to find her own answers.

Xander thought she should be cautious with her money and with her life. He wasn't anxious for her to move on, which she found interesting considering he hadn't liked her husband in the beginning. In fact, Xander had vehemently disapproved of him until just before Lukos found out that he was sick—

Stasia halted her thoughts. She didn't want to go down that road. She needed to focus on the here and now. It was the only thing she could control.

"What am I supposed to do with this?"

Stasia held up a cruise ship ticket while sending her big brother a puzzled look. She didn't have time for a vacation. Now that she was on her own, with no husband and no other family besides Xander, who now had a wife and baby, she needed to pull herself together and carve out a life for herself. That had to be her priority. As it was, she'd put it off for too long.

"Use the ticket and go on vacation." Xander frowned at her as though he was concerned about her.

She shoved the ticket back across the table. "I don't have time—"

"Sure you do." Xander wasn't a man used to hearing the word *no*. "Now that our real-estate deal fell apart—of which I am sorry—you have all the time in the world." He sent her a reassuring smile. "And don't worry. By the time you get back, I'll have a new deal lined up that we can go in on together."

How did she tell him that she no longer wanted to be involved in a deal without hurting his feelings? After all, she was the one who had come up with the idea of them working together in the first place. He'd initially been resistant to the idea, but she'd kept after him until he'd finally given in.

Of course, she'd had some help getting him to change his mind—Roberto Carrass, her brother's best friend, who'd recently been elevated to the role of business partner. He'd sided with her, convincing Xander to let her be a part of the business.

Stasia pulled her thoughts back to the relevant subject. "I don't want you going into a deal because you think it'll suit me." When he didn't respond, she raised her voice just enough to gain his attention. "Xander, you aren't listening to me."

"Sure I am. I always listen to you."

She blatantly rolled her eyes. Her brother barely heard a word she said and they both knew it. "Please—"

"Okay. Maybe I get distracted sometimes."

She arched a brow. "Isn't that how you ended up with your new family?"

"Ah, but see how well that worked out." He sent her a smile that lit up his whole face. "I saw a good thing and I went for it."

She couldn't help but tease him. "Is that the story you're going with?"

He shrugged and sent her a guilty smile. "It's how I like to remember it."

Stasia nodded. She didn't mind him rewriting the rocky start of his romance with his now wife, Lea. In fact, Stasia found it endearing. Who knew her brother could be romantic? She never would have guessed it till now.

And as much as she wanted to confide in her big brother about her quandary, she couldn't find the words. She'd been visiting Infinity Island for the past few weeks, reconnecting with her brother and learning more about her sister-in-law, Lea, while playing with the baby, Lily. Stasia had volunteered to babysit while Xander and Lea were working. And though Stasia's days were now full, she still felt as though she was missing something.

As appealing as it was to remain here on this idyllic island with its clear blue water, gentle sea breeze and charming village, she couldn't hijack her brother's life. She'd been here long enough. It was time to head home to Athens.

"Let's go for a walk." Stasia took the last sip of her iced coffee.

Xander scooped up the cruise ticket and then got to his feet. "Lead the way."

She didn't have any particular destination in mind. She just needed to move. "I've never seen you happier."

"I am happy," he said. "My life is complete. And… and I feel guilty."

Stasia stopped walking and faced her brother. "Why should you feel guilty?"

"Because when you were so happy with Lukos, I was being foolish and getting in your way. And by the time I got my head on straight about your husband, he was… well…"

"He was dying." She never thought she'd be able to say those words without breaking into a fit of tears. The memory of losing Lukos far too soon still hurt. She supposed it always would, but she was learning to live with the loss. "It's okay, Xander. You can say he died. I won't break into a million messy pieces."

The look in his eyes said he wasn't sure he believed her. "I miss him too. You do know we got to be good friends at the end."

"I know." The friendship between her husband and brother might not have happened as soon as she would have liked, but she was grateful they'd worked out their differences. She wasn't sure how she'd have made it through that dark period without her brother by her side. "Lukos thought of you like a brother when he died."

Xander reached out and gave her a great big hug. Lukos had made her promise that, no matter what happened in life, she wouldn't let anything come between her and Xander. She'd made the promise. It hadn't been hard. She loved her brother and she always would. She couldn't imagine anything coming between them. He was stuck with his little sister for life.

Xander pulled back and placed the ticket in her hand. "This is your birthday gift. Please take it. I have it on good authority that you always wanted to take the cruise."

She'd only told one person about her desire to cruise around Greece, Montenegro, Croatia and Italy. It would be her trial run to see if she enjoyed voyages before booking something a little farther from home, say the Caribbean, or possibly something a bit cooler, like Norway.

"Lukos told you?" She said it matter-of-factly.

Xander nodded. "He was disappointed he never got to take you on a cruise."

Xander's words took the fight out of her. She'd forgotten all about the things she'd wanted to do before Lukos got sick. They somehow seemed so trivial after all that had happened. Maybe Lukos somehow knew she would feel that way and this was his way of propelling her forward.

And now there were no more excuses—no more reasons to cling so tightly to the past. She needed to fulfill her husband's final wish. She needed to look to the future and find her new path in life.

Her choice needed to be something meaningful. She needed a purpose, a compelling reason to get out of bed in the morning.

Her husband had done his best to watch out for her, leaving her enough money that, when combined with what she'd inherited from her family, it would keep her quite comfortable for the rest of her life. But she couldn't wake up in the morning, enjoy her coffee and drift through the rest of the day. That wasn't how she'd been raised.

She needed a reason to get excited. She needed a goal to strive for and even some setbacks to overcome to remind her of life's many blessings. But what she didn't

need was being patted on her head and dismissed because
people thought she wasn't up to the challenge.

"Okay. I'll go." She forced a smile to her lips. All the
talk of Lukos had deflated her mood. He should be going
with her on this adventure, but she knew he would always
be in her heart—it just wasn't the same.

"And when you get back, I'll have a business deal or
two for you to look over. If one of them isn't to your liking, I'll keep looking until we find the right deal for you."

She didn't say anything about her waning interest in
the real-estate market and wanting to strike out on her
own. But she wanted a firm plan before she said anything to anyone.

"Thank you." She hugged him again.

This cruise was going to be a turning point in her life.
She'd take her laptop with her and make it a working trip.
When she got back, she'd have her life all planned out.

DAY ONE

Two weeks later... Athens, Greece

"DID YOU MAKE IT to the ship in time?"

"Why would I be late?" Stasia stood on the busy deck. She pressed the phone to her ear, straining to hear her brother over the voices of dozens of excited travelers.

Xander sighed. "Must you answer a question with a question?"

A smile pulled at Stasia's lips. "Why must you act like the overprotective brother?"

She knew the answer. Xander felt guilty because he was happily married with a baby girl, not to mention living on a private Greek island. And she, well, she was alone now.

Not so long ago, she'd been happy when her college sweetheart had become her husband. Back then, they'd had dreams—lots of dreams. However, it was all cut short when a stomachache turned out to be so much worse than the flu.

From that point, their dreams radically changed. Instead of wishing for exotic vacations, they started wishing for just one more Christmas, one more birthday, one more month, one more day. Stasia halted her thoughts. She pushed away the heart-wrenching memories before she drowned in them.

She'd been on her own for nearly two years now. There had been a lot of tears shed over that time—her first Christmas alone, her first anniversary alone. And when filling out forms, her hand would hover over the *married* box before ultimately checking *single*. It hadn't been easy learning to be a widow—not at all.

Eventually she'd been able to donate Lukos's clothes, including his tailored suits and silk ties. It took a long time until she could bear to slip off her wedding ring and place it with Lukos's in the back of her jewelry box.

Her thumb nervously rubbed over her ring finger. It was something she'd started to do when she'd waited in the doctors' offices and hospital waiting rooms. Feeling the smoothness of her wedding band and knowing the love behind it had somehow bolstered her strength to face the horrible diagnosis Lukos had been given.

She glanced down at her now bare finger.

She was on her own. Each step had taken time. Some steps were big and some were tiny. Each of them had pulled on her heartstrings.

"I…I worry about you." Xander's voice cut through her thoughts.

"I know you do." And she knew it wasn't easy for him to admit it. Xander had always held his feelings close to his chest. "And I appreciate it. But it's okay. I'm okay."

"So you're on the ship?"

She nodded, and then, realizing he couldn't see her, she said, "Yes, I am."

"Good. Now watch out for any smooth-talking men. Don't fall for their lines. Tell them to push off or else your big brother will take care of them—"

"Xander, I'm not in school anymore. I'm a grown woman. I can take care of myself."

Her brother sighed. "I know."

"But you worry."

"Is that a bad thing?"

"No." How could she reprimand him when she'd done something similar when he'd hooked up with Lea? Stasia had posed as a potential buyer of Infinity Island in order to find out if Lea was a gold digger. In the end, Stasia had learned that Lea had a heart of gold. "But you have to trust me. I can take care of myself."

"If you need anything, I'm only a phone call away."

And then a movement out of the corner of her eye caught her attention. It was a tall man with dark hair. Though she could only see the back of him, there was something familiar about the way he held himself and the way he moved with sure, steady strides.

She told herself she shouldn't stare even if it was from across the deck, but she couldn't turn away. Or maybe she was using this distraction to keep from thinking about what her brother was saying. Did Xander really think she was incapable of caring for herself?

She knew then and there that she had to prove to him— to herself—that she could stand firmly on her own two feet. She'd thought she'd been doing that ever since Lukos passed, but it seemed that wasn't so clear to everyone. She promised herself that by the time the cruise ended, she would have a firm life plan for herself.

In the beginning of this horrible nightmare, she'd had her doubts about facing life alone. But one day faded into two, and with each passing day, she'd somehow mustered up the strength and determination to put one foot in front of the other. And now nearly two years later, she was feeling strong and determined. She just needed a direction.

As Xander spoke of the bungalow he could build her on Infinity Island, her gaze focused on that tall, dark man across the way. He was busy speaking with a striking young woman. No doubt it was his girlfriend or wife.

And then the man turned. She was curious to see if his face was as handsome as she'd imagined it to be. And it was, but the surprise didn't end there. The breath caught in her throat.

It was Roberto.

Her heart stuttered. What was he doing here?

Xander had his hand in this. She was certain of it. Her brother couldn't even send her off on a cruise for a birthday gift without feeling the need to send along someone to keep an eye on her.

"What's Roberto doing here?"

"What?"

"Don't act like you don't know what I'm talking about." She was angry. This was too much. "I'm looking right at him."

"I bet he's probably flirting with some beautiful young woman."

"How did you know?"

"Because that's Roberto. He's a *love 'em and leave 'em* kind of guy. If any woman is foolish enough to think he'll commit himself to her, she'll just end up getting hurt. But as far as a friend, they don't come any better than him."

"Xander, I want to know what he's doing on this cruise."

Xander's voice was muffled as though he had his hand over the phone. "Okay. I'm coming." He spoke back into the phone. "Sorry, sis. I've got to go. Lea needs me."

"Xander?"

And with that, the phone went dead.

Stasia inwardly groaned in frustration. What had her brother done? Enough was enough. And she wasn't going to play his game, whatever it was.

This ship was big—big enough for her to avoid Roberto. Which was a shame because she'd always liked Roberto. Even when they were growing up, he'd been kind and thoughtful. And now as an adult, he was the most amazing eye candy. She hadn't known it was possible for a man to look that good in a suit.

But if he was here to babysit her, then she didn't have

time for him. Stasia turned her back to him and walked in the opposite direction. Wherever he was, she would not be.

This was the absolute last place in the world he wanted to be.

Why couldn't a work emergency have come up?

Ding.

Roberto Carrass checked his phone for the ninth time in less than five minutes. The emails were stacking up, each one more important than the last. He didn't have time for a vacation. There was work to be done.

His fingers moved fluidly over the face of his phone. He composed a response to his assistant about a pending acquisition.

Ding. Ding.

Now that he was a full partner with Xander, their business was taking off. There were no more delays, waiting on approvals. When he spotted a good deal, he could move on it—if he wasn't stuck on a two-week cruise with his big Greek family.

Roberto sighed, louder than he'd intended. His phone was not the best way to deal with emails. He really needed to go to his cabin and work on his laptop.

His grandmother elbowed him. "Would you put that contraption away?"

"Yaya, it's a cell phone." With great reluctance, he slipped it in his pocket. "And if you would quit being so stubborn, I would get you one. They aren't that hard to use."

She lifted her chin. "I already have a perfectly good phone at home. I don't need one when I'm out and about. Whatever people want can wait until I get home. Now stop frowning. We're here to have fun." His grandmother smiled brightly. It was so hard to believe she was about to have her eightieth birthday. Most of the time, she acted half her age or younger.

"I'm going to get myself a drink."

Yaya arched a penciled brow. "Don't hide in some corner. Or worse, go to your cabin to work. This is a vacation. Look at all these lovely ladies. I'm sure you'll find someone to spend your time with."

While wearing a forced smile, he inwardly groaned. He was in so much trouble. They'd just pulled out of the dock and they were to be at sea for two weeks—two weeks of matchmaking torture.

"Yaya, I'm fine. I don't need to find someone to spend time with."

His grandmother's gaze narrowed. "Roberto, is there something you haven't told me?"

"Yaya, I—" And then out of the corner of his eye, he thought he saw a young woman he recognized. "I need to go say hello to someone."

The worry lines on his grandmother's face eased. "Don't let me hold you up. I need to go check on your grandfather."

There was something in the tone of his grandmother's voice that caught his attention. "Is he feeling all right?"

His grandmother didn't say anything at first. "I shouldn't say anything."

"It's me. No matter how much he and I argue, I still care. Surely you know that."

"I wish things were different between you two." She sighed. "I don't know what is going on. He won't talk about it. Every time I bring it up, he tells me not to worry."

"But you're still worried?"

She nodded. "Maybe it's nothing."

"Don't worry." He gave her a brief hug. "I'm sure if it's serious, he'll talk to you about it."

"Maybe you could speak to him." Her hopeful gaze implored him.

Roberto gave a quick shake of his head. "I don't think so. It'll just lead to another argument—"

"You don't know that."

"I do. It doesn't matter the subject—eventually it leads back to me abandoning both the company and him. Then an argument ensues."

"Don't you think it's time you two make peace?"

"Tell him. Not me."

She sighed. "I just wish… Oh, never mind. Go mingle."

She didn't have to finish her thought. He knew what she wished—that he was still working with his grandfather. That there was peace in their family.

He leaned over and placed a kiss on his grandmother's cheek. "I'll see you later."

Yaya patted his arm and smiled before she headed off in the opposite direction.

As Roberto walked away, he couldn't stop thinking about his grandparents. They were getting on in years. Was his grandfather doing too much?

This was his grandfather. Obviously he was doing too much. And the look on his grandmother's face said she was more concerned than she let on. With his complicated relationship with his grandfather, he wasn't sure what he could do to help, but for his grandmother's sake, he'd give it some thought.

Roberto didn't waste any time making his way across the deck toward the open-air bar where he'd caught sight of someone who looked quite familiar. Still, the day was quite beautiful with a clear blue sky, warm sunshine and a gentle breeze. Even if he didn't catch up with someone he knew, he might grab a cool drink and find a quiet spot to return a phone call or two before they got too far out to sea and the connection became spotty. He'd been so busy helping Xander spin off a new arm of his real-estate empire, as well as relocating the headquarters to Infinity Island, that he'd forgotten what it was like to have free time. He could once again have a social life.

Roberto intended to stick with his bachelor status— even if some incorrectly labeled him a playboy. But he couldn't deny his preference for no-strings-attached flings. He didn't have a lot of them, but he wasn't exactly a hermit either.

His bachelor status didn't please his grandparents, who thought he was the age to settle down with a family. All his life there had been expectations set for him. It started back when he was barely out of diapers. He'd been enrolled in the most prestigious preschool. He had to excel at everything so he could attend the top boarding school. And then he was expected to graduate at the top of his class. As the only grandson, his grandparents had high expectations for him.

It was a lot of pressure to put on a kid. By high school, he resented his family's expectations. By college, he was interning at the family construction business. When nothing he did lived up to his grandfather's high standards, Roberto knew he needed to forge a different path—one of his own choosing. And that was what led him to join forces with a childhood friend in the real-estate business, much to his family's disappointment.

Having lost sight of the elusive woman, he moved to the bar and ordered a drink. While he waited, he glanced around once more. Maybe it was just wishful thinking that he'd recognized someone. Still, it had been a good excuse to get away from his grandmother.

He was on his way to an open table off to the side when he spotted her again. This time he was certain he knew her. It was Stasia Marinakos. No other woman carried herself quite like she did, with her slender shoulders pulled back, her head held high and a warm smile on her face. How she could smile after all that she'd been through was beyond him. But she hadn't lost her zest for life. And he applauded her.

"Stasia?" he called out. When she paused and looked around, he called out to her again.

At last, their gazes met. Her big brown eyes widened. He waved her over to join him at the empty table. It took her a moment or two to work her way through the crowd of people all eager to enjoy the morning sun.

"It's so good to see you." He gave her a brief hug.

Was it wrong that he wanted the hug to last a little longer? Of course it was. Stasia was his best friend's younger sister. And if that wasn't enough to discourage any interest, she was a grieving widow. Enough said.

He moved to pull out a chair for her. Once again, her eyes widened with surprise. Was getting her chair for her that unexpected? He mused over this as he returned to his own chair. He supposed that in all of the occasions that they'd spent time together over the years, he hadn't actually spent one-on-one time with her before. There had always been a group of people with them.

She frowned at him. "You don't have to act surprised to see me."

"But I am surprised."

She studied him for a moment. "My brother didn't set this up?" She motioned between them. "Being on the same cruise so you can babysit me?"

"If he did, he didn't mention it to me."

"Oh." She still looked perplexed. "He surprised me with the ticket. He said it was my birthday gift."

"It's your birthday?"

"Not yet. It's next week."

"We'll have to do something special."

"You mean more special than taking an extended cruise?" Her eyes twinkled with amusement.

"Maybe not. But we'll have to mark the occasion." And then he realized she might not be on the ship alone. After all, she'd been a widow for…what was it? Two years. Maybe she was moving on. "Are you sailing alone?"

"I am. How about you? Are you here with someone?"

He wondered if she'd noticed that the passenger list had an overwhelming number of young, beautiful women who appeared to be alone. "I'm not here with anyone. Not exactly."

Stasia arched a brow. "You came on this cruise alone?"

Roberto nodded and surprise flickered in her eyes.

Xander had warned him that he was getting a reputation of always having a beautiful woman on his arm. He'd thought Xander was just having some fun at his expense. Maybe Xander had been serious after all.

"You wouldn't believe that I just wanted to get away from the hustle and bustle of the office?"

She shook her head. "You're just like my brother. You both thrive on the chaotic energy of business. Without it, I think you'd both be bored. In fact, I know it." Her beautiful eyes studied him as though if she stared long enough, layers would peel back, and she'd be able to see what truly made him tick.

Roberto glanced away. Under her gaze, he felt exposed and vulnerable. That was a first for him. He'd sat through a lot of tense meetings with some of the toughest businessmen. They'd all sized each other up for the other's weakness, but none had made him feel like an open book.

He cleared his throat. "Actually, I'm here at my grandmother's request."

The twinkle of surprise showed in Stasia's eyes. "Your grandmother is on the ship?"

He nodded. "So are a number of my family members."

"That must be so nice."

He remained quiet. He knew Stasia only had her brother these days. She didn't know what it was like to have a bunch of well-meaning but intrusive family members delving into her personal life.

"It must be something special to get you out of the office. I hope you have a great time."

And then he realized there wasn't any reason to be secretive. "We're here for my grandmother's eightieth birthday celebration and my cousin's wedding in Venice."

"Wow. That's a lot to celebrate."

He nodded and then glanced around to make sure none of his family were within listening distance. Once he was sure the coast was clear, he leaned closer to Stasia and lowered his voice. "I should probably tell you that my cousin and her fiancé applied to Infinity Island but were turned down."

Stasia's brows rose but she didn't say anything.

"I just wanted to forewarn you because this ship isn't that big, so you're likely to run into them."

"No problem. Thanks for the warning."

He nodded. "I just wonder if it's a good idea for them to get married."

"Why? Don't you like who your cousin is marrying?"

"It's not that." If anything, he really liked Anthony. "He's a great guy. But Xander told me a little of how the system works on Infinity Island. Do you know how the process works?" When she shook her head, he continued. "It seems pretty involved. The legend or folklore or whatever you call it says if you don't pass the test, it means you're ill suited for each other."

"Really? Do you think it's true?"

He shrugged. Weddings were never of interest to him. "I just don't want my cousin to be hurt. She's a great person. Loving and caring."

"I'm sure it'll all work out for her."

This was his turn to study Stasia. It definitely wasn't a hardship. He could stare at her all day. She was beautiful in a very classic and stylish way. Her dark hair was straight and cut in a sleek bob that brushed over the tops of her shoulders. Her makeup only emphasized her vibrant eyes and her high cheekbones. She went for more color when it came to her lips. They were a deep rose shade. Her lips were pouty and inviting.

"Roberto?"

He jerked his gaze back to her eyes. He'd been busted staring. He cleared his throat and glanced away. What had they been discussing?

It took him a second to recall the conversation. "I'm not normally one to give in to such superstitious kind of stuff, but this is my cousin. She's the closest thing I have to a sister."

Stasia reached across the table and squeezed his hand. "I wouldn't worry. There's also this saying that love can overcome everything."

"I sure hope you're right." And then he had a question for her. "If it were you, would you take the test? Would you want to get married on Infinity Island?"

Her eyes didn't give away anything. "That's not a fair question. After all, I'm related to the owners of the island. And as such, I've spent quite a bit of time there. It's a gorgeous place."

"And you still haven't answered my question." It was only then that he realized he was asking a widow about getting married again. He inwardly groaned at his thoughtlessness. "Never mind. I shouldn't have probed. I guess it's just a side effect of my job, always digging for information."

He was about to take a drink when he noticed she didn't have anything in front of her. "Can I get you anything to drink or eat?"

"Actually, yes. I'd love an espresso. I need the caffeine."

It was only then that he noticed the shadows beneath her eyes. They were faint, as though they were covered up, and you wouldn't even notice them unless you were looking for them. Something was keeping her up at night. And then he realized what it might be. She was still grieving for her husband. Sympathy welled up in him.

"I'll be right back with caffeine." He got to his feet and walked away.

He couldn't even imagine what she was going through. It was just one more reason that remaining a bachelor was a good idea. Families were messy with entanglements, emotions and responsibilities. It was easier to just deal with himself.

He ordered two coffees. Though he didn't rely on caffeine to get him up and going in the morning—that was what running was for—that didn't mean he didn't appreciate the flavor and warmth of a cup of coffee.

He'd picked up the coffees and started back to the table when he noticed a young guy headed straight for Stasia. He couldn't blame the guy. She was a beautiful woman. And if she weren't his friend's sister as well as being a widow, he definitely would have pursued her. Nothing serious, but they'd have made some great memories together.

Roberto slowed down, unsure what to do. Maybe Stasia knew the man. Maybe she'd welcome the company. As Stasia smiled at the man, Roberto's body tensed. He knew it shouldn't bother him. It wasn't like the guy was horning in on a date. They'd merely bumped into each other.

Maybe he should head over there and take his seat. After all, this was his time with Stasia. Was that a thing? Could friends claim time with each other?

Or perhaps he should head to his cabin. He could get some work done before meeting up with his family for dinner. Just then his phone vibrated, letting him know a new email had landed in his inbox.

But instead of withdrawing his phone to find out what required his attention, he continued gazing in Stasia's direction. He wanted to be sure everything was all right before he moved on.

Stasia's smile faded. He couldn't hear what was being said, but the shake of her head let him know she was no longer interested in the man's company. And yet the man didn't move on. Instead the man reached out to touch her. Stasia quickly withdrew her arm.

That was it. The decision had been made for him.

Without giving himself time to reconsider what he was about to do, Roberto headed across the busy deck, weaving and bobbing around the vacationers. He did his best to keep an eye on the situation—it was what Xander would want him to do.

He wondered if Xander had picked this cruise specifically for his sister because he knew Roberto would be on it. If so, it was strange that Xander hadn't mentioned anything to him.

The young man made himself comfortable in his chair and that wouldn't do. Roberto walked up to Stasia. The easiest and fastest way to get rid of her newfound admirer was simple.

"Sorry it took so long, darling." Roberto placed the coffee on the table and then kissed Stasia's cheek.

He noticed the softness of her skin and wondered if her lips would be just as soft. The thought of sneaking in another kiss crossed his mind, but just as quickly he dismissed it.

As Roberto straightened, he noticed the gentle floral scent of her perfume. It was pleasant and fresh like spring. It so suited her because anytime he'd been around Stasia, she'd been sunny and energetic.

The man across the table sat there with his mouth slightly agape as his gaze moved between the two of them. Was it so hard to believe they were together? Sure, he was a few years older than Stasia, but he wasn't an old man by any stretch of imagination.

"I…uh…" The man practically tripped getting to his feet. "Gotta go."

And that was it. The guy turned and made a quick retreat to the bar. Roberto could only wonder if he was seeking a drink to calm his nerves or if he was about to try his luck with one of the young women sitting at the bar.

"What did you do that for?" Stasia's eyes reflected her confusion.

The lack of a smile on her face led him to wonder if he was in trouble. "I saw the guy bothering you." The guy had been bothering her, hadn't he? He hadn't misread her agitation with the young guy, had he? "You weren't interested in him, were you?"

For a moment, Stasia didn't respond. Roberto started to worry he was going to have to track that guy down and apologize. That was about the last thing he wanted to do on this trip.

At last, she shook her head. "I think he was hitting on any available woman on the cruise. I tried to tell him I wasn't interested, but he was the type that didn't take no for an answer." And then her gaze narrowed in on him. "And you couldn't think of any other way to get rid of him other than to act like we're a couple?"

Roberto smiled. "It worked, didn't it?"

She sent him a funny look as though she wasn't sure what to say. Luckily, she didn't know how that innocent kiss had affected him. He'd make sure not to do that again. Getting sucked into Stasia's orbit did strange things to his mind.

Had that just happened?

Stasia resisted the urge to touch her cheek where just moments ago Roberto's lips had been. They'd known each other for years, but they'd never shared a hug, much less a kiss. Usually, it was a passing hello or a nod of recognition.

And it wasn't like he was the first man to kiss her cheek. Why was she letting it get to her like this? When he'd kissed her, her heart had pounded, her mouth had gone dry and her palms had dampened. Sheesh! She really needed to get out more.

She assured herself that it was just the shock of Roberto acting like her significant other. It had caught her completely off guard. Everything would be fine now.

Stasia's mouth suddenly felt dry. She took a large gulp of the strong coffee. That might not have been her brightest idea. She coughed.

Roberto sent her a concerned look. "Are you okay?"

She nodded, then coughed again. "Swallowed the wrong way."

She took a more conservative sip and it calmed her throat. "I should be going. There's so much on the ship to explore. I'm not even sure where to begin."

"They have an app. Did you load it to your phone?" When she looked at him with a blank look, he said, "Could I have your phone?"

She pulled it from a pocket in her black purse and handed it over. He quickly downloaded the app and handed it back to her. "There you go. It'll give you a schedule so you know what's available. Oh, I almost forgot. You should switch your phone to airplane mode to avoid premium roaming charges."

She swiped her finger over the phone until she had the right screen. "Got it."

"And one more thing. You'll want to hook up to the ship's Wi-Fi."

He talked her through the process, and in no time, she was set to go. "Thank you. I wouldn't have thought of that. You must go on a lot of cruises."

"Actually, this is my second. But I do a lot of research. It's one of my hobbies. I research locations, periods in history, all sorts of things. I guess you could say my mind is filled with all sorts of trivia."

"That will come in handy for you."

Lukos had always known how to do those types of things for her. It was just one more thing that she needed to learn to do for herself. The more she did for herself, the more confident she felt.

She smiled at Roberto. "Thank you. I'm sure we'll see each other again."

"I'd like that."

She reluctantly walked away. If given the opportunity, she would have liked to sit and talk the rest of the morning. Roberto had always been easy to be around.

But she had a life plan to brainstorm. Socializing would have to wait for another time. Besides, she couldn't impose on Roberto's time with his family.

DAY TWO

Katakolon, Greece

So FAR THE TRIP was okay.

Stasia's image came to mind. Maybe the trip was better than okay. Roberto smiled. Much better.

But then there was his grandmother. She was a lady who didn't accept the word *no* from anyone, including him. And right now, she was more interested in his love life than he found comfortable.

Why exactly had he agreed to come on this cruise? Oh, yes, it was his cousin's wedding. And he loved his cousin. But still, wedding bells and his matchmaking grandmother were not a good match. He really should have given this more thought. Perhaps he could have flown in for the ceremony and had the helicopter wait for him after the reception. That would have been much better than enduring the entire trip.

Still, he did have the opportunity to get to know Stasia better. The thought brought another smile to his lips. She was a nice surprise on this ship. At least he had an ally on this voyage.

It was as though his thoughts of Stasia made her appear. She entered the passageway just ahead of him. This trip was definitely looking up.

"Hey, Stasia."

She turned.

He rushed to catch up with her. "Did you make plans for dinner?"

Her forehead scrunched up. "Is this something I should check on my app?"

He chuckled. "I meant to say, do you want to have dinner with me? But if you don't want to or you have other plans, that's fine—"

"No. I mean no, I don't have other plans, and yes, I'd enjoy having dinner with you."

"Roberto! Roberto!"

He didn't have to turn around to know the perky voice belonged to his cousin. If he had a sibling, he'd want them to be just like Gaia. She was so full of life that it bubbled out of her and spread to those around her.

Roberto paused in the passageway. Stasia stopped next to him and they both turned. His cousin rushed up to him with one of her great big warm smiles. And then she wrapped him in a big hug. He hoped her future husband realized how lucky he was to have Gaia in his life.

When Gaia pulled back, she was still smiling. "We kept missing each other yesterday and I was starting to wonder if you were really on the ship. But I'm glad you're here." It was then that her gaze moved to Stasia. "I'm sorry. I didn't mean to interrupt."

Remembering his manners, he said, "Gaia, I'd like you to meet Stasia Marinakos. Stasia, this is my cousin Gaia, the blushing bride."

"It's so nice to meet you," Stasia said, holding a hand out to Gaia.

"We can do better than that." Gaia hugged a surprised Stasia.

Roberto smiled as Stasia experienced the Gaia effect. When it came to making people feel comfortable and welcomed, his cousin knew how to do it. They may be opposites, but he couldn't love her more if she were his sister.

When the two women parted, Stasia said, "Roberto told me about the wedding in Venice. Congratulations. I'm sure it will be absolutely beautiful."

Gaia's dark brows drew together. "You sound like you won't be there."

"I...I won't be."

Gaia's puzzled gaze moved from Stasia to him and then back again. "Consider yourself invited. You will be Roberto's plus-one." Gaia's phone buzzed. She glanced at it. "I've got to go. It was so good to meet you." Gaia turned to him and mouthed, "She's great."

Without waiting for anyone to speak, Gaia took off down the passageway.

"What just happened?" Stasia's eyes reflected her confusion.

"That was my cousin. She's kind of like a force of nature."

"But she thinks you and I...that we're a couple. Why didn't you correct her?"

He smiled. "Because she wouldn't care what I said. She likes to come to her own conclusions. She's a lot like our grandmother. She'll figure out the truth eventually."

"And the wedding?"

He paused. His cousin didn't have such a bad idea after all. Weddings made him uncomfortable, especially when his family started asking when he was going to walk down the aisle. His answer was always the same—never.

"What do you think?" he asked. "Would you like to go to the wedding?"

Stasia immediately shook her head. "I couldn't impose."

"You wouldn't be. My cousin is expecting you to be there."

Stasia paused as though considering the idea. "I always did like weddings, and one in Venice has got to be beautiful."

"Good. That's settled." He glanced at his phone and the growing number of emails in his inbox. "I have some work to do, but I'll see you at dinnertime."

They exchanged room numbers and he said he'd pick her up at seven for dinner. Why did that seem so far away? After all, it was already after eleven. After eleven? That meant he didn't have long to work before meeting up with his family for lunch shortly.

This is great. Some downtime to relax and regroup. Maybe Xander had the right idea all along.

Stasia decided not to go ashore at Katakolon. Instead she grabbed her laptop and headed to the deck to enjoy some sun while she did research on her computer. It was time for her to make a plan for the future.

She moved to one of the lounge chairs and sat down. She glanced at her phone and thought about checking out the ship's app. On second thought, she placed her phone in her bag. She didn't have time for fun. She wanted to have a life plan or at least a five-year plan by the time they returned to Athens.

She wondered what Roberto was doing at that moment. Was he having fun with his family? Or was he checking his phone every minute for a new business email? Probably the latter. She smiled. They'd make a good pair on this voyage—each busy with their own endeavors.

The warmth of the sun was so relaxing. Each stiffened muscle loosened. For just a moment, she leaned her head back and closed her eyes.

She hadn't realized until then how much time she'd spent indoors in the past few years. Other than her time on Infinity Island, she'd been inside, at first taking care of Lukos, and then for a number of months after that, she wasn't sure what she did. It was all a blur of tears, regret over all the missed opportunities and then the finality of the paperwork. She never knew there could be so much paperwork involved with a death.

A gentle breeze rushed over her body, cooling it from the sun's rays. If she didn't have so much to do, she could be just like a cat and curl up for a nap in the sun. She really should get to work.

She opened her laptop. Realizing that it was too sunny where she was, she moved to a shaded spot. It was so much easier on her eyes.

She would start with a search engine. She did searches on her interests that included reading and teaching, but she lacked the appropriate degree... Maybe she could go back to school. But the more she thought of it, the more she decided against it.

The afternoon wasn't without its interruptions. It appeared she must have a sign on her forehead that said Single and Alone. Because she was hit on numerous times. Thankfully, the men were charming and respectful when she said she wasn't interested. Still, it was awkward and time-consuming. And the last thing she wanted to do was stay in her cabin for the whole cruise. She could have stayed home if she were going to do that.

It was almost time for her to get ready for dinner and she still didn't have an idea of how she wanted to focus her life. At the age of twenty-nine, weren't people supposed to have these things figured out? Well, she'd thought she had it all figured out, but then Lukos had been diagnosed with cancer, and it hadn't just affected his life—hers had changed dramatically too.

She shoved the thoughts to the back of her mind. She had a dinner date. Not a *date* date, but dinner with a man who wasn't her brother. The thought spurred her into action. She was actually looking forward to this dinner. Roberto seemed so different outside of the office—much more relaxed and, dare she say it, fun.

* * *

At last it was dinnertime.

Roberto couldn't remember the last time he'd been so anxious for a meal. He made his way down the passageway toward Stasia's cabin. His footsteps grew faster.

After a day of touring Katakolon with his family and being introduced to one available woman after the next, he couldn't wait to have the company of an ally. His grandmother had been so upset when he'd almost gleefully told her that he had dinner plans. When his grandmother pushed, he'd admitted that it was Stasia. His grandmother had given him a suspicious look. He hadn't revealed any details, letting her think whatever she wanted so long as she didn't set him up with any other granddaughters of friends.

He had firmly decided that was his last trip ashore with his family. He'd rather stay on the ship the remainder of the cruise than be subjected to his grandparents' tag-team approach to dissecting his life.

The one question he did want to ask his grandmother was how she was able to get all of these single women on this cruise. But he figured he was better off not knowing and pushed the whole matchmaking scenario to the back of his mind.

He double-checked the note he'd made on his phone to remind him of Stasia's cabin number. This was it. He'd just knocked on the door when it was jerked open a crack.

Stasia peered out at him. "You're here?"

He frowned. Had he been so rattled today by his grandmother's blatant matchmaking that he'd mixed up the time in his head? "Weren't we supposed to meet at seven?"

"Oh. Is it that late?" The look on her face was one of panic.

He'd never seen Stasia anything but cool and collected—

even at her husband's funeral. Her eyes had told another story, but on the outside, she was elegant and graceful. He'd never known how she'd held it all together so well. If he'd been in her shoes, he'd have been a total wreck, inside and out.

He cleared his throat. "If you need more time, I can come back."

She worried her bottom lip as though considering what to do. And then she shook her head. "You might as well come in."

He wasn't sure what he'd be walking into considering her worried expression. As she swung the door wide open, he took in the sight. On the bed was a pile of dresses that looked like they'd been tried on and then discarded.

"I...I couldn't decide what to wear." Her face bloomed with pinkness that looked totally adorable on her. "I haven't gone to dinner with a man that wasn't my brother since...well, since Lukos."

Roberto nodded in understanding. "It's okay. You can relax. After all, this isn't a date. Right?"

The look on her face was not telling. "Right."

"Do you want help cleaning this up?"

She shook her head. And that was when he noticed she was wearing a strapless black gown with a sequined bodice and a flouncy skirt. She looked... He struggled for a word that did her beauty justice.

"You look amazing." His gaze met hers. The color in her cheeks intensified. "Shall we go?"

"I...I can't. Could you help me?"

"Sure. Whatever you need."

She turned around. "Could you pull up my zipper?"

He told himself not to, but he couldn't resist the temptation of taking in the sight of her bare back. Her smooth skin had a warm bronze tone to it. And in that moment,

Stasia had gone from being the sister of his friend to a woman that he desired. He swallowed hard.

He stepped toward her. He told himself that if he did this quickly, it would be all over. The temptation would be gone. And they could return to being nothing more than friends.

Stasia lifted her long hair and swiped it off to the side, revealing her long, slender neck. It was so tempting to lean forward and plant a kiss on the gentle slope where her neck met her shoulder. He wondered what her reaction would be.

"Roberto? Is there a problem?"

Yes! A great big problem. How am I to remain a perfect gentleman when you look so utterly desirable?

"No. No problem." His voice came out deeper than normal.

Now he had to touch her and act like it was nothing. Otherwise, she would suspect something. And there was no way he wanted to risk their fledgling friendship. He told himself that their friendship was so important to him because she was his only true ally on the ship. Even his cousin was telling him to give romance a chance. Gaia was so happy and she wanted everyone to be just as happy.

He reached out for the zipper. In the process, his fingertips slid across the small of Stasia's back. He noticed the ever-so-slight intake of her breath. So, it wasn't just him who was uncomfortable with this intimate situation.

He grasped the zipper, but it wouldn't budge. How could that be? He pulled harder. Nothing. Though he didn't want to, he used his other hand to pull the material together, being careful not to touch Stasia's back. He pulled again. Still nothing.

"What's wrong?"

"It's the zipper. It's stuck."

"Stuck?" She attempted to turn around.

"Don't move! You're making it worse."

He pulled gently on the material, clearing it from the teeth of the zipper. He gave it another go. It started to move. He breathed a sigh of relief. His relief was short-lived as the zipper got stuck again.

"This is ridiculous," Stasia said. "I'll just put on something else. Pull down the zipper so I can get out of it."

He tried pulling it the other direction. "It won't budge."

"What?" Concern rang out in her voice. "You mean I'm stuck in this dress that is only half-zipped?"

He needed to get a better view of the zipper. "Move over here."

He walked over and sat on the edge of the bed. This gave him an eye-level view of the problem.

She turned around and took a step toward him. When her heel caught on the carpeting, she lost her balance. Roberto reached out to her, wrapping his hands around her slender waist. He guided her to him. She landed on his thigh.

She turned to look at him. At this point, her face was mere centimeters from his. The breath caught in his throat as his heart hammered against his ribs. He couldn't ever remember experiencing this powerful of an attraction.

His gaze lowered to her lips. They wore a rosy shade of lip gloss. They reminded him of sun-ripened berries just perfect for picking. But dare he?

When his gaze rose to meet hers, he saw the flames of desire flickering in her eyes. In that moment, she was no one's widow, no one's little sister. She was just a very desirable woman who wanted the same thing as him.

He leaned forward. His mouth lightly brushed hers. He had to move with caution. And then he stopped. Too much, too fast, and she'd bolt. The only sound in the room was the beating of his heart echoing in his ears.

He wanted her so badly, but he wasn't going to rush her. If it killed him, he would sit here and let her walk away. If this kiss were to happen it had to be wanted by both of them.

And then she was there, pressing her lips to his.

At first, her touch was tentative, unsure. He let her lead the way. Right now, he would follow her just about anywhere. Her kiss was sweet and yet it was also spicy. This was a kiss unlike any other—and he'd been kissed a lot. But he knew going forward that Stasia had ruined him for any other woman.

His hand moved to her back. With her zipper stuck, it left her back completely bare. His mouth grew dry. His fingers grazed over the silky-smooth flesh. A moan swelled in the back of his throat. If this didn't stop soon, it would go so much further than either of them was ready for. And he didn't want to lose Stasia—as a friend.

It took every bit of willpower in him to grip her bare shoulders and pull back. Desire and confusion warred within her eyes.

"I'm sorry," he said. "I didn't mean for that to happen."

"Um…you're right." She got to her feet and started to walk away.

"Wait."

She turned back to him. The confusion was still evident in her eyes, but in place of the desire there was now something else. Could it be disappointment? In a blink, whatever he saw was now gone.

He ran his fingers over his mouth. "Your zipper. I need to get it unstuck."

She shook her head. "I'll just change."

"But I don't think you can get out of it until the zipper is fixed."

A distinct frown settled over her beautiful face. He could tell she was considering ways to get out of the dress that didn't involve him touching her again. And it made him feel bad that he'd let go of his common sense and caused this rift between them. He wondered if—no, he hoped—they could move past it.

"Come here." When she didn't move, he said, "The kiss, it won't happen again."

Her eyes reflected the uncertainties churning within her.

"I promise."

That seemed to be enough to get her to move toward him. When Stasia stopped in front of him, he noticed she'd kicked off her high heels. And when she stood with her back to him, she left a modest distance between them. It saddened him that he'd ruined the easiness between them. He would have to work extra hard throughout dinner to gain her trust back.

It took him a few minutes to work the delicate material out of the teeth of the zipper. He slowly pulled on the zipper until it was to the top.

Once she gathered her shoes and purse, he presented his arm to her. For a second, she didn't move. And then she slipped her hand into the crook of his arm. It was a small thing, but it was a start.

What in the world had happened back there?

Stasia's heart still hadn't returned to its normal rhythm. She wasn't sure it would as long as she was with Roberto. She'd always been aware of his devastatingly handsome looks, but she never thought he would be interested in her. She'd seen him in photos on the internet with fashion models, pop stars and countless other beautiful women on his arm, but she never thought she'd be one of them.

The only vision in her mind was of that kiss.

That kiss, it was mind-blowing. It was sinfully delicious. And she hadn't wanted it to end—not ever.

And now that it had, she was struck by a tsunami of guilt. She knew it didn't have to be that way. After all, she'd been a widow for almost two years now. It was past the time for her to move on—at least that was what her friends had been telling her. But it was easier said than done.

Now she was filled with elation that this very sexy man desired her, which was tempered by the thought that she was somehow being unfaithful to her husband's memory. How could she just act like she hadn't pledged her heart and life to Lukos?

Her heart continued to beat wildly in anticipation of feeling Roberto's lips once more. It was traitorous. She was a terrible person.

But then in the back of her mind, she could hear the echo of Lukos's voice. He'd told her she was too young to live the rest of her life alone. He'd insisted she find someone to love and have those kids she wanted. Two of them. A boy and girl.

She'd told him that she would always love him—that their memories would be enough for her. At the time, she'd been unable to imagine her life without Lukos.

He'd pushed and prodded until she'd promised to go on with her life and love again. Tears had been involved on both their parts, but Lukos seemed to relax, knowing she wouldn't give up on life. She wondered what he'd think of her being with Roberto.

Her gaze moved to Roberto. There was absolutely nothing about his stylish haircut, designer suit or flirty smile that said he was ready to settle down. She was worrying too much. It had been a kiss. Nothing more. Everything would be all right.

Once they were seated at their table in the enormous dining room, she ordered a glass of wine. Maybe it would help her relax. She didn't want the evening to be filled with an awkward silence.

"Can we just pretend that it didn't happen?" She hoped he'd agree.

His gaze met hers, and just by looking into his eyes, her pulse raced. What was it about this guy that could make her whole body react to him? It was more than just his great looks. Or maybe she was lonelier than she'd thought.

She needed to focus more on her future and then she'd be less distracted by the Robertos of the world. But right now, there was only one Roberto on her radar. And he didn't seem keen to disregard that steamy kiss.

His voice lowered. It held a sexy rumble to it. "Is that really what you want?"

Her one-word response rushed to the tip of her tongue and teetered there. No. She wanted more of those kisses. Lots more. She would never get enough of them.

But then what? They'd have a steamy onboard affair, and by the time the boat docked back in Athens, she would be left with what? Memories? Would that be enough?

And if she let herself become distracted, she would have no five-year plan for her life. She would be in exactly the same position that she was in now. She couldn't let that happen.

Renewed in her determination to forge her own path in life, she said, "Yes, that's what I would like." But she didn't want to draw a firm line in the sand. "I'd also like it if we could continue our friendship."

There was a flicker of something—could it be disappointment in his eyes? Or was she just seeing what she wanted to see?

"I would like that very much." He sent her a warm, reassuring smile. "Now wait until I tell you about my day."

It didn't take long for the awkwardness to fade away. They ordered their dinner and relaxed. Roberto's day had been anything but boring. And Stasia felt bad for him, not only being set up on a lunch date, but also two other dates that afternoon. And if it hadn't been for their dinner plans, he would be having dinner with some other young woman.

Stasia sipped her wine. "And here I thought my brother was bad with his overprotective tendencies."

"Xander just wants what is best for you."

"Don't start sticking up for him or I might have to rethink this whole arrangement." And then she sent him a teasing smile.

Roberto held up his hands in surrender. "I have no interest in getting between two siblings."

"Smart man. I knew there was a reason I liked you."

They both smiled and the rest of dinner was filled with light conversation as well as laughter. By the end, Stasia had to admit that she hadn't had this much fun in…well, in a very long time. And she hated to see it end. But she knew she couldn't occupy all his time.

"Would you like dessert?" Roberto offered.

She shook her head. "I'm full. The meal was delicious. I must admit that I had my doubts about onboard dining, but they have most definitely put my worries to rest."

Roberto set aside his napkin. "Thank you for joining me. This dinner was definitely the best part of my day." His smile faltered and she had to wonder if he was recalling their kiss. "Would you like to do anything else?"

She best not press her luck. "Thank you for the offer, but I should be going."

"Maybe we can share a meal again while we're sailing."

"I'd like that." She would like that a whole lot—so much so that it scared her.

And with that, they parted company. She went one way and he went the other. She should head back to her cabin to start reading some of the self-help books she'd purchased. Some people would think that she was silly or perhaps frivolous for not having a clear path in life. But when your future was stolen away by cancer you had to regroup. That was what she was doing.

But she found that she was too wound up to concentrate on reading just yet. She told herself it was the lively dinner conversation and that it had absolutely nothing to do with that earth-moving kiss back in her cabin. Either way, she decided a walk around the deck might be nice.

She found that she wasn't the only one wanting to enjoy the warm evening under the stars. But most of the people around her were coupled up. Some were arm in arm; others were stealing a kiss in the moonlight.

Stasia, in that moment, felt profoundly alone. There was no one waiting back in her cabin for her. Her thoughts turned to Roberto, but she halted them. She would be fine alone.

"There you are."

Roberto paused in the hallway. "Hello, Yaya."

"Did you have a good dinner?"

"I did. Thank you. And how was yours?"

She gave a nonchalant shrug of her shoulder. "It was nothing special. Marissa was sorry you couldn't have joined us."

Marissa must be another attempt at matchmaking. "Like I said, I had a prior commitment. And I didn't want to cancel at the last moment." He knew how his grandmother felt about manners—even when it foiled one of her matchmaking schemes.

"Perhaps tomorrow when we dock, you could make it up to Marissa." His grandmother's eyes twinkled with renewed hope.

"I have plans." He was going to ask Stasia to go sightseeing with him. The idea had just come to him, but he liked the idea of spending the day with her. He liked it quite a lot. "I'm sorry, Yaya. I must go. I have to meet someone."

His grandmother's eyes narrowed. "Is this someone a female?" When he nodded, she asked, "The same one you dined with?" When he nodded again, she asked, "And you still maintain that you're nothing more than friends?"

The answer to that question was more complicated than the last time she'd asked it. He drew in a deep breath as he considered his options. He never lied to his grandmother. He might not always give her full and complete answers, but never an outright lie.

He continued to meet her inquisitive stare. "It's complicated."

His grandmother's eyes widened. "You have feelings for this girl?"

Ding.

He'd never been so happy to receive an email.

"I have to go. I have some business that needs my immediate attention." The truth was that he didn't know how he felt. That kiss, it had affected him more than he'd expected.

He headed for the deck to get some fresh air before he spoke with Stasia. He didn't want to do anything foolish. The more time he spent with Stasia, the more he liked spending time with her. And therein lay the rub. He stepped out on the spacious deck, and as though his thoughts had summoned her, there stood Stasia, staring out at the vast sea. Like a magnet, he was drawn to her.

He stepped up behind her. "We meet again."

Stasia turned to him and smiled, making his chest get that funny, warm sensation again. "I was just going to take a walk. Would you like to join me?"

"I can't think of anything I'd like more." Because it was the gentlemanly thing to do, he offered her his arm.

And this time, without hesitation, she accepted. When she slipped her hand into the crook of his arm, he could feel the warmth of her touch through the fabric of his dinner jacket. He liked that feeling—very much so.

They set off, strolling along the moon-drenched deck, looking like every other star-crossed lover enjoying their evening with the one they loved. Except they weren't in love, he reminded himself. Sure, they'd kissed, but that had been a mistake. The best mistake he'd ever made.

As the other couples headed inside, they strolled for a while in the quiet of the evening. The only sounds around them were of the sea and occasionally when a door was opened, voices from within trickling out to them.

"You know, we're docking in Corfu tomorrow. Would you like to go with me on the guided tour and check out some ancient ruins?"

Stasia shook her head. "Thank you. But I don't think so."

"What? You don't like history?"

"It's not that. It's just that I have some stuff I need to do."

She made it sound like work. And he couldn't imagine what work she would have to do while on vacation. Xander had sent his sister on this trip for her to relax and unwind. Her sitting in her cabin working while he was out sightseeing didn't seem right.

"Come with me for just a little while."

She turned a questioning glance his way. "You really want me to go sightseeing with you?"

He nodded. "It'd be nice to see it with a friend."

She hesitated. He implored her with his eyes. He didn't know why this was so important to him, but it was.

"All right. I think an outing would be nice." Stasia smiled at him, making his heart pound harder than normal.

"It's a date." Once the words had left his lips, he knew it was a mistake. But when she didn't correct him, he let it go.

He escorted Stasia back to her cabin, and it seemed so natural to lean in and give her a kiss good-night, but he caught himself just in time. After they agreed on where to meet in the morning, they said good-night. Stasia slipped inside the cabin and a feeling of disappointment fell over him by missing out on that kiss.

Corfu, Greece

THERE HAD BEEN so much to see.

And they'd hardly covered much of the Mediterranean island, even though they'd set off first thing in the morning. It was now late in the day.

They'd joined a guided tour that took them to one of the island's picturesque beaches. They didn't tarry long as they moved on to the Royal Palace, also known as the Museum of Asian Art, with its stunning collection of artifacts from China, Japan and India.

From there they'd visited Corfu's old town, with its narrow roads and older homes. It was like an archaeological treasure trove.

And Stasia's feet were sore from all of the walking. "That was beautiful."

"Yes, you are." Roberto smiled at her.

Stasia couldn't help but laugh at his very obvious flirting. He had been the perfect date today. He'd been fun, distracting, and most of all, he hadn't treated her like she was fragile, like her brother and friends did. While touring Corfu, she hadn't thought about all the things that had been weighing on her mind. The museum was interesting and the artifacts were definitely worth a closer look.

But now with evening approaching, they boarded the ship with the other tourists. Stasia was exhausted from all the walking, but she didn't regret a moment of it. Who knew Roberto had such a relaxed side to him? In his short sleeves and khaki shorts, he looked like a laid-back tourist. At this particular moment, he was the exact opposite of the serious businessman who she'd gotten to know over the years.

Once on the deck, Stasia moved off to the side and turned to Roberto. "Thank you for today."

He was still smiling. "So you're not mad that I practically twisted your arm to go?"

"Not at all." And just so he knew she meant it, she lifted up on her tiptoes to give him a hug.

At first, he didn't move. And she wondered if she'd overstepped in their friendship. But then his arms wrapped around her, pulling her close. She breathed in his masculine scent mixed with a light whiff of spicy cologne. She longed to lean in closer to inhale the intoxicating combination—

"Hello, Roberto."

The woman's voice had Stasia jerking back out of his embrace. Heat swirled in her chest and raced to her cheeks as she turned to face the person. The older woman's silver hair was trimmed short and not a strand was out of place. Diamond earrings adorned her ears. And her face was made up. But it was her gray-blue eyes that caught and held Stasia's attention. They were the exact same shade as Roberto's. She didn't have to be told. This was his grandmother.

"Yaya, what are you doing here?" Roberto asked.

"Why, dear, this is a ship. And I was out for a stroll." Her gaze moved between him and Stasia. "Maybe I should be asking the questions. What is going on here? You have a dinner date with Marissa."

"We already ate while we were ashore," Roberto said.

His grandmother's eyes darkened. "You knew you had obligations."

Stasia couldn't believe his grandmother was really going to push her agenda, even in front of her. Stasia's heart went out to Roberto. At least Xander wasn't pushing her into some man's arms to get her out of his hair. In fact, Xander would probably do the opposite and keep her away from any men.

But she just couldn't stand there and let Roberto's grandmother push him to do things he didn't want to do. And he loved his grandmother too much to stand up to her and cause a rift. So that left Stasia. She could fix this problem. But did she dare?

Catching sight of a beautiful woman headed in their direction with her gaze set on Roberto, Stasia slipped her hand in his. Roberto turned a surprised look at Stasia.

"You might as well go ahead and tell your grandmother," Stasia said.

"Tell me what?" His grandmother's gaze moved between the two of them.

Roberto's eyes reflected his confusion. He stared deep into Stasia's eyes, searching for answers. She hadn't thought this was going to be so stunning for him. Perhaps she needed to help him a bit.

"Go ahead and tell her about us." Was it her imagination or had his complexion lost a bit of its color?

He shook his head. "I don't think this is a good idea."

"Roberto, tell me what is going on," his grandmother demanded.

Roberto was still staring into Stasia's eyes. "You're sure about this?"

She sent him a reassuring smile and nodded.

He turned to his grandmother. "Stasia and I are involved."

"You are a couple?" His grandmother's gaze narrowed. When they both reluctantly nodded, his grandmother asked, "Then why did you tell me that you weren't involved when I asked before?"

Stasia tightened her grip on his hand, sensing the tension coursing through his grandmother's inquisition. Stasia had never done anything like this before, but she'd never met anyone quite so pushy. What was Roberto going to tell the woman?

Roberto cleared his throat. "Stasia is my friend's sister. I don't think Xander will be happy to know we're involved. In fact, I'm quite certain he'll be anything but happy. So, you see, it's for the best that we keep this quiet."

The beautiful young woman stepped up next to Roberto's grandmother. "Is it time?"

"Not now, dear." Roberto's grandmother never took her gaze off Stasia and Roberto long enough to look at the young woman. "I'll catch up with you later."

The young woman frowned. "But I thought—"

"I'll explain later. Now go." His grandmother's voice brooked no room for argument.

With a dark look at Stasia, the young woman turned on her stilettos and strode away. It was then that Stasia wondered if she'd helped or hindered Roberto. After all, that young lady was amazingly beautiful.

The older woman's eyes held a glint of skepticism. She narrowed her view in on Stasia. "Is this true? Are you seeing my grandson?"

"Yes."

"Hmpf…" The woman's gaze moved from her to Roberto. "We'll talk more about this later." And with that, his grandmother strode away.

When the woman was out of earshot, Stasia asked, "Do you think she believed me?"

"I don't know. It's tough to get anything past her."

"I feel bad about deceiving her."

"So do I, but it wouldn't be necessary if she'd give up on trying to find me a wife." His gaze met hers. "She isn't the only one to worry about. If your brother finds out, he truly isn't going to be happy."

"You're right. If he ever found out, he would be furious with both of us. He can be so protective. Did you know that when I got married we had to elope because Xander didn't approve of Lukos?"

Now, why had she gone and dredged up that memory? Perhaps because Lukos was such a big part of her life and pretending otherwise was impossible.

Their wedding had been simple but romantic in a small rustic chapel in the rolling hills of Tuscany. She'd worn a simple white dress while holding a bouquet of wild-flowers. Lukos had worn a dark suit and tie while wear-ing a huge smile that lit up the whole world. Stasia stifled a resigned sigh.

She should have known then that something was wrong with him. But she explained away his symptoms as being stress over fighting with her brother and then the wed-ding. How was she supposed to have known—known that he was dying? Still, she should have suspected that it was something more.

Stasia drew in an unsteady breath as she slammed the door on her memories. And the pain, she tucked away deep inside her heart.

Roberto studied her with a frown on his face. "I'm sorry. I didn't mean to upset you."

"I…I'm fine." She said the words, trying to convince herself as much as him. "It's just sometimes I wish I could go back and do things differently."

"I knew back then there was some trouble between you and Xander. I just didn't know the details."

"Xander later apologized, saying he'd misjudged Lukos. But in the beginning, you could slice the tension in the room with a knife." She shook her head, chasing away the unhappy memories. "I know Xander loves me and only wants the best for me, but I wish he'd trust me to figure that out on my own. My whole life, it's felt like he's been smothering me with his overprotectiveness. He'd scare off the guys when I was in school. I used to have to sneak around to date."

"As I recall, you did some butting into his romance with Lea."

Roberto was right, but she'd had her reasons. "That was different. He didn't even know her all that long and all of a sudden he's moving to Infinity Island."

"He didn't move there in the beginning—"

"It sure seemed like it. How was I to know if Lea was telling the truth about being pregnant? And it being his child?"

"But it wasn't up to you to know the truth. That was his situation to settle for himself."

Stasia frowned. Roberto was right. She had done exactly what she'd accused her brother of doing—butting in. "So, what do we do about Xander?"

"We don't tell him about our little shipboard arrangement."

"I don't want to lie to him."

"You won't be. It's not like we're actually involved. What my grandmother makes up in her own mind is all up to her."

Stasia's mind was still stuck on them pretending to be romantically involved and what all that would entail. "We'll be a couple for the voyage and then what?"

"We break up. It isn't that far-fetched. Couples do it all of the time."

"But why would we break up?" She was having a hard time imagining why any woman would walk away from Roberto.

"I work too much. I'm too much of a neat freak. I'm no fun."

"As for the first one, that could be changed with enough encouragement." She smiled at him.

He smiled back. "Perhaps with the right person."

As he continued to look directly at her, her heart raced. Surely he didn't mean she was the right person. Of course not. Right?

She averted her gaze. It was the only way she could string words together. "As for the second reason, I admire a man who cleans up after himself."

"Oh, so that's a positive quality."

"Very much so." She was having fun with the flirty banter. It'd been so long since she'd felt like a desirable woman and not like a nursemaid or a fragile widow. "As for the last reason, well, that is obviously not true. I had a lot of fun today. And I'm looking forward to more excursions."

"I must admit that when I first suggested the tour of Corfu, I wasn't so sure about it. You're the one who made it fun."

"I think we made it entertaining together. So when do we arrive in Venice?"

"Not for a few days."

And then she came to a stop outside her cabin. "Can you believe I've never been to Venice?"

"Really? I would have thought you'd have visited the beautiful city at least once."

"I've always meant to. But for one reason or another, I've never been there."

He smiled at her. "I'm honored that your first visit will be with me."

She gazed into his eyes and her heart skipped a beat. Again, she was swept up in the desire to lift up on her tiptoes, press her hands to his broad shoulders and touch her lips to his. Stasia stifled a sigh.

At the very least, it would be nice to invite him into her cabin for a nightcap. She knew what would happen if she did. This pretend relationship would take on a very real tone. And she knew that would not only jeopardize Roberto's relationship with Xander, but it would also gravely injure her brother-sister relationship. That was a lot to risk for a shipboard romance that would end as soon as they returned to Athens.

Left with no reasonable option to prolong their time together, her gaze lifted to his. "Good night."

"Night."

She remained right there in her doorway as he turned and walked away. Her gaze lingered on him. He looked just as fine going as he did coming. Mighty fine indeed.

DAY FOUR

Kotor, Montenegro

KEEPING UP APPEARANCES surprisingly wasn't hard.

Roberto liked spending time with Stasia. In fact, it was quite possible he liked it too much. But Stasia wasn't quite as enthusiastic. Granted, his boisterous family could be a lot to take in all at once. But every chance Stasia got, she would escape to her cabin. Or perhaps it just felt that way to him because he missed her when she wasn't around.

"You're a hard man to catch up with," said a familiar male voice.

Roberto turned to find his grandfather standing behind him. "I don't mean to be. There are just a lot of activities on this ship and then there are the daily tours and there's also work to catch up on. I'm always on the go."

"I understand. Your grandmother has tried to get me to go on the tours with her, but she doesn't understand that I have work to do."

Roberto felt bad for his grandfather. He wasn't getting any younger, and at his age, he should be able to enjoy life instead of having to worry about work and deadlines. But there was this thing about control. His grandfather didn't want to give it up. His successor would have to meet his stringent requirements. As of now, no one in the family wanted the position or was willing to meet his grandfather's standards—including himself.

His goal since childhood was taking over his grandfather's commercial construction business. But in college, when he'd gotten into it with his grandfather over the man's unreasonable expectations, Roberto had walked away. He'd joined Xander and he'd helped his friend build up his real-estate company.

His grandfather cleared his throat, drawing Roberto from his thoughts. "I have to be going."

"To meet Yaya?"

His grandfather shook his head. "I told her I didn't have time for a cruise right now."

He knew his grandfather was a workaholic, but this seemed excessive even for him. "Is something wrong?"

His grandfather frowned. "Don't start sounding like your grandmother. She's always on me about slowing down."

When Roberto was younger, he would have let the subject drop, but now that he was older, his grandfather was still stubborn and quite set in his ways but not nearly as intimidating. "Maybe she has a point."

His grandfather's mouth pressed in a firm line as he glared at Roberto as though he were some sort of traitor. When Roberto refused to back down, his grandfather sighed.

"It's not like you care. You left."

"I left the company because you didn't give me a choice." Before his grandfather could vocalize his protest, Roberto continued. "But let's leave it in the past."

"You had a choice." His grandfather liked to have the last word. Roberto braced himself for an argument, but then his grandfather said, "I suppose there's no point in rehashing it."

For a moment, Roberto wasn't sure he'd heard his grandfather correctly. Considering his grandfather's congenial mood, Roberto decided to extend an olive branch. He knew it was risky because his grandfather's responses were so unpredictable. But then he thought of his grand-mother and knew he had to try to help.

"You know, I have some time during the cruise and I'm not much of a sightseer. If you have some work to throw my way, it'd give me an excuse to get out of some of the planned excursions."

His grandfather frowned. "If this is some sort of charity—"

"It's not." Roberto shook his head in frustration. He should have known his grandfather wouldn't change. "Never mind—"

"Wait." His grandfather stared at him as though try-ing to decide if this was the right decision. "If you're seri-ous, I could use another set of eyes. But this has to remain confidential. I don't want your grandmother to worry."

It was a little late for that, but Roberto decided to play along. It must be bad if his grandfather was willing to give in that easily.

This was the first time his grandfather had ever asked for his input. "Sure."

His grandfather gave him a brief idea of the large proj-ect taking place on the outskirts of Athens. And then using his smartphone, his grandfather forwarded Roberto the pertinent files. The fact that his grandfather used a smart-phone impressed him. Not everyone his grandfather's age kept up with technology. But then again, not everyone his grandfather's age was still running a multimillion-dollar corporation. Roberto promised to get back to his grand-father by the end of the cruise.

"Now that we have that out of the way, tell me how serious this relationship is with…what's her name?" his grandfather asked.

"Stasia. Did Yaya tell you that we're involved?"

His grandfather was a tall man with a full head of gray

hair. The lines of time that marked his face only made him look more distinguished and wiser. He arched a brow as he stared at his only grandson. "Wasn't she supposed to tell me? Seems like the rest of the family is getting to know her."

Roberto resisted the urge to shrug his shoulders. It was one of those gestures that got on his grandfather's nerves. He thought that it was lazy and ill-mannered. When Roberto was a child, his grandfather would always correct him and insist Roberto use his words.

Roberto cleared his throat. "I'm just surprised is all. The relationship is new. And Yaya didn't appear pleased about it."

"She doesn't think you're serious about this woman. She thinks you're avoiding the opportunity to meet some nice young ladies." His grandfather's pointed stare met his. "Is she right?"

"Why does it have to be serious?"

His grandfather narrowed his gaze on him. "What you're saying is that this isn't going to be anything permanent either. I have to wonder if you're even involved with Stasia."

Heated words rushed to the back of Roberto's throat. Why did his grandfather always look at him like he was a failure because he refused to do things the way his family thought they should be done? At least he was still here, unlike his parents, who were married but lived separate lives in separate parts of the world—separate from him.

Roberto wasn't going to do what his grandfather wanted just to fit in and not make waves. His parents had done that, and now they were unhappier than any two people he knew. As it was, his grandparents had raised him because his parents couldn't stand being at home for any length of time.

His early childhood had been a series of nannies. His parents had worked in the family business and socialized regularly. They were either too busy or too exhausted to deal with him.

At one point, Roberto recalled overhearing his mother saying that she regretted having him. Those words had been seared upon his heart. He withdrew from people. Even at the age of seven, he knew not to trust people because in the end they'd hurt you.

And then a huge fight between his father and grandfather had his parents packing and leaving—without him. Much later, Roberto learned there had been accusations against his parents of mismanagement and harassment.

Roberto spent the remainder of his youth moving between his grandparents' vast estate and boarding school. His grandmother tried her best to fill the void in his life, but being abandoned by his parents left a scar that couldn't be erased, no matter how hard his grandmother tried.

Roberto had vowed long ago not to have a family. He didn't want to find out after the fact that he wasn't cut out to be a father—just like his parents. He refused to subject a child of his own to a life like that.

But what about Stasia? Did she want a family? Sure, she'd made moves to join Xander in the business world, but something told him her heart wasn't in it. He'd noticed her sometimes at the meetings with Xander. She'd been attentive and interacted, but she hadn't smiled. Her face hadn't been animated like it was when she got truly excited about something.

However, she had seemed happy when she was married. Was that what she wanted again? If it was, he'd have to be careful. If things between them escalated, he didn't want to get her hopes up that he could offer her a diamond ring. It would never happen.

His gaze met his grandfather's. "You don't have to wonder. Stasia and I are together. She'll be attending the wedding with me."

"We'll see how long this lasts." And then his grandfather strode away.

Roberto shrugged off his grandfather's disappointment. It was something he'd grown accustomed to over the years. Some things didn't change.

His thoughts turned to Stasia. He wondered what she was doing right now. He thought of seeking her out, but then changed his mind. It was best not to spend too much time together—even if a part of him wanted to spend all his time with her.

It was too beautiful to stay in the cabin.

Stasia lifted her face to the warm sunshine. Maybe she should have taken Roberto up on his offer to take her on today's tour. Where had they stopped? It took her a second to figure out which port they were at that day. With them sailing at night and docking at a new port each morning, it was a lot to remember. But then she recalled that today they were in Montenegro. Though exploring the old Mediterranean town appealed to her, she was holding out for Venice. She couldn't wait to explore as much of it as time allowed.

In the meantime, she'd spent the morning in her cabin poring over aptitude tests and college catalogs and then running internet searches. She stared at her computer until her head started to pound.

She wondered what Roberto was doing, but she didn't want to disturb him, as she didn't want to take up all his time. It wouldn't be fair. He deserved to spend his vacation any way he pleased—even if it meant working.

She'd made her way to the pool. There were a lot of

young families around. The echo of children's voices surrounded her. As she found an available lounge chair, she
couldn't help thinking she'd been robbed of this experience with Lukos. They'd been planning on having a baby.
In fact, they'd just started working on a family when he'd
received the most devastating news that he had cancer. For
a man who'd exercised regularly and led a healthy life-
style, this diagnosis came as quite a shock to both of them.

A little boy moved past her chair, holding on to his
father's hand. The little boy must be around two...about
the age her child would be if their attempt at starting
a family had been successful. An arrow of pain shot
through her heart.

While Lukos had been in the hospital, he got to the
point where he would send her away. Lukos liked to read
or as he grew sicker he'd listen to audiobooks during his
treatment. She never wanted to go far from him and so
she'd made her way around the hospital. She'd ended
up learning about all the volunteer programs out there.
They'd intrigued her as she'd visited with the children as
well as the elderly.

"Stasia?" Roberto's voice drew her attention.

She turned to the side, finding him heading for her. He
was wearing shorts that showed off his long, lean runner
legs. Her gaze rose up over his trim waist, broad chest and
strong arms. When she reached his clean-shaven chiseled
jaw, she paused. Her gaze lingered over his very kissable
lips. With a bit of a struggle, she drew her attention up-
ward past his straight nose and stopped at his gray-blue
eyes. There was amusement reflected in them.

She swallowed hard. She didn't normally get caught
checking someone out. In fact, she wasn't in the habit
of checking anyone out. But there was something about

Roberto—something that had her thinking about what it'd be like to start over.

"Find something you liked?" he asked in a teasing tone.

Heat rushed to her face. "I…I just didn't expect to see you today."

"I can leave if you want—"

"No, please stay."

He took a seat next to her. "I took care of some emails this morning, but I didn't have anything else planned for the day."

"So you aren't a businessman twenty-four-seven?"

His brows lifted. "Is that what you think?"

She shrugged. "It kind of seems that way."

He didn't say anything for a moment as though mulling over her words for some validity. "I guess you've only seen me at the office and at business events. But I do other things."

"Such as?" She was genuinely curious to know the other side of this man.

"I like to go running early in the morning just as the sun is rising."

"It shows in those shorts. You have very nice legs." Was that a bit of color in his cheeks?

"And I like to cook, but I must admit I don't bother very often. More times than not I eat takeout at my desk. I always tell myself I'm going to leave the office at a reasonable hour but then I get engrossed in a project and lose track of time."

"Or is it that you don't have a reason to go home?" That was what happened when she visited Infinity Island. It was so hard for her to leave her adorable niece and family in order to return to a house full of nothing but memories.

It was funny how life played out. In the beginning, she was the one who found love at an early age, and for a long time, she worried Xander would never know such happiness. And now Xander was the one with the love of a family and she was the one walking through life alone. Life could be so unpredictable.

Roberto averted his gaze. "I've chosen work over a home life. It's the way I like things."

She wanted to argue, but she couldn't. Choosing a career over having a family sounded much safer. "Maybe you're right."

This time his gaze did meet hers. Questions reflected in his eyes. "I'm right?"

She struggled not to laugh at his shocked expression. "Why do you look so surprised?"

"Because, well, no one has ever agreed with me before."

There was a time when she wouldn't have agreed with him either. But that boat had sailed, so to speak. Maybe it was time to let him in on her special project. "I've been looking for a job—but not just any job. I want one that fulfills me the way work does you and my brother."

"I thought you were going to join Xander in some real-estate deals."

She glanced away, catching sight of a little boy and his father rolling a bright red ball back and forth. "Don't tell Xander, but real estate, it's not for me."

"Really? Because you seemed so anxious to work on the resort in Italy."

"You're right. I was, in the beginning. But I was mostly excited about being able to work side by side with my brother."

"So what happened?"

It'd been a long time since someone was truly interested in her and her feelings. "I don't know. Somewhere along the way, I figured out that this deal was really involved and long lasting. I just couldn't imagine having my life tied to the project for years. It was just too cold—too impersonal." She caught the frown flitting across Roberto's face and realized how her words might hurt him. "I'm sorry. I didn't mean you and my brother can't find happiness in the work. It's just not for me."

"Fair enough. So what do you want to do?"

"That's the problem. I don't know. I know how ridiculous that sounds for an almost twenty-nine-year-old to not know what they want to do with their life. I married young, and with Lukos's job, I knew we would be traveling a lot. I was all right with putting aside my career to support him, and we were talking—well, we were doing more than talking—about having a family. And then, well, you know…he got sick." She sucked in a steadying breath. "So now I have no husband, no baby and no idea what to do with the rest of my life."

Roberto reached out and took her hand in his. He gave it a squeeze. "I'm sorry. Life isn't fair."

"Agreed." But they'd been talking about her for far too long. "So how about you?"

"What about me?"

"I don't know, but we've discussed my life enough for one day. Tell me something new about you."

"Well, I just spoke with my grandfather. He needs my help."

She wasn't sure what to say at this point. His furrowed brow told her that whatever his grandfather had asked of him must be weighing on him. She wasn't sure if it was her place to press him for information.

Roberto turned to her. "You have to understand that my grandfather has never asked for my help. My grandparents stepped up and raised me when my dysfunctional parents abandoned me. I don't know what I'd have done without them. But I'm afraid I've failed them. I haven't followed the path they wanted for me—working in the family business."

"I always wondered about that. But I knew you had your reasons."

Roberto got quiet. He stared off into space as though he were thinking something over. By the creased lines on his forehead, it was troubling him.

"It must be serious."

Roberto shrugged. "I'm not sure. He said he had some reports for me to look over, but he was reluctant to go into details."

"That's rather mysterious, isn't it?"

"Yes, very. My grandfather isn't one to play games. He's a straight shooter. But I'm sure you don't want to hear about my family business."

"I'm interested in whatever you want to share with me. And it's nice to focus on someone else's problems for once. I'd like to think that we're friends besides being fake lovers."

"We're definitely friends."

"Good. I was hoping you'd be up for touring Venice with me. We'll arrive there in a couple of days." It was heralded as one of the most romantic cities in the world and it just seemed like a place that she would like to share with someone—even her fake boyfriend.

He reached out and gave her hand a squeeze. "You can count on it."

His touch warmed her skin and sent a shiver of excitement over her. What was it about this man that got her body all excited with just a touch?

Her gaze met his and held. She knew she should turn away, but she lacked the willpower. There was something mesmerizing about his eyes, as though they could see straight through her and read her very thoughts.

She wondered if he could sense that all she wanted to do on this beautiful day was get lost in his arms and re-visit the kiss he'd laid on her the other day. If only some-one would come flirt with her, perhaps Roberto would kiss her again.

All too soon, Roberto released her hand and got to his feet. "I've taken up enough of your day. I'll let you get back to your planning."

As he turned to walk away, she wanted to call out to him to stay. She wanted to tell him that she could figure out her future another time. But wasn't that what got her in this tough spot in the first place? And without a defi-nite plan by the time the cruise ended, she would end up caving to Xander's plans because she wouldn't want to hurt him.

And there was another reason she needed to hold back. This rush of emotions felt so new—so foreign. How could she possibly be falling for Roberto? Or was she just try-ing to fill that void in her heart?

Either way, she needed to slow things down. She didn't trust herself where Roberto was concerned. And so she remained quiet as he moved out of sight.

DAY FIVE

Dubrovnik, Croatia

VENICE SEEMED SO far away.

Luckily Roberto hadn't meant to keep his distance until then.

Stasia sat across the table from him. They'd just had lunch. Neither felt like going ashore. Instead they'd moved to the deck beneath the light blue sky. To keep up appearances with his family, they were spending a lot of time together. Every day they gravitated toward each other, and to Stasia's surprise, she didn't mind. In fact, she was enjoying having a friend on board.

While Roberto enjoyed an iced latte that she'd convinced him to try, she was sipping on a fruity umbrella drink. A gentle breeze rushed over her sun-warmed skin as they sat in comfortable silence.

"Roberto?" a female voice called.

In the next moment, his grandmother and a gentleman with silver hair who resembled Roberto, from his handsome face to his tall stature, approached. The man had some white in the temples that only accentuated his classic good looks. It was definitely Roberto's grandfather. However, neither grandparent was smiling.

Roberto rose to his feet and gave his grandmother a hug. "Yaya, happy birthday."

"Thank you," his grandmother said. "Everything is arranged for the party this evening." And then his grandmother smiled. Not one of those friendly, doting grandmotherly smiles, but one of those I-know-something-you-don't-know smiles. And even though Stasia didn't know the woman, it made her nervous.

"Good." The straight line of Roberto's shoulders eased. "Is there anything you need me to do—"

"Yes." His grandfather spoke up. "I thought you'd be in your cabin working on that project I gave you." The man frowned. Displeasure was written all over his face. "I should have known better—"

"I was just headed that way to get my laptop."

His grandfather's eyes widened in surprise. "I'm looking forward to hearing your thoughts."

"And you don't want to give me a heads-up about what I'll be looking for?"

He shook his head. "I want your unbiased opinion about the numbers."

"Okay. I'll do my best."

"You have until the end of the cruise."

Stasia felt for Roberto. How was he supposed to do what his grandfather wanted when the man was being so vague? And by the look on Roberto's face, no matter what he said, pleasing his grandparents was important to him. He may have fooled himself into thinking otherwise, but she could see the love he had for them written all over his face. And she couldn't blame him.

Family was something special—something she no longer had. And now that Xander was married with a child of his own, he felt further away than ever before. And that was why she needed to carve out a life for herself. She needed to find a job that she was as passionate about as Roberto was about his work.

"We should be going," his grandmother said. And then she turned to Stasia. "It's so good to see you again. I hope we'll get a chance to speak more this evening at the party."

"But, Yaya, she...she wasn't invited," Roberto said, looking utterly flustered.

His grandmother reached out and patted his arm. "All the details have been taken care off. We'll see you both there."

And then his grandparents strolled off toward the double doors leading to the interior of the ship.

Stasia turned to Roberto before he could say anything. "I don't know about this."

"She's suspicious of us. I mean, if we were really a couple, you'd come with me, right?"

Stasia hesitated and then nodded. "I'm just having a problem thinking of us, you know, that way."

"If you've changed your mind—"

"No. I said I'd do this." Even though she was now having second and third thoughts about what she'd agreed to. But she refused to let Roberto down.

"Forget it. I'll go tell her the truth." When he started after his grandmother, Stasia rushed after him.

"Roberto, don't. I really wouldn't mind attending the party. Those of your family who I've met, I like. And I've always loved big get-togethers." She really missed her own grandparents and their extravagant parties. They'd always been so much fun, with singing, storytelling and dancing into the wee hours of the morning.

"You're sure?"

She nodded. "I am."

She hadn't been to a party since...since Lukos was alive. A pang of guilt and a dose of pain washed over her. This would be another first for her since he'd passed.

"Now, I'd better go look over the reports for my grandfather. I have a feeling this evening's activities will include a Q&A with him." Roberto started to walk away.

"Good luck."

He glanced back. "Thanks."

Now was her time to run and do some research and reading before she had to get ready for the party, but instead she remained seated. Roberto had her so confused that she didn't know if she was coming or going.

That evening there were no wardrobe malfunctions.

Roberto was disappointed, as the last time had led to such delicious consequences. He told himself it was for the best that they didn't kiss again. It was better for everyone if they remained friends without benefits.

He'd have preferred an excuse to avoid a big, loud family affair. These things always made him uncomfortable.

When Stasia finished speaking with his cousin Gaia, he leaned in close. "Are you ready to call it a night?"

She turned a puzzled look in his direction. "Since we arrived that's the second time you've asked me that question—what's wrong?"

He shrugged. How was he supposed to explain how awkward he felt around his relatives?

"I have work to do." It was the truth. He always had work to do. And there was a report he needed to review about a prospective piece of property.

"It's more than that. You've been unusually quiet this evening. Do you regret bringing me?"

"No. Not at all." He glanced around to make sure no one could overhear him. "You're the only thing that's made this evening bearable."

"What?" Her gaze filled with confusion. "But this is your family. And they're all happy you're here."

"But I don't fit in."

"That's so sad." Sympathy reflected in her eyes.

That was the last thing he wanted. He shouldn't have said anything. "Forget I said that."

"I can't. Talk to me."

He never told anyone as much as he'd told Stasia. There was something about her that made confiding in her so easy. And she wanted to hear what he had to say, unlike some of the women he'd dated who only cared about listening to themselves talk.

Stasia continued to stare at him expectantly.

He cleared his throat. "You probably noticed that my parents aren't here." When she nodded, he continued. "They dumped me on my grandparents when I was young. I used to wonder what was wrong with me that they didn't want me. I was the only one in my large extended family who didn't have an active mother and father. I always felt different, estranged from everyone else. So I spent my youth studying and reading. And when I got older, it was easier to always be working instead of attending family functions."

"I'm sorry." She reached out and squeezed his hand. Her touch was warm and gentle. It sent a wave of awareness through him.

"Don't be." He shook his head. "I'm used to it after all these years." But it was the reason he held back a part of himself in every relationship.

"Your parents, they're still alive?"

He nodded. "They rarely show up for these sorts of events."

"Gaia is really happy you're here. So are your grandparents." She nudged him. "Maybe you could smile and act like you're having a good time."

Guilt assailed him. He avoided a lot of the family functions. Maybe in the future he would make more of an effort to attend the gatherings. After all, his grandparents weren't getting any younger, and to his surprise, his grandfather was mellowing a bit.

Not wanting to talk any more about his family, Roberto turned to Stasia. "Would you like to dance?"

Surprise lit up her eyes. "I would."

"I have to warn you that I don't dance often."

"I bet you're better than you think."

He shook his head. He knew his limitations. Why exactly did he suggest dancing? It was obviously a moment of desperation.

To his relief, the music switched to a much slower, romantic ballad. He was a little better at this pace. And then Stasia stepped in front of him. She was so close. His heart beat faster. He wrapped his arm around her slender waist and automatically drew her closer. His heart pounded his ribs. His other hand reached for her much smaller hand, enjoying the feel of her smooth skin touching his.

Her jasmine scent wrapped around him. All the bad memories, stress and guilt disappeared as if in a puff of magic. The only thing on his mind now was Stasia and how much he enjoyed holding her as they moved around the floor. He'd never get enough of this.

All too soon the music stopped as the band took a break. Disappointment assailed him as he released her. His family and friends joined them at a large round table in the middle of the room. The birthday girl was at the center of the crowd. She looked ten years younger than her eighty years. And his grandmother continued to smile as she'd done all evening.

People pulled up chairs until they were sitting two and three chairs deep. He and Stasia were at the front, across the table from his grandparents. Moods were light and festive as champagne flooded.

"You two looked so amazing out on the dance floor," his cousin said.

"I don't know about me," Roberto said. "I have two left feet."

"You do not," Stasia piped in. "You are quite talented."

"All I know," Gaia said, "is that you two look so much in love. Maybe you'll be the next ones to get married."

Stasia reached under the table and squeezed his hand. He knew she was nervous and he couldn't blame her. His cousin could get carried away at times. But with his grandmother watching them like a hawk, he didn't say a word.

As the party wound down and they made their way to their cabins, they were hand in hand. It just seemed like the thing a couple would do. And he found that he liked the physical connection—being tied to someone else. Even though it was a fake relationship, he liked that they were in it together. It was a confidence that was shared just between the two of them. It was a link he'd never shared with anyone, as he usually kept people at arm's length.

And as hard as he tried to tell himself it was just a blossoming friendship, unlike the cordial relationship they'd entertained in recent years, this was so much different. She was warmer, funnier and livelier than he'd originally thought. In the beginning, she was reserved with people until she got to know them. Like with his grandmother, Stasia had held herself back. But something told him that if she spent much time with his outgoing grandmother it would all change. He wasn't sure how he felt about it.

Because the more Stasia became comfortable with him and his family, the more comfortable he'd get with keeping her around for the long term. And he didn't do long terms. He refused to end up like his parents, who were involved in a relationship, which was supposedly based on love, but they could barely stand to be in the same room with each other for more than five minutes.

But then there were his grandparents. They seemed to have overcome their problems. He couldn't help but wonder if it was because they came from a generation that believed you toughed out the rough times no matter how bad or how miserable. That didn't sound like something he wanted to try.

It was best for him to remain a bachelor, answering to no one and not having to worry about disappointing anyone.

DAY SIX

Split, Croatia

SHE JUST COULDN'T FOCUS.

Stasia sat in her cabin, having to reread the same paragraph three times. Each time she would get distracted with thoughts of Roberto. What was he doing now? Was he regretting their arrangement?

For as much work as she'd accomplished, she might as well have gone ashore. She had to admit, she'd been tempted. After all, there was Diocletian's Palace, with its cathedral and bell tower to explore. But if she kept running off exploring, she'd never devise her five-year plan.

She turned her attention back to the self-help book about finding what truly made a person happy. Because she was frustrated with herself—with her life. It wasn't that she didn't have enough to do to keep herself busy during the day. She had friends to lunch with. She liked to cook—though cooking for one was a challenge. She was also learning to knit. She'd started with socks—funny-shaped socks. And she had a sister-in-law and niece that she could visit. All in all, she had enough to keep her from growing bored, including enough money that she could travel the world. But she felt driven to do something important with her life—something to make a difference.

And then there was Xander to take into consideration. She knew he wanted her to be happy. She didn't think he'd want her to go into business with him out of some sort of sense of loyalty and obligation. Besides, she was fairly certain her brother was just drawing her into the business because he was worried about her and not because he actually wanted her help.

She glanced down at the book in her lap and had absolutely no idea where she'd left off. With a frustrated sigh, she closed the book and placed it on the table next to her chair. So much for reading.

Stasia got to her feet. Maybe some fresh air would do her good. She headed for the door and walked until she reached the sun-drenched deck where there was a light breeze. This trip was not going as she'd planned. She thought she'd have her goals listed out by now. Potential employers all sorted into a list from her favorite to her least favorite. A résumé put together. A five-year plan detailed and ready to go as she exited the ship.

And all she'd done so far was get drawn into a fake relationship with Roberto, of all people. If Xander was here now, he'd have a fit. She couldn't help but smile at the image of her brother flipping out over a relationship that wasn't even real.

Xander didn't like when things didn't go his way. In fact, he didn't take it well at all. Just like when his now wife had turned up pregnant. That hadn't been in his plans and it had turned his whole life upside down overnight.

Maybe that was what she needed. Not a surprise pregnancy. Definitely not. But something to turn her life upside down. Maybe then she'd be able to see the path she was supposed to take in life. Why did she feel like the answer was just out of her reach?

"What's the matter?" asked a male voice.

The familiar voice drew her from her thoughts. She stopped walking and found Roberto sitting at a nearby table with his laptop open. How was it that on such a large ship they kept running into each other?

If she believed in signs, she would think this was one.

But of course, neither of them was interested in starting anything. She wasn't even convinced that Roberto was thrilled with the idea of her being his fake girlfriend.

"Hey," she said, trying to sound happy. "What are you up to?"

"Working on that project for my grandfather."

"I won't keep you." She started to walk away.

"Don't go."

She turned back to him. "I don't want to disturb you."

"You won't be. I'm stuck. So maybe a distraction will do me some good."

He wasn't the only one spinning his wheels. Since she couldn't concentrate on her planning, maybe she could help him. She wasn't sure what she could do, but she was willing to be a sounding board while he talked through his thought processes. Perhaps that would give him some new ideas.

She moved to the seat across from his. "What are you working on?"

"Spreadsheets. Itemized income and expense statements."

That didn't sound very interesting, but there was obviously something of importance in those numbers or his grandfather wouldn't have him going over them. "And does anything jump out at you?"

"No. That's the problem." He leaned back in the chair. "I thought something was wrong and that's why I was asked to look at them. But nothing seems to be out of place." He sighed. "My grandfather didn't tell me what he suspected because he didn't want to influence my findings. Is it possible I'm on a fool's errand?"

"Your grandfather doesn't seem like the type to waste another person's time with looking for a problem that doesn't exist. And if he wanted you to know how well the company was doing, I'm sure he would have come straight out and told you."

Roberto raked his fingers through his dark hair, giving it a tousled look. "Then I don't get it. On the surface, the numbers all add up."

"Then maybe you have to look beneath the surface."

He stopped and looked at her for a moment. "You make a good point. I started with the consolidated report. I figured it would give a full overview of the business. But there are some other files. They have the backup information. The very detailed information. But it would take days for me to comb through. And I don't have that much time before the end of the cruise."

"You seem to like what you're doing. Do you miss working at your family's business?"

He shrugged, not answering the question one way or the other. "I should get back to work."

Since she wasn't having much success with her five-year plan, why not help Roberto? She could see how important this was to him.

"I could help you," she said, not sure he would take her up on the offer.

He arched a dark eyebrow. "You don't want to waste your vacation combing over reports."

"But I want to help you. And between the two of us, maybe we can find whatever it is your grandfather thinks is important." She paused. Maybe he was just trying to turn her down gently. "Unless, of course, those are secret files."

He shook his head. "I mean yes, they are confidential. But I trust you. I just hate having you do something so boring."

"You aren't making me do anything. Remember, this was my idea."

"Thank you. I don't know what I'd do without you on this trip."

His words filled her chest with warmth. Maybe he did want her around...just as much as she wanted to be around him.

"Wait here. We might as well work outside on this gorgeous day. I'll just run and get my laptop." She stood. "I'll be right back."

She had no idea what they'd be looking for on those spreadsheets. But she liked being able to help Roberto. It felt good to be needed. Everyone needed to be needed sometimes. And it'd been a long time since she was needed.

A few hours later, the answer was still elusive.

He knew what the problem was... Stasia.

Roberto was good at business. He was avid with spreadsheets. And he was great at numbers. But for the life of him, he couldn't come up with the reason his grandfather had him going over these reports. There was something lurking in the figures. He was certain of it.

But every time he stared at the numbers for more than a minute or two, his mind strayed to the dark-haired beauty who for the duration of this cruise was his fake girlfriend. And the biggest problem he was having was that he was enjoying their time together. He was curious to see what it'd be like if they were truly dating.

He halted his thoughts. Was that what he really wanted? Because Stasia was nothing like the other women who had passed through his life. Those women had known up front not to expect anything long-term from him. They knew he didn't do commitments—aside from the business kind. And he never ever uttered the *L* word.

He remembered how his parents would banter around the

word *love* as he was growing up. They loved his art projects from school. They loved his grades. They loved how well he did on the polo team. They loved him. And then they were gone. As soon as the school holiday was over, they jumped on their respective flights and headed who knew where. If that was love, he wanted no parts of it.

It was like his parents used the word to make up for being absent in his life. They seemed to think if they said it enough times it would make up for everything. It didn't. It never would.

And so the *love* word had become meaningless to him.

"Hey, did you find anything?" Stasia's voice drew him from his thoughts. When he shook his head, she said, "I've found something but I don't know if it'll mean anything to you. It's probably nothing."

Considering he still had no clue what his grandfather suspected was wrong, he was willing to look at just about anything. He got up and moved to her side of the table. "Let me see."

"It's this." She pointed to a number on the screen. "I can't tell if it's just a transposed number."

She had two screens open at once. One was the consolidated file and the other was the backup information. The consolidated file was supposed to draw from the detailed files, but perhaps his grandfather didn't have the links automated. It seemed a bit odd to him because everything at Roberto's office was monitored with oversight controls.

He checked the next number. It tied to the original file. As did the next one. Maybe it was, after all, just a typo.

"Can you make a notation of the number, where you found it and the information from the source document?"

"So it's something?" There was a hopeful note in her voice.

"It's definitely wrong. But the numbers surrounding

it appear to be correct. So I'm not sure yet. But it's worth noting."

"Would your grandfather really pick up on a nine-dollar difference?"

He didn't think so. That would be something for the accountants to hash out. But he didn't think they'd escalate nine dollars to his grandfather's attention. There had to be more.

"I think we're still missing something." A big something.

"I'll keep combing through the numbers," Stasia said.

He appreciated how dedicated she was to helping him. She was easy to work with and she didn't ask too many questions. In fact, he was thinking of asking her to come work with him.

Then Stasia would always be close. He wouldn't have to miss her after this cruise ended. Because he was quite certain he would. She was so easy to be around. She didn't make him uptight because she wanted something from him that he wasn't willing to give. And she listened to him with avid interest.

He wondered what Xander would think about the working arrangement. He knew how worried Xander was about his sister. Maybe this would give his friend some peace of mind because Roberto would be able to keep an eye on Stasia and make sure no one took advantage of her while she sorted through the aftermath of her husband's death.

The more he thought about this idea, the more he liked it. And if he was able to think of Stasia as a colleague, it would rid him of these other thoughts—the ones about wanting to pull her into his arms and smother her lips with kisses before tumbling into bed.

Yes, this plan to offer her a job was much better.

"Oh, no." Stasia's voice filled with worry.

"What's the matter? Did you find another mistake?"

She shook her head. "It's not that. It's the time. If I'm going to be ready for us to meet up with your cousin and her fiancé for dinner, I have to start now. And I haven't finished reviewing the report you gave me. There were just so many numbers and the trail back to the source documents can be quite lengthy."

He was having the exact same problem. There was nothing fast about this analysis. And he had a feeling his grandfather knew it.

"I think what you discovered will be enough for today," Roberto said.

"You do?"

He nodded. "My grandfather is a very wise man. He knows it'll take more than an afternoon to uncover whatever it is he thinks is amiss in these reports. That's why he gave me until the end of the cruise."

"Which isn't that far off."

Her concern touched him. "Don't worry. It'll all work out."

"If he asks about it, what will you tell him? Will you mention the typo?"

"I'll tell him enough to let him know we're on track."

She shook her head. "You shouldn't mention me. He didn't ask us both. He wanted you to work on this. Alone."

Perhaps she was right. He didn't like taking credit for someone else's work, but if she accepted his business proposal, he knew this would never happen again.

And so he sent her off to get ready for the dinner. He wouldn't take nearly as long to prepare. It was only after she'd gathered her things and headed for the door to the interior of the ship that he realized he hadn't asked her to be his official assistant.

He'd turned to find her disappearing through the doorway and then she slipped out of sight. The question would have to wait for later. He just hoped it would be the answer she was searching for as far as her future. He knew she didn't have to work. Her family and husband had made sure that she would be well cared for, but he understood the need to have a goal in life, a reason to get out of bed in the morning.

But he didn't want to rush things. He was not a man to be rushed into things. His normal way was to let it simmer at the back of his mind as he weighed the pros and cons of such a decision.

Though part of him was certain they'd make a good match, the other more cautious part of him said to rush things was an opportunity to make a mistake. And a mistake might lead to Stasia getting hurt. And that could not happen, not on his watch.

Perhaps it was best to give it some more thought. Maybe once this project was complete, he would know for sure just how well they worked together.

He decided to work a bit longer on the reports. Who knew what he'd find, but his curiosity was piqued now. Thanks to Stasia.

"Roberto." It was his grandmother's voice. He turned to find her headed toward him. She wore a serious expression. "I've been looking for you everywhere."

He thought of mentioning that she could have called his cell phone, but he refrained. "Now that you've found me, what can I do for you?"

"I'd like you to walk with me back to my cabin."

He turned back to his computer. He thought of telling her he was busy working on the project for his grandfather—

"Whatever you're doing can wait," she said in a firm tone. "This can't."

That got his full attention. He gathered his things and walked with her. She made idle chitchat about the cruise and the upcoming wedding. All the while, he wondered what was really on his grandmother's mind.

If it had something to do with Stasia, he would have to stand up to his grandmother and put a halt to her meddling—easier said than done. His grandmother was fiercely strong and he loved her dearly. But it was saying something when he was more worried about a meeting with his grandmother than he was with fourteen lawyers and a shrewd billionaire.

He paused outside her cabin door and took a deep breath. He sensed his grandmother had something serious on her mind. And that was never a good thing.

"Come in," she said. "Don't loiter in the hallway."

He stepped inside and closed the door behind him. Her suite was the most luxurious and spacious on the ship. She moved to sit at the head of the dining room table where a teapot and service were awaiting her.

She held a cup of what he presumed was her favorite tea. "Would you like some?"

He shook his head. Anxious to get this over with, he asked, "What did you want to discuss?"

She poured him a cup of tea anyway and then waved for him to have a seat next to her. "We need to talk."

He took a seat. Normally, he wasn't a fan of tea, but right about now, he welcomed the fact that he had something to do with his hands. He stirred in some sugar and waited quietly for his grandmother to have her say.

She leaned back in her chair. "You know I'm not easily fooled." His gaze met hers but he remained quiet and she continued. "I know you were not happy that I invited some young women on the cruise to attend the wedding—and for you to meet."

"You shouldn't have done that, Yaya." It was time to make some things clear with his grandmother. "When or if I decide to settle down, I am quite capable of finding my own wife."

Her knowing smile broadened. "Are you ready to admit that you're not really involved with Ms. Marinakos?"

"Why do you presume it's all a pretense?" The truth was he did feel something for Stasia. However, he was reluctant to examine those feelings too closely.

"Because you told me very bluntly that you were a confirmed bachelor. Why should I believe you are suddenly involved with this young woman?"

"It isn't sudden. I've known Stasia for a while now. She's Xander's younger sister. And she's been involved with the business."

His grandmother's eyes widened. "So you're saying you've been seeing her for quite a while?"

He paused. It all depended on what she meant by "seeing." He'd spent quite a bit of time with Stasia since her husband passed away. Xander had been trying to get Stasia started in his business, and when he was preoccupied with working things out with Lea, Roberto had strived to make Stasia feel welcome.

"What is this inquisition all about?" He cut to the chase. "If you want me to end things with Stasia, it's not going to happen."

He surprised not only his grandmother but himself with such a declaration. The fact it was true was all the more startling. He didn't want this thing with Stasia to end.

His grandmother's gaze widened. "So you're telling me you care about this woman?"

He nodded. It was true. But caring was different than loving someone. He was a long way from that.

His grandmother's gaze searched his. "In that case, I have something for you."

She reached over and pulled a small black velvet box from her purse. She placed it on the table and pushed it toward him. The box sat there in front of him like some ominous apparition.

"Go ahead and open it. It won't bite you."

He had a feeling it would do much worse. He knew what was in the box without opening it.

His grandmother was calling him out on his story. She was going to make him prove his commitment to Stasia. Could he do something like that?

He reached forward and took the box in his hands. He pried it open and found a stunning diamond ring inside set in white gold. His first thought was that it would look perfect on Stasia's delicate hand. And the next thought was that he was in trouble—very big trouble.

He tried to form words to say something and utterly failed. There was a disconnect between his shocked mind and his dry mouth. He sat quietly staring at the dazzling ring.

"That belonged to your great-grandmother. My mother. I've been saving it all these years and now I want you to have it. I want you to give it to the woman who you pledge your heart and life to." She glanced at her wristwatch. "Look at the time. I have to go meet your grandfather."

And with that, they parted ways. He slipped the ring box in his pocket. It felt like it was burning a hole through his clothes. He'd had absolutely no idea that his grandmother had been saving this for him.

Part of him was touched that his grandmother entrusted him with a family heirloom, but another part of him was angry that she had his life planned out for him. His grand-mother had this ring and this ship full of women because she was bound and determined he should be married be-cause it was the way things were done—even though he'd told her marriage wasn't for him. It obviously wasn't for his absent parents either and look where that had got-ten them.

And then there was his grandfather with this problem that needed to be solved. Was there a problem? Or was his grandfather trying to lure him back into the family business?

Roberto got the distinct impression that he was being played. And he didn't like it one little bit. And the more he thought about it, the less guilty he felt about his fake engagement.

DAY SEVEN

Venice, Italy

WHY HAD HE worked so late?

Today there was no room for tiredness.

This was their first day in Venice. And most important, it was Stasia's birthday.

After a cold shower and two espressos, Roberto was feeling so much more like himself. And he couldn't think of anything he wanted to do more than to make Stasia smile. When she was happy, her radiance lit up everything in her orbit, including him.

He'd wanted to throw her a party with all the trimmings, but she'd firmly refused. He would have to do something low-key, but that didn't mean it couldn't be special. And he had the perfect thing in mind. He was keeping it a surprise.

They weren't the only ones going ashore. The ship practically emptied at this stop. He glanced over at Stasia. She was beaming with anticipation.

"Where are we going?" Stasia watched as some passengers went one direction while Roberto took her hand and headed in the opposite direction. "Roberto?" She dug her heels in and they came to a stop. "I'm not going any farther until you speak to me."

He turned to her with a smile on his face. "Do you want to hit a couple of the highlights with a paid tour or do you want to have the most amazing day?"

Like that was a hard question to answer. "Of course I want to have an amazing visit. This is my first time in Venice."

"But it's not mine." Sure, he'd been here for business purposes, but he'd never had anyone to share the magic of this very special city. "I want to show you around. I want your birthday to be memorable."

She removed her hand from his hold. "You don't need to do that. It's too much."

Was she making a point that, since he wasn't truly her boyfriend, he was overstepping? The thought didn't sit well with him.

During the past week, it felt like they'd moved beyond friends. But where did that leave them? He wasn't sure of the answer and now certainly wasn't the time to evaluate it.

"Relax," he said. "It's just one friend showing another a good time on your birthday. Nothing more." When he saw the worry disappear from her eyes, he said, "We need to catch a vaporetto."

"What's that?"

"It's like a floating taxi."

"Oh."

He reached out to take her hand again but caught himself and lowered his arm to his side. He took off again with rapid steps. When he noticed her lagging behind, he slowed down for her.

The water taxi was crowded as it chugged down the Grand Canal. But Roberto was able to claim the last two seats in the open prow, which provided a sweeping view of the majestic canal. There wasn't much room. When he sat down, his thigh rubbed against Stasia's. A bolt of attraction shot through him, settling in a tightness in his abdomen.

He willed away the unwanted sensation. He attempted to put some space between them but that only succeeded in rubbing not only his thigh but also his shoulder against her. He was becoming increasingly aware of her—of wanting her—in a much friendlier manner than was appropriate. He stopped moving.

"Are you all right?" Stasia asked.

"I'm fine." He was anything but fine. However, that was his problem, not hers.

"I could stand."

As she started to get up, he reached out to her. "No. Stay where you are."

And then realizing he was touching her, he withdrew his hand. She settled once again, next to him. Why had he thought being "just friends" was going to be easy?

It didn't help that this ride seemed to go on and on. There were a few stops along the way before they finally exited at the Rialto Bridge, one of the oldest bridges that spanned the Grand Canal.

Stasia snapped photo after photo on her smartphone. All the while, she wore a big smile that made her eyes twinkle with happiness. Thankfully, his uneasiness hadn't ruined her good mood. The more she smiled, the more relaxed he became. He could just stare at her for hours. It was then that she turned to him and snapped his photo.

"I hope you don't mind. I couldn't resist," she said. "You smile so little when you're conducting business, which is when I see you the most. But on this trip, I've seen a new side of you. The relaxed, fun side of you."

"And this new side, do you like it?" His breath hitched as he waited for her answer.

"I do." Her gaze caught and held his a little longer than necessary. "I like it very much."

"Then I'll make a point of relaxing more often." So long as he maintained a respectable distance between them.

"And don't forget about having fun. The smile on your face looks good on you."

He didn't think her admission would affect him one way or the other, but her words zeroed in on his chest and a warm sensation filled it. She had a way of sneaking past his best-laid defenses. His smile broadened.

They meandered around until they came to the Campanile di San Marco, where they took the elevator to the top of the bell tower. Stasia continued making the pictorial history of their outing. And he had to admit the view from the top of the bell tower was awe-inspiring, with all the historic architecture, but the most amazing view of all was the look of awe reflected on Stasia's face.

With so much to see, they didn't linger long. They hurried to nearby Saint Mark's Basilica, with its most amazing mosaics. And then they were off to the Doge's Palace, where they arrived early enough to tour the hidden rooms followed by a tour of the public rooms. There was just so much history in this amazing city that it was hard to take it all in.

But he had to admit it was so hard to concentrate on the historical artifacts and the culture when the most amazing person was right next to him and all he could think about was pulling her into his arms and kissing her. But completely impossible. He'd promised her they would tour the city as friends—nothing more. It was best for both their sakes.

They shared lunch at an outside café serving authentic Venetian fare, as Stasia insisted they soak up as much of the culture as possible during their brief visit. Stasia chose spaghetti *alle vongole* and he chose to go with a rice dish, *risi e bisi*. And with witnessing her bubbly enthusiasm, he was incapable of denying her just about anything. Seeing Venice through Stasia's eyes was like seeing it for the very first time.

And for dessert, he surprised her with glasses of prosecco as well as some tiramisu. Her face lit up with happiness and he'd never experienced such joy just by watching someone smile.

"Roberto, what have you done?"

"It's your birthday. We have to celebrate."

"But I told you not to make a big deal of it." But the twinkle in her eyes let him know she wasn't upset with him.

He wasn't well versed at buying birthday gifts, so he'd called his assistant for some advice. She'd assured him that jewelry was the way to go and the salesperson at the jewelry store at one of the ports had concurred. Now that he was sitting here with Stasia, he hoped they'd been right.

He reached in his pocket and pulled out a small box. He placed it in front of her. "Happy birthday."

Her eyes widened.

When she didn't move to take the box, he worried that he'd done the wrong thing. "Don't you want it?"

She nodded, then opened the box. Inside were diamond-and-blue-sapphire earrings. For a moment, she didn't say a word and his body tensed. He'd messed up. She didn't like them.

"If you don't like them, I can exchange them."

"They're gorgeous." Stasia looked at them in awe. "And way too extravagant."

When she attempted to hand them back, he frowned at her. "Weren't you taught that it's not polite to return birthday gifts?"

"Then what am I supposed to do with them?"

"That's a silly question. Put them on."

Her mouth gaped slightly. And then to his surprise, she took off her earrings and put on his gift. Talk about dazzling—the woman, not the earrings. No wonder his thoughts and vision kept straying back to her succulent lips.

He forced his gaze back to her earlobes. "The earrings are almost as pretty as the birthday girl."

She flushed and glanced away. "Thank you."

"You are quite welcome."

The afternoon they spent meandering through the Rialto Market, where a kindly older woman offered to take their photo.

Roberto tried to bow out. Having his photo taken wasn't his thing. But when Stasia pleaded with him, sticking out her bottom lip, he turned to putty in her hands. He moved to her side.

The woman held up Stasia's phone. "Closer together."

He hesitated. Stasia inched toward him, still leaving a little space between them.

The woman lowered the camera and frowned. "Closer."

He stifled a groan. This woman had no idea how hard she was making this for him. Stasia moved until their shoulders brushed together.

The woman still didn't take the photo. *"Bacio! Bacio!"*

Suddenly someone stepped up next to the woman and joined the woman in chanting *bacio*. They wanted them to kiss. Other people in the market added their voices.

Roberto grew uncomfortably warm. He resisted the urge to undo a button on his shirt. What had gotten into these people? Didn't they have anything better to do than to torture him?

Stasia leaned close, making his heart race. She said in his ear, "I think she's planning to hold my camera hostage until we, um, you know…"

"Kiss?" His voice rose a couple of octaves.

Color filled Stasia's cheeks. "Yes, that."

Somehow her discomfort with this whole scenario eased his own uneasiness. "Do you really need your phone?"

She gave him an *are you serious?* look. "Yes."

His gaze moved to the woman holding the phone. She arched an expectant brow at him. "It looks like we really don't have any other choice. If we don't kiss, we'll have to get you a new phone."

"What?" Stasia blinked a couple of times as though processing his answer. It obviously wasn't what she'd been expecting. "But, no, we can't. I have all my photos on there. And my contacts. My life is on that phone."

"What you're saying is that it's important? So important you'd do almost anything to get it back?"

She frowned. "I can't leave here without it."

"What do you want me to do?"

"Just do it."

"Kiss you?"

"Yes."

It certainly wasn't the response he'd been hoping for. Not taking time to consider all the reasons this was a bad decision, he dipped his head and claimed her soft, pliable lips. The chanting stopped and a silence fell over the crowd. He'd only meant it to be a brief kiss, but once he felt her mouth pressing to his, thoughts of pulling away escaped him.

As Stasia's lips opened to him, he was utterly and totally caught up in the moment. The fact they had an audience also slipped from his thoughts. He could only think about the woman who was now in his arms. She was definitely not as immune to his kisses as she had let on.

He drew her closer. His mouth moved over hers, slowly at first, as he didn't want to scare her away. Because there were so many ways this kiss was wrong. And yet nothing had ever felt so right. It was as though Stasia had been made to be right there in his arms.

Her hands slid from his shoulders and wrapped around

his neck. A deep moan of longing and excitement swelled in his throat. Could she hear him? Did she know how much he wanted her?

And then the sound of applause broke through his hazy thoughts. Bit by bit, reality came back to him, from being in the market to the woman taking their photo to the growing audience. Audience? He pulled back.

Stasia's eyes blinked open. She looked at him with confusion reflected in her eyes. Apparently, he wasn't the only one to be caught up in the moment. He refused to contemplate what that should mean to him.

The older woman stepped up to them with a big smile on her face. She went to hand Stasia the phone, but Stasia didn't reach out to take it.

"You didn't take the photo yet," Stasia said.

"Oh, but I did. In fact, I took more than one." The woman placed the phone in Stasia's hand. "You two are going to have an amazing future together."

"But we're not together," Stasia said too late.

The woman had disappeared into the crowd. In unison Roberto and Stasia stared at her phone. There was a photo of them kissing. Not just kissing but getting utterly lost in the moment. If he didn't know better, he'd swear they looked like they were lovers—like they were head over heels in love. But of course that wasn't the case.

The crowd dispersed and Stasia slipped her phone in her purse. Neither said a word about the photo. And Roberto fought the urge to ask her to send him a copy of the photo. It shouldn't mean anything to him, but for some reason it did. It was best he didn't have a copy. Otherwise, the only thing he'd get done would be staring at the photo.

"How about some gelato?" Roberto gestured to a gelato shop. He needed something to cool him down after that rousing kiss.

"I don't know. We just had that delicious lunch."

"But it's your birthday. You're allowed to indulge."

Buzz. Buzz.

"Do you need to get that?" Stasia asked.

"It can wait."

Surprise reflected in her eyes. "But you didn't even check to see who the message is from."

"It can wait. But celebrating your birthday can't wait."

She smiled brightly as she continued to stare at him.

Starting to feel self-conscious, he ran a hand over his mouth. Perhaps her lip gloss had rubbed off on him. "What? Do I have something on my face?"

She shook her head. "Maybe there's hope for you."

"Hope?"

"To learn that there's more to life than work."

As they entered the small shop, he couldn't stop thinking about his conversation with Stasia. He grew uncomfortable with her peeling back his layers and figuring out how he ticked.

Wanting to change the subject, he said, "It's your turn to order."

She ordered *limone* and let Roberto have a taste of the lemon indulgence. In turn, he shared some of his *gianduja*, with its creamy chocolate and hazelnut flavors.

As they ate, Roberto couldn't help thinking how Stasia's presence in his life made everything feel so different. Until this point, he'd traveled all over the world but he'd never slowed down long enough to savor the gelato. But with Stasia next to him, he wanted to slow down and take in everything about this marvelous day.

When they'd finished, Roberto removed another small box from his other pocket and placed it in her hand.

Her eyes grew wide. "Roberto, this is too much."

"No, it isn't. I don't have anyone in my life to do these things for. Please indulge me."

She opened the box and gasped. "It's gorgeous." Her gaze met his. "You do know that you're spoiling me."

"What can I say? I like to make you smile."

When she went to put on the necklace, she had a problem with the catch. His instinct was to help her, but he hesitated. Getting close to her so soon wasn't a good idea. But when her frustrated gaze met his, he moved into action.

She swept her hair out of the way and tilted her head to the side. The nape of her slender neck was right there just begging him to press a kiss to it. His jaw tightened as an inner war waged within him.

None too soon, he'd latched the matching diamond-and-blue-sapphire necklace. He quickly stepped back as though sprung from a trap. It fit her perfectly, stopping just above her cleavage. The gems caught the sunlight and sparkled.

"Thank you, again. This is a birthday I'll never forget."

"And it's not over yet."

He'd visited Venice before but he'd never appreciated its beauty. But today, seeing it through Stasia's eyes, it was like he was seeing it for the very first time.

This was such a different side of him.

A more down-to-earth version of him.

Stasia smiled as they continued their exploration by visiting the Accademia Gallery, taking in the great masterpieces. She kept glancing at Roberto to make sure he was having a good time. She never would have guessed he'd be content in an art museum. She knew he was doing it for her and she appreciated it more than she could say.

Lukos never had the patience for this stuff. He was an active guy, from running marathons to playing European football at the park. He always had to be on the go, and strolling through a museum wouldn't qualify.

But Roberto was different. He was interested in what appealed to her. Or at least he'd give the activity a chance.

"This was an unforgettable birthday." She smiled at him. "And it's thanks to you. If it wasn't for you, I'd probably be hidden away in my cabin for most of the cruise. Thanks for being such a great friend."

His gaze delved into her, making her heart beat faster. "I'd like to think we're a little more than friends."

"Does fake girlfriend count?" She was trying to lighten the mood; after the thoughts of Lukos, she needed some levity to alleviate some of the weight on her heart.

"I've never had a fake relationship, so that makes you special."

"And I've never had a fake boyfriend."

"Earlier you mentioned that you wanted to discuss something—what was it?"

"You know how I've been working on my life plan?" When he nodded, she continued. "I see how passionate you are about your work and that's what I want for myself. I want to wake up in the morning with a purpose—one that gets me motivated and ready to hit the day with all of my energy and passion."

"And you're sure that isn't real estate?"

She shook her head. "It's just not me."

"So, what is you?"

"That's the thing—I don't know. I mean, I thought I did at one time. I loved being a wife, and with Lukos's job taking him to many places across the globe, I always had a new adventure. And then we started talking about having a family, but then that dream crumbled. And now I have to find a new dream. A dream that's all mine and not dependent on someone else. Does that make any sense?"

"It does. Do you have any idea what it is you want to do?"

She shook her head. "That's what I thought I would sort out on this trip."

He stopped next to a magnificent marble statue. "And then I interrupted you with all of my family drama. I'm sorry."

"Don't be. I've had a really good time with you and getting to know your family."

"But it doesn't help you find a career."

"No, it doesn't. But I still have the rest of the cruise to come up with something."

"And how's the search going?" There was avid interest reflected in his eyes.

She shrugged. "I know a number of things that I don't want to do."

"Such as?"

"Singing. I can't carry a tune. And I'm not artistic, at all. Though I do love visiting the galleries and admiring other people's work. But I'm lucky if I can draw a decent stick figure."

"Are you considering something in the business world?"

"I don't know."

The more time she spent with him, the more she found she wanted to spend with him. She told herself that she was just lonely. Since Lukos died, her life had become quiet and routine. The only laughter in her life was when she was with Xander's family and her adorable niece.

Now wasn't the time.

Roberto decided to refrain from asking Stasia to work with him. He didn't want to pressure her into a job that didn't suit her. He was certain she would eventually find her way.

As amazed as Stasia had been by the artwork, Roberto was just as amazed by her. There was definitely a deep, abiding strength within her.

She turned a curious look in his direction. Their gazes met and his heart thumped harder. Did she know what he'd been thinking?

Of course not. She wasn't a mind reader, even if she did have a way of reading him quite well.

"You're not even looking at the painting," she said.

"I'm not?"

She smiled. "No. You're not."

"Sorry. I got distracted."

Her cheeks pinkened. "Maybe we should get going. What's next on this tour?"

"Something I think you'll like a lot." He held out his arm to her. "Right this way, signorina."

She smiled up at him as she slipped her hand into the crook of his arm. And just that small gesture felt so right— as though they had been doing it forever.

There was one more thing burning a hole in his pocket— the diamond ring.

His grandmother expected Stasia to wear the ring, but that would take this charade to a whole new level—

"What has you so quiet?" Stasia's voice drew him from his musings.

"Um, nothing." Nothing he wanted to discuss with her.

Before they could continue the conversation, they'd arrived at the gondola. Roberto turned to her. "Your ride awaits you."

Stasia's face beamed and his heart thumped hard and fast. What was it about this woman that just a smile could make his body react?

Once she sat down on the cushioned seat, he took his place next to her. The ring box dug into his thigh, reminding him that he needed to do something with it. Not now. Definitely not in this romantic setting.

He shifted on the seat, allowing space between them. The gondola was ornately decorated with gold trim and small statues of seahorses. There were red ropes along the sides and fluffy, colorful pillows on the seats. Stasia was quiet as she took it all in.

He hadn't told her but this was his first gondola ride too. In the past when he'd visited this beautiful city, he hadn't felt the urge to ride the gondola. For some reason, it just felt too romantic to ride alone and he didn't have anyone he wanted to ask to accompany him—until now.

Off they went down the canal, gliding over the peaceful water. They took in the striking architecture of the surrounding buildings. They crossed under footbridges and past other gondolas.

His hand moved to the ring box still in his pocket. It dampened his mood. It was like an albatross around his neck. Stasia turned to him with the brightest smile on her face. He moved his hand and returned her smile.

"Are you enjoying the ride?" he asked.

"I am. This is amazing—the whole day has been amazing." She gazed deep into his eyes. "Thank you."

"For what?"

"Making this amazing day."

It had been amazing for him too.

"Roberto…" Her voice was soft as it floated through the air.

Or perhaps it just seemed that way because the loud pounding of his heart drowned out most of what was going on around them. Right now, all he could concentrate on was Stasia.

He reached out to her, tracing his hand over her cheek. "You are the most beautiful woman in the world."

Her lips parted but no words came out.

He lowered his head and claimed those sweet lips. He knew he'd never tire of her kisses. In fact, he was quite certain he would remember this moment for the rest of his life. He didn't care if he got old and forgetful. This would be one of those memories that he would cling to—Stasia in his arms, pressing her lips to his.

As she leaned into him and opened her mouth to him, her arms slipped up over his shoulders, wrapping around his neck. She tasted sweet like the prosecco and gelato they'd indulged in earlier. This was in fact the sweetest, most stirring kiss he'd ever experienced.

A cheer from observers stirred him from the kiss. It was with great reluctance that he pulled back ever so slightly. Stasia smiled up at him—a smile that made her eyes sparkle.

He would never visit Venice again without thinking of Stasia. This was their city.

That was so much better than working.

Wait. Had that thought really crossed his mind? Roberto smiled. He never expected anyone could convince him that sightseeing could be more interesting than business.

Hours later, they walked along the deck. Neither seemed anxious to go to their cabin and put an end to the day. He moved his hand and it brushed over the ring in his pocket. He needed to do something with it. What would Stasia say when she saw it?

Stasia stopped walking and turned to him. "I should head to my cabin, but I want to thank you again for making this the very best birthday." Her gaze caught and held his. "I know you'd rather have been working, but you didn't complain once or rush us at all. That was very kind of you. I'll never forget it."

He continued to stare into her beautiful eyes as his heart raced and his fingers tingled to reach out to her. "There was no other place I wanted to be—"

"Hey, guys." Gaia rushed up to them with a giant smile on her face. "Did you have a nice day?"

Roberto sensed his cousin was up to something, but he couldn't put his finger on what exactly she had on her mind.

"It was absolutely a beautiful day," Stasia said before briefly mentioning some of the places they'd visited.

"Any other news to share?" Gaia probed.

"News?" Stasia sent them both a confused look. "Are you talking about the wedding tomorrow?"

"Not exactly. At least not mine."

And then Roberto realized what his cousin was hinting at. "Gaia, can I talk to you?" When she didn't move, he added, "Alone." He glanced at Stasia. "We'll just be a moment."

They moved off to the side of the deck. Gaia turned to him. "Didn't you ask her? What are you waiting for? Venice is the most romantic city."

"You've been talking to Yaya."

"She told me about the ring. It's so romantic. What are you waiting for?"

He frowned. "I'm waiting for the right moment."

"Can I see it?"

He glanced over his cousin's shoulder to where Stasia was waiting for him. It really had been a nice day. He didn't want to ruin it.

"Roberto?"

"No. You can't see it. At least not now. And don't tell anyone about it—"

"Too late." When his gaze narrowed in on her, Gaia

added, "No one said it was supposed to be a secret. You're going to ask her, aren't you?"

He sighed. "Not with you standing here."

Gaia's face lit up with excitement. "Oh. Okay. I'm out of here." She let out a squeal of delight. "This is so exciting. Yaya is going to be so happy."

He pressed his hands to his sides and gave his cousin his most intimidating glare.

"Okay. Okay. I'm going." She gave him a brief hug. "Good luck."

Once Gaia was gone, he glanced around to make sure no other family members were lurking about. The coast was clear.

He returned to Stasia. "Sorry about that."

"What has your cousin so excited? Or was she celebrating her nuptials early?" Stasia hand signaled that Gaia might have been drinking too much champagne.

Roberto shook his head. The time had come. He withdrew the ring box from his pocket and held it out to her. Stasia didn't move as she stared wide-eyed at the box.

"My grandmother gave it to me for you."

"Me?"

He nodded. "And now everyone in my family thinks we're getting married."

"Married?"

He nodded, feeling the weight of the moment. "I think they all have wedding fever because of Gaia."

Stasia's astonishment reflected in her eyes.

He opened the box for her to see the ring.

"It's gorgeous," she said.

"You can put it on." When she cast him a questioning glance, he said, "They already think we're engaged. You should have a ring."

He withdrew the ring from the cushion of black velvet. "May I?"

She lifted her hand. As he slipped the ring on her finger, he noticed her slight tremble. It fit as though it had been made for her. They both stared at the diamond as it sparkled in the last rays of the setting sun.

"Roberto, what are we doing?"

The earlier happiness and fun had been replaced with tension and uneasiness. "It's only for a few more days."

Her gaze searched his. "I never thought it'd go this far."

"Neither did I. But I don't want to cause a scandal with it being Gaia's wedding. But it's up to you. We can end this here and now."

"I...I need time to think."

"Of course."

She walked away and his gaze followed her. He understood how much he was asking of her. After all, she hadn't signed on for a surprise engagement.

Had that really happened?

Stasia replayed the events of the day as she made her way back to her cabin. She was constantly checking that the heirloom ring was still on her finger.

Roberto had no business giving her something so precious. He should have saved it for the woman he truly loved. And then she realized there was nothing stopping him from doing just that once their charade was over.

Her gaze moved to the ring. This ring was absolutely stunning. The white-gold band had a unique and delicate design. A couple dozen diamonds surrounded a large square-cut diamond. It was fit for royalty—or the woman Roberto truly loved.

The thought of another woman wearing this ring gave

her an uneasy feeling in the pit of her stomach. She quickly dismissed the troubling thought.

Once she stepped inside her cabin, she leaned back against the closed door. She closed her eyes and expelled an uneven breath. What was she doing?

Her mind replayed scenes from the day. There were images of Roberto smiling at her and holding her hand. Stasia's heart raced. And then there was the kiss—the very stirring kiss.

Her eyes sprang open, vanishing the thoughts. Instead her attention moved to the diamond ring. It was dazzling. Its setting was so feminine and delicate. It was the type of ring she could imagine being worn by a princess.

But it didn't belong on her finger.

She slipped it off and moved to the bedside table. She gently placed it next to the lamp. Then she sank down on the edge of the bed.

The last rings she'd worn had been the ones Lukos had given her. Her heart squeezed with the familiar pain of loss. What would he think of the mess she'd gotten herself into?

He had been a lighthearted guy. There wasn't much that got to him. That was one of the things she'd loved about him. Would he understand about this? Would he insist on fixing it for her as he'd done for her time and time again? Or would he shake his head and ask what she'd been thinking?

That was a good question. What had she been thinking? She laid her head on the pillow. She'd be helping a good friend who had gone out of his way for her. That couldn't be a bad thing, right?

Roberto wasn't going to fix this for her. He was stepping back and letting her take the lead. Unlike Xander and

Lukos, who freely offered their advice, Roberto was trusting her to make up her own mind without his influence.

And the more decisions she made for herself, by herself, the more confident she was becoming in her own decision-making. She smiled. Roberto was helping her more than he knew.

Her gaze returned to the ring. But she still had to decide whether they should continue this charade. If they ended things now, she knew it would cast a shadow over Gaia's wedding. She didn't want to do anything to hurt his cousin.

And if they let it continue, what? Would it change anything? Not really. She'd still find herself being drawn closer and closer to Roberto. And when the cruise ended, so would their relationship. Was she willing to risk getting hurt again?

So what was the right thing to do?

This charade was becoming so confusing. It was increasingly difficult to tell what was fiction and what was real.

DAY EIGHT

Venice, Italy

THINGS HAD CERTAINLY taken an unexpected turn.

She was Roberto Carrass's pretend fiancée.

She picked up the ring, letting the sunlight catch the angles of the many diamonds, sending a cascade of colors over the wall. What should she do?

Today was Gaia's wedding in Venice. And she was Roberto's plus-one. She couldn't think of anyone she'd rather experience a wedding with in such a romantic city—

And then her thoughts clouded with Lukos and Xander. What would they think if they could see her now? She took in her short black dress with the plunging neckline. It wasn't anything too fancy, as she had never envisioned when she'd packed for the cruise that she'd be attending a wedding.

She recalled Lukos's words not long after he'd been diagnosed. He'd made her promise that if he died, she would go on living and not walking around in the shadow that had once been their life.

She hadn't wanted to promise. She hadn't wanted to admit that he might not make it through this battle with cancer. But Lukos had been firm and he wouldn't let her walk away until she'd made that promise.

He'd told her it was easier to make the promise then while he still had his hair, while he could still walk and do most everything he'd done before. It was making the promise later when he was bedridden that would have ripped her tattered heart to shreds. And he'd been right. The end had been—

She shook her head, chasing away the heart-wrenching memories. She refused to let them ruin this occasion.

Even though Lukos had wanted this for her, it still felt not quite right. And she didn't know what to do about that. But every day she was with Roberto, she felt as though she was letting go of Lukos's memory a little more. Not that she could or would ever forget him. He was her first love. But she was starting to wonder if there was room in her heart for the love of two men—

She gasped. What was she thinking? She did not love Roberto. Did not. Impossible. But she was attracted to him. There was no denying that.

And there was her brother to think of. Xander would be furious to know she was involved with his best friend. And she didn't want to damage her relationship with her brother—not for a shipboard fling. Right?

Knock. Knock.

"Stasia, are you ready?" Roberto's voice vibrated through the door.

Her heart raced. Her palms grew damp. This was it. A date.

Not a real date. But it sure felt like a real date. After all, Roberto's family thought they were getting married. And as this charade continued, the lines of their relationship were becoming increasingly blurred.

She was just as nervous as she'd been on her first date with Lukos. No. Correction—she was more nervous.

She tried to calm herself with a deep breath as she slipped on the ring. The harder she tried to calm her breathing, the faster her heart pounded. Maybe she shouldn't have agreed to this charade. Maybe it was too soon.

But she knew it was just an excuse. It'd been almost

two years since she'd lost her husband. She glanced down at her finger where not that long ago she wore a wedding band, which was now replaced with a diamond ring. Would Lukos understand—

Knock. Knock.

"Stasia?"

She swallowed. "I, uh…um, I'll be right there."

She shoved aside the troubling thoughts, along with the reference to love. She was just letting this wedding stuff get to her. That was all.

She gave herself one last glance, making sure she hadn't missed anything. She smoothed a hand down over the skirt. Maybe she should have picked a more cheerful color for a wedding. Maybe the hemline was too short for the occasion.

Another knock drew her from her thoughts. With a sigh, she moved to the door. When she opened it, she marveled at how good Roberto looked. Usually…no, always, he looked so put-together and sharp. But tonight, he looked devastatingly handsome in his dark suit and silver tie.

Her mouth opened but no words came out. Her mind was overwhelmed with how attractive she found him and how much she wished this was a real date.

Roberto's dark brows drew together. "Is something the matter?"

She shook her head. "Um, no. You look great."

"Really? Because you have this look on your face, like…well, I don't know, but obviously you were thinking something."

Not about to delve into how attractive she found him, she turned, grabbed her black clutch purse decorated with tiny crystals and then pulled the door shut behind them. "I was thinking we don't want to be late for the ceremony."

As they made their way through the passageway, he said, "If you changed your mind and don't want to go with me, I would understand. I won't hold you to the arrangement we agreed upon."

It was so tempting to back out. This was her chance. But there was another part of her—a part that wanted to spend the evening with Roberto as his fiancée. After all, when this cruise was over, they'd each be going their own way.

And most of all, she didn't want to let him down. She'd told him that she'd act as though they were a couple in front of his family and she wasn't going to back out now.

"I didn't change my mind."

He stopped and turned to her. "Thank you. Whatever you want tonight, it's yours. Just say the word. And when you're ready to leave, it's fine by me."

Her gaze met his. "I appreciate that."

They continued to stare into each other's eyes longer than was necessary. Her heart started to race again. Then again, she wasn't sure if it ever slowed down.

He took her hand in his and gave it a reassuring squeeze. "It'll be good having a friend by my side."

A friend? He was reminding her that was all they'd ever be. "Yes, it's always good when a friend has your back."

"Agreed. And I certainly never had a friend who was so beautiful. You've got all of the single guys on this ship jealous that you're with me."

Heat rushed to her face. Where exactly was this evening in the floating city going to lead them? The possibilities both excited and terrified her.

Roberto didn't know what to do with himself.

Weddings made him uncomfortable. His whole family made him uncomfortable with their expectations of him.

Still, he'd told Stasia that he'd try harder to spend more time with his family and that was what he was doing. Any other time, he would have quietly slipped away long ago.

He knew this wasn't going to be easy. But if the smiles Stasia had bestowed upon him throughout the evening were any indication, he was doing okay.

But he'd noticed the sadness that filled Stasia's eyes when she didn't think he was looking. He didn't have to ask her what was wrong; he knew. She was missing Lukos. Her heart still belonged to her departed husband. And Roberto didn't know how to deal with the ghost who stood between them.

Roberto's gaze strayed around the room, searching for Stasia. And then he spotted her, deep in conversation with his grandmother. She appeared to be having a good time.

As Roberto continued to sit alone in the ballroom of an exclusive hotel, he glanced out at the crowded dance floor. His gaze strayed across the happy newlyweds. Gaia had been a radiant bride. In fact, he'd never seen her look happier. He just wondered if it would last. Or if she would end up taking separate trips from her husband like his parents did.

But then he'd watched his grandparents. They were definitely devoted to each other. He'd always considered them the anomaly. They were that perfect couple that everyone dreamed of being when they said *I do*.

Roberto knew what his grandparents had was rare. And he didn't want to change himself, to the point he didn't even recognize himself, to fit in a relationship. If that was what it took to make a successful marriage, no wonder his parents lived apart.

But he didn't want to marry someone just to see them on holidays. That seemed like an impossible situation. The only way he could imagine being happy was to maintain his independence. He couldn't rely on anyone to go the distance with him.

He continued to observe Stasia as she talked to his

grandmother. She looked happy now. He wanted her to stay that way.

Part of him wanted to pull her into his arms and make some new memories with her. But Stasia would expect more from him. She wasn't one of those women who lived in the moment and then moved on to the next man to catch their eye.

Stasia was more grounded. She liked strings and commitments. She didn't take relationships lightly. And her brother certainly wouldn't approve of a fling—even if it got Stasia over the hurdle between her past and her future.

Roberto could almost talk himself into the fact that them getting together would be good for her. It would show her that there was still so much life for her to live. He so desperately wanted to believe what he was saying to himself. And yet he couldn't.

Stasia had been through so much in her twenty-nine years. She was so young and yet she had lived more of life than he ever had. And she'd experienced enough pain and loss for a lifetime.

He wouldn't hurt her. He didn't need Xander to threaten him. He could take care of that all by himself. He wanted to protect Stasia from any further heartache—from the guys on the ship who eyed her up—from himself.

"Hey, what has you so quiet over here?" Stasia leaned in close to speak to him over the music.

He'd gotten so caught up in his thoughts that he hadn't seen her approach him. With her so close, he inhaled a whiff of her jasmine scent. He resisted the urge to close his eyes and savor the scent. But he couldn't meet her gaze either. He didn't want her to read too much in his eyes.

Instead he turned to watch his family out on the dance floor. His family loved to celebrate. The young, the old and the in-between were out there dancing, smiling and having a great time.

"Roberto?" Stasia's voice again drew him from his thoughts. "What's wrong with you tonight?"

"Uh, nothing."

"Really? Because it looks like you're sitting over here frowning and downright miserable."

He toyed with his water glass. "I guess I just don't do well at weddings."

"Are you sure?" There was a heavy dose of doubt in her voice. "You won't even look at me."

He pressed his lips together in a firm line and turned to her. When their gazes met, there was this funny warm feeling that filled his chest. He ignored it as he forced a smile to his lips.

She gave him a strange look. "Really? You can't even muster up a real smile for me?"

How did she know? Could she really read him that well?

"Stop trying to figure out how I know these things," she said.

There she went again, reading him like an open book. He was growing uncomfortable with her being able to sense his thoughts. He'd always thought he was a master at keeping his thoughts under wraps. That was what made him such a good businessman.

He glanced away, not sure what to say.

"You're not that big of a mystery," she went on to say. "You don't want to be here and you regret inviting me."

His head quickly turned. "You would be wrong."

"About what? Being here? Or bringing me?"

"Bringing you. You're the highlight of my evening."

A smile pulled at her glossy lips. "It's about time you admit it."

Wait. Had he just fallen into a cleverly planned trap? If the twinkle of amusement in her eyes was any indication, he most certainly had. Who knew that sweet, innocent Stasia had a much more devious side to her? He was most certainly intrigued.

He held out his hand. "Would you care to dance?"

She placed her hand in his. "I'd love to dance."

This time no words were necessary. He guided her to the dance floor, where he took her into his arms. In fact, the lack of conversation made the dance less stressed and a lot more enjoyable. Except for the fact that Stasia was standing awkwardly away from him.

He told himself that his arms were growing tired with the distance and that was why he tightened his hold on her. But he'd miscalculated, and the next thing he knew, Stasia was snug against his chest. Not that he was complaining or anything.

She tilted up her chin to look at him. Questions reflected in her eyes, but no words were spoken. He'd been mucking up this whole evening and he'd really wanted to give her a good time.

"I'm sorry."

"Don't be."

And then because she kept staring up at him with a look in her eyes that said she could feel the desire that ignited every time they were together, he lowered his head and claimed her lips in what started as a quick kiss, but quickly grew into something more.

Roberto was learning that he would never get enough of Stasia or her sweet kisses. They were utterly and totally addictive.

There was a pat on his shoulder. "Way to go."

Roberto jerked back to find some distant cousin, who was in college, smiling at him.

And then his grandmother passed by him. "Really, Roberto."

His gaze moved from his grandmother to Stasia. He

needed to apologize again for losing his head in front of his family. So much for thinking before he acted.

Stasia lifted a finger to his lips. "Don't say it."

He pulled her hand away and wrapped it up in his hand. "How do you know what I was going to say?"

"You were going to apologize for kissing me but I don't want you to ruin the moment. Please."

She enjoyed the kiss? She wasn't upset that he'd over-stepped his bounds as a friend—as her brother's friend? What did she think it meant? Was she expecting more from him?

The last question cooled his heated blood. He didn't want her to assume anything. He didn't want to get her hopes up that something more was to follow that kiss.

"Listen, Stasia," he said. When she went to say something, he rushed on. "Don't worry, I'm not going to apologize for the kiss. I enjoyed it too. I…I just want you to know that it was spontaneous—"

"And part of our cover story." She came to his rescue, making this confession so much easier than he deserved. "After all, we want your grandmother to believe we're engaged, so why wouldn't we kiss? It'd be a little strange if we didn't, don't you think?"

How did she do that? Make him go from being totally uncomfortable to immediately putting him at ease. The woman was very good with people. It was definitely one of her greatest strengths.

And so they continued to dance, this song and the next song and even the one after that, which was a fast song. By the end of it, they were both a little winded and returned to their table.

"When's the wedding date?" the bride asked.

He restrained his inclination to frown at Gaia and get her to quiet down. Why in the world would she bring up this subject in front of their grandmother? The woman needed no encouragement when it came to her efforts to marry him off.

"Oh, yes." Yaya's expression filled with eagerness. "Tell us when the big day is."

Everyone pulled out their phones and ran their fingers over them as though preparing to input the wedding date on their calendars.

"We haven't set a date," he said as Stasia's grip on his hand tightened. Apparently, she was feeling as cornered as he did at the moment.

His grandmother looked crestfallen. "I should have known."

"Known what?" His grandfather looked confused.

"Our grandson isn't getting married. In fact, they probably aren't even in a real relationship. This is just an attempt to keep from meeting the young women on the cruise."

His grandmother had read him so well. Was he that obvious? He was between a rock and a hard place. If he disagreed with her, she would expect them to set a wedding date. And if he admitted she was right, then she would have him on a blind date before the night was over.

Stasia let go of his hand and sat up straighter. "It's true. We are serious about each other."

His grandmother's gaze narrowed on them. "How serious?"

Stasia met his grandmother's gaze without flinching. "Well, you know how your grandson doesn't like to do big public displays of affection? He likes to keep things low-key. And so we've been keeping everything quiet—until now."

His grandmother's mouth opened in an O as her eyes twinkled with hope and she clasped her hands together. "So, you are getting married?"

"Yes."

Roberto looked at Stasia. What had she said? He replayed the conversation in his head. Had Stasia really just told his grandmother they were getting married? He opened his mouth but no words would come out. There was a disconnect somewhere between his racing thoughts and his mouth.

Stasia turned to him. "I'm sorry. I know you wanted to keep it quiet for a while, with the transition at your office and all."

"Don't be upset with her," Gaia said to him. "You couldn't expect her to keep that kind of news to herself."

The next thing he knew, people were throwing around dates. Dates that weren't that far off. And then his arm was around Stasia's shoulders as his whole family debated what date would work best for each of them. He moved and spoke in a dazed robotic motion. Since when was his wedding date up for debate by his family members? Not that he was getting married for real or anything.

When all was said and done, his wedding was set for the beginning of August. His grandmother was over the moon, and Stasia, well, she looked happy. And his family loved her. By the time he found his voice, he didn't have the heart to embarrass Stasia by telling his family that the wedding would never take place.

He knew Stasia had only said those things to keep him from disappointing his grandmother once again. He knew she was even less interested in getting married than him. After all, she'd had her heart ripped out when her husband had passed away. No one would want to risk that sort of pain again. But she'd stepped up, putting herself out there, just for him. No one had gone out of their way for him like she had done. He was truly touched.

"Would you like some fresh air?" he asked, anxious for someplace a little quieter.

"I'd love some."

He once again held his arm out to her, enjoying when she was touching him. And they strolled outside beneath the big, brilliant moon that reflected off the calm water. Apparently, they weren't the only ones with this idea, as there were many couples strolling along the canal.

They walked a bit until they found a stretch of rail where they could be alone. Roberto wasn't in the mood to share Stasia any longer. He couldn't explain it to himself nor anyone else what it was about her that had him rethinking the whole bachelor thing. What had he found so great about it when he could spend amazing evenings like this with a woman who was as beautiful as she was generous of heart?

"Are you thinking about the project for your grandfather?" Her soft voice broke through his thoughts.

How could she think he was pondering work on such an amazing evening? Perhaps he'd had his emotions suppressed for so long now that even she couldn't see he was profoundly moved by this evening, by this trip—by her.

He turned to her, finding her standing closer to him than he'd expected. It was all he could do not to reach out and take her in his arms. But he couldn't overstep again. She'd gracefully forgiven him once this evening. He knew he wouldn't be so lucky a second time.

That thought dampened his mood.

"I was thinking that tomorrow we have one last day in Venice and I was wondering if you would want to see some more of it."

A smile lifted her lips. "I would love it."

"Then it's a date?"

Before he could correct his slip of the tongue, she said, "It's a date."

He smiled. Stasia really did make things easy. He could get used to having her around.

"So I'll meet you on the deck first thing in the morning?" she asked, while staring into his eyes.

"Yes." Resisting the urge to wrap his arms around her and pull her soft curves in for a very long, very deep kiss, he said, "Would you like to return to the wedding? I'm sure it'll keep going until very late."

She shook her head. "If you don't mind, I think I'd like to stay here just a bit longer before heading back to the ship."

The problem with lingering here beneath the star-studded sky was that he wasn't sure how long his determination to keep his hands to himself would hold out. And he didn't want to mess this up—whatever this was.

He forced his thoughts to the work that awaited him. However, the last thing he wanted to do that night was to work. The thought startled him. He was always up for work. It was his driving force in life—until now.

This trip had opened his eyes. He knew that was a lie. It was Stasia who had shown him what he was missing in life. He wasn't sure his work would ever be enough to fill his life again.

What he really wanted to do was pull Stasia into his arms. He wanted to kiss her without limitations, without his family watching them and without any restraint. He wanted to drink in her sweetness and show her that there was still so much in life for her to experience.

And then he recalled his prior conversation with Xander, promising to watch out for Stasia. Roberto stifled a frustrated groan. Why did Stasia have to be his friend's sister? Because she was the first woman to thoroughly intrigue him. She was the only one to make him question if his permanent bachelor status was really the right choice for him.

DAY NINE

Venice, Italy

WHERE WAS HE?

Stasia had walked the entire length of the deck twice now, but there was no sign of Roberto. She was beginning to wonder if she'd gotten their plans mixed up in her head. But the more she thought about it, the more she was certain they'd agreed to meet up here.

So where was he?

She tried his cell phone, again. And once again, it went directly to voice mail. That was strange. That man lived on his cell phone. He never turned it off.

The touring party had already departed the boat about fifteen minutes ago. It was too late to catch up with them. And honestly, she didn't want to. She'd been looking forward to her private, guided tour with the sexiest man on the boat.

In fact, she'd had the hardest time getting to sleep last night and it was all his fault. Every time she'd closed her eyes, she saw his face. And then she would relive the moment when his lips pressed to hers. Even though it was only a memory, her heart would race.

Maybe she was so anxious for today because she hoped he would follow up that all-too-short kiss with a much longer one. Was that wrong? After all, she was supposed to be on this ship figuring out her next step in life.

She knew Xander wouldn't approve of her hitting it off with Roberto. But what her brother didn't know wouldn't hurt him. She knew her brother's heart was in the right place, but she was all grown up and it was up to her to figure out what came next. And who she did it with. Well, if he showed up.

She sighed. Where was Roberto? She sent him a text. And she waited and waited. There was no response to it either.

Roberto wouldn't ignore her, not unless something was wrong. Could that be it? Was he sick?

She took off toward his cabin. With most of the passengers having departed the ship in order to go on a tour, she didn't have to wait for the elevator or have to wade her way through a throng of people in the passageway.

Once she got to Roberto's cabin, she rapped on the door. "Roberto? It's Stasia."

She waited. When he didn't immediately open the door, she pressed her ear to it. She didn't hear any movement inside.

She knocked again. "Roberto, are you okay?"

Thunk. Crash.

"Roberto? What's going on?"

"Coming."

She breathed easier, hearing his voice. Thank goodness he was safe and sound. Though she had absolutely no idea what had kept him and what caused him to forget that they had a date today.

At last the door swung open and Roberto stood there. His hair was mussed up. His normally clean-shaven jaw now had a shadow of stubble. He was still wearing the same clothes as last night, but they were a bit disheveled just like the rest of him.

"Are you sick?" She'd never seen Roberto unprepared. She'd have sworn he was born ready to take on the world.

He ran a hand over his face and then his hair, scattering the dark strands every which way. "Uh, no, I'm not sick." It took him a second as though she'd literally just roused him from a deep sleep. He glanced at the time on his wristwatch. "Eight twenty. Oh, no. I was supposed to meet up with you at eight o'clock."

"Yes, you were." She crossed her arms and looked at him. Part of her wanted to be angry with him for standing her up and making her worry. The other part of her was relieved to see that nothing was the matter. Which led her to her next question. "Why are you still in your dress clothes?"

An older couple passed them in the passageway. The woman's eyes widened as she took in Roberto's appearance. And then she turned her attention to Stasia and gave her an approving nod. "Good for you."

Stasia stifled a laugh.

He cleared his throat and opened the door wider. "Come in."

She wasn't sure what to expect as she entered the luxury cabin. Everything about Roberto struck her as him being neat and orderly. But the room didn't appear to be as she would have expected.

Though the bed was perfectly made, there was a black suitcase tossed on top of it. The case was open. Clothes and accessories were strewn across the bed as though he had been in a hurry to get out the door and didn't have time to put things where they belonged.

And then there was the table. It was covered with a laptop, portable printer and tons of printouts. Some of the pages were lying flat on the tabletop and others were crumpled and tossed toward the garbage can but had missed their target.

"I don't understand." She turned a puzzled stare his way. "What's going on? It looks like you worked all night."

"As a matter of fact, I did. Not all of it. But a lot of it." He rubbed his neck and then rolled his shoulders.

"I'm guessing you didn't make it to bed."

He shook his head.

"You work too hard. And too often."

"I'm fine."

Her gaze narrowed in on him. She saw the tired lines etched around his eyes. And the way his broad shoulders sagged ever so slightly as though he were carrying a heavy burden.

Someone had to be honest with him. Someone had to tell him to slow down—that there was more to life than work. And she knew all too well how fleeting life could be.

She lifted her chin ever so slightly. "You're not fine."

Roberto crossed his arms over his chest as his steady gaze met hers. A muscle in his jaw twitched. "I'm sorry my life isn't to your liking, but it's the way I like it. My work is important to me."

"Even though you're all alone?" She hadn't meant to say that out loud. But she never understood why such a good-looking, successful man would choose to be alone.

His gaze darkened. "Did you ever consider that I like it that way?"

Her mouth opened but nothing came out. She hadn't meant to say that. What was wrong with her?

"I'm good this way. Love and marriage, that may be the way for other people, but it doesn't work for me."

That was one of the saddest things she'd ever heard in her life. "I'm sorry you feel that way because you don't know what you're missing."

His gaze searched hers. "How can you say that after all you've been through?"

"And what? By not falling in love, by not marrying, that I would be better off?"

He hesitated as though realizing he too had said more than he'd meant to. And then he gave a nod.

Was this what everyone thought? That she'd have been better off by never loving Lukos? Well, it was time to set the record straight.

"I am better off for having known and loved Lukos. He showed me how great love can be through the good times and the really rotten, horrible bad times." Tears pricked the backs of her eyes as moments from their life together flickered through her memory. "But I wouldn't trade one single moment I had with him. Not any of it. He helped me to become a better person—at least, I'd like to think I am."

Remorse reflected in Roberto's eyes. "Of course you are. I shouldn't have said that—I shouldn't have dredged up the past. I know how hard this is for you."

"How hard what is?"

He shrugged. "Moving on alone. Mourning his passing."

She wanted to argue and tell Roberto that it wasn't hard, that she was doing just fine. But that would be a lie. It was like waking up one day and having everything you knew about your life and routine being totally altered. It had taken her a while to find her footing again, but she was now able to stand on her own two feet. Now she just had to find a new path to walk down.

"I did mourn Lukos for a long time. He had been such an important part of my life. But I'm moving on now." And then she wondered if she should share her thoughts with Roberto. She wanted to tell someone—someone who wasn't her brother, who thought he had all the answers where she was concerned.

"Do you really think you can do that? Move on, that is?" Roberto's gaze searched hers as though he could see the truth reflected in her eyes.

"Lukos will always have a place in my heart, but he

made me promise him that I would move on. That I would have a life and all it entails. And that's what I'm trying to do. It hasn't been easy and there were days when I really regretted making him that promise because all I wanted to do at that point was to wrap myself up in his memories and stay there. But now, well, I'm feeling a little more confident and I know I have to move on, for the promise I made and most of all for myself."

Roberto reached out to her. His fingers gently stroked her cheek. "You are the strongest person I know."

His kind words made her heart swell. "Thank you. But I'm not anything special."

"You are to me."

Her pulse raced and she longed to lean forward and press her lips to his. But perhaps she was reading this moment all wrong. And she didn't want to mess up this special friendship.

After an awkward moment of silence, Roberto said, "I need to get ready for our last day in Venice."

"I…I should go." She moved toward the door.

"You can wait here." He grabbed some clothes from the bed and headed to the shower. "I'll only be a few minutes."

Stasia felt guilty for dragging Roberto away from his work. It was so evident last night that his grandfather was looking forward to Roberto's findings. She remembered her own grandfather and the close link she'd shared with him. She would do anything to have him in her life again. She missed him dearly.

Stasia's gaze turned to the table with the stack of papers and Roberto's laptop. She felt guilty for coming between him and his bond to his grandfather. She moved to the table and sat down. She had to admit she was curious to unravel the mystery.

Her gaze moved to the bathroom door. It was closed and

the sound of running water could be heard. Would Roberto mind if she took another look? She didn't think so.

She opened his laptop and one of the files she'd worked on the other day appeared on the screen. In fact, she noticed that Roberto hadn't gotten much further. She set to work. Maybe, just maybe, she could uncover something more than a transposed number.

"What are you doing?"

Stasia's head jerked up. Her gaze met Roberto's questioning stare with his arched brow. A guilty smile pulled at her lips. She felt like she was back in primary school reaching for a second cookie when only offered one.

"I was bored. I thought I'd look at the spreadsheet some more." As their gazes continued to connect, she said, "You really care, don't you?"

His eyes widened. The color drained from his face. As time passed without him saying a word, she realized how her words might have sounded.

"I meant you care about the company."

The worry lines on his handsome face smoothed. He shrugged, just like he'd done when they'd had a similar conversation. "I've tried to tell myself that I don't care, but the more I work on this project, the more I realize how much I enjoy this business."

"Maybe it's time you went back."

He shook his head as he slipped on his socks and shoes. "I offered to help, but I couldn't work for my grandfather again. We disagree too much."

"Maybe it'll be different this time." She was hoping during the cruise that the two men would repair their relationship—maybe it was too much to hope. "Show me what needs to be done."

"You don't have to do that. I told you I would take care of it."

"I know I don't have to, but I want to." She thought about mentioning how it would please his grandfather to finish this project early, but then she decided to tell him the honest truth. "The thing is, I'm curious. There has to be something here that we're not seeing."

His eyes widened. "You're really that curious?"

She nodded.

"Maybe you found your calling," he said, coming to stand next to her. "Maybe you are meant to be an accountant or perhaps a forensic accountant."

She thought about it for a moment. She did like numbers, but not enough to devote a large portion of her life to it. "I don't think so. I just can't imagine me sitting and staring at numbers day in and day out. But right now, the curiosity is eating at me."

He ran a hand over his still-damp hair. "What about Venice? It awaits us."

She worried her lip. She was torn. Was it wrong that she wanted to do both things?

He held his hand out to her. "Come on. There's gelato to taste and perhaps another gondola ride."

"But—"

"And if you still feel like it when we get back to the ship this evening, we'll work on the reports—together. Deal?"

She liked the idea of working alongside him. They did make a pretty great team. She closed the laptop and placed her hand in his. "It's a deal."

He gripped her hand as she got to her feet. She expected him to let go once she was standing, but instead he laced his fingers with hers and headed for the door. For the first time in a very long time, she didn't feel alone, even when she was in a crowd of people.

When Lukos had gotten sick, she hadn't noticed it at first, but over time, she started doing everything alone.

When he'd been resting, she would grocery shop. When he'd been awake but had no energy, she would clean and cook. As time had passed, she'd grown used to going it alone. She'd forgotten what it was like to be part of us.

Roberto was helping her to remember how life could be. And for that she was grateful. And when it was over, she would help him with his project. Together it would be a good day.

DAY TEN

Sibenik, Croatia

EVERYONE WAS HAPPY.

Too happy. And that made him worry.

His grandmother sat across from Roberto at the table in her suite. They'd just finished a light breakfast. And he had yet to learn why he'd been summoned.

His grandmother held up the teapot. "Would you care for some?"

He shook his head before checking the time. He was supposed to meet Stasia soon for another excursion and he didn't want to be late.

"I can see that I'm keeping you," his grandmother said. "So I'll get to the point. I owe you an apology."

He sent her a puzzled look. "No, you don't."

"But I do. When you first told me about Stasia, I didn't believe you. I thought you were dodging my attempts at matchmaking, which your grandfather said would never work. But I watched both you and Stasia over the course of the cruise. I've seen the way you look at each other and the way your face lights up when she's around. I've never seen you happier. And I'm sorry I doubted your love for Stasia. You obviously didn't need my help after all."

Roberto sat there taking in his grandmother's words. She was a wise woman. Had she seen something he'd missed? Was it possible he was falling in love with Stasia?

"Don't let me keep you any longer. I'm sure you're anxious to get to Stasia."

It was true. He was anxious to see her. But did that equate to love?

He hugged his grandmother and left. All the while he wondered how he had let things get so far out of control. He replayed every moment they'd spent in Venice from her birthday to the engagement to dancing with Stasia at his cousin's wedding. He knew he'd never ever visit that city without thinking of her. From this point forward, they were indelibly entwined.

Venice had changed everything for them. First, there had been the photo—the romantic photo—that had led to the kiss. He could still clearly recall the tenderness of Stasia's lips pressed to his. His blood warmed at the memory of her curves pressed up against him.

She'd felt so right, there in his arms. And then as she'd opened herself up to him, it was all he could do to hang on to some semblance of reality.

How exactly had he gone from showing her the sights to giving her his grandmother's ring?

He knew he'd gone a little over the top for her birthday, but there was just something about that day that had him acting out of character, or maybe he should say that he was in character as the besotted lover. He wanted to blame it on the prosecco, but he knew that wasn't the case.

And ever since, they'd fallen into a comfortable companionship that included clasped hands, warm smiles and a mounting number of kisses. But where was it leading? Where did he want it to go?

The walls started closing in on him. He made his way down the passageway, not paying much attention to his surroundings or the people he passed. He kept moving up the steps, through the doorway and across the deck until he was at the rail. He stared out at the water.

He inhaled the sea air, wishing it would clear his thoughts. But thoughts of their three days in Venice kept replaying in his mind. He should have called a halt to this relationship a long time ago.

And then at the wedding, it was like it had made their engagement official. For all intents and purposes, it was—at least as far as his family was concerned—

Ding.

It was a text message. Roberto was tempted to ignore it, but he knew he was expected to accompany Stasia along with his family into Sibenik today. He wasn't in any frame of mind to put on a show for everyone.

The question he couldn't answer was what exactly did he feel for Stasia? When they departed the boat back in Athens, they'd each go back to their life as though none of this had happened. Wouldn't they?

Ding.

He removed his phone from his pocket and glanced at the screen. It was Stasia.

Where are you?

I've changed my mind. I'm not going.

Then neither am I.

Go ahead. Enjoy yourself. I've got work to do.

I'd rather stay with you. I could help.

Go with the family. They adore you. I'll see you later.

Silence. Then he sent another message.

We okay?

Sure.

Roberto slipped his phone back in his pocket. He started walking. He had no particular destination in mind. Maybe some physical activity would help wear away his frustration.

Time passed slowly. For all of the walking he was doing, he should have gone with Stasia into the city. But he told himself the distance was for the best. Being together day in and day out was confusing things, making this little fantasy they'd concocted seem like reality instead of fiction.

Later, he'd have a talk with Stasia. He'd reaffirm that this thing between them—it couldn't last. There was no way. He was a sworn bachelor. And she was a widow still mourning her husband. And then there was Xander, who would not be pleased about any of this. Definitely too many hurdles for them to cross.

"Roberto?"

He stopped walking and glanced around, not sure who'd called his name. And then he spotted a young woman waving at him. She looked slightly familiar, but he couldn't put a name to the face.

She rushed up to him. "Alone at last."

He wasn't sure what to say to that, so he pretended he hadn't heard her. "Do we know each other?"

She smiled at him. "It has been a number of years, but we used to see each other when I visited my grandparents."

He studied her for a moment. Upon closer look, she did look familiar. It took a moment, but then it came to him. "Little Petra?"

Her smile broadened. "Not so little anymore."

They hugged. It seemed like forever since he'd recalled those days. Petra's grandparents used to live down the road from his. A lot had changed since those days, but so much had stayed the same. It was funny how life worked out.

"Did my grandmother invite you on this cruise?" When she nodded, he continued. "I'm so sorry. She had no right to do that."

Petra shook it off. "It's no big deal. I needed the vacation. But it sounds like you were holding out on your grandmother. I hear congratulations are in order."

"Um...thanks."

She arched a brow. "That doesn't sound very excited."

Petra had been cool to hang out with when they were kids. She always seemed to have her life together and there wasn't any argument she couldn't win. It only seemed natural she would become a litigator. His grandmother had made sure to keep him up to date on Petra's accomplishments and the fact that she was still available.

"I should be going," he said. "It was good to see you again."

When he started to walk away, she reached out to him. "Wait. That's it. You're just going to leave?"

He turned to her. She was still the spitfire he remembered. "Listen, Petra, I have a lot on my mind."

"Let's grab some lunch, and if you want, you can talk to me. I'm a pretty good listener."

He wasn't sure about opening up to Petra, especially about Stasia, but the thought of sharing a meal and reliving some memories appealed to him. What could it hurt?

What was up with Roberto?

Why had he insisted she go on this day trip while he remained on the ship?

The questions whirled around in Stasia's mind as she walked with Roberto's family to the center of Sibenik. The city had that historic village feel, with monuments representing the past and architecture that had definitely been around for quite a while. There was lots to see and learn, but Stasia was having problems concentrating on what the tour guide was saying. And so she finally bowed out of the group, claiming a headache, which wasn't far from the truth.

As she made her way back to the boat, she tried to figure out what to say to Roberto. Everything had been fine until they became engaged. With each passing day, it was becoming increasingly complicated.

Obviously Roberto had second thoughts about things—about her. After all, she did come with baggage. She was pretty certain none of the other women he'd dated had been widows.

But the thought of him backing out of her life after all they'd shared was unacceptable. She liked Roberto—really liked him. And she thought he really liked her too.

Maybe things had gotten off track. Maybe he was confused about the kiss at the wedding as much as her. If they talked, they could work things out. She was certain of it.

She went straight to his cabin and knocked on the door. "Roberto, it's me, Stasia."

No answer.

She knocked again but didn't hear a word.

That was strange. She thought he'd been in his room working, but then again, it was a beautiful sunny day. Perhaps he'd decided to move to the deck. So off she went to find him.

She pulled out her phone and texted him.

Am back. Where are U?

There was no response. That was odd.

She kept walking and looking around. Surely he

wouldn't have gone ashore, would he? No. He was very
determined to unravel the mystery of those files that
his grandfather had given him. He had to be here somewhere—

And then she spotted him. He was smiling. He was
laughing.

Her gaze moved across the table at the café to a beautiful woman who was laughing too. And then the woman
reached out to Roberto, covering his hand with her own.
The breath stilled in Stasia's throat. What in the world
was going on?

Roberto didn't pull away. Instead he leaned toward the
young woman and said something that Stasia couldn't
hear from this distance. He continued to smile and stare
into this woman's eyes.

Something cold and dark churned in the pit of Stasia's
stomach. Her body tensed and her hands clenched. This
was why he'd blown her off today?

Why did she think he had changed? He was the same
playboy bachelor he'd always been. Playing her besotted
fiancé must be killing him with all these single beautiful
women on board.

Not wanting to get caught staring at the happy couple,
she turned on her heels and headed for her cabin. If he
was already moving on from the moment they'd shared,
then she needed to do the same. She had a career to settle
on—a reason to get out of bed every morning—something
to fill the emptiness in her life.

And Roberto obviously had nothing to do with her
future.

DAY ELEVEN

Bari, Italy

THE FOLLOWING MORNING had come and gone.

And yet there wasn't any sign of Stasia.

Roberto was certain she was upset with him for skipping out on the outing yesterday with his family. He didn't blame her. And if he hadn't been so conflicted about the chemistry coursing between them, he would have gone with them.

He didn't know why spending time with Stasia was getting to him. He was thinking about things that he had no business considering where she was concerned—like pulling her into his arms and kissing her until she couldn't think of anyone but him. And no matter how many times he reminded himself of all the reasons that getting involved with her wasn't a good idea, when he closed his eyes at the end of the day, it was her face that he saw. And when sleep finally claimed him, she was in his dreams warming his bed.

For days, they'd been inseparable, and now she was nowhere to be seen. And it was because of him. She was avoiding him. He'd overstepped with one too many kisses.

He should have respected her space, but he'd thought she'd wanted him too. And when their lips had met, he was certain she'd wanted him just as much as he wanted her.

He wanted to call her, but his phone was dead. He'd checked the ship's courtesy shop, but they didn't have a replacement battery. He'd have to wait until they got back to Athens to have access to his phone.

Having grown tired of pacing in his cabin, he'd moved to the sunny deck. Maybe a bit of fresh air would help him relax. As he took a seat at a vacant table, he heard a familiar voice.

"Good morning." His grandmother placed a hand on his shoulder before passing by him and taking a seat across from him.

"Good morning, Yaya." He slipped his dead phone back in his pocket. "I thought you'd be off on another tour."

His grandmother sighed. "I'd love to, but my body, it's not as young as it used to be. It needs a day of rest."

Roberto nodded in understanding.

"I thought you'd be with Stasia."

"I, uh, haven't seen her since you went off exploring yesterday."

A concerned look came over his grandmother's face. "How strange."

"Wait. Why do you look so worried?"

"Because she left the tour early yesterday. She said she had a headache, but I suspected she missed you." His grandmother's gaze searched his. "So she didn't come back here to see you?"

He shook his head.

"That's very odd."

Concern coursed through him. If she hadn't come back here to see him then perhaps she truly did have a headache. And then guilt assailed him. All this time he'd been sitting around worrying about himself and how the engagement had changed things between them. What if something was wrong and she'd tried to call him? With his phone dead, her call would have gone straight to voice mail.

He got to his feet. "Excuse me."

"Go. Go." His grandmother waved him off. "I hope everything is all right."

He was already in motion before his grandmother finished speaking. He couldn't imagine Stasia needing him and not being able to reach him. As he strode down the passageway, he realized there was a cabin phone. She could have used it to get ahold of him. Unless she was too sick.

Not having the patience to wait for the elevator, he opted to take the steps. He moved swiftly, dodging around the slow-moving vacationers. He had to get to Stasia. He had to be certain she was all right.

When he finally stopped in front of her door, he knocked rapidly. "Stasia? Stasia?" When the door didn't open right away, he knocked again. "Stasia, open up."

The door flung open and there stood Stasia. Her face was devoid of makeup and her hair was pulled back in a messy ponytail. She was still wearing what he assumed were her pajamas—a black cami that hinted at her cleavage and matching satin shorts that showed off her long legs. She looked so good, so very good.

"Roberto, what's wrong? Why did you almost pound the door off its hinges?"

With great effort, he lifted his gaze to her face. On second glance, he realized she was a bit pale and her eyes were dulled. Something was definitely amiss.

"Yaya said you weren't feeling well. I wanted to check on you."

Her gaze narrowed and she didn't open the door enough to let him in. "Would you have noticed if your grandmother hadn't said something?"

"What is that supposed to mean?"

"It means this arrangement is over. Let that woman you were enjoying a leisurely lunch with yesterday, after you blew me off, be your fake girlfriend. I quit." She attempted to close the door.

He stuck his foot in the way, stopping the door. "Stasia, what are you talking about?"

She let go of the door and walked farther into the room. He followed her.

"Stasia, I don't understand."

She turned to him, anger flashing in her eyes. "Don't try to deny it. I left the tour early because I felt bad that you were back here on the ship working hard while I was out having a good time. And imagine my surprise when I find my fake fiancé having a romantic lunch with some beautiful woman."

"You saw that?"

She nodded. "Did you think you were being so sneaky?"

He'd had absolutely no idea that she'd been there. "If you had walked over to the table, I would have introduced you."

Stasia shook her head. "I don't need to be introduced to your lovers."

That was what she thought? That he was involved with Petra? He studied Stasia's beautiful face and the way her big brown eyes reflected her anger and pain. Was it possible their kiss at the wedding had meant something to her? Was she jealous?

"Her name is Petra. And she's not my lover."

Stasia's mouth opened but nothing came out. She pressed her lips together into a firm line as though she was making sense of what he was saying. Emotions flickered through her eyes as reality started to take hold.

Stasia pressed her hands to her hips and lifted her chin until they were eye to eye. "Are you saying you aren't interested in her?"

Roberto couldn't help but laugh. "I think of Petra like a little sister."

"Sister?"

He nodded in affirmation. "She grew up on the estate next to my grandparents'. When we were kids, she played with me and my friends."

"You…you were childhood friends?"

He smiled and nodded.

"You aren't romantically involved?"

He shook his head. "The idea never even crossed my mind. I don't think of Petra that way and she doesn't see me that way. My grandmother invited her on the cruise, thinking there was a chance for something more. She was wrong."

"So if Petra isn't interested in you, why did she agree to come on the cruise?"

"She was in need of a vacation and she is good friends with Gaia. So, basically, she was here for the wedding."

Stasia's eyes widened with hope. "Not you?"

"Not me." He stepped closer to her and caressed her cheek. "The only woman I have eyes for on this cruise is you."

"Really?"

"Really." And he didn't stop to think of the right or the wrong of it; he just acted.

He reached out to her, placing his hands on her slender waist and drawing her to him. And she willingly moved closer to him. He lowered his head and pressed his lips to hers.

For so long, he'd been fighting his feelings for her. But after seeing that she cared enough about him to get so worked up—so jealous—he'd been moved. He'd never had another woman in his life stir him the way Stasia did.

His mouth moved over hers. With the heated emotions,

it didn't leave room for a soft and gentle kiss. Instead their lips moved hungrily over each other. Her hands moved to his shoulders before moving to the back of his neck. He'd never get enough of her touch.

Roberto reached behind him and pushed the door shut. He was going to show Stasia that there was no other woman in his life. All he could think about—dream about—was her.

As the kiss deepened, he scooped Stasia up in his arms. He carried her to the bed and laid her down. He leaned down, continuing to kiss her.

But before this went any further, he had to be entirely sure it was what she wanted too. It took every bit of willpower he could muster to pull away from her sweet, sweet kisses.

Stasia's eyes fluttered open. Confusion reflected in her eyes. "What's the matter?"

"Stasia, are you sure this is what you want?"

Her gaze met his. In its depths desire flickered. "I want you. All of you."

And then she drew him to her, smothering his words with a kiss. A kiss that was sweeter than anything he'd ever imagined. How did he get so lucky to have Stasia in his life?

DAY TWELVE

Crotone, Italy

THE NEXT MORNING, before Stasia opened her eyes, she reached out for Roberto. Her hand landed on an empty spot in the bed. Her eyes fluttered open. Her gaze searched the cabin.

He was gone.

She closed her eyes, trying to keep her emotions under control. Why did she think it would be different? She knew about his *love 'em and leave 'em* reputation. Why did she allow herself to believe that he was different than people thought?

She opened her eyes and reached for the blankets. With a big yank, she pulled them up to her chin. That was when a slip of paper fluttered in the air. What in the world?

It landed on the other pillow—the pillow where not so long ago Roberto had been. She picked it up.

> *Good morning, beautiful! Had some things to take care of before we head off on our next adventure. See you soon. Roberto.*

The note should have made her smile. It didn't. The knowledge that their night together had meant more to Roberto than an itch he needed to scratch or a casual fling scared her.

It wasn't the reaction she'd been expecting. The truth was that she'd had no idea how she would react to their lovemaking. She hadn't let her mind jump that far ahead.

He was the first man she'd been involved with since

Lukos. For so long, she'd sworn there wouldn't be another man. And now there was Roberto.

She should feel guilty for moving on, shouldn't she? But she didn't.

After all, Roberto wasn't a stranger to her. She'd known him for quite a long time, and while on the cruise, they'd grown close as friends. Still, what had happened went beyond friendship—far beyond it.

Last night, their relationship had been irrevocably changed. Their fake relationship was now a real one. Her stomach shivered with nerves. Where was this leading? Where did she want it to lead?

She didn't have the answer to those questions. The only thing she knew was that her life had just become even more complicated.

History abounded around them.

But all Roberto could think about was the woman standing next to him.

They'd just toured the sixteenth-century Castle of Charles V. And, if asked, Roberto couldn't tell anyone what they'd seen. His attention was distracted by Stasia's quietness.

He knew their night together had been a huge step for her. He'd been so worried that in the aftermath she'd pull away from him—so worried that he hadn't taken time until now to realize how significant the moment had been for him.

For so long, he'd kept everyone at a distance, but that was impossible to do with Stasia. There was no wall, no barrier that she couldn't scale. She saw through him—straight through to his damaged heart.

He didn't know what to do about it. Stasia had already been hurt so deeply when she lost her husband. Roberto didn't want to do anything to cause her more pain. Or was it too late?

Not liking the direction of his thoughts, he started to talk about his project for his grandfather. It seemed like a safe enough topic.

But after a while, he noticed Stasia's distinct lack of input. "Enough about me," Roberto said. "You've been quiet. Is everything all right?" He stopped and turned to her. "Are we all right?"

She sent him a smile that didn't quite reach her eyes. "We're fine."

He nodded in understanding. It was going to take them both some time to make sense of what was happening between them. He took her hand in his and they began to walk.

"We've talked a lot about me and my stuff—it's time we focus on your future."

"I don't think so."

"You've helped me so much. Now I want to return the favor." He really did want to help her. "If you just need someone to bounce ideas off, I'm your guy. If you need me to make a phone call and pull some strings, I'm there for you. If you need—"

"Okay. Stop." Stasia smiled. "I appreciate your support. I really do. But this is something I have to figure out on my own."

"I can't imagine that a little help will hurt."

She glanced over at him as they continued to walk around Crotone with no particular destination in mind. "Maybe a little."

"Okay. What can I do?"

She paused as though thinking over her answer. "What career do you think I should pursue?"

The fact she wanted his input touched him. Sure, people wanted his opinion when it came to business—to making a deal. But this was different. This was so much more personal. And that was something he'd been avoiding...until now.

"I can't tell you what to do." When she went to say something, he stopped her. "But I can ask you a question. In your past, when were you happiest?"

They continued walking in silence as though she were giving the question some deep thought. After a while, she said, "That's not an easy question to answer. I did retail when I was a kid."

"Really?" The word slipped out before he could stop it.

She turned to him and frowned. "What? You think I've always been spoiled?"

He opened his mouth but realized this was a trap. Knowing no matter what he said he would be in trouble, he closed his mouth without saying a word.

"Well," she said, "the truth is my grandfather believed in teaching my brother and me what it's like to fend for ourselves."

"Okay, then. Is retail work something that appeals to you? You could open your own boutique."

She tilted her head to the side as though recalling those memories. And then she shook her head. "I don't think so."

"What else is there?"

"I worked in the library in college. And as much as I love to read, well, that isn't for me."

"Keep going."

She sighed. "There isn't anything after that, I'm afraid. Because Lukos and I got married straight out of college. And then he got sick and that took up our lives. Except..."

Roberto stopped walking and turned to her. There was something in her voice. She'd had a thought and something told him that it was important. "What is it?"

She shook her head. "It's nothing."

"It's definitely something. Tell me."

She sighed. "I was just thinking about when Lukos was in the hospital."

"Oh." He'd totally misread her. He didn't mean to lead the conversation in this direction. What had made him think he knew her so well?

"No, it's not that. Lukos didn't want me hanging over him while he was getting his treatments, so I had time on my hands. One thing led to another and eventually I ended up volunteering my time." She smiled. "I met some of the most amazing people. They had every reason to be gloomy and yet they cheered me up. Can you believe that?"

"It sounds like they touched you."

"They did. They really did."

"The way your face lit up talking about them says a lot."

"But I didn't do anything special. I took a cart around the oncology ward. I handed out books, snacks, games, anything to take the patients' minds off their problems for a moment."

"And how did that make you feel?"

She shrugged. "I loved seeing people smile and knowing I had something to do with it. More than anything, they just wanted someone to listen to them."

"Then you have your answer."

"What answer?"

He took her hands in his own. "You are the most giving, caring person I know. When you speak of your volunteer work, your whole face lights up. I think that's what you should do—help people."

"You think I should go back to pushing the cart around the ward?"

He shrugged. "You could do that. Or you could head up your own foundation that would help people."

Her mouth gaped and then she shook her head. "I couldn't do that."

"Why not? You understand people. You're good with numbers. And if you need donors—and you will need donors—I'll be the first in line. Your brother will be the second in line."

Her gaze searched his. "You're serious, aren't you?"

"Of course I am. This world needs people like you—people who are willing to help others in need. I couldn't think of anything more rewarding—"

"Or painful. I've already lost a husband."

He grew quiet. He'd seen how she got excited over the memory and he'd let himself get caught up. In that moment, he'd forgotten what she'd been through. He knew that losing her husband had been devastating for her. What was he thinking to suggest that she deal with those memories on a daily basis?

"Forget I said anything." He started walking again and she fell in step next to him.

She didn't say anything, but he sensed her thoughts were on that traumatic period of her life. Here he'd been trying to get her to let go of the past and focus on the future. And now he'd undone everything.

The day had gone by way too fast.

And now the sun was starting its slow descent toward the horizon.

Stasia and Roberto made their way back onto the ship. They weren't the only ones returning from a day excursion. All around them people were laughing, talking and just enjoying the day. She couldn't blame them; it was wonderful. So was the company.

"Wasn't that beautiful?" Stasia said with a smile on her face.

"Yes, you are quite beautiful." Roberto tightened his arm over her shoulders, drawing her close.

"Today was amazing."

"Last night wasn't too shabby either."

Stasia couldn't believe this side of Roberto existed. Today he was sweet, thoughtful and fun. As they'd toured the ruins around Crotone, he'd been a different man. From him suggesting they pose in front of the Castle of Charles V for a photo, to taking his time to view sacred parchments, books and icons at the museum. Today there was no rushing around. The fact he was genuinely interested in the same things thrilled her.

Roberto had reminded her that she hadn't died with Lukos, even though it had felt like it at the time. Roberto had let her enjoy herself without the guilt of still being alive while Lukos wasn't. Roberto didn't rush her. He didn't expect things of her. He just accepted her as is.

Stasia moved off to the side of the deck, out of the way of the returning tourists, and turned to Roberto. He'd been so different since they'd cleared the air last night. She hadn't known it was possible to be so jealous. And it had all been for naught. Thankfully.

"You know, if you're not careful, I'm going to fall for all of your compliments."

Roberto's eyes reflected his playful mood. "You deserve to be complimented every single day and night."

She shook her head and lowered her gaze, feeling uncomfortable with his blatant flattery. "No, I don't."

Roberto placed a finger beneath her chin and lifted until their gazes met. "I mean it, Stasia. You are very special."

And then his head lowered, capturing her lips with his. Her heart pounded with excitement. She leaned into his embrace. It would be so easy to believe this was the beginning of something—something special.

The echo of voices faded into the background. The fact they were standing in a crowd of people while kissing didn't matter. The only thing that mattered in that moment was him and her.

"Roberto."

The stern, disapproving male voice had them jerking apart. Stasia immediately missed the feel of Roberto's touch. She longed to sidle up next to him—to wrap her arms around his trim waist—to lean into him.

Instead she turned to find his grandfather frowning at them. It appeared his grandfather didn't believe in public displays of affection. That was too bad because she couldn't promise she wouldn't give in to her desire to share a kiss with Roberto in public again.

"I'm surprised to find you out here." His grandfather's voice held a note of disapproval. "I've been looking for you. I called your cell but it went to voice mail."

Roberto smoothed his fingers over his mouth. "Hello, Grandfather. My phone died."

When a strained silence ensued, Stasia spoke up. "We just got back from sightseeing. Did you have a chance to visit Crotone?"

His grandfather's gaze flickered to her. "I did not." Just as quickly, the older man's attention returned to his grandson. "I attempted to catch up with you this morning, but it appears you had other priorities."

"I just wanted to see the sights with my fiancée." Roberto reached out and took her hand in his.

His grandfather's suspicious gaze moved between the two of them. "Are you trying to tell me this relationship is real? It's not just a ruse to keep your grandmother off your case?"

"What?" Roberto's gaze moved to her before returning to his grandfather. "Of course this is real. You just saw us kissing."

It was like the sweetness of the kiss had been wiped

away and now the kiss was nothing more than part of their charade. Was that right? Was she just getting caught up in the show they were putting on? Or was there a genuineness to what they'd shared last night?

The frown lines on his grandfather's face smoothed. The man turned to Stasia, who remained by Roberto's side. "I'm sorry for interrupting your day. It looks like my grandson makes you very happy. And you do the same for him."

"He does—make me happy, that is." Stasia smiled brightly as though to confirm her words. It wasn't a lie to keep the charade going. It was the truth.

"I'm sorry to intrude—" his grandfather took on a more serious tone as he turned back to Roberto with a direct stare "—but I wanted to discuss those files with you. I assume since you have time for sightseeing that you've completed the project."

Roberto's body tensed. His grip on Stasia's hand tightened. His grandfather was calling him out for not spending every moment working and it was her fault. She was the one who'd lured him out for a day of leisurely strolls, delicious food and good times beneath the Italian sun.

The tension coursing between the two men was palpable. Stasia's mind raced for something—for anything—that would break the rising tempers.

"It's my fault," she uttered. Both men turned to her and she knew she had to keep going. "I asked Roberto to go sightseeing today. If you're angry with anyone, it should be me—"

"It's not her fault." Roberto gave her a stern look as though telling her to back off—that this was his fight. "I should have stayed and worked today."

Not one to be warned off, she said, "But I promised him that I would help him—"

"Help him?" His grandfather's gray brow arched. "Is that true, Roberto? Do you need help?"

Stasia inwardly groaned. "That isn't what I meant—"

"Stasia, stop." Roberto released her hand. "You don't owe my grandfather any explanations."

Immediately her lips pressed together in a firm line, holding back all the words she now wanted to say to Roberto. She'd been trying to help him. If he didn't want her help, she didn't know what she was doing here.

Roberto straightened his shoulders. "You didn't say how I was to complete your project. In fact, I don't even have to work on this thing for you."

Now she could see why Roberto had opted to work with her brother. Both Roberto and his grandfather had iron wills. Neither wanted to back down.

"Are you saying you're quitting?" his grandfather asked.

There was a moment of silence as though Roberto was weighing his options. "I plan to work on your reports the rest of the evening. And before you ask again, yes, Stasia is assisting me."

"Those are confidential reports."

"And I trust her explicitly." He turned to her. "Would you mind giving us a minute alone?"

Stasia nodded before walking away. She hoped the two men would make peace with each other. Everyone needed family—whether it was by blood or by choice.

Roberto's back teeth ground together.

Instead of his grandfather being grateful for the help, he could only criticize the way he'd gone about accomplishing it. Roberto remembered exactly why he'd quit working for his grandfather all those years ago.

Once Stasia was out of earshot, Roberto turned to his grandfather. "Don't ever do that again."

"Do what?" And then his grandfather's eyes widened in understanding. "You really do care about her. Your grandmother said it was real. I should have trusted her instincts. She's pretty good at spotting these things."

"Not when it came to my parents," Roberto muttered under his breath.

"That was different."

Roberto hadn't meant for his grandfather to hear him, but now that he had, Roberto had some questions. "How was it different? My parents can hardly stand to be in the room together."

"What you don't know is that your grandmother and I vehemently opposed their marriage. But the harder line we took, the more insistent your parents were about marrying."

Having a very strained relationship with both parents, he would never broach this subject with either of them. "So why don't they get divorced?"

His grandfather sighed. "That's a question I've asked myself many times. And the only thing I can figure out is that they truly love each other."

"No." Roberto shook his head. "I've seen them. They don't touch. They hardly talk to each other."

"But when you see them, they are with the family. They feel awkward and don't want any pressure put upon them."

"And what? They get along when they are off on their own?"

His grandfather smiled and nodded. "Your father told me they've found a way to be happy together."

"But without me."

His grandfather walked over to him and briefly touched his hand to Roberto's shoulder. "I am sorry about that. Not all people are meant to be parents. Your grandmother and I, we did the best we could, but we weren't your mom and dad. And…and I worried that I'd make the same mistakes with you that I made with your father. So I overcompensated by being harder on you. Too hard. I...I'm sorry."

His grandfather's explanation and apology were like a balm on his scarred heart. Maybe there was a possibility for a new beginning for them. He could finally allow himself to admit that he missed his family.

As frustrated as Roberto had been with his grandfather, he loved him even more for always being there—even when Roberto didn't make the choices his grandparents wanted him to make.

"Thank you for being the steady presence in my life."

His grandfather was quiet for a moment. "Maybe this can be a new start for us."

Roberto nodded. He liked the thought of being closer to his grandfather—of returning to the family business.

His grandfather gave his shoulder another squeeze. "I should be going. Your grandmother will be looking for me." His grandfather started to walk away but then paused and turned back. "Don't plan your future based on your parents' choices. You are your own man and quite capable of anything you set your heart and mind on."

And that was it. His grandfather moved toward the interior of the ship, leaving Roberto to grapple with the realization that his parents loved each other in their own way. Maybe he should have seen this—should have suspected this, but he'd been so angry with them most of his life that he was oblivious.

Even though they loved each other, he would never want a life like theirs. And he knew that Stasia wouldn't want that lonely life either. Not that he was considering truly marrying her or anything.

There were still a few more days of the cruise. And he knew that when the ship made port in Athens this whole fantasy would come to a screeching halt.

He wasn't ready to deal with that now. He had enough on his mind with his grandfather and his looming deadline.

Together, he and Stasia quietly made their way to his cabin. Once the door closed, Stasia asked, "What in the world happened back there?"

"My grandfather was just being himself."

"But he was so kind and friendly before."

"And he was trying to get me to do something for him. Now that I'm doing what he asked, he doesn't have to play nice." He didn't want to discuss what he'd learned about his parents. He was still trying to make sense of it.

Stasia pursed her lips. "Is it possible it was something else?"

"Something like what?"

"Like he's worried and anxious to find out what you've learned."

Instead of quickly rejecting her speculation, Roberto paused. Did she have a point here? He rubbed the back of his neck. "I don't know. I've been butting heads with him for so long now that there's where my thoughts naturally go. But maybe you're right. I do know that he looks more tired than I've ever seen him."

"Is it possible there's more to those reports than a few transposed numbers?"

"I know there is. My grandfather wouldn't send me on a fool's errand. There is something definitely wrong. I can feel it in my gut. But it might be more serious than I originally suspected."

"Or maybe you want there to be something there for you to find so you can prove yourself to your grandfather."

There she went again, seeing more of him than he wanted anyone to see. "I don't have anything to prove."

"Says the man working at another company instead of his family business."

He stepped up to her. He needed to look her in the eyes when he set the record straight. "I work with your brother because he's my friend and I like what I do. You don't know me as well as you think."

Stasia's eyes grew round as her mouth slightly gaped.

He inwardly groaned. That had come out much gruffer than he'd intended. He didn't want to hurt Stasia's feelings. In fact, that was the furthest thing from his mind.

He just needed her to stop pulling back the scabs on his life's traumas. One by one, she was revealing the real Roberto, and he felt exposed. It was not a situation he was used to finding himself in.

The truth was he never left the family business because he wanted to leave. He'd done it to stop the daily arguments with his grandfather. He'd never said he wouldn't go back. It just had to be on his terms.

"I'm sorry," he said.

"No. I'm the one who's sorry. Sometimes I forget myself and I venture into subjects that are none of my business." She glanced off to the side. "Maybe I should leave."

He sighed. He was single-handedly ruining this most perfect day. But it wasn't over yet; there was still a chance to salvage it.

"Don't go. I know I took my frustration with my grandfather out on you. I shouldn't have done that."

Stasia hesitated. "And I pushed you more than I should have."

"How about we start over?"

"Do you think it's possible?"

"I could order us some dinner," he said.

"And I could get started on those reports."

"You don't have to."

"I want to."

He smiled and nodded. "Thank you."

DAY THIRTEEN

Sicily, Italy

THIS WAS UNBELIEVABLE.

She was standing on a volcano.

Stasia felt giddy inside. It was exciting to push herself and try new things. A year ago or even five years ago, she would have played it safe. Lukos had been a cautious man. When she'd push for them to be more adventurous, such as going on a weeklong hiking trip along the Amalfi Coast in Italy, he'd countered with a long weekend in wine country in a five-star hotel. She hadn't argued, perhaps she should have, but she'd preferred to make him happy. And the spa at the hotel had been out of this world.

But thanks to Roberto, she was finding she was capable of so much more. He didn't hold her back. He encouraged her to explore—to take chances.

Stasia couldn't believe she was seriously considering Roberto's idea of starting her own foundation. The man seemed to have a way of convincing her she was capable of doing anything she set her mind to. As this trip went on, she was learning that she was capable of far more than she'd previously given herself credit for. She wouldn't make that mistake again.

Still, she worried about letting herself get closer to him. She had to learn to count on herself for her happiness. But as her gaze moved to Roberto, she had absolutely no desire to put any distance between them.

And then his gaze caught hers and her stomach dipped. He flashed her a smile, causing her to smile back at him. If it weren't for Roberto, she wouldn't have thought to chal-

lenge herself—to go beyond what she thought were her
limits.

"What has you smiling?" Roberto's voice cut into her
thoughts.

"You. You have me smiling."

"I do?" His voice came out as an enticing deep growl. He
moved to stand in front of her. His hands wrapped around
her waist as her hands came to rest on his shoulders.

She nodded. "Standing at the foot of a massive volcano
is something I never thought I'd do. I'm beginning to feel
like anything is possible."

"You can do anything you set your mind to."

As the breeze rushed past them, she leaned her head
back. She stared up at the clear blue sky. She couldn't believe this cruise was almost over. She wanted to make the
most of every moment they had left.

It was then that she felt Roberto press his lips to her
neck. A shiver of excitement coursed through her body.
Apparently she wasn't the only one who wanted to make
the most of the time they had left.

When she straightened up, she realized their tour group
was getting away from them. "We better hurry across this
lava field before they leave us behind."

"Would that be such a bad thing?"

She lightly slapped his arm. "Seriously? And miss the
best part."

"The best part?"

She started walking. Roberto fell in step next to her.
She moved as quickly as she could, considering they were
in a lava field.

"Don't you want to wear a helmet and take a flashlight
to explore a lava cave?" She glanced over at Roberto, who
was smiling and shaking his head. "What? It sounds exciting."

"Until something creepy and crawly comes out and attacks you."

She visibly shuddered. "It doesn't matter what you say—it's not going to stop me."

"Are you sure? I hear the spiders down there are big. Really, really big. With long, hairy legs and googly eyes—"

"Stop!" She frowned at him. "How did you know?"

"That you're afraid of spiders?" When she nodded, he said, "It was a calculated guess."

"Calculated? Are you saying I'm predictable?"

"I'd never say that. Because I never would have predicted you'd become my fiancée."

She smiled. For just that moment, she wanted to give in to the fantasy, imagine what it'd be like to really be Roberto's true love—his destiny. Her gaze moved to the heirloom diamond on her hand. It was meant for Roberto's wife—the woman he was meant to spend the rest of his life with.

In that moment, she realized that she never wanted to give up the ring. Because to surrender the ring would be to surrender the blissful fantasy. And she didn't want this to end.

The breath stilled in her chest. Her heartbeat slowed. What was she saying? Did she really want this engagement to continue?

And then she knew the answer. It wasn't some mysterious answer that she had to wrestle with. The answer came to her so quickly, so easily that it was startling. No matter how much she wanted to fight it—deny it—she was falling in love with Roberto.

She glanced at the ring again. Ever since he'd put it on her finger, it was like it had pulled the blinders from her eyes. And now she was able to see what was clearly in front of her—Roberto.

He took her hand in his. "What are you thinking about?"

"Um, nothing."

"That look on your face says otherwise. Must be something good."

She glanced at him. "I was just thinking this is such a lovely day."

"It is a really nice day. But I think there's more going on in that mind of yours than that."

She shrugged but didn't elaborate. Some thoughts were best to keep to herself until she decided how to tell him. She didn't know what he'd say. Would he be happy?

What was she saying? They'd just made love. He must feel the same way or he wouldn't be here with her in a lava field about to descend into a cave.

Roberto played his emotions so close to his chest that sometimes it was so hard to read him. But with them reaching the mouth of the cave, it was best to leave the subject alone until they returned to the chalet.

What was going on?

She'd been acting strange all day.

Roberto couldn't shake the feeling things had shifted with Stasia. He wanted to say that escalating their relationship had been a mistake, but he couldn't dismiss such an amazing night. But it wasn't just Stasia who was confused.

And this was why he worked rather than trying to have a relationship. For the most part, his work was straightforward. But this thing between him and Stasia was anything but straightforward. He didn't know what to say or how to act.

At lunch at the nearby chalet, when she didn't think he was looking, she would stare at him. She didn't say anything, but there was a different sort of energy coursing between them. And it had nothing to do with the fresh air or bright sunshine. Nor did the change between them have to do with the delicious meat-and-cheese tray or the local wine. No, this change had to do with him letting go of his common sense and giving in to his desires. And now he didn't know how to rewind the clock.

"You're awfully quiet," Stasia said as they made their way onto the ship.

"I am?" He hadn't noticed because there were so many conflicting voices in his head.

She nodded. "What are you thinking about?"

He glanced around. A lot of people were returning to the ship at the same time as them. This wasn't the place for a serious talk. But they had to talk. He couldn't let things spiral further out of control.

"I was thinking that I'm almost out of time to tell my grandfather what is going on with his business."

"And that's all?" She arched a fine brow.

"I didn't know you were the suspicious type." He sent her a teasing smile.

"Suspicious, huh?"

They kept walking and he kept the conversation light, which was the exact opposite of how he was feeling at the moment. And somewhere along the way, Stasia had slipped her hand in his. It felt so natural for their fingers to be entwined that it drove home the reason they had to talk.

Stasia wanted more from this relationship than he could give her. He wasn't the right man for her. He didn't know how to have a long-term relationship. His parents were terrible role models. And he was a workaholic. Not exactly the criteria for a faithful, devoted companion.

When they reached Stasia's cabin, she opened the door and stepped inside. He paused at the doorway, not sure he trusted himself to go any farther. All his good intentions were likely to go out the window if she were to turn those big brown eyes on him. He would be putty in her hands, but he couldn't let her see his weakness because in the end, this thing between them, it wasn't real.

"Aren't you coming in?" she asked.

He shook his head. "I can't stay."

"Of course. You need to get back to work—"

"Stasia, it's not that." Although he did need to find the answer for his grandfather—prove that he was the rightful heir to the Carrass dynasty. But first he had to put right what he'd broken. "We need to talk."

The smile faded from her face. "It sounds serious."

"It is." He wasn't sure where to begin. "I owe you an apology."

Her brows rose. "For what?"

"The other night." He raked his fingers through his hair, scattering the short strands. He searched for the right words.

"The other night was what?"

There was no way to sugarcoat this. His gaze lowered because he just couldn't stand to see the pain that would be reflected in her eyes. "It was a mistake."

"A...a mistake?" Her voice was hollow.

When he lifted his gaze, he found she'd turned her back to him. She busied herself by taking off her shoes. Every bit of him longed to go to her—to wrap his arms around her waist—to plant a kiss on the slope of her neck—to hold her in his arms until the sun came up.

Stasia was amazing. If he ever imagined falling in love and starting a family, it would be with someone like Stasia. She was kind but insightful, beautiful but down-to-earth.

She turned to him. "You were saying why this was a mistake."

He couldn't read her thoughts. Her expression was blank.

This was not the reaction he had been expecting. Still, she stood there staring at him, waiting for him to speak.

"I'm sorry. I acted without thinking. It shouldn't have happened."

She crossed her arms. "You don't think we're good together?"

That was the real problem. He did think they were good together, but he couldn't tell her that. "I think I'm not the man for you. And I don't want to hurt you."

"I appreciate you trying to let me down gently, but it's not necessary."

"It's not?"

She shook her head. "I didn't think we were anything serious. We agreed to be a couple for the length of the cruise. It's only natural being so close that one thing might lead to another, but I didn't expect this—" she waved between her and him "—to last."

He breathed a sigh of relief. This was going so much easier than he'd ever imagined. "So then we're still on track?"

She nodded. "Don't worry. Everything is good."

It didn't feel good. His gaze met hers and he still wasn't able to get a handle on her feelings. "Then I'll go."

"I'll freshen up and then I'll meet you at your cabin."

Really? This seemed too good to be true. "Are you sure you want to do that?"

She didn't say anything as though considering her choices. "I said I'd help and I will."

He pulled the door closed behind him and then started down the passageway. He'd noticed how the light in her eyes had dimmed. No matter what she said, he'd hurt her. And that was the last thing he'd meant to do.

DAY FOURTEEN

Naples, Italy

"MAYBE WE'RE GOING about this the wrong way," Roberto said.

Stasia leaned back in her chair and stretched her sore muscles. Leaning over a laptop for hours made for aches and pains. "What do you mean?"

"I mean, we're going about this with a micro view. Perhaps we should pull back and go about it with a macro view."

"But we already went over the balance sheet. It tied in to the supplemental files." She wasn't getting his meaning, but she did agree that what they were doing now wasn't working.

It didn't help that she was distracted by their earlier conversation. His words had been like nails driven into her heart. But she had no one to blame but herself. She knew from the start that this relationship was temporary.

"I don't know." Roberto's voice drew her attention. "Maybe we have to do spot checks on the expenses because if there's going to be something unscrupulous, it's going to be with the outgoing funds. Let's hope we get lucky."

"Spot checks? You mean like pick a random number—"

"Or entry. And track it back to its origin."

She could feel his rising desperation. The cruise was over in less than two days and he so desperately wanted to have the answers for his grandfather. And she wanted to help him find those answers. But was this really the right way to go about it?

His fingers were already moving over the keyboard

when she said, "Isn't this like throwing a dart at a board and just hoping it hits the bull's-eye?"

Roberto paused and glanced up at her. "If this business were smaller. If the numbers didn't run in the hundreds of millions, then yes, I would agree with you, but we just don't have time to do a full-fledged audit. My grandfather wants answers now."

"And you want to show him that you're the man to give him those answers."

His gaze met hers, but he didn't say the obvious.

After a few minutes, he said, "Okay. I've just printed off a couple of pages of entries. Pick a few numbers on each sheet and trace them back to their invoices."

"Invoices? We don't have that sort of detail."

"No. But I have the password and access to the company's servers. We'll be able to pull everything, as the system is automated and all the invoices are stored digitally."

And so they set to work. Time passed quickly with few results because it was a big task. They started with a vendor and then tracked the payments back through the system.

The first number was tracked back to a legitimate invoice.

The second tracked back accordingly.

The third and the fourth did, as well.

Stasia was beginning to think this was a fruitless mission. And the hour was getting late. Dinner had been a number of hours ago and she was starting to get tired as well as hungry.

As though he sensed her restlessness, Roberto glanced up from his laptop. "You should call it a night."

The idea was so tempting. This was the last place she wanted to find herself. Being so close to Roberto and yet so far apart was excruciating. But she'd told him that she would help him find answers and she wasn't going back on her word.

Her gaze met his. "What about you? Do you want to get some sleep and tackle it again tomorrow?"

He shook his head. "I want to get through a few more numbers."

She restrained a sigh. "That's what I was thinking too."

He arched a disbelieving brow. "Are you sure? I'd totally understand if you want to go."

She shook her head. "But can we call for food? I'm starved."

He smiled. "I like the way you think."

They continued to work, verifying number after number. Then something didn't quite add up. Stasia had an expenditure on the reports that tied to an invoice. When she took it a step further, she could not locate a company that went by the name on the invoice.

Knock. Knock.

Stasia was so confused. She refused to give up until she resolved this mysterious company. Because there was a lot of money charged off to it over the years for construction materials.

"I'll get the door," Roberto said.

She didn't say anything as she was caught up in what she was reading on the internet. The company name did not have a website that she could find, and in this day and age of technology, that threw up a red flag for her. And then she typed in the phone number from the invoice. It said it belonged to a woman by a totally different name.

Roberto closed the door and set the food on the nightstand next to his bed since they had the table covered with their computers and papers. "I thought you were hungry."

"I, uh…" She typed in the physical address listed on the invoice.

Roberto moved to her side. "You what? Did you find something?"

"I don't know." Using online global mapping, she tracked the address down to an empty lot. "This invoice, it's not making sense."

He crouched down next to her. "You mean the amount isn't matching up?"

She shook her head. "It matches. But I decided to go a step further with each invoice and check out the company. This particular company, I don't think it's legit."

"Do you mind?" He gestured to the computer.

"Look for yourself. Maybe I'm more tired than I thought."

He swung the laptop around and started moving through the various reports that were all open on the screen. He repeated all her steps, from doing an internet search for the company name to the phone number and the physical address. All were the same results.

Then he asked to borrow her phone.

"What are you doing?" she asked.

"I'm calling the number." His finger moved over the screen.

"But it's late."

"And this is too important to wait around." He pressed a button and put the phone on Speaker.

It rang a few times, and just about the time that Stasia thought no one was going to answer, a female voice came on the line. Roberto asked if this was the company name on the invoice. The woman said it wasn't. He asked if she'd ever heard of the company. She said she hadn't and asked who he was and what he wanted. The woman was very nice, but she was no help as far as finding the company.

After Roberto disconnected the phone call, he dialed again This time turning off the speakerphone.

"Who are you calling now?"

He held up a finger as he pressed the phone to his ear this time. "Grandfather, I hope I didn't wake you."

Roberto asked him if he had ever heard of the company. They continued to speak for a few minutes, after which Roberto told him he wasn't prepared to report anything on his findings just yet.

After Roberto disconnected the call, she looked at him. "Well…"

"My grandfather said there used to be a company by that name, but they'd gone out of business a number of years ago."

"Which explains why they don't have an internet presence. So then why is your grandfather's business still paying them?"

"That's what I intend to find out."

"But first food." She got to her feet and led him to the food. "Eat," she said in a firm tone.

Roberto's brows lifted. "Has anyone ever told you that you're bossy?"

"If you're trying to charm me—"

"You think being called bossy is charming?"

She thought about it for a minute. "Sure. I like being taken seriously."

"Oh, I take you seriously. Especially when you uncover what is surely a case of embezzlement." He stepped closer to her. "This is it. My grandfather will at last take me seriously and offer me the CEO position."

"It's your birthright. Of course he will."

Roberto shook his head. "You don't know my grandfather. It's his way or no way. But this revelation changes things. This is exactly what I needed. Do you have any idea how amazing you are?"

"Stop." She couldn't have him flirting with her. It was too painful. He had his answer. Her job was finished. "I have to go."

She turned and headed for the door.

"Stasia. Wait."

She kept going. If she were to stop now—if she were to look into his eyes—her bravado would crumble. And she refused to make a fool of herself in front of him by letting him know that she'd fallen for her pretend fiancé.

DAY FIFTEEN

Rome, Italy

THE CRUISE WAS almost over.

And she'd concentrated on everyone but herself.

Stasia realized that was a pattern she'd developed in her life. First, it was Lukos. She'd given up her dream of a career in order to follow his career. And after she lost Lukos, she let Xander have a say in her future. Even on this cruise, she'd let Roberto distract her from her goals. It had to stop.

Stasia had stayed in her cabin that morning, not venturing on the tour of Rome and all its many splendors. She didn't have any other excuses—any other distractions.

Everything was taken care of with Roberto. His project for his grandfather was complete. And he was about to step into his birthright. She couldn't be happier for him.

She would miss him. More than she'd ever imagined possible. Her heart ached at just the thought of not seeing Roberto every day. And even worse, she could imagine him avoiding her at every turn after the way things on this cruise got way more involved than either of them planned.

She sighed. Worrying about the future wasn't going to help anything. The best thing she could do was to make a final decision on her future.

At last she knew what she wanted—a chance to help people. It fulfilled her. It gave her a purpose. And it would help so many others.

She didn't have to think any further. She knew what to do. But now she needed to take action—put motion behind her words.

Stasia grabbed her phone. She looked up the email correspondence from the woman at the hospital where Lukos had been treated and she placed the call. When she told the woman she would like to expand on their services and create a foundation, the woman promised to do everything she could to help smooth the way.

By the time Stasia hung up, she was smiling. This foundation would carry her late husband's name. It seemed so fitting and she hoped Lukos would be proud of her efforts.

For so long she'd told herself she'd secluded herself because she had to figure out her life's path, but the truth was she wanted a chance to lick her wounds—her deep wounds. And they hadn't gone away, but they were healing now. The scars would always linger but they were now a part of her, just like Lukos would always be a part of her. She would never be the woman she used to be, but she hoped she would be a better person for having known and loved Lukos.

Now she was ready to start life once again.

And she'd foolishly thought she'd found the right person to share it with.

And she'd been totally wrong.

She might have said all the right things to Roberto when he'd declared their night together a mistake. A mistake? Really?

Because it'd felt like anything but a mistake. He'd been so passionate, so thoughtful, so giving. It was like the wall between them had fallen away and it was just the two of them on even ground.

She'd thought it had been the beginning of something real for them. She glanced down at the diamond ring on her finger. It felt so heavy. She slipped it off and placed it on the table next to her laptop.

She'd known what the deal was when she'd agreed to

play his fake fiancée. Why should she think that would change? Her heart cried out: because it was what she'd wanted. Each day she'd spent with Roberto, they'd grown closer and she'd found out that he wasn't the shallow playboy that she'd initially thought him to be.

He was so different—so much deeper—than she'd ever imagined. But there was one thing that hadn't changed—his determination to remain a bachelor. His grandmother couldn't change his mind. The flood of vivacious single women on the ship couldn't change his mind. And she couldn't change his mind.

She had to accept that he knew what was best for his life. And it didn't include her—

Knock. Knock. Knock.

"Stasia? Are you in there?"

It was Roberto. She had thought he'd be off sharing the information they'd uncovered with his grandfather. She didn't want to see him again.

Knock. Knock.

"Stasia," he yelled. "I'm not leaving until we talk."

She jumped to her feet and rushed to the door. "Roberto, keep it down." She glanced around to see if he'd disturbed any of her neighbors. She didn't see anyone in the passageway. "Come inside." Once he was inside, she closed the door. "What are you doing here?"

His brows rose. "Am I supposed to be somewhere else?"

"I thought you'd be with your grandfather. You know, to go over things."

"My grandfather and I are getting together this evening. My grandmother dragged him off to Rome and she wouldn't take no for an answer."

"I can definitely see your grandmother doing that. She's a very determined lady."

"Looks like you've been busy." He moved to the table. "What are you doing?"

"Working on my five-year plan."

"Anything I can do to help?"

She shook her head. "Not at this point. I'm finally getting started with the foundation."

He approached her. "And that's my fault."

"Why would that be your fault?"

"Because I kept you busy worrying about my life and my problems." He gazed into her eyes. "And I haven't thanked you nearly enough."

She shook her head. "You don't have to thank me."

"I disagree."

Knock. Knock. Knock.

Stasia ran a hand over her hair. "If I knew I was going to have this much company, I would have gotten dressed up."

She moved to the door and opened it to find one of the ship's crew standing there with a cart. What in the world?

"I'm afraid you have the wrong cabin," she said. "I didn't order food."

Roberto rushed to her side. "Actually, you do have the right place."

Stasia stepped aside while Roberto opened the door wide for the cart. And then he rushed to the table and cleared it so the man could set up what appeared to be two covered plates, a bottle of bubbly on ice and a dozen red roses. What was this man up to?

Once the table was set and the man was gone, Stasia turned to Roberto. "What are you up to?"

"Isn't it obvious? You need lunch and I need lunch. So I thought we would eat together." He approached her. "What do you say? Shall we eat?"

"Roberto—" she shook her head "—this isn't a good idea."

He held up the diamond ring. "Does it have something to do with this sitting on the table instead of being on your finger?"

Her gaze moved to the ring that twinkled at her, but she made no move to take it. "The cruise is almost over. You need to take it back."

"And I've done a lot of thinking. What would you say if I said I didn't want this to end?"

"What? But you just got done telling me that this was only temporary—a show for your grandparents."

He reached out to her. His hands gently gripped her upper arms. "I made a mistake. You and I, we make a great team. If my grandfather offers me the CEO position, which I think was his motive behind this project, it'll mean moving to Alexandroupoli. We can start a life there."

Her head was spinning. A life with Roberto? He was saying all the right things except for the *L* word. And there was no way she would plan a future with someone who couldn't say he loved her.

Wait. He said that he was moving. Alexandroupoli was quite a way from Athens. And she'd just made a commitment to start her foundation in Athens. It'd taken her a long time to figure out just the right thing to do with her life and this felt right. She couldn't—she wouldn't give it up. She had to break the pattern.

And there was the crux of the problem. Everyone wanted something from her. His family wanted her to marry Roberto. He wanted her to give up everything to follow his dreams.

She couldn't do it. She couldn't give up on herself again. She needed this foundation. She needed to know that she could do it. She needed to know that she could stand on her own two feet and follow through with her dream.

"Roberto, I said I'd be your fiancée for the length of the cruise. Not any longer than that."

He stared at her for a moment. "I didn't mean for you to continue being my fake fiancée. I want you to be there with me, by my side, in a real relationship."

Her gaze searched his. There was nothing about love. He didn't feel the same for her.

"I can't do that. I'm staying in Athens. I'm starting the foundation. It's something I need to do on my own."

His expression hardened. "And what about us?"

"There is no us." The words tore at her heart, but she knew in the long run that it was for the best. Roberto was not a man to be tied down. "We got caught up in the charade. It's over now. We have to go back to reality. Alone. It's the only way."

His eyes grew darker as a muscle in his cheek twitched. He surely couldn't be mad that she'd beat him to the punch. He couldn't actually think they'd last. Did he?

"I should go." And with that, he stormed out the door, closing it with a solid thud.

DAY SIXTEEN

Athens, Greece

TODAY WAS THE end of their cruise.

The end of their engagement. The end of seeing her every single day.

He'd been up all night. Every time he'd closed his eyes, Stasia's image came to mind. And he couldn't forget her final words to him. They'd been sharp and had cut right through him.

Early that morning, he'd meandered to the deck, where he'd watched the sun rise. Though it should have filled him with some sort of joy, it had done nothing for him. The brilliant colors of the sunrise were like a taunt to his gray mood.

"Roberto?"

He inwardly groaned. The last person he wanted to talk to was his grandmother.

"Roberto, what are you doing out here?" His grandmother stopped at his table and looked at him with confusion reflected in her eyes. "Shouldn't you be packing?"

"I already did it." He didn't want to talk. He just wanted to sit here alone with his thoughts.

Yaya glanced around. "Where's Stasia?"

He shrugged, looking down at his lap, where he was holding the engagement ring. "I don't know."

She sat down. "Roberto, what's wrong?"

He sighed. "It's over. It's all over."

"What is? I don't understand."

He started at the beginning, telling his grandmother

about the charade and how it somehow became real—or at least he thought it had turned into a real relationship. Obviously, he'd been mistaken.

He handed her the engagement ring. "You need to take this back."

Yaya accepted the ring. She stared at it a moment. "Are you sure about this?"

"Positive. She dumped me." The acknowledgment was like an arrow through his heart.

"And that's it? You're just going to let her walk away?"

He frowned at his grandmother. "You want me to go back so she can do it again?"

Yaya shook her head. "That's not what I meant." She reached out and placed a hand on his arm. "I know that this isn't the first time you've been dumped. That was the exact word you used when your parents left you with us—"

"I don't want to talk about them. This has nothing to do with them."

"But I think it does. What your parents did was wrong and they hurt you deeply. You learned how to protect yourself by keeping others out. And you stopped telling people how you feel."

He turned to her. "What are you saying? That I'm the reason Stasia dumped me?"

"I just want you to think about it. Did you give her a reason to stay? Did you tell her that you love her—really love her?" His grandmother looked at the ring and then placed it back in his hand. "You hang on to this a while longer. I have a feeling you might need it." His grandmother stood. "Now I'm off to find some more bags. I've bought more things than I thought. Your grandfather is having a fit because there's no room in the luggage."

Roberto didn't hear his grandmother leave. He was too

busy considering what she'd told him. Was she right? Had he been holding himself back?

Would Stasia feel different about him if he told her the truth? Just the thought of baring his deepest feelings to her with the chance that she'd reject him—much like his parents had rejected him when he'd begged them not to leave—left him feeling more vulnerable than he ever had in his whole life. Could he do it?

Ending things with Roberto was one of the hardest things she'd ever had to do.

Stasia had cried herself to sleep. And now in the morning light, her face was still puffy and her head hurt, but not as much as her heart.

As she exited the ship, her feet felt as though they were weighted down. Each step she took away from the ship—away from Roberto—was like another piece of her heart being torn away. What was she doing? Why was she walking away from him?

She'd been telling herself that Roberto didn't love her, but would a man who didn't care about her put a family heirloom on her finger? She had to admit that was pretty extreme even for a fake fiancée.

And then there was the way he'd spoiled her on her birthday, making her feel like a princess. And the way he'd talked with her about her future. And then there was their lovemaking. It had been so gentle and giving. That most definitely hadn't just been sex. It had been the closest she'd ever been to a person—heart, body and soul.

She glanced over her shoulder as though Roberto would be standing there. He wasn't. Was it possible she was remembering what she wanted to?

"Stasia?"

She turned her head forward, finding her brother standing there. "Xander, what are you doing here?"

"Looks like I'm just in time." He came to a stop in front of her. "Why are you crying?"

She touched her cheek, finding it damp. She hadn't even realized the tears had slipped down her cheeks. She rubbed at her face. "It doesn't matter."

"It's a guy, isn't it?"

She couldn't deny it.

"Stasia, what's going on?" Xander looked at her with concern reflected in his eyes. "Who upset you?"

Maybe if she'd been more willing to be honest with herself, with Roberto and with her brother about her feelings, she wouldn't feel so terrible now. This was supposed to be her chance to turn over a new leaf in her life. She would start with the truth.

She leveled her shoulders and lifted her chin. "Xander, there's something I need to tell you."

"Okay. I'm listening."

"I've made a decision. I'm not going into business with you." Disappointment reflected in his eyes but she didn't let that stop her. "I'm sorry. I know you've tried to include me and I really appreciate all you've done. But I have to follow my heart."

He arched a brow. "Follow your heart, doing what?"

"I'm going to start a foundation to help support the families of cancer patients. There are so many programs for the ill, but there's not a lot for the caregivers. I want to do something to support them so they can give their all to their ill loved ones." She paused. Her breath caught in her throat as she waited to hear what her brother thought of her plans.

"I think that's a great idea. When you're ready, let me know and I'll donate or do whatever you need."

A smile pulled at her lips. "Thank you."

"But that still doesn't explain what had you so upset when I first saw you." His gaze searched hers. "If some guy has hurt you, tell me. I'll take care of him."

She glanced away, finding Roberto standing on the deck of the ship speaking to his grandfather. She'd love to know what was being said. She hoped there would be peace between the two men.

She turned her attention back to her brother. She was on a roll. She might as well keep going. "Xander, thank you for being there after Lukos passed. I really needed you, but I need you to understand that I have to figure things out on my own. I need to be able to make my own decisions without you watching over my shoulder and without worrying you'll be disappointed with my actions."

"You never disappoint me." He rubbed the back of his neck. "I just worry about you. I don't want you to be hurt again."

"But I will be and you have to be okay with that. I don't want to live in a glass house where no one can reach me and where I don't feel anything. I want to takes chances and live life to its fullest."

Her thoughts circled back to Roberto. If she were going to take chances, it should be with him. If she were going to live life to the fullest, it should be with him. So why exactly was she walking away from the man she loved without asking if he felt the same way about her?

Her gaze met her brother's. "I've got to go. I have something to do."

She turned and rushed off in the direction of the ship. She heard her brother call to her but she didn't care. She had to do this. She had to take this chance.

As she drew closer to Roberto and his grandfather, she overheard his grandfather say, "You strike a tough bargain, but I think we can make this work." His grandfather held out his hand to him. "Welcome back to the company."

Roberto shook his hand, all the while smiling.

Stasia came to a halt. Roberto was smiling. He was happy. Maybe it would be best just to leave well enough alone.

"Stasia—" her brother's voice came from behind her "—what's going on?"

It was then that Roberto and his grandfather noticed her standing off to the side. Roberto's gaze caught and held hers. Her heart pounded in her chest. She should say something, but no words came to mind.

Xander stepped forward. His gaze moved between her and Roberto. "It's him?"

Stasia was done keeping secrets. She nodded.

Xander's expression hardened. He moved toward Roberto in determined steps. "You were supposed to watch over her—keep her from getting hurt."

Stasia rushed to stand between the two most important men in her life. "Xander, I love you. But this is none of your business."

"I can explain," Roberto said.

"We don't want to hear it." Xander pressed his fists to his sides with a glare written all over his face. "You screwed up. Big-time."

"Ignore him," Stasia said to Roberto. "I want to hear what you have to say."

Just then Roberto's grandmother joined them. "What's going on?"

"Shh…" Roberto's grandfather said. "You don't want to miss this."

Roberto approached Xander. "First, Xander, I resign. I'm sorry for the short notice, but with you moving most of the operations to Infinity Island, this is probably the best time for a change."

When Xander went to say something, Stasia glared at him and he closed his mouth without saying a word. She didn't want her brother to ruin one of his closest friendships.

"And second—" Roberto moved to stand directly in front of her "—thanks to your support, I am taking the CEO position. However, my grandfather and I have hammered out a deal where the headquarters are to be moved to Athens."

"Really?" A big smile pulled at her lips. The thought of Roberto being close by, the thought of being able to see him regularly, almost offset the sadness of calling off their engagement. "But I don't understand. Why would you do that?"

"You honestly don't know?" When she shook her head, he said, "Because I love you. I love the way you smile. I love your laugh. I love your generous heart. I love everything about you. I'm sorry I didn't tell you sooner, but someone set me straight." He glanced at his grandmother, who had happy tears in her eyes. Roberto turned his attention back to Stasia. "And I plan to stick around until you realize that you love me too."

Her heart swelled. "You won't have to wait long because I already love you."

A smile lit up Roberto's face as he pulled her into an embrace and kissed her. The kiss was short but it left no doubt in her mind that there would be more to follow soon.

When he pulled back, he said, "I think I have something that belongs to you." He pulled the engagement ring from his pocket. He bent down on one knee.

Her heart lodged in her throat. She had never expected

this. His gaze held hers. When her gaze blurred from happy tears, she blinked repeatedly.

"I know I did this once before, but I want to do it over again, the right way." He took her hand in his and held the ring at the end of her finger. "Stasia, you've shown me what true love is. You've shown me that some risks are worth taking. I want us to walk through life side by side with no one in the lead. If you give me the chance, I'll be your biggest cheerleader. I believe you're capable of anything you set your mind to." He stared deep into her eyes. "Stasia, I love you with all my heart. Will you be my partner in life?"

"Yes. Oh, yes." Happy tears splashed onto her cheeks as he slid the ring on her finger.

After Roberto stood and kissed her again, they turned to Xander, waiting for his reaction.

"What's everyone looking at me for?" Xander's stony expression burst into a big smile. "I couldn't be happier for either of you." He hugged each of them.

And then Roberto's grandparents stepped forward. She'd forgotten they were still there. A puzzled expression was written over his grandfather's face. "I don't understand. I thought you were already engaged."

Everyone started to laugh. Roberto promised to fill his grandfather in later, but right now he had plans with his fiancée. They had wedding plans to make because August wasn't that far off.

EPILOGUE

August... Infinity Island, Greece

THEY'D PASSED THE TEST.

Stasia smiled. Not that she ever had any doubt about their compatibility. Still, not everyone passed the wedding test issued by Infinity Island. They were meant to be.

She stood in what used to be Popi's bungalow. But now that she had married the love of her life, Apollo, and moved to the Drakos estate, where she had started her own wedding business, this bungalow had been designated the bridal suite. It was where the brides came and stayed until the big day.

Stasia had been here for a week. Not only did she want to take part in the wedding preparations, but she also wanted to spend some time with her family before Roberto swept her off on a monthlong honeymoon in Alaska, of all places. He said they had sun and sand whenever they wanted, but snowy peaks and cozy fires were for snuggling. She had a distinct impression that they'd be doing a lot more than snuggling in the luxury cabin that he'd reserved for them.

Roberto had been tying things up at the office all week and she couldn't wait to see him. Now that he had taken over the family business, he had been working long hours to undo the damage the former accounts manager had done. The authorities had arrested the man and were still working on tracking down the funds that had been meticulously siphoned from the company.

But in the end, Roberto's grandfather was able to retire in peace. He knew the company was in good hands. And with the safeguards Roberto had implemented since taking the reins, the likelihood of anything like this ever happening again had been greatly reduced.

And Roberto's grandfather was so thrilled that they were tying the knot that he had agreed to step back in and run the company while Roberto enjoyed a nice long honeymoon. Stasia was thrilled to see the two men drawn back together.

Roberto's parents, on the other hand, were coming to the wedding, separately. Though some things changed, others stayed the same. At least Roberto had accepted that marriage and love didn't have to be as complicated as his parents' relationship with each other and with him.

Knock. Knock.

"Stasia, are you in there?"

Her heart leaped with joy. It was Roberto, at last.

She rushed to the door and swung it wide open. "You arrived just in time."

"What? Did you think I'd be late for my own wedding?"

The thought had crossed her mind. She knew how wrapped up he could get when he was working, but she also knew he could be just as devoted to his family. And that was something she loved about him, his passion for the things that mattered most to him.

"You did?" He glanced at her with an astonished look on his face. "You really thought I'd forget our big day?"

"No, of course not." When he arched a disbelieving brow, she said, "But I know how distracted you can get in your work."

"Not enough to forget you." He leaned forward and kissed her. Not a brief peck, but a long deep thorough kiss to prove to her just how much she mattered to him.

When he finally pulled away, her heart was hammering in her chest. And the news she had to share with him had somehow escaped her.

Not wanting to stay inside on such a beautiful day, she said, "Let's take a walk."

Hand in hand, they made their way to the beach. This was where their wedding was to take place. White chairs were already set up on either side of the sandy aisle that would be lined with white rose petals just before the service began.

And at the end of the aisle stood an arch draped in white tulle. It would have small blue flowers alongside white roses adorning the arch. Both Lea and Popi had come together once more to make this a very special wedding. And they had outdone themselves. It was everything Stasia had been hoping for and more.

"Do you think we should be here?" Roberto asked.

"Why not? After all, it is our wedding."

And wait until he saw the strapless dress she'd chosen for the big day. Her hair would be pulled back in a loose braid with small flowers inserted. On her feet would be sandals with beaded lace over the tops of her feet.

Roberto smiled at her. "Does this mean you'll stop worrying now?" When she nodded, he said, "Good. Because I'm not going anywhere. And in just a couple of hours we're going to be husband and wife." He studied her face for a moment. "You still have something on your mind. What can I say to convince you that absolutely nothing is going to go wrong today?"

"I'm not worried. Honest."

"There is something on your mind—I can see it in your eyes."

And then it came back to her, the big news she had to share with him. She just hoped that he was as excited about it as she was.

"I have some stuff to discuss with you and I didn't want to do it over the phone."

His dark brows drew together in a worried line as he reached out and took her hands in his. "What is it?"

"First, the paperwork for the foundation has come through. We're all approved and everyone I invited to be on the board has accepted."

Relief eased the worry lines on his face, and in their place, a smile lifted his lips. "That's wonderful." He leaned down and gave her a brief kiss. "I'm so proud of you. I knew you could do anything you set your mind on." He paused. "You said the first thing—that implies you have more news."

"I…I do." She gazed into his eyes, finding the added strength she needed to put the words out there. "Roberto, I have something to tell you that I hope you will find as exciting as I do."

A guarded look crossed his handsome face. "And this news, would it have anything to do with expanding our family?"

Her mouth gaped. "How…how did you know?"

A smile covered his face and lit up his eyes. "Call it wishful thinking."

"Call it whatever you want, but the doctor says in seven months and one week, we're going to be calling you Daddy."

"Woo-hoo!" He picked her up in his arms and swung her around. When he settled her feet back on the ground, he said, "I didn't think it was possible to make this day any better, but somehow you found a way. Thank you for making me see that life can be more than I ever imagined. I am truly living a dream."

"You are my dream too. I love you."

"I love you too."

* * * * *

THE MAVERICK'S
WEDDING
WAGER

JOANNA SIMS

Dedicated to Sandie Weiss

I wanted you to know how much I love you,
so I dedicated this book to you!

I love you, Aunt Sandie, and I always will.

Chapter One

"You are late."

"I *know*," horse farrier Genevieve Lawrence said to her phone as she stepped on the gas. She hated to be late and yet, here she was, running behind again on the way to her next client. Spotting one of her favorite off-road shortcuts ahead, Genevieve downshifted her four-wheel-drive Chevy Colorado, jerked the steering wheel to take a hard right and then floored it once the hind end of her truck stopped fishtailing. Laughing as she sped over a large bump in the road that sent her truck airborne for a split second, Genevieve knew she was taking a risk using this dirt road. It had been a rainy late August in Montana and there would be mud hole mine traps everywhere. But she'd been off-road racing since she was a teenager and knew this road like the back of her hand. If she didn't get stuck, she'd shave a good fifteen minutes off her time.

"What's life without a little risk?" Genevieve gave a rebel yell, fighting the steering wheel to keep it straight when the back tires hit a slick pocket of mud that sent her sliding sideways.

"Now you are really late," her phone gave her another verbal reminder.

"Nobody likes a know-it-all, Google!" Genevieve snapped as she went careening through a large puddle of standing water, splashing brown water onto her windshield and temporarily blinding her view.

Putting her wipers on high so she could see, she saw the end of the dirt road up ahead and, instead of slowing down, she floored it again. In Genevieve's mind, this was the best part. This was the most dangerous, and therefore, the most exhilarating, part of this shortcut. If she got up enough speed and momentum, she would really catch some air off a large mound of dirt right before she had to make a sharp left onto the main road.

"Woo-hoo!" she shouted, loving that wonderful sinking feeling in her stomach that she always got when all four wheels left the road.

A loud honk of a horn brought her smashing back into reality and made her tighten her grip on the steering wheel. She had successfully navigated the sharp left turn onto the highway, but miscalculated how close the next vehicle was to her entry point and she ended up cutting them off—just a little.

"Sorry!" She waved her hand out of the window with another laugh. She had cut that one a bit too close for comfort. But in her mind, no harm, no foul. This was what living was all about! Taking risks for big payoffs.

By the time she pulled into the driveway to the Crawford's cattle spread, the Ambling A, her heart was still pounding and her body was still crackling with adrenaline. She parked in front of the twenty-stall stable. When Maximilian Crawford, the patriarch of the Crawford family, purchased the ranch, the barn had been just a plain metal structure. Maximilian refurbished the barn, matching the exterior to the main house's log cabin design, and now the once plain barn was an impressive showpiece by anyone's standards. Everything about the updated stable wreaked of money—from the custom Ambling A windmill perched atop the cupola to the red brick rubber pavers in the long, wide aisle that provided a cushion for the horses' legs and joints. The Crawford cowboys had already begun to fill that fine stable with some of the highest pedigreed Montana-bred quarter horses money could buy.

Working with those horses was an honor Genevieve never thought to have. In fact, she had been completely shocked when Knox Crawford, one of Maximilian's six sons, had called to hire her as part of the Ambling A's horse care team. From her experience, most ranchers still had a mindset that being a horse farrier was a job for menfolk. And that mindset went double for her father.

As she was shutting off her engine, Genevieve spotted Knox up in the hayloft above the barn. The two large doors to the hayloft were open and Knox was restacking bales of hay, presumably getting ready for another shipment. The moment she spotted Maximilian's fifth-born son, she felt that same wonderful shot of adrenaline that she normally only experienced when she was bungee jumping from a bridge, off-road racing or winning a wager with some cowboy who thought that he couldn't ever lose to a chick.

Knox Crawford was tall and lean with intense brown-black eyes; his body appeared to be carved out of granite from years in the saddle. When Genevieve saw Knox as he was now, shirt unbuttoned with the glistening sweat from his muscular chest making an eye-catching trail down to the waistband of his snug-fitting, faded jeans, it made her almost change her mind about leaving Rust Creek Falls for more open-minded pastures in California.

Almost.

Knox heard the crunching sound of tires on the gravel drive and that got his heart pumping just a little bit faster. He'd been checking his watch, anticipating pretty Genevieve Lawrence's arrival. In fact, he'd found himself looking forward to seeing her all week. Knox hoisted one last bale of hay onto a tall stack nearby before he walked over to the wide opening of the hayloft to greet the horse farrier. Genevieve's truck, white with a colorful horse mural painted on the side, was covered in brown mud. The petite blonde got out of the driver's side door, looked up at him with an easy smile and waved.

"Sorry I'm late!" she called up to him and the sweetness in her voice rang some sort of bell in the deep recesses of his mind.

Ever since his father had tasked him with the job of finding a veterinarian and farrier for their horses, and Knox had stumbled upon Genevieve's Healing Hooves website, something in his soul seemed to hone in on this woman like a heat-seeking missile aimed at its target. Surprisingly for him, it wasn't the fact that she had long wavy, wheat-colored hair that framed her oval face in the most attractive way—even though he had always had a weakness for blondes. And it wasn't those wide cornflower blue eyes and full lips that seemed to always be turned up into a smile when she looked at him. It was more than just her looks. She fascinated him; she made him laugh. In his mind, that was a mighty potent combination.

"Not a problem." Knox took his cowboy hat off so he could wipe the sweat from his brow with his sleeve. "Did you get stuck in a mudhole?"

Genevieve had walked around to the back of her truck so she could get her tools as she always did. With a laugh and a cocky smile, she said, "I took a shortcut."

"Must've been one heck of a shortcut."

"It sure was," she said with another laugh.

While the farrier buckled on her scarred-up leather chaps that covered the front part of her thighs and knees, Knox tugged his gloves off his hands with his teeth so he could button his shirt. He never took his eyes off Genevieve. She was the sexiest darn tomboy he had ever met. Whenever he saw her, it made him sorely regret that he was dedicated to sticking to his self-imposed dating moratorium. His father was paying big bucks to a matchmaker to marry off his sons and Knox had no intention of going along with the plan quietly. If he had to give up dating for a good, long while, then that's what he was going to do—but he'd do it *his* way.

As she finished her task of putting on her chaps, she looked up to find him staring at her. There was no use trying to play it off—she had caught him dead to rights.

"How many do we have today?" Genevieve asked, all business. She was the one woman in his new hometown of Rust Creek Falls that he'd like to flirt a little with him, and yet she seemed to be the only one who *didn't.* When she came out to the Ambling A, she was friendly but always professional and on task.

"Four," he told her.

"You know," she said, "we could get all of these horses on the same trimming schedule. It'd be easier on you."

"Naw. Then I'd only get to see you once a month." He said with a smile. "I'll meet you down there."

Genevieve had a routine and he knew it well. She had a policy that the owner, or an owner's representative, had to be on site when she trimmed hooves, and from her very first visit back in June, Knox had been the one to greet her. There was something special about the time he spent with Genevieve while she worked; he could talk to her in a way he'd never been able to talk to another woman. In fact, he could talk to her like she was one of his brothers. She liked to do guy stuff and she wasn't overly concerned with her nails and her hair and she was as pretty as they came without makeup. Perhaps the confident, no-nonsense way Genevieve comported herself was why he felt, for the first time in his life, like he had begun a genuine friendship with a woman. The fact that she was easy on the eyes was just a bonus.

Knox slipped the halter on his big dappled gray gelding, Big Blue, and led him down the wide aisle of the barn to the cross ties where Genevieve had set up her hoof stand.

"How's Blue today?" The farrier ran her hand down the horse's neck as she always did, checking out the horse's body and stance before she moved to the hooves.

"No complaints." He hooked the cross tie onto Blue's halter to keep the horse standing in one place while Genevieve worked.

"He's got a good weight on him."

"He's fit, that's for sure."

Genevieve finished her inspection, circling back to the horse's left front hoof. Unlike any other farrier he had ever seen, she knelt down beside Blue's front left leg, lifted it and let it rest on her thigh while she took one of her tools from a pocket of her chaps. On the first day she'd come out to the ranch he'd asked her about her unusual trimming posture—kneeling instead of standing, which was the standard because it was safer for the farrier. Genevieve's answer had stuck with him—she had said that it was all about the comfort of the horse for her. Yes, it was more dangerous, but she trusted the horses and they trusted her. If she had to get out of the way, she knew how to do it. That night he had gone to his father, who was convinced that hiring a woman farrier was bad business, and told him that he had just met one of the most talented farriers he'd ever known. And to this day, he hadn't changed his mind about Genevieve.

"How's he looking?" Knox moved closer to Genevieve, liking the way she would flip her long, thick braid over her shoulder.

"He looks great." She glanced up from her work to nod at him. "The walls of the hoof are strong, the frog has got good give, and it's been so rainy and wet these last few weeks, I've been seeing a lot of thrush out there, but Blue's don't have any signs of that."

"All good news then."

"All good news."

After that brief exchange, Knox leaned back against a nearby wall and watched Genevieve work. She was fast and efficient, another trait he appreciated about her. She didn't smoke or spit tobacco, or take extended breaks in between horses to shoot the breeze about hunting or to recount worn-out rodeo stories like the past farriers he had hired. Genevieve kept her focus on the horse, even during the times when they had a conversation going.

"He's ready to go back to his stall." She unhooked Big Blue from the cross ties.

Knox had been so lost in thought that he hadn't even noticed that she had finished. Those moments when he had been brooding about the conflict he was having with the father had raced by without him noticing.

"He's already done?" He pushed away from the wall. "That was quick."

"Quick and competent." She handed him the lead rope with a smile. "Bring me my next victim, please."

Knox led Big Blue back to his stall before he grabbed a dun mare with a black mane and tail and a tan body his father had just purchased for breeding.

"Who's this beauty?" Genevieve's face lit up at the sight of the new addition to the stable.

"Honey."

Genevieve rubbed the mare between the eyes, and the mare, who had been head shy and skittish around most of the ranch hands at the Ambling A, lowered her head and nuzzled the farrier's hand.

"And, you're sweet like honey, aren't you?"

After her standard body and leg check of the mare, Genevieve went to work. The first order of business was pulling the mare's shoes; Genevieve had a reputation of being one of the best "barefoot" farriers and could often get a horse sound without shoes. Some horses required shoes, but it was best for the horse if they could have their hooves natural like God made them.

"Walk her forward for me so I can see her walk," Genevieve instructed once she pulled the last shoe off the mare. "Let's see how she does."

After a couple of cautious steps where the mare was trying to get used to the odd sensation of walking without metal attached to her hooves, she began to walk naturally without any signs of lameness.

With a pleased smile, Genevieve waved her hand. "Bring her on back. She's going to do just fine without shoes."

It didn't seem like any time at all that Genevieve handed the new mare off to him as she prepared for the third horse of the day. She was halfway done and he had wasted their time together lost in his own thoughts.

"I'm sorry I haven't been much company today." He didn't know why he felt like he owed her some sort of explanation. Most visits they had a lot to say to each other. But today he couldn't seem to get out of his own head.

Genevieve, in keeping with her easygoing manner, said, "Don't worry about it. There're plenty of days I don't feel like talking, trust me."

That was just the thing—he *wanted* to talk to somebody about his situation with his father. In fact, he felt like he *needed* to talk to somebody about it. It was eating him inside out keeping it all bottled up. Lately, he swung like an erratic pendulum from furious to just plain fed up and he was always thinking about a way to show his father, once and for all, that he couldn't meddle in his life. He was a full-grown man and he was dog tired of his father thinking that he could control him like a puppet on a string.

Knox had chafed under his father's rule for most of his life. Even as a kid he had wanted to set his own course, to make his own decisions. Max ruled the family with a proverbial iron fist—he was the boss and his word was first, last and final. There had been plenty of times when Knox thought to take a different path in life and leave the family business behind but one of his brothers would always reel him back in to the fold. In fact, his decision to move to Montana in the first place was touch and go. This move would have been the perfect excuse to start a new chapter in his life without having to always bend to his father's will. Yet, here he was, in Montana, once again, doing it Maximilian's way.

And, perhaps that would have been okay for him. The Ambling A had plenty of elbow room and he had his own cabin. The town of Rust Creek Falls was nice enough and the women sure were pretty. But, then his father dishonored him, and his brothers, by offering to pay a local matchmaker, Vivian Shuster, a million bucks to find brides for his sons. Knox felt humiliated and the wound was deeper because the source of that humiliation was his own father. More than any time in his life, Knox wanted to send his father a message: stop meddling in my life!

In no time at all, Genevieve was finished with the third horse and ready for the last one. Perhaps it was the fact that their visit was about to be over—or perhaps it was because he had grown so comfortable with this woman. Either way, when Knox placed the last horse in the cross ties for Genevieve, he broached a subject with her that he had sworn he'd never broach with anyone other than family.

"I suppose you've heard all about the million-dollar deal my dad made with Viv Shuster." Knox had his arms crossed in front of his body and he watched Genevieve's face carefully.

She was about to kneel down and begin working, but his words must have caught her off guard. Genevieve looked up at him with what could only be read as embarrassment—not for her, but for *him*. Of course the pretty farrier had heard all about the million-dollar deal Max had made to marry off his six sons. Of course she had.

Genevieve had hoped that the subject of the Viv Shuster deal would never come up between Knox and her. Everyone in Rust Creek Falls had heard about Maximilian's quest to marry off his six eligible bachelor sons. It was the talk of the town! Most of the towns-folk were rooting for Viv so she could keep her sagging wedding business afloat. And there was a good chance Viv could pull it off. There were a lot of single women in town who wanted in on the Crawford action. Because Knox had become a friend of sorts, Genevieve never wanted to bring up what might be a sore subject for him. After all, she knew too well what it was like to have an overbearing father determined to control the lives of his adult children.

"I heard," she said simply, not wanting to sugarcoat it. Knox didn't seem like the type to want things sugar-coated for him. She took a moment to look directly into his intense, deep brown eyes so he would know that she was sincere when she said, "And I'm sorry."

His heavy brown brows lifted slightly at her words. "Thank you."

She nodded her head. Perhaps she was the first to say that to him. Instead of starting right away on the last horse, Genevieve opened up to Knox in a way she hadn't before. "You know, I do understand how you feel. My dad's been trying to marry me off for years. He thinks that my profession is unladylike." She made quotation marks with her fingers when she said *unladylike*. "He thinks my expiration date for making babies is looming like an end-of-the-world scenario. As if that's the only thing I'm good for." She frowned at the thought. "I've gone out with every darn made-in-Montana cowboy within a fifty-mile radius—"

"You haven't gone out with me," the rancher interjected.

The way those words slipped past Knox's lips, like a lover's whisper full of promise of good things to come, made Genevieve's stomach tighten in the most annoying way. She did *not* need to get involved with anyone in Rust Creek Falls. That was not the plan.

Wanting to laugh off the suggestion in his words, she smiled. "Well, that's because you are a made-in-Texas cowboy. That doesn't count."

Knox took a step closer, his eyes pinned on her face in a way that had never happened before. This new line of conversation had seemed to open something up between them, and Genevieve wasn't all too sure that she shouldn't slam the lid shut real quick on what might turn out to be a giant Pandora's box.

"Well," the rancher said, his voice lowered in a way that sent a tingle right down her spine. "You know what people say about things from Texas—"

"I know, I know." She cut him off playfully. "Everything is bigger in Texas."

"Now, that's a dirty mind at work." Knox smiled at her, showing his straight white teeth. "I was going to say *better* but if you want to say bigger, then I'm not going to object."

The banter seemed to break the odd tension between them and they both laughed. And that's when she noticed that when Knox took a step toward her, she had mindlessly taken a step toward him. With a steadying hand on the neck of the horse patiently waiting in the cross ties, Genevieve said, still laughing, "Do you know that I even agreed to go out with your brother on a date, just to get my father off my back?"

In the rancher's eyes, there was a fleeting emotion that Genevieve could identify only as jealousy. It was brief, but she saw it.

"Not that anything happened between us," she was quick to add before she got to work on the final horse of the day. If she got lost in conversation with Knox, she would lose the time she had made up and then she would be late for her next client. "I knew that Logan had it bad for Sarah. As a matter of fact, I told him to quit being such a chicken on our date. It was just a one and done for me. I told Viv to take my name officially off the list and I told my dad I tried."

"So... Logan wasn't your type?"

Genevieve glanced up to see that same intense, focused, almost examining expression in Knox's eyes.

"No," she said with an easy laugh. "And obviously I wasn't his! He's married to Sarah and everyone in town knows how much he loves being a father to baby Sophia."

Genevieve gently moved the horse's hoof onto her stand so she could smooth out the rough edges left behind by her nippers. "My dad says I'm too picky, but is there really such a thing as being too picky when you're looking for your soul mate? I mean, unless I meet that exact right guy, I'm not even all that sure that I want to get married and have kids. I have my business and my career to build. I'm happy. Why fix what ain't broken, right? That's why I'm living in the apartment above my parents' garage—I'm saving money so I can move to California. There's a lot of really exciting stuff happening with holistic approaches to horse care there and I want to be a part of it."

"So, you're not even planning on hanging around Rust Creek Falls?"

"Nope."

"That might just be perfect, then."

The cryptic tone Knox used to say those words made an alarm bell go off in her head, but she didn't ask him about it. Some things, in her experience, were better left alone.

Genevieve finished her work and unhooked the last horse from the cross ties, hooked the lead rope to its halter and handed the horse off to Knox.

"You can tell your father that all the horses got a clean bill of health today. I can see these four again in four to six weeks."

Knox nodded rather absentmindedly. He led the horse back to its stall, and then he headed back to her, covering the distance quickly with his long-legged stride. There was a new determination in the way he walked, and there was a glint of mischief in his dark brown eyes that caught her attention and made her feel a little queasy in her stomach, like she had just gotten a mild case of food poisoning.

Instead of handing her a check as was typical, Knox stood in front of her, his hat tilted back a bit so she could see his eyes, and asked her, "How would you like to get your dad off your back while you're earning your way out of here?"

"How would I *like* that?" She shook her head with a laugh. "Are you kidding me? I'd *love* to get Lionel Lawrence off my back."

"Then you and I are in the same boat. Because I would love to get Max off my back and out of my business."

Genevieve heard, and understood, the frustration in Knox's voice. Having an overbearing, meddling parent as an adult could strain even the most solid of parent-child relationships.

She shrugged. "I hear you, Knox, but so far, nothing I've tried has worked. If I could find a guy who would just be a no-strings-attached boyfriend for a while, that would placate dad for a while I think. But, all the guys around here want a commitment. Something weird in the water around these parts, I think."

"I wasn't really thinking about a boyfriend," Knox said.

"Oh, no?" Her brow wrinkled curiously. "What were you thinking?"

Knox pinned her in place with those deep, dark eyes of his and his lips—very nice, firm, masculine lips—curled up into a little smirk. "I was thinking more along the lines of a husband."

Chapter Two

The idea that she would leap from single to married struck Genevieve as laughable.

"Giant fat chance of that!" She laughed as she swept up the leftover fragments of hoof that were scattered across the red rubber pavers. "Marriage? To a local guy? How would that get me closer to my goal of getting to California?"

When she finished cleaning up her area and dumping the hoof fragments into a nearby trash can, Knox still hadn't moved from his spot. Usually, as was their established routine, he would have gone to the office, written her a check, and by the time she was finished packing up her small cache of tools, the check would be in her hand. Genevieve slid her phone out of her back pocket and glanced down at the screen; she had gained a couple of minutes of time and if she left the Ambling A shortly, she would actually be back on schedule for her next client.

"Well…?" she prompted, hoping the fact that she had her hoof stand in one hand would be a silent signal to Knox that, as enjoyable as his company was, it was time for her to move along.

As if it just dawned on him that he was holding her up, Knox gave a quick nod of his head. "Let's go to the office and I'll write you a check."

Fine. We'll do it this way.

Genevieve set her hoof stand down on the rubber pavers and followed Knox the short distance to an office space that had been incorporated into one of the tack rooms. Knox opened the door for her and let her walk in first. The room, which had rows of Western saddles and bridles lining the far wall, smelled of leather and soap, along with the sweet smell of hay from the small stack of bales just inside the door. Genevieve walked over to a black saddle with ornate designs carved into the leather and fancy-edged silver conches as accent pieces. From the smoothness of the leather on the seat, along with the craftsmanship, she knew that this was a classic saddle from the 1950s.

"That's my dad's saddle," Knox said as he closed the door. "Seen a lot of work over the years."

At the sound of the door closing, Genevieve's Cat Woman senses started setting off alarm bells in her brain and she spun around to face the rancher. Knox had a strange look on his classically handsome face. She didn't like the fact that he was blocking the door and she *especially* didn't like it when he reached behind his body and locked them in the tack room.

"Listen here, Knox Crawford." Genevieve scowled at him, moving her body into a defensive stance. "I've had six weeks of self-defense training when I was in college and if you make so much as one wrong move, cowboy, I will hurt you!"

Knox lifted his hands as if he were surrendering, a slightly lopsided grin on his face that she hadn't seen him use before. "I promise you, I only want to talk business."

She pointed at the door. "We don't need a locked door to talk business, Knox. I trim the horses' hooves and you write me a check. Simple."

"The delivery of hay is here," Knox noted distractedly. Earlier she had heard the piercing sound of squeaking brakes on a large delivery truck backing up to the opening in the hayloft and the sound of deliverymen yelling to one another. But she didn't understand what the heck that had to do with the fact that Knox wanted her *alone* in the office.

"I have a proposal for you and I don't want us to be overheard or disturbed."

Her arms crossed in front of her body, Genevieve's interest was piqued in spite of herself. Even though he had locked the door, Knox wasn't giving off any creepy stalker vibes, so her defenses lowered ever so slightly. Knox had always been gentlemanly, kind, consistent and had never come on to her in all the months she had been working with him. It wasn't beyond reasonable to give him the benefit of the doubt.

"What proposal is that?"

Knox took his hat off and tossed it on the nearby desk, his dark brown eyes so serious.

"Marriage." He said it so plainly and simply she almost thought she had misunderstood.

Genevieve's arms tightened around her body, and her heart, without her permission, began to beat rapidly in her chest. This wasn't her first marriage proposal, but it certainly was the strangest.

"Gen." Hands in his pockets he took a small step toward her. "I want to propose marriage. Let's get married."

Today was the first day he had ever called her by a nickname, and she had to admit it sounded kind of nice when he said it in his raspy baritone voice.

Genevieve stared up at Knox and he stared right back at her. The only sound was the ambient noise of the scraping and stomping of men's feet as they moved bales of hay into the hayloft above them.

After a second or two, her arms fell away from her body as she laughed. "Very funny, Knox. Ha, ha. Yeah—let's get married. That makes total sense."

But Knox wasn't laughing.

"You're right. It does make perfect sense."

"You're serious?" She stopped laughing. "You want us to get *married*?"

"Yes."

Now she was frowning at him. They had started a friendship over the last several months and she liked him. But what in the world had possessed him to propose marriage out of the blue? He had never even so much as flirted with her!

"Are you going through some sort of mental crisis, Knox?" she asked seriously. "Because you can get help for that."

"I'm perfectly sane." He wasn't smiling but there was now a conspiratorial gleam in his eye. "Just hear me out."

"No." She scooted around him, unlocked the door and swung it open. In the open doorway, she held out her hand. "I'll take my check, please, and then I'll be on my way."

He didn't move to the desk to write her a check. "What if I told you I had a way for us to help each other get exactly what we want?"

Now that the door was open and any passing ranch hand could overhear their conversation, Knox had lowered his voice. She had to lean in slightly to hear his next words.

"You want to move to California." It was a statement of fact.

She nodded.

"How much does a move like that cost?"

His words touched a raw nerve in her body. From her calculations, to move her and her horse to California and get her business established it was going to take much deeper pockets than she currently had. In truth, as much as she hated admitting it, she was most likely years away from moving out of her parents' garage apartment.

"A king's ransom," she admitted gloomily.

"I just happened to know a king."

Everyone in town knew that the Texas Crawford cowboys were wealthy; if Knox wanted anything in his life, he just had to go out and buy it. It seemed to her, in this moment, that he was trying to buy himself a bride.

She wasn't for sale.

"Hear me out, Gen. If you don't like what I have to say—no harm, no foul." When he used one of her favorite expressions, her eyes moved back to his face. "We'll never speak of this again."

In spite of herself, she just couldn't say no to at least listening to a plan that could possibly shave off years of saving for her move to California. She would be crazy not to at least listen, wouldn't she?

Genevieve stepped back inside the tack room and closed the door behind her. "You've got five minutes."

"We elope," he told her in a no-nonsense manner. "Now that Logan is married to Sarah and Xander is happily married to Lily, my father will think he's three sons down with only three more to marry off. And when my other brothers get engaged, we'll get the marriage annulled."

"You really want to get back at your dad that much?"

She saw a shift in Knox's eyes, a flash of anger that disappeared as quickly as it had arrived, like a quick flash of light in the darkness.

"Nobody controls me. He needs to learn that lesson, yes." The rancher continued, "After the annulment, I'll make sure you get to California. All expenses paid. In the meantime, as a bonus, you'll be free to live your life without any hassle from your dad."

"As your wife." She scrunched up her face at the thought. She had never equated *marriage* with *freedom*.

"As my *fake* wife," he said. "A marriage in name only. You do your thing and I'll do mine."

"You know what, Knox? This is absolutely the most extreme way a man has tried to lure me into his bed. And there have been some doozies, let me tell you."

"I don't want to sleep with you, Gen. I want to marry you." He said it seriously, and then added as almost an unimportant aside, "Not that I don't think you're attractive."

"Gee thanks, Crawford." She rolled her eyes at the way he delivered the compliment. "You really know how to make a woman feel all girly inside. Am I blushing?"

As if the sarcasm didn't register, he asked, "So, what do you think?"

"What do I think?"

He nodded.

"I think," Genevieve said in a slow, thoughtful tone, "thank you, but no thank you." She gripped the doorknob. "Do me a favor, would you? Please put that check in the mail. My next client awaits."

Before she could open the door and walk out into the hall, she noted that Knox's expression was cloudy. He had his head tilted downward and he was tapping his finger on the top of the desk, as if that action would help him find a way to change her mind. Logan had told her that Knox didn't like to be wrong, he didn't like to lose and he didn't like to be told no. She and Knox had those three things in common.

He looked up and pinned her with eyes that looked more black than brown in the moment.

"I suppose all of those things I heard about you must've been a pretty big exaggeration then." Knox's words were laced with a challenge that made the small hairs on the back of her neck stand up.

"What's that supposed to mean?"

"I heard that Genevieve Lawrence never backs down from a challenge."

Knox caught her off guard by skillfully tapping into one of her weaknesses.

"I don't."

"I also heard that Genevieve Lawrence has never lost a wager in the town." This was said with a small challenging smile, as if he knew that he had just sunk the hook.

"You heard right." She found herself still standing there, gripping the doorknob. "I haven't."

She had always been a tomboy who felt more comfortable hanging out with the boys than the girls. And, for the most part, the boys had accepted her as one of their own. But they thought, wrongly, that because she was a girl she would be easy to beat. She wasn't. The boys in town had always made bets with her and they had always lost. When the boys grew into men, they still lost. What she lacked in strength, she more than made up for it with an innate desire to win. She had been competitive since she was a kid and that had never changed. Everyone knew Genevieve was the reigning champion for winning wagers in Rust Creek Falls; it was a title she wore with pride. And she planned on leaving this town undefeated.

There was a cockiness lurking behind Knox's dark eyes that made her jaw clench. This was the exact look cowboys gave her right before she beat them at tractor chicken. No matter how big or tough, the braggadocios all blinked and ended up driving their tractor into a ditch while she kept right on driving her tractor on the road. She *never* blinked.

"Then," Knox said as he took a step toward her, his tone steady and serious, "I dare you to marry me."

She'd always had a bit of a temper and it had gotten her in trouble more times than she could remember. She took a step toward Knox.

"You *dare* me?"

"That's what I said."

"You *dare* me?" she repeated, surprised that he

had thrown down a gauntlet that he had to know she wouldn't be able to resist picking up.

"You'll be married by morning, Crawford, so you'd better watch who you're daring to do something." She jabbed her finger in his direction, her cheeks flushed.

"Naw, I doubt it. I bet you won't marry me." She hated the fact that there was smugness in his tone now. "You'll chicken out."

Chicken out? Did he actually know that those words were like waving the proverbial red flag in front of the meanest bull in Rust Creek Falls? "I *never* chicken out, Knox."

"Neither do I."

Genevieve slipped her phone out of her back pocket, typed in a search, and then scrolled through the information on the website she chose. She held out the phone for Knox to see. "We can drive to Kalispell tomorrow, get a license and get married the same day. No waiting."

"That doesn't scare me." He smiled at her. "Does it scare you?"

"Nothing scares me." She kept searching for information about getting married in nearby Kalispell. "There's a problem."

"What's that?"

"We need someone to officiate the wedding and it says here we need to book months in advance."

"That's not a problem. I know a guy I can call."

"You know a *guy?*"

"Yeah. I know a guy. I'm sure he'll be able to squeeze us into his schedule."

"How romantic." Genevieve slipped her phone back into her pocket. "Meet me tomorrow morning, eight o'clock outside of the Gold Rush Diner." Genevieve pushed open the door, bristling mad. "*If* you show up, we'll go get ourselves hitched."

"I like the sound of that." Knox held out his hand. "Shall we shake on it?"

Her hand slipped easily into his. "We enter into a *platonic* marriage and then when we get an annulment you pay all of my expenses to move to California— including moving my horse, Spartacus."

"My word is my bond as a man."

"My word is my bond as a woman," she countered as she tugged her fingers free.

She had meant to call his bluff, but it had backfired. Instead of backing down, he'd stepped up.

He picked up a long piece of greenish alfalfa hay off the floor, quickly tied it into a small circle and, with his straight white teeth showing in a genuine smile, he knelt down before her on one knee and extended the makeshift ring.

"Genevieve Lawrence, will you do me the honor of being my fake bride?"

"You're being ridiculous."

"Don't ruin this special moment for me." He moved the hay ring back and forth for her to see. "It's not every day I get engaged."

"Fine," she said with an annoyed sigh as she held out her left hand. "I will be your fake bride, Knox. But only if you show up tomorrow."

The cowboy stood up and slipped the crude ring onto her finger. Did she imagine it, or did a small shock pass between them when he took her hand in his? She looked at the ring encircling her finger; she had never thought to see any type of ring on that finger for years, if ever. Even a hay ring made her feel boxed in like a trapped wild animal.

Genevieve swayed backward and put her hand on the door to steady her body. She pushed the door open quickly so she could get some air into her lungs. When she stepped out into the wide aisle of the barn, she took in a deep breath, wanting to fill her lungs with as much air as possible to fend off the dizziness that had sprung up out of nowhere. She forced her brain to will her body to get it together and calm down. She was well-known for her nerves of steel when she was off-road racing or vaulting on the back of her horse—why were those nerves failing her now? Perhaps because this was the most serious bet she had ever made in her life—and if she was wrong, and Knox actually showed up, Genevieve knew that she wouldn't be the one to back down. If she was wrong and he showed up, she would be married by sundown tomorrow.

Genevieve closed her eyes for the briefest of seconds; when she opened them, she had her game face firmly back in place. To Knox, she said in a clipped, no-nonsense tone, "Don't forget to put that check in the mail, Crawford. I've got bills to pay."

"No need, darlin'," Knox called out after her with a pleased laugh in his voice that made her shoulders stiffen as she walked away. "I'll just bring it to you tomorrow."

The next morning, thirty minutes before their planned meet time, Knox parked his truck in the crowded lot of the Gold Rush Diner. He spotted Genevieve's truck, still caked in mud from her off-road shortcut, parked nearby. He hadn't been able to sleep the night before, thinking about the moment he would arrive at the diner, not knowing if Genevieve would really show up. It surprised him that the sight of her truck didn't make him feel nervous in the least. In fact, his stomach had been churning all morning at the thought of her *not* showing up. Now that he knew she was here, all he felt was relieved. And hungry.

Knox pushed open the door to the diner and nodded his head in greeting to the folks he knew. Rust Creek was a small town; it was typical to run into folks he knew everywhere.

"Find a seat where you can," the waitress pouring coffee behind the counter called out to him.

Knox had already spotted his target. Genevieve was sitting in a booth in the back of the diner, her long, wavy blond hair freshly washed and cascading over her shoulders. She wasn't dressed for an elopement, but then again, neither was he. Just like him, Genevieve had on her work clothes—jeans, boots and a T-shirt. No doubt she assumed he was going to back out of the wager, just as he assumed she would. He couldn't explain it fully, but the moment he spotted her sitting alone in that booth, his spirits lifted and all of the nerves and anxiety he had been feeling slipped away.

"Mornin'." Knox sat down in the booth bench opposite his fiancée. He took off his hat and placed it on the table. From the pocket of his T-shirt he took out a folded check, unfolded it and slid it across the table.

Genevieve, who seemed to be stiff as a statue, her hands seemingly glued to the sides of her steaming coffee mug, stared at the check for a second before she snatched it off the table and put it in her jeans pocket.

"You're early." She stated the obvious in a harsh whisper.

"So are you."

"Do you really think that it's a good idea for us to be seen together like this?"

He caught her drift. There were some town gossips in the diner who stared curiously in their direction.

Feeling happy, Knox smiled at her. "May as well start giving them something to talk about."

"I can feel them staring at us," his bride-to-be said under her breath.

"They sure are."

The waitress swung by their table with her order pad and a pen. "What can I get you folks?"

"Are you hungry?" he asked Genevieve.

"No."

He took the menu out from behind the salt and pepper shakers. "Really? Suddenly I'm famished." He winked at the pretty, frowning blonde sitting across from him. With a teasing, private smile, he asked, "What do you suggest for a man who's about to eat his last meal?"

Chapter Three

They had decided to take his black decked-out GMC truck for the thirty-minute trip to Kalispell. Was Knox bluffing or was he truly pleased that they were on their way to get married? She had watched the man put away scrambled eggs, bacon, three biscuits with butter and honey, grits and two large glasses of orange juice. She had no idea how he could eat at a time like this! Her stomach felt like a washing machine on a spin cycle; the coffee she had drunk at the diner was just adding to the acid backing up in her throat. She felt miserable while he hummed contentedly behind the wheel.

"You played me pretty good, Knox. I have to admit it."

For two people who normally had a lot to say to each other, the first half of the ride to Kalispell had been a quiet one.

"How do you figure?"

"You knew I wouldn't be able to turn down a wager. You knew my weakness and you exploited it."

"That's true. I did."

"That's a move right out of my own playbook. I don't like it but I have to respect it," she admitted grudgingly.

After a moment of silence she added, "I've never lost a wager before." She had her arms crossed in front of her body as she stared out at the pastureland dotted with grazing cows on either side of the highway. "It galls me to lose to a Texan of all things."

"You didn't lose," Knox said with an easy smile turned her way. "I'd call this one a draw."

"Draws are for losers."

"That's not how I see it. We're both winners, as far as I can tell."

"The only way I win is if you back out. I can still win. There's still time."

He laughed. "I'm not backing out of this wedding wager, Gen. If someone's gonna back out of this deal, it's gonna have to be you."

Genevieve glanced over at Knox's profile; she took in the strong jawline and the straight nose. Had she finally met her match? Was this cowboy crazy enough to really elope today? Was she so pigheaded that her ego wouldn't let her back down for a bet? She suspected the answer to her first two questions, but she absolutely knew the answer to the last. Her ego wouldn't ever let her back down—not when she was racing, not when she was bungee jumping and not even when she was about to elope with one of the Crawford cowboys on a dare.

"Then," she said with a pensive frown, "I guess we're really going to get married today."

"Darlin', that's music to my ears."

"Quit being so darn cheerful," she snapped at him. "And quit calling me darlin'."

Genevieve had hoped for a long line to apply for their marriage license. There was a line, but it seemed to be the swiftest moving line she had ever seen. How did it even make sense that two people could just walk up to a counter and get a license to get married? But that's what they did. They went to the third floor of the Flathead County Justice Center, showed their driver's licenses, paid fifty-three dollars and left with a state sanctioned "permission slip" to become husband and wife.

"This is why there's so much divorce in this country," Genevieve complained as they stepped out into the sunshine with their marriage license in hand. "They make it too darn easy for just anyone to say *I do*."

"Lucky for us." Knox carefully folded up their marriage license and tucked it into his wallet.

Genevieve had stopped waiting for the cowboy to back out—she could see that he was full-steam ahead on this deal while her mind was whirling with a thousand consequences. What were her parents going to say? What was his family going to say? Of course, she could hear her mother now. *Genevieve, when will you ever learn to look before you leap?*

"We aren't exactly dressed for a wedding, are we?" Knox asked as they walked to the sidewalk outside of the Kalispell courthouse.

"I didn't expect you to show up," she admitted. In fact, she had only stuffed some things into a backpack at the last minute before she headed to the Gold Rush on the off chance he did show. In her backpack she had a toothbrush, a hairbrush, her laptop and a Swiss Army pocketknife. Not exactly the most practical of wedding trousseaus.

"Well, I did." He kept on smiling at her like the cat that ate the canary. "So, why don't we find some wedding duds? There's got to be a place where a man can get a suit and a bride-to-be can find a dress."

She wasn't quite sure why Knox wanted to make such an event of a civil ceremony for their marriage-in-name-only, but the thought crossed her mind that her family, particularly her two sisters and her mom, would want to see pictures. Her family would totally buy her eloping in her barn clothes—they almost expected that kind of behavior from her—but what about Knox's kin? Would they believe their elopement was the real deal if they didn't look like a head-over-heels couple sneaking off to make their secret romance official?

"I suppose," she said, looking up the main street of Kalispell to a row of shops. "If we're going to convince your father that we eloped because we're crazy in love, we had better look the part."

After a quick search on her phone, they headed toward the Kalispell Center Mall on North Main Street. They found their way to Herberger's department store for one-stop shopping. First, they purchased simple white gold wedding rings, just plain bands without any embellishment. After all, those rings were just costume props and would be discarded once Viv Shuster managed to get the last three Crawford cowboys engaged.

Knox hadn't wanted to scare Genevieve off, but it could take a while for Viv to make matches for the final three brothers. His brother Finn, older by only one year, might be the easiest to pin down with a bride. Finn didn't seem to mind their father's plan all that much and he was always falling in and out of love anyway. But, his one younger brother Wilder was going to prove extra challenging for Viv—he was a busy bee that loved to pollinate all the lovely flowers of Rust Creek Falls and it was going to be a neat trick to get Wilder to dedicate himself to one special rose. And, Hunter, well, he was a single father who wasn't focused on finding love in the least. Hunter's heart, mind, and soul were all wrapped up in six-year-old Wren.

Knox pocketed the wedding rings as they parted ways—he headed to the men's clothing section, while she headed for women's dresses. They agreed to meet back at the jewelry counter in one hour. Genevieve wasn't much of a shopper but she was quick to make decisions, so one hour suited her just fine.

"Hi! Welcome to Herberger's." A petite salesclerk with a blond bob and bangs popped out from behind a tall rack of dresses. "How may I help you?"

"I need a dress."

"Special occasion?"

"My wedding," Genevieve said. "I suppose."

"You suppose?" The salesclerk's name tag read Kimber. "That's a first. Don't you know?"

She didn't have any intention of sharing the details of her wedding wager to Knox Crawford with a stranger in Herberger's department store, so she ignored Kimber's question and focused on the dress.

"Do you have something you could show me? I'm in a bit of a time crunch."

"Of course, I do." Kimber beamed with pleasure. "I love dressing brides. White, off-white?"

"White." That was for her mom—it was a small token but it was the least she could do.

"Indoors or outdoors?"

Not wanting to say "I don't know," she just took a guess. "Outdoors."

Kimber marched her over to a section of white dresses that could be worn as a casual-ceremony wedding dress.

"You are short-waisted and petite like me," the salesclerk said as they sifted through the rack. "If we aren't careful, we'll have you looking like you're a little girl playing dress-up in your mama's clothes. What size do you wear?"

"In a dress? I have no idea." She hadn't put a dress on her body since high school graduation. "A four maybe?"

"Ooooh, look at this!" Kimber pulled a gauzy white dress off the rack. It was a high-low dress with spaghetti straps and a sash at the waist. "What do you think?"

Genevieve felt the material—it was light and airy and it wasn't too fussy or girly. "I think, yes."

The moment she saw herself in the mirror with this flowing hippy-girl dress skimming over her body, she knew. This was her wedding dress. Kimber's beaming face was further confirmation that the first dress she had tried was the only dress she needed to try. They found a pair of cowgirl boots in white in the shoe department, which worked perfectly with the gauzy dress. Kimber insisted that Genevieve go over to see her friend at the makeup counter just for a touch of mascara, blush and a light lip gloss. By the time she left the makeup counter in her new dress, her hair wavy and loose, Genevieve saw a bride in the full-length mirror.

"Thank you." She hugged Kimber. "I couldn't have done this without you."

"You look absolutely, positively gorgeous, Genevieve!" the salesclerk gushed. "Congratulations."

Knox was early to the jewelry counter, feeling slightly awkward in his new dark gray suit, crisp white shirt and a bolo tie. The suit wasn't a perfect fit—it was a little tight in the shoulders and the pants and the jacket sleeves were almost too short—but it was the best the store could do. He checked his watch before he tugged on his shirtsleeves and adjusted his bolo tie for the sixth time. He couldn't remember ever feeling this nervous to see a woman before, yet Genevieve wasn't just any woman. She was about to be his wife. At the moment, it didn't matter that it wasn't a genuine marriage—in the eyes of the State of Montana, their families and God above, they were about to be husband and wife.

One minute to the hour, Knox looked up from checking his watch and saw Genevieve round the corner in a filmy white dress with thin straps that showed off her tanned arms, toned from years of working with horses. Genevieve always presented herself as a confident, assured woman. Today, there was hesitancy in her cornflower blue eyes—a fleeting vulnerability that touched him. She wanted his approval; he could see it in her eyes. He didn't have to fake what he was feeling in the moment—he had never seen a more beautiful bride.

"Gen," Knox said, his eyes drinking her in. "You're a vision."

A pink blush stained her cheeks, so lovely and sweet that it made him want to reach out and touch her, but he resisted that urge.

"Thank you," she said. He had never seen this almost shy side to this woman and he had to admit that he liked it.

"I like that tie."

Knox looked down at the bolo tie. He hadn't been too sure about that fashion choice, but the salesman swore it was the item of choice for many Kalispell grooms.

"When in Kalispell…" he said, making yet another attempt to adjust the tie to make it less tight around his neck. Giving up, he held out his arm to his bride-to-be. "Shall we?"

Genevieve looked at his extended arm and he could almost see her thoughts as she stood there considering. A shift occurred on her pretty oval face. He witnessed the exact moment she decided, once and for all, to be his wife.

"Okay," she finally said. "Yes."

When Genevieve tucked her arm through his, a calm flooded his body. He had never felt so comfortable with a woman on his arm before. It was as if having this petite, strong-willed woman beside him made him feel more at home with himself. He didn't understand it exactly, but he knew that it meant something more than he could figure in this moment. All he knew was that Genevieve was special and she was going to be his bride.

"Where are we going to do the deed?" she asked him as they left the mall.

"It's a surprise."

"I have to tell you, I'm not a huge fan of surprises."

"This one you'll like."

"Lawrence Park." Genevieve read the sign at the public park entrance. She had been to Kalispell many times in her life, but she had never known that there was a park that shared her last name.

"There's a walking trail that leads to Stillwater River. I know you like the outdoors, so I thought that would be a good place to get married."

Knox's thoughtfulness caught her off guard. She had always gotten the impression that he was a hardworking man—a good man—but he had never really come across as an overly romantic or thoughtful man. This gesture showed her a different side of Knox Crawford—a side that she had to admit that she liked very much.

"There's Sonny." Knox nodded through the windshield at a heavyset man with a long white beard standing in faded overalls by an antique Ford truck. Beside Sonny was a woman in a long flowered dress and tennis shoes, her salt-and-pepper hair in a single thick braid down her back. In the woman's hands was a simple bouquet of Montana wildflowers.

"Is he officiating the wedding?"

Knox nodded. He came to her side of the truck and helped her out. "He goes way back with my dad. I knew he would be willing to help us out on short notice."

"Hello, young man!" Sonny raised his hand in greeting. "You picked a mighty fine day to get married."

Knox clasped hands with Sonny, then hugged his wife, Cora, before he introduced them to Genevieve.

"Knox wanted me to bring these for you." Cora handed her the flowers. "He's always been such a thoughtful boy."

Genevieve took the flowers, with a quick glance up at Knox who was watching her closely. She smiled down at the bouquet. Wildflowers were the perfect flowers for her.

"Young love is always in such a hurry." Cora smiled at her. "We were so surprised to get Knox's call."

"You're father's not gonna be too pleased with me, what with all of this secrecy," Sonny said as he thoughtfully tugged on his beard.

"I appreciate you doing this for us." Knox put his arm around her shoulder and she had to force herself to stand still and plaster a smile on her face. From this moment forward, she was Knox Crawford's blushing and loving bride and she had to act like it.

"Yes," she said. "Thank you. This all happened so fast for us." She met her fiancé's eyes. "We just want our first moments as husband and wife to be *ours*."

"My Cora and I eloped, so I can't really say I don't understand your thinkin'," Sonny said, still tugging on his beard. It seemed to Genevieve that there was a possibility that Sonny wouldn't agree to marry them after all. But, in the end, Cora gently persuaded her husband to go forward with the ceremony.

The four of them walked along the narrow path to the edge of the Stillwater River. They picked a spot where a small group of tall trees lined the bank of the river, shading them from the afternoon sun. With the sound of the water rushing over the rocks, Genevieve held her wildflowers tightly in her hands and stood before Knox, facing him, as Sonny began the intimate ceremony. Cora moved around them with her camera, capturing candid moments as her husband opened his bible to read a suitable verse from Corinthians on the patience and kindness of love.

It was difficult for Genevieve to keep her focus on Knox's eyes. It did not escape her that she was getting ready to commit herself to him on a dare—on a *wager*.

Her parents had been married for over thirty years and they took their marriage vows seriously. They would be so disappointed in her for taking a vow, saying that she intended to love Knox for life knowing full well that the marriage would end sooner rather than later. That thought of her parent's disappointment and the sad expression on her mother's face when she found out that she had missed the moment her daughter took her wedding vows almost made her turn away and bolt down the path back toward the truck.

Sonny closed his bible and added his own thoughts to the occasion. "The commitment you made here today will be the foundation upon which your marriage will be built. Don't ever go to bed mad. Forgive each other and move on. Say I love you every day and never get too old to hold each other's hands."

Sonny smiled at his wife for a brief moment before he continued. "You've got to give each other room to grow because, in the end, it will be the two of you, standing together, facing the challenges of everyday life. If you always remember this moment and the love you have for each other right now, this sacred union will last you a lifetime and beyond."

Cora stepped quietly forward and took the bouquet of flowers from Genevieve as Sonny prepared for the ring exchange. Knox took her hand in his and it flashed in her mind that she liked how strong, large and rough this man's hand was. It was the hand of a working man.

"With this ring, I thee wed." He slid the simple white gold band onto her ring finger. She detected the slightest tremble when he did so, and realized that, beneath the seemingly calm exterior he was presenting, Knox was feeling as uncertain, off balanced and flustered as she was. A split second later, it was her turn. She didn't look up at him as she slipped his wedding band over his knuckle until it was snugly seated on his ring finger. Then Knox squeezed her hand and when she looked up into his face, he was smiling at her kindly with his eyes.

"Knox and Genevieve, you have come to this beautiful place to vow to love each other for the rest of your lives. You have exchanged rings as a symbol of this commitment."

"Genevieve, do you take this man to be your husband? Do you promise to love him, comfort him, honor and keep him, in sickness and in health—and, forsaking all others, be faithful to him as long as you both shall live?"

It took Genevieve several seconds to make the words "I do" come out of her mouth. The moment the words finally did come out, Cora snapped a close-up photograph of her face and she hoped only that her internal turmoil wasn't captured for everyone to see.

"I do." When she said those words, there was a waver in her voice that she didn't recognize. It wasn't her way to be uncertain about anything in her life; she lived her life as she raced off-road vehicles—pedal to the metal and full steam ahead.

"Knox, do you take this beautiful woman to be your wife? Do you promise to love her, comfort her, honor and keep her, in sickness and in health—and, forsaking all others, be faithful to her as long as you both shall live?"

Knox lowered his head so she could see his eyes— eyes that were so steady and intent on her face. "I do."

"Well, then," Sonny said as he rolled back on his heels a bit, "by the power vested in me by the glorious

State of Montana, I am tickled pink to pronounce you husband and wife. Knox, my boy, you may kiss your lovely bride."

She couldn't get her heart to stop beating so fast. Her chest was rising and falling in the most annoying way as Knox, still holding on to her hands, with a question in his eyes that only she understood, leaned down and lightly kissed her on the lips.

It was their first kiss; it was their only kiss.

It occurred to her in that moment, as she stood there with her eyes closed, focusing her attention on the first feel of her husband's lips pressed gently upon hers, that she didn't want that kiss to end.

Chapter Four

"Well, we did it."

She looked over at Knox who was sitting in the driver's seat of his truck, his hands resting lightly on the steering wheel as he stared out the window.

They had just said their goodbyes to Sonny and Cora and now they were alone again, this time as husband and wife, when just the day before they had been employer and employee. Two people who were developing a friendship but who didn't really know each other all that well.

"Yes, we certainly did," Genevieve agreed, twisting the odd-feeling gold band around and around on her finger. She didn't wear jewelry—not even earrings. Now she had this ring on her finger that she was supposed to wear all the time?

Knox took a deep breath in through his nose and then let it out slowly. Out of the corner of her eye, she saw him staring at the new ring on his finger.

"What now?" she asked him. The postnuptial euphoria, with Sonny and Cora and a small group of strangers walking the path by Stillwater River clapping and cheering for them, had subsided. When she had let her ego dictate her decisions, when she had thought this whole thing was a lark, this moment didn't feel like a real possibility. And yet, here she sat, in a wedding dress in Lawrence Park as Mrs. Knox Crawford.

In the quiet of the truck, with only the distant sound of children playing on a playground, her stomach rumbled. The loud sound made her laugh and it made Knox look over at her with a smile. She had felt too sick with nervous tension to eat when she was at the diner that morning, but now that the deed was done and she was officially wed, she was feeling famished. Hungrier perhaps than she had ever felt before in her life.

"Hungry?" Her husband—wow, that was weird—kept on smiling at her.

Her hands went to her stomach. "Starving. You?"

"I can always eat," he said. "What are you hungry for?"

"Barbecue."

"In that white dress?"

"Why not?" She made a face at him. "I'll put on a bib. I don't care."

Knox studied her face in a way that made heat come to her cheeks.

"I knew you were my kind of woman," he said as he turned the ignition key. "Any place in particular?"

"DeSoto Grill is my favorite."

"Then DeSoto Grill it shall be." Knox shifted into Drive. "A woman should have exactly what she wants on her wedding day."

* * *

Knox found a parking space on 1st Street and turned off the engine. But he didn't move right away to get out of the truck. Instead, he wanted to put Genevieve at ease. This whole marriage-by-bet, his idea to thwart his father and establish himself in his father's eyes as a full-grown man had been a whirlwind for both of them. Yesterday he came up with an outrageous plan and today they were married. It was enough to make anyone's head spin with crazy thoughts.

"Do you know what I think?" He turned his body toward his bride.

"Huh?"

"I think that I like you, Genevieve Lawrence."

"That's Genevieve Crawford to you," she said with a teasing tone.

Knox laughed. Gen had always made him laugh, from the first day they had met.

"My apologies. I think that I like you, Mrs. Crawford."

"Well, that's good, Knox, because you're stuck with me until Viv manages to hog-tie your last three brothers. And neither one of us knows how long that will be." Genevieve rolled her eyes and shook her head, and under her breath she added, "Leap before you look."

"What I'm trying to say is that I always liked your company when you came out to the Ambling A."

She sent him a small smile for his trouble.

"And you seemed to like mine…?"

That garnered him a nod.

"So, why don't we just have fun with this?" he asked her. "Why not just keep on enjoying each other's company, keep on being friends?"

"Okay," Genevieve replied, her tanned exposed shoulders lifting up into a quick shrug.

"So you agree with me." He wasn't used to the women in his past being so easy to get along with.

"I just said so, didn't I?" She frowned. "Now, can I eat?"

"Yes." He laughed, wanting to reach out and squeeze her hand affectionately. He had wanted to ask Genevieve out on a date and now, oddly, he didn't have to ask her because he had married her.

When he came around to her side of the truck, Genevieve had already hopped down onto the sidewalk and was shaking out the skirt of her gauzy white dress. They walked together, side by side instead of hand in hand, to the door of the DeSoto Grill. At the entrance to the restaurant, it occurred to Knox that this was his wedding day, albeit a fake marriage, and he wanted to celebrate. Without even warning her, because he wanted to catch her off guard and get her laughing, Knox bent down and swung Genevieve into his arms.

"What the heck are you doing?" His bride's bright blue eyes, so close to his own now, were wide with surprise.

"I'm carrying you over the threshold."

She didn't struggle to get out of his arms; instead, she reached out so she could tug on the door handle to open it just enough that he could get his foot inside.

"This has been a very strange day." Genevieve tilted back her head and let her long blond hair fall over his arm.

"Do you mind?" Knox asked as he managed to open the door and then quickly carry her inside.

"Not at all. I like strange."

The barbecue joint was half-full and when Knox walked in carrying his bride in his arms, some of the patrons began to clap and hoot and holler.

"We just got hitched, y'all!" he called out to his fellow Montanans. "Drinks are on us!"

He held his bride in his arms a little while longer, liking the way her body felt pressed up close to his. Genevieve was a willing partner in the spectacle—her face was glowing with excitement and she was happily waving to the crowd. He had already begun to notice that Genevieve was at her best when she was performing for a crowd. It was making him feel more confident about how she would play her role as "blushing bride" in front of his family. Watching her now, Knox was pretty convinced that his family didn't stand a chance when it came to Genevieve Lawrence. Er, Genevieve Crawford.

The DeSoto Grill had a large selection of Montana beer and everyone in the bar got a free cold one on them. Sitting cross-legged in the chair with a napkin bib tucked into the front of her dress, Genevieve gulped down a second beer before she attacked a second rack of ribs.

"Oh, my goodness, this is soooo good." She grinned at him with a little barbecue sauce on the side of her mouth.

"I've never seen anyone other than my brothers eat that many ribs."

"Getting married must've made me hungry," Genevieve said between chewing, without a hint of self-consciousness. She didn't seem to care one way or another if he disapproved of her large appetite—and he just added that to the list of things that he already liked about her.

"Here's to us." Knox held out his glass after the waitress brought him water—because he had to drive them home—and a fresh beer for Genevieve.

"To us!" She clanked her glass with his. "Just two crazy kids in love."

"You know the next stop for us is the Ambling A."

"Uh-huh." She nodded. "I figured. First, your people and then I suppose we can go face the music with my folks tomorrow."

"Did you pack what you need to stay at my cabin tonight?"

They had gone through with this wager so quickly, so recklessly, that they hadn't even discussed the logistics. The truth was, he hadn't really expected to have a bride today—he figured she wasn't going to show.

His bride took a big napkin and swiped it over her mouth. "Not really. I mean what was I supposed to pack for a wedding night I really didn't expect to have? Let's see—what did I put in my backpack this morning? My toothbrush, a hairbrush, my laptop and my favorite Swiss Army knife."

"A knife? Why do you have that?"

"Are you kidding? Only for *everything*. I can fix a broken radiator hose or open a bottle of beer with one awesome tool. I think you're question should really be, why wouldn't *every* bride have one?" She laughed a big laugh. "Hey! Do you have a dollar? I want to get that jukebox going."

Now that Genevieve had cleaned her plate and had a few beers, her spirits were flying high from his perspective. She seemed to have shed the worry and the stress of their elopement and replaced it with good spirits and

the desire to have a good time. He pulled a couple of
dollar bills out of his wallet and handed them to her.

He watched Genevieve walk away, liking the way
the material of her wedding dress hinted at the curve
of her derrière and legs. No doubt, he was attracted to
his bride—he always had been since the first time he
had seen pictures of her on her website. He had agreed
that this marriage was in name only—he had said it
more to convince her to go along with his scheme—
but would he really be able to keep it platonic between
them? He hadn't ever acted on the physical attraction
he had for Genevieve because he was on that self-
imposed dating hiatus, but that physical attraction had
always been there.

"Garth Brooks or Kenny Chesney?" His wife had
spun around to ask him a question.

"Brooks!"

With a nod, Genevieve pushed a button and waited
for the music to begin to play before she headed back
his way. She gathered up the sides of her long skirt in
her hands and began to sway the material back and forth
to the rhythm of the music. When she arrived back at
the table, Knox stood up.

"Do you want to have that first dance?" he asked her.

Her surprised smile reached those pretty eyes of hers.
Genevieve craned her head so she could look up into
his face. "You know how to dance? Really?"

"Darlin', I've been doin' the Texas Two-Step since
I could walk."

"Well, all right then, cowboy. Let's do this." She
gave him her hand.

There wasn't a real dance floor so he pushed a nearby
table out of his way and pulled Genevieve into his arms.

If he hadn't come up with this wager, how long, if ever, would it have taken him to be able to hold this woman as he was right now?

While the patrons looked on, they danced. They danced until they were both sweaty and out of breath and laughing. He had taken off his too-snug jacket and bolo tie, and he noticed the tendrils around her face had escaped from the sparkly hair clip and framed her face in the loveliest way. Several times while they danced Knox had to stop himself from kissing her. He wanted to kiss her. But they had made a deal and he was determined not to violate that agreement. This was to be a platonic marriage, no matter how hard it was on him.

"Kiss, kiss, kiss, kiss!" the crowd started to chant.

Her chest rising and falling from the exertion of dancing, her cheeks flushed pink, Genevieve looked around at the chanting crowd.

He leaned down, put his cheek next to hers, and asked in a voice that only she could hear, "It's your call."

"This won't be the last time people ask," she told him pragmatically and he knew she was probably right. The suddenness of their relationship would no doubt make people speculate about their sincerity. There would be times that they were going to have to be affectionate with each other because that was how most genuine newlyweds behaved. They may as well start practicing now.

Before he could respond, Genevieve threw her arms around his neck and planted a big kiss on his lips to gratified cheers in the background. Not thinking, only acting, Knox picked his bride up into the air and kissed her back, long and hard, before he let her slide down the length of his body until her toes touched the floor. Knox couldn't have known how he would feel about marrying a woman based on a wager—but he did know now. He felt more grounded today, in this moment, with this woman, than he had ever felt in his life. He'd always played the field and he had the reputation of never being in a hurry to settle down with just one woman. But the way he felt about Genevieve was already so different than he had ever felt for anyone else. He sensed that he could be himself around her—being around Genevieve was like being around a best friend that you really liked to kiss. And, even though Knox knew that this relationship wasn't meant to last, this petite firebrand of a woman had already changed how he felt as a man. And, maybe—just maybe—she had begun to change how he felt about settling down.

"Ugh!" Genevieve held her stomach, this time not because it was empty but because it was way too full.

She had eaten two racks of ribs on her own with a side of potato salad, corn bread and three beers. Their waitress had given them each a slice of cheesecake on the house in honor of their marriage and how could Genevieve say no to that?

"Am I waddling? I feel like I'm definitely waddling."

She was wearing Knox's jacket over her shoulders because the air conditioner had given her a bit of chill in her bones. She was also feeling a tad tipsy, so she naturally linked her arm with her husband's arm for support.

"You're not waddling," he reassured her. "You're weaving a bit, but not waddling."

"I knew I shouldn't have had that last beer."

Knox walked her over to the passenger side of the truck. When they had gone into the DeSoto, it had been bright and sunny outside. Now it was late afternoon. They had managed to laugh and dance and eat their way through several hours. Knox unlocked the truck door and opened it for her.

"You do know I'm perfectly capable of opening my own door, right?"

Knox, unfazed, held on to her hand while she swayed onto the seat.

"I was raised to be a gentleman and you're darn well going to enjoy it, Gen."

Genevieve groaned again as she closed her eyes. "Have it your way."

"Thank you. I will."

Her companion reached across her body, grasped hold of the seat belt and buckled her in. When he climbed behind the wheel, she could sense him looking over at her. She cracked open her eyes.

"What?"

"Next stop is the Ambling A."

"Uh-huh."

"You going to be okay to face the rest of the Crawfords?"

Genevieve pushed herself more upright in the seat. "I'm a pressure player, Knox."

"Meaning?" he asked as he backed out of the parking spot.

"I work better under pressure. In fact, that's when I'm at my best. I never crumble."

"That's good to hear because I'm giving you fair warning, Gen. They're gonna interrogate the heck out of us. Bugs under a microscope."

She closed her eyes again. "Trust me, hubby. I'll have your family believing that we are the most in-love couple they've ever seen. I'll have them wondering how we managed to put off the elopement as long as we did! And your dad?" She held up her pointer finger. "I'll have him wrapped around my little pinky in no time flat."

"Well, I'm certainly looking forward to seeing that," he said in response. "Of course, you do realize that's not your pinky, correct?"

"Smart-ass."

It was dusk when Knox pulled onto the long drive leading to the main house at his family's ranch. Throughout the day, they had both been texting periodically with their friends and family so no one would suspect that the day was anything other than ordinary. The sky behind the sprawling log cabin main house was glowing orange and pink and purple while the clouds were shadowy shapes drifting overhead. Knox parked the truck and turned off the lights. Genevieve was breathing deeply beside him; soon after he had buckled her in, she'd fallen asleep. He almost hated to awaken her, especially when he knew that they were about to be bombarded with questions and comments and, no doubt, suspicion from his brothers, his father, as well as Logan and Xander's new wives.

Knox reached out and put his hand on Genevieve's arm and gave it a gentle shake. His wife mumbled something in an irritated tone but she didn't open her eyes.

"Gen," he said quietly with another shake of her arm. "We're here."

That time she opened her eyes. She yawned loudly, stretched and then pushed herself upright, looking around groggily.

"I slept the whole way back?"

He nodded.

"Sorry about that." She wrapped her arms tightly in front of her body. "Not much company, huh?"

"I'm glad you slept. Hopefully that battery is recharged because behind that door is a roomful of critics and skeptics."

"You sound worried."

"I am absolutely worried. If we don't convince them we're the real deal, this whole day was a waste of time."

Genevieve unbuckled her seat belt, tugged her arms free of his jacket and seemed to perk up quickly. She checked her reflection in the mirror on the back of the sun visor, gave her long blond wavy hair a quick brush through, and then declared, "I'm ready."

It was strange—he was about to bring his "bride" home for the first time and he appeared to be the more nervous of the two. Genevieve didn't seem nervous or anxious at the idea of facing his family. In fact, she seemed perfectly calm.

They walked up to the front door to the main house and Knox paused to take in a deep breath to calm his nerves. Genevieve reached over and took his hand in hers.

"Don't worry, Knox. We've got this."

He looked down at the top of her golden head. This petite woman seemed to have all the confidence in the world. And her confidence actually made him believe that they could pull this off. She had told him that she was a pressure player and now he was seeing that firsthand. His nerves were on the verge of getting the best of him but Genevieve was completely calm.

"They're a tough crowd." He felt the need to reiterate this point—to prepare her for what was to come.

Genevieve had a very serious expression on her face when she said, "Maybe they are. But they're not tougher than trying to shod a stallion with a stable full of mares in heat. If I can handle that, I bet I can handle them."

Chapter Five

"Here goes nothin'." Knox let out a long breath before he opened the heavy front door of the main house.

"Here goes everything," she countered.

With her arm firmly linked with Knox's arm, Genevieve didn't have to fake a smile. The idea of meeting Knox's family and pulling off the nearly impossible—convincing them that their whirlwind romance and sudden elopement was on the up-and-up—was a challenge. And she dearly loved a challenge.

Stepping into the foyer at the main house was like stepping into an architectural magazine for men who wanted rustic chic with a sophisticated flair. Yes, the inside of the log cabin mansion was full of dark wood and Western motif touches, but there was an overarching sophistication, from the paintings on the wall to the light fixtures, that gave a nod to the Crawfords' Dallas roots. On every other visit to the Ambling A she'd been the hired help. This was the first time that Genevieve had been invited into the main house.

"Sounds like a party," she noted as the sound of loud talking and laughter greeted them.

"We all try to get together at least one night a week for dinner," Knox explained. "So everyone's here."

She looked up into Knox's face, noting the tension in his jawline and his unsmiling lips.

"You don't look like a man who just married the love of your life, Knox," she whispered. "Smile."

Knox followed her instruction and smiled as he walked with her toward the sound of the voices. Gathered in an informal family room were her new in-laws. Standing by the window, holding an unlit cigar and a glass tumbler, was the man she immediately recognized as the patriarch of the family, Maximilian Crawford. The Crawford cowboys were famously handsome, Knox included, and it was easy to recognize that those six apples hadn't fallen far from the paternal tree. The Crawford patriarch was tall and solidly built with broad shoulders and a shock of silver hair combed straight back from his tanned, Hollywood-handsome face. Her eyes swept the rest of the room, taking inventory of all of the people in the room, and ending with Logan, the eldest Crawford brother, and his bride Sarah.

"Knox! Where the heck have you been?" Logan was the first to notice them standing in the entrance of the family room.

"Hey! Why do you have the hot farrier with you?" A brother with longish brown hair was lounging on a nearby couch, his hands behind his head, his booted feet propped up on the coffee table.

"What's with the get-up, Knox?" another brother,

tall as Maximilian with mussed dark hair and his arm around a pretty petite redhead, asked. "Did you just come from a funeral or something?"

"No," Knox said with a slight waver in his voice that she hoped only she could hear. "A wedding."

Genevieve's eyes were on Knox's father. As far as she was concerned, he was the most important audience member. He sipped from his tumbler.

Logan, with his closely cropped dusty-brown hair and blue eyes, seemed to be catching on to the meaning behind Knox's words more quickly than the rest. The eldest Crawford brother, his eyes narrowed curiously, asked, "And whose wedding was that?"

Genevieve looked up at her husband and was gratified that he looked right back at her. When he winked at her, she laughed, genuinely laughed, which was perfect for the show they were presenting for the family.

Before he answered, Knox unhooked her arm from his, wrapped his arm possessively around her shoulders, dropped a quick kiss on the top of her head and then said, "Mine."

That one word was all it took. The entire crowd in the family room—one patriarch, five brothers, two women, a baby, and young girl playing with a chubby puppy in front of an unlit fireplace—who had pretty much ignored them when they'd walked in, now turned to them in silence. The only sound for a couple of heartbeats was the sound of the baby cooing in Sarah's arms.

"What did you just say, son?" The look on the patriarch's face said it all—he wasn't happy.

"I said," Knox, repeated loudly and clearly without the waver in his voice, "I just got married. I would like to introduce you all to my wife, Genevieve."

She had never known what it felt like to be a celebrity, but Knox's announcement, made her feel like she was being mobbed by paparazzi. They were suddenly surrounded by the five brothers, all of them bombarding them with shocked questions interlaced with congratulations. Sarah wove her way through the throng of brothers, holding baby Sophia tightly in her arms, so she could give her a hug.

"Welcome to the family," Sarah said warmly. "It's so nice to have some more estrogen in this place."

Genevieve knew Sarah in passing and she had always liked her friendly, sweet personality. And it didn't seem that the fact that Viv Shuster had set Genevieve up on a date with Sarah's now-husband, Logan, bothered the young mother in the least.

"Thank you, Sarah." She smiled and reached out to touch baby Sophia's soft little hand.

Knox kept a protective arm around her shoulders while she said hello to her new brothers-in-law. Xander, the tallest and second oldest, had a skeptical look on his face. He pulled the petite redhead closer to his side.

"Logan and I just got married and now *you* turn up married out of the blue? Something smells to high heaven."

"So, what's the story, Knox?" Logan prodded. "None of us even knew the two of you were dating. How'd the two of you end up married?"

"Yes." Maximilian finally spoke, his tone rippling with anger. "I'd like an answer to that too."

Knox stiffened beside her and she instinctively pressed her body reassuringly into his. "I'd thought you'd be happy, Pop. Isn't this what you wanted? All of your sons married. Well, three down, three more to go, right?"

When Maximilian walked toward them, the rest of the family parted like when Moses parted the Red Sea. Perhaps the patriarch was accustomed to intimidating people with his stern, formidable, unsmiling countenance, but Genevieve had been facing tough male competitors ever since she was a teenager. She thrived on this kind of head-to-head matchup.

"Is this Viv Shuster's doing?" Maximilian now stood in front of them.

"No," Knox said with a satisfied rumble in his voice. "She can't claim credit for this one."

The older man's scowl deepened.

"Pop," Knox said, "I'd like to introduce you to my wife, Genevieve Lawrence Crawford."

"It's a pleasure to finally meet you, Mr. Crawford." She held out her hand, which he refused.

"That's real polite." Knox frowned at his father.

"Wait a minute." Maximilian stared down into her eyes and she stared right back at him. "Do you mean to tell me that you married that lady farrier I told you not to hire?"

"I wasn't aware that you had any objection to my services," Genevieve said before Knox could reply.

"You'd better know I did," Max snapped back at her.

"And you'd better know that you're talking to my wife." There was a heat behind Knox's black-brown eyes that she had never seen before. This power struggle between Knox and his father was real and it appeared to have very deep roots. Suddenly, the reason behind Knox's desire to break the grip his father had on his life with this fake elopement came into sharp focus for

Genevieve. Knox had to win this one if he was ever going to truly be his own man.

There was a tense silence in the room, before Finn, one of Knox's older brothers, said, "Come on, guys! We can give Genevieve a better welcome than this, can't we? Knox is married! We need to drink to that!"

Finn, who seemed to always be brushing his scruffy bangs out of his eyes, grabbed her free hand and tugged her loose from Knox's side.

"We Crawfords can make a lousy first impression, sis," her new brother-in-law confessed. "But we aren't all that bad once you get to know us."

"I can handle it," she assured him.

Finn smiled down at her, his boyish hair in his eyes. "I just bet you can."

Hunter, the only brother who had been married before and who was now a single father to his daughter, Wren, had quietly retrieved a couple bottles of champagne from Maximilian's collection. Genevieve found herself standing beside her husband with a glass of champagne in her hand. All of the brothers and the two wives had glasses in their hands, ready to toast them. Maximilian was the only one who refused to participate in Hunter's toast.

"Here's to Knox and his beautiful wife, Genevieve! We had no idea the two of you were even dating, but who can argue with love? Congratulations!"

"Congratulations!" the rest of the family shouted.

"Why didn't any of us know you were dating?" Xander asked, his eyes still suspicious.

"I can keep a secret," Knox said with an easy shrug.

"As can I." She put her empty champagne glass on a coaster on the coffee table.

"Tell us the whole story." Xander's wife, Lily, leaned closer to her love.

Knox looked down and met her eyes. They had discussed their backstory over their postnuptial barbecue but this would be the easiest place for the family to find discrepancies if they didn't get it right. "Do you want to tell them, or should I?"

"I think you should tell them."

They sat together on a nearby love seat and Genevieve reminded herself to keep her body close to Knox's as any new bride would. She put her hand on his thigh and looked at her husband frequently while he told their story, making sure that her gaze was always admiring.

"All of you know that I first saw Genevieve's picture on her website when I was looking for a farrier." Their eyes met when he continued. "I liked the look of the website and the message—her mission statement was all about treating the whole horse, not just the hooves, with a holistic approach. And, without knowing her, I liked her. She was interesting…and beautiful."

The way his eyes roamed her face let her know that these were his true feelings. He was speaking from the heart in that moment.

"Did you hire her just so you could date her?" Knox's other brother Wilder asked in a booming, teasing voice.

Knox gave his brother a little wink. "I'd be lying if I said that the thought didn't cross my mind."

This was news to her, and with all the fibs they were telling, it was hard to know if Knox was telling the truth about that.

"The minute I met Genevieve, we hit it off."

That was true—they had.

"We became friends…" Knox put his hand over her hand.

That was also true.

"And then one day it hit me like one of those cartoon characters that gets hit over the head with a ton of bricks—I had found the woman I wanted to marry."

The way Knox had skillfully worded that last sentence was also the truth. He had all of a sudden decided she was the one he wanted to marry. But he left out the crucial part—the word *fake*.

"Why keep it a secret?" Xander pressed him.

"That was my idea, Xander," Genevieve piped up. "I knew that eventually we would be the talk of the town. I just wanted some time for us—to be *us* and to make sure that what we were feeling was real."

"It's so romantic." Lily's emerald green eyes were sparkling. "I love the fact that you eloped."

"We wanted to start our lives together in our own way, on our own terms," Knox added. "And we couldn't be happier with how things have turned out. Isn't that right, sweetheart?"

Genevieve scanned the faces of her new in-laws, noting that most appeared to be convinced that the marriage was the real deal. For extra effect, she put her head on Knox's shoulder. "We couldn't be any happier if we tried."

"What do you love about our brother?" Xander still wasn't thrown off the scent.

She lifted her head so she could look into her husband's face. In his deep brown eyes she saw a curious question about what she might say. The best way to get Xander to back off was to tell the truth.

"What's not to love?" This was her honest answer.

"He's handsome and smart and talented. He shares my passion for horses. From the very beginning, he's made me feel like I belong in my career, that I have a right to be who I am."

The slow smile Knox gave her let her know that he liked what he was hearing.

"And," she added, "he's a cowboy and a gentleman."

There was sincerity in her words because they were the truth. Had she directly said that she was madly in love with Knox? No. But she had said enough to shift the suspicion in Xander's eyes. That was a step in the right direction. Now all she had to do was win over Maximilian.

Genevieve had a feeling that he was going to be a much tougher nut to crack.

Knox couldn't believe that they had really pulled it off. Genevieve had played the part of the loving new wife to perfection. By the time the family began to disband, everyone in the room, with the exception of his father, seemed accepting of the surprise relationship and elopement.

"Why is it that even when you get your way, you're miserable?" Knox had followed his father to his study.

Max shut the door to the study behind them and took a seat behind a heavily carved wooden desk.

"Sit, son."

Knox sat down in a chair opposite the desk, always aware of the power dynamic—the one behind the desk had the power, and that, as usual, was Max.

"I was expecting a bit more of a hero's welcome from you, Pop."

"Is that right?"

"Sure." He smiled broadly. "I gave you what you wanted."

"This isn't what I wanted," Max leaned his arms on top of the desk, his expression serious. "I don't know what kind of trick you're trying to pull."

"No trick." Knox took the marriage certificate out of his wallet and slid it across the desk. "I'm married."

Max studied the certificate, a muscle working in his jaw. Then he folded the certificate and shoved it back toward Knox.

"You've made a big mistake here, son."

"You're entitled to your opinion."

"What do you even really know about this girl?"

"I know that when you meet the right one you know."

Max's dark eyes were stormy as he said, "Marry in haste, repent in leisure."

Knox understood the reference. Max had been quick to marry their mother and his father had never made it a secret that he considered his marriage to be one of the biggest mistakes of his life. Years ago, their mother had run off with her lover, leaving Max a single father to six young boys. They never really talked about it, but Knox believed that Max had never fully recovered from his mother's betrayal.

"I'm not you," he said seriously. "I'm nothing like you."

"That's where you're wrong, son. You're exactly like me." Max stabbed the desk with his pointer finger. "Did you even bother to get a prenup?"

Knox stood up. "That's none of your business."

His father stood up and slammed his palms on the desk. "Everything about this is *my* business."

They stared each other down for several tense seconds before Knox gave an annoyed shake of his head. "Not this time. You disrespect my marriage, you disrespect my wife, you are disrespecting me. I don't want to hear one more word about a prenup."

While Knox went with his father for a one-on-one meeting, Genevieve made her way over to the rug in front of the fire where Hunter's six-year-old daughter, Wren, was sitting cross-legged.

"Hi," Genevieve said. "Do you mind if I join you?"

Wren nodded her blond head. She was a slight girl with lopsided pigtails and a pale complexion.

"Who's your friend?" Genevieve sat cross-legged as well, reaching out to pet the head of the sleeping puppy.

"Silver."

The chubby puppy opened its eyes sleepily, wagged its tail at Genevieve, before it yawned, rolled over onto its back and fell back asleep.

"I like your puppy," she told the quiet little girl.

"He's not mine," Wren said. "He's Uncle Knox's. I just get to play with him."

The young girl looked at her with the directness only a child could achieve. "How come you don't know that?"

Of course, out of everyone in the room, it took a six-year-old child to stump her. She didn't have a good explanation for that. She *should* know that her husband had a puppy.

Knox marched back into the family room with an unsmiling expression on his face. He walked directly over to her and held out his hand. "It's time for us to go."

Genevieve stood up quickly, glad that she didn't have to answer Wren's question. "Everything okay?"

"Everything's exactly as it should be."

"Can Silver stay with me tonight, Uncle Knox?"

Knox kissed his niece on the top of her head before he scooped the sleepy puppy up into his arms. "Not tonight, sweet pea."

Her husband held out his free hand to her and she accepted it. They said their quick goodbye to the family and then Knox made a beeline for the front door.

Once back in the privacy of the truck, Genevieve held Silver in her arms while Knox cranked the engine.

"What happened in there?" she asked about the meeting that took place between father and son.

"What happened?" Knox echoed with a big, pleased smile on his face. "We pulled it off, that's what happened. Every one of them bought it hook, line and sinker."

"Even your father?"

"Especially my father." Her husband winked conspiratorially at her. "You set the hook and I pulled him right into the boat."

Chapter Six

It was dark when they left the main house and took a gravel road to Knox's small log cabin located on the Ambling A ranch. Genevieve held the puppy tightly in her arms, her stomach twisting into an uncomfortable knot. The excitement of putting on a great show for the Crawford family had been an adventure—a challenge— and she had thrived under the spotlight. But now, on this pitch-black road with only the headlights to light their way, it was starting to sink in that she had just, at least for the short term, completely changed her life. She was now Knox Crawford's wife, and as such, would be living under the same roof with him.

"Here she is." Knox pulled up in front of his cabin, which had been built back in the woods with a small stream nearby. It was a mini version of the main house, fashioned out of rustic logs with rocking chairs on the front porch. If this had been a real marriage, Genevieve would have been pleased to call this her first home with her husband.

"Nice." The word came out of her mouth and it sounded hollow to her own ears. How could she swing so quickly from feeling triumphant to feeling horrified?

Genevieve opened the truck door and then repositioned the puppy in her arms. Dried leaves crunched beneath her feet as she slid out of the passenger seat onto the ground. The air was crisp and the familiar sound of field crickets singing all around them worked to settle her nerves. She followed her husband up the porch stairs, the wood creaking beneath their feet. Silver began to wiggle in her arms and whine, licking at her face to get her attention.

"I think he needs to go to the bathroom."

"I've got a fenced-in area out back."

Knox opened the door, flipped on a switch just inside the doorway and held the door open so she could walk through. In that moment, Genevieve realized that she had just walked into Knox's world—a world she had never thought to experience. The cabin, like Knox, was masculine and neatly appointed. From her experience, the cowboy was always well put together, even when he was working. In contrast, her garage apartment looked like a bomb had exploded inside. She was always just about to get around to cleaning it up but never quite got there.

"Make yourself at home," he said.

Silver finally wiggled free, ran over to Knox, stood up on his hind legs and began to paw at the rancher's leg.

"Hey, buddy. Let's go out."

Knox dropped her backpack on the couch in the

small living room before he walked through the tiny kitchen to the back door. Silver bounded out the door, down the back porch steps and into a dimly lighted fenced-in area.

Genevieve followed them outside and stood on the back porch next to her husband. Her arms crossed in front of her body, she said, "This is just plain weird."

Knox looked over at her, his features in shadow. "You're right. It is."

They both laughed when Silver came galloping back toward them, his fat legs churning as he worked his way up the stairs.

"I didn't even know you had a dog. Wren caught me on that one."

"She's smart as a whip."

Genevieve nodded.

Back inside, she stood awkwardly in the living room, taking in the sparse decor. Knox, it seemed, was a no-frills kind of guy, which fit the picture she had always had of him. The cowboy shrugged out of his jacket and dropped it on the butcher-block counter top in the kitchen.

"What now?" she asked him.

He unbuttoned his white shirt exposing his tanned, corded neck and part of his chest. Knox then unbuttoned his cuffs.

"Now?" he asked. "I'm going to get some shut-eye. I get up before dawn. How 'bout you?"

She was exhausted and wired and disoriented.

"I meant, what's next?" she clarified. "For us."

"What do you mean?"

"What do you mean, what do I mean?" she snapped, the exhaustion beginning to make it difficult to keep her tone friendly. "Are you prepared to face my family tomorrow?"

"Yes. I'm prepared. We've got to tell them before they hear it from someone else. Will they worry if you don't show up tonight?"

She shook her head. "No. I come and go as I please. Sometimes I don't get home until they've gone to bed and I can be gone before they awaken."

He joined her on the couch, lifting Silver up and putting him on the cushion between them. "Then we're covered for tonight."

She yawned with a nod. "A short reprieve."

When she opened her eyes, Knox was staring at her quietly.

"We actually did it."

She took a deep breath in through her nose and let it out. "Yes, we actually did."

"We haven't really discussed sleeping arrangements."

"We haven't discussed much of anything really," she interjected.

"I'll take the couch. You can have my bed."

"Thank you. Can I have your puppy too?"

She liked the way that the sides of Knox's eyes crinkled when he laughed. "I suppose, technically, he's your puppy now too."

"I may just ask for him in the divorce," she teased.

"Along with puppy support?"

"Absolutely."

Knox gave her the top to his pajamas and showed her where the toothpaste was kept in the medicine cabinet above the sink. The bathroom was cramped but clean and there was a claw-foot bathtub that would have been calling her name if she wasn't so weary. She quickly brushed her teeth and her hair, slipped on Knox's pajama top, which looked like a minidress on her, and then opened the door slowly.

"I'm coming out," she warned him.

"The coast is clear," he promised.

Genevieve quickly crossed the narrow hallway to the bedroom and closed the door partway so she could call Silver. Silver came bounding down the hall, squeezed his roly-poly body through the crack in the door and greeted her with unconditional love. The bed was made, of course, with dark blue–and–green–plaid linens. She got under the sheets and flopped back onto the pillows. The mattress was much softer than the one she slept on in the garage apartment, and surprisingly comfortable.

With the puppy curled up beside her, Genevieve switched off the lamp next to the bed and stared up at the ceiling. She had never really imagined herself married—but alone in a strange bed with a puppy wouldn't have made the short list of scenarios for a wedding night if she were to ever have one, that was for sure.

"Please," she said into the dark. "Let sleep come quickly."

Knox tried to sleep but he couldn't. Everything was going according to his plan, yet he couldn't have known what it would actually *feel* like to have a wife in his cabin. For the last hour, his mind had been fixated on the image of Genevieve wearing the top part of his pajamas. The fact that he hadn't seen her in the garment hadn't stopped his mind from imagining it. She was in his bed, in his pajamas, and he had promised not to touch her. He had given his word. What was he *thinking*? Now he had a beautiful, sexy wife with whom he had to maintain a hands-off policy. Living with Genevieve in such close quarters, it seemed like a monumental challenge he would have to fight to overcome every day.

"Wake up, lovebirds! It's time for your shivaree!"

Knox sat up at the sound of his brothers' voices. They were banging on what sounded like pots and pans, hooting and hollering at the top of their lungs. Knox threw off the blanket, stood up, switched on the light and stomped over to the front door. He yanked open the door and was greeted by Finn and Wilder.

"What are you doing?" he yelled at them, holding his hands over his ears.

"The shivaree, bro! From the movie Oklahoma." Finn laughed, banging his pot with enthusiasm.

"We're welcoming your bride to the family!" Wilder tipped his head back and hollered.

"Knock. It. Off!" Knox grabbed for the pots and pans but missed.

Wilder and Finn pushed their way into the cabin and it seemed that they all looked at the blanket on the couch at the same time. Knox turned back to his brothers, who now had a perplexed, wondering expression on their faces. At that moment, Genevieve came out of the bedroom in his pajama top. All three of them stared at her. Her long blond hair was mussed, her blue eyes blinking against the light and her tanned, muscular legs were exposed.

Instinctively, Knox stepped to her side and put his arm around her body. "My wife and I would like to spend our wedding night alone. Now take your *shivaree* and get the heck out of here."

Wilder lifted his eyebrows, his eyes shifting to the

blanket on the couch. "It doesn't look like we were interrupting anything, bro."

If Finn and Wilder walked away thinking that they were having a platonic wedding night, the entire plan would be ruined. Knox couldn't let that happen. He took Genevieve's face in his hands and kissed her. He kissed her the way he had always thought about kissing her—slow, sweet and full of promise for good things to come. For a split second, she stiffened in his arms, but then she put her arms around his neck and kissed him back like a woman in love. By the time the kiss ended, his brothers were slamming the door behind them.

Knox let his arms fall away from Genevieve's body and took a step backward. "I'm sorry. I had to do something."

His wife looked a bit dazed, as dazed as he felt. That kiss—so unexpected and unplanned—had got his juices flowing and made his body stand at attention.

Genevieve touched her lips as if she were still feeling the kiss before she said, "You had to."

Knox tried not to notice the shape of her legs or the outline of her breasts beneath the thin material of his pajama top, but he couldn't avoid it. His wife was a beauty. How could he not notice?

"Were you able to sleep?" she asked him.

He shook his head.

"Do you think they'll come back?"

Knox took a glass out of the cupboard and got some water out of the tap. "Knowing them? It's possible."

"We can't let anyone see us sleeping apart," Genevieve said. "We can't risk it."

He brought her a glass of water, which she accepted with a thank you.

"What do you suggest?"

"We share the bedroom."

Knox's mind immediately went to the thought of sharing a bed with Genevieve and not being able to act on any desire that was surely to arise. Could he handle it? Would he ever be able to get any sleep with her just an arm's length away?

"Are you sure about that?" he asked.

Genevieve finished the water and put the glass in the sink. "I'm not sure about anything we've done, Knox. But we're here now, so we have to just find a way to make it work."

"Do you really think that you can share a bed with me and keep your hands to yourself?"

His wife laughed—a natural, sweet-sounding laugh that he enjoyed. "I will certainly give it my best shot."

"See that you do."

"Are you a right or a left?" Genevieve followed Knox back to the bedroom.

"Middle."

"Not tonight, you aren't," she said. "Silver is the middle."

The puppy's head popped up and he wagged his tail.

"Silver is our chaperone?"

"Yep. We'll keep the puppy between us like an adorable chastity belt."

Genevieve ended up getting the right side of the bed. She hurriedly slipped under the covers and pulled them up to her chin. Right before Finn and Wilder had barged in on their wedding night, Genevieve had just drifted to sleep surrounded by Knox's scent. The pillows and sheets and blanket all had the faint scent of Knox's body. Now that he was in bed next to her, the scent of his warm skin made it difficult for her to remember that this was a marriage in name only. The man was built for a woman's appreciative eyes and the sight of him naked from the waist up, the feel of his hard body and his soft lips on hers, awakened feelings in her that she had worked to push aside.

"Gen?" Knox said her name in the dark.

"Hmm?"

"If I had asked you out—you know—before we got married, would you have said yes?"

Genevieve hesitated to answer. "No."

The bed moved beneath him as he shifted his body toward her. "No?"

"No."

"Why not?"

"Are we really having this conversation now?"

"Why *not*?"

"Because, Knox," she said. "You're too young for me."

The bed wiggled because he sat upright. "Too *young*? You're thirty-two."

"Which you just learned today…"

"And I'm twenty-eight."

"Exactly."

"I'm only four years younger than you!"

"Which means that you're really ten years younger than me because men are about six years behind women as far as maturity. Hence why I don't date younger men."

"You just marry them."

Genevieve curled her body around Silver, rubbing his soft warm belly. "Touché, husband. Now go to sleep. Being your fake bride is exhausting."

* * *

Genevieve awakened to the smell of rich coffee and the feel of a wet puppy tongue licking her face. Giggling, she grabbed Silver and wrapped him up into her arms.

"How are you this morning, puppy breath?"

Silver barked and thumped his tail back and forth. Then he shimmied out of her arms, leaped off the bed and went racing out of the room. She pushed herself upright in the bed and checked her phone for the time.

"Oh, my goodness." She squinted at the screen, shocked. It was after eight! She never slept in like this.

"Good morning." Knox appeared in the door, freshly showered and shaved. He was wearing dark jeans and a button-down shirt tucked in neatly. "Coffee?"

"God, yes."

"If you want to jump in the shower, I put a fresh towel out for you and there's shampoo."

Knox had seen her in his pajama top the night before, but in the light of day, she suddenly felt self-conscious.

"Can I borrow your deodorant? Didn't think of that when I packed."

"What's mine is yours," he said. "Help yourself."

Genevieve quickly took a shower and changed into the jeans and T-shirt she had worn the day before. It seemed like a lifetime ago that she had been waiting for Knox at the diner. The simple gold band around her finger felt foreign but she knew that, at least for the time being, she would have to get accustomed to wearing it.

"You cook?" she asked as she walked barefoot out to the kitchen.

"Enough to survive." Knox handed her a cup of coffee. "Cream? Sugar?"

She shook her head and blew on the piping hot coffee.
"I can do scrambled or fried. Pick your poison."

"Scrambled."

Knox cracked an egg. With his back to her, she admired the way his jeans hugged his hips and his legs. He turned his head to look at her and caught her checking him out. He smiled at her with a wink.

"Enjoying the view?" he teased her.

"No. I was trying to read the label, that's all."

"If you say so," Knox said. "But I think this platonic marriage may just prove too difficult for you, Gen."

He brought two plates of scrambled eggs to the table and joined her.

"I can't believe how late I slept." She took a forkful of eggs. "How long have you been up?"

"A couple of hours."

"Did you sleep?"

"Like a rock once my two knucklehead brothers left."

"Do you think they bought the kiss?"

Knox caught her eye and held it. "It felt real to me."

Genevieve looked down at her plate and pretended to be preoccupied with moving the eggs from one spot to another. That kiss had felt real to her as well. It wasn't the kind of kiss that two platonic friends would share; it was a lover's kiss. Knox had felt it and so had she.

"How do you think your family's going to react?" Knox asked, bringing her eyes back to his handsome face.

Genevieve looked out the window for a moment, thinking. Then she gave a little shake of her head. "My mom will think it's typical. I've been impulsive since I was a kid. But my dad? I think he's going to freak out."

"Good to know. Looking forward to it." Knox stood

up and took both of their plates to the sink. "I suppose we should go and face the freak-out then."

She had to agree. Putting off telling her parents was only making her stomach churn. And the thought of them finding out from anyone else was a serious concern. Rust Creek Falls was a small town with a big mouth. They had to get to the folks before the news of their elopement reached them by a gossip or a well-wisher.

Genevieve looked down at Silver who was on his back on the couch with his fat paws up in the air. "Let's take Silver. I mean, seriously. Who can stay mad when there's a puppy in the room?"

"Only a monster," Knox said.

"Exactly!" She nodded. "It's not the least bit cowardly to hide behind a puppy shield."

Chapter Seven

Knox hadn't been in too many serious relationships in his life, so meeting-the-father moments had been far and few between. This was the first time he was meeting his in-laws and it didn't seem to matter that this was a marriage based on a wager. He was still nervous.

"You'd better fill me in more about your family," he said to his bride as he drove his truck to the Lawrences'. From their previous conversations, Knox knew that Genevieve was the oldest of three daughters and the only one who wasn't married with kids. He was well aware of the fact that Lionel, Genevieve's father, could be rigid, old-fashioned and didn't approve of his daughter's chosen profession.

"I don't know…" his wife said. "What can I really tell you in ten minutes?"

Their decision to elope without a plan had come back

to bite them several times and they weren't even a whole day in to the ruse.

"Just tell me what you think I should know."

"My mom, Jane, stayed at home with the kids. Lionel sold industrial farm equipment until he retired. The man was absolutely horrible at being retired, so we were all thrilled when he started going to farm equipment auctions with his friends, buying old equipment and refurbishing for resale. It keeps the man busy and out of my mom's kitchen," Genevieve said with a smile. "I have a sister Margo—married with four kids. I told you about her. And then there's Ella—she's my youngest sister— married, of course, with two kids and one on the way. I am the only Lawrence daughter who isn't married."

"Not the case anymore."

"Hey! That's true. I *am* married." Genevieve held up her hand to look at the gold band on her left hand. "One less thing for the folks to complain about."

The Lawrences owned a small homestead on the outskirts of town. The house was a classic two-story whitewashed farmhouse; there was a wraparound porch with a swing and the front door was decorated with heavy leaded glass. Next to the house was a two-car garage with a flight of stairs leading up to an apartment.

"This is home," she said as they pulled up and he detected the slightest catch in her voice. On the outside his new wife appeared calm, but she was, beneath the surface, understandably rattled.

"We're in this together." Knox wanted to reassure her.

She sent him the slightest of smiles but it disappeared quickly.

"Oh! Shoot! Let me get Oscar before he spots Silver."

Genevieve hopped out of the truck and jogged over to the front porch where a giant orange tabby cat was sitting as still as a statue. Genevieve scooped up the massive cat, hugged it to her body and then disappeared inside the house.

Knox looked down at Silver, who looked up at him and then tried to lick him on the chin. "She is going to come back, isn't she?"

After a couple of minutes waiting, Genevieve reappeared on the porch and waved her hand for him to join her.

"All right," he said to his canine companion. "Here goes nothing."

With Silver cradled in his arms for extra protection, Knox walked up the porch stairs to meet his bride.

"You're going to meet my mom first. She's the easy one."

Knox stepped into the Lawrence home and it was like stepping into his grandmother's hug. The house was tidy and decorated with farmhouse decor—chickens and roosters and cows. The old wide-planked wood floors were dinged up from years of use, but an obviously recent coat of polish brought out their color and luster. There was something that smelled mighty good cooking in the kitchen at the back of the house. They walked past a stairwell leading to the second floor on their way to the kitchen and Knox noticed that there were framed pictures of family everywhere—on the walls, on the fireplace mantel, on every surface.

"Is that you?" He stopped to look at one of the framed pictures on the wall. The young blond girl was executing a perfect handstand on the back of a horse.

"Yes."

"You were a wild child even back then, weren't you?"

Genevieve laughed and he was glad to hear the sound. "Always, much to my mom's dismay."

As they approached the kitchen, Genevieve called out, "Mom!"

Knox had never met Mrs. Lawrence before, so he didn't really know what to expect. A heavyset woman appeared at the end of the hall wearing an apron covered in yellow flowers. She threw open her arms, a welcoming smile on her face.

"Ladybug! What are you doing home this time of day?"

"Ladybug?" Knox asked under his breath, loving the fact that his tough-as-any-cowboy wife had such a sweet nickname.

"Not one word, cowboy," Genevieve ordered.

"Oh!" Jane Lawrence noticed him but first enveloped her daughter in a tight hug. "This is such a wonderful surprise."

"Mom." His bride untangled herself from her mom's hug and turned to him. "I want you to meet Knox Crawford."

Genevieve had inherited her mother's lovely cornflower blue eyes; Jane's eyes twinkled with pleasure as she welcomed him into her home. Genevieve had also inherited her mother's smile. It was a smile he had always appreciated from the first time he'd met the pretty farrier in person. Knox was invited into a crisp white and cheerful yellow kitchen that was filled with refurbished 1950s appliances. Stepping into Jane Lawrence's kitchen was like stepping back in time.

Jane clasped her hands together, her eyes darting excitedly between her daughter and him. Knox got the distinct feeling that Genevieve didn't bring men home very often.

"I had no idea we were going to have company." Jane touched her short blond hair self-consciously. "I didn't even put on lipstick."

"It's fine, Mom." Genevieve scooped Silver out of his arms.

"It's a pleasure to meet you, ma'am."

"Oh, it's such a pleasure to meet *you*." Jane smiled. "You know, I saw your father at the post office once. He's so tall!"

Knox didn't think it was possible, but he felt immediately at home in Jane's kitchen. She offered him a cup of coffee and made a place for him at her small round kitchen table. Then she filled a bowl of water for Silver. He'd never experienced such a warm welcome as he received from Genevieve's mom; he only hoped it would continue once she found out that he had eloped with her daughter.

"Where's Dad?" Genevieve, who had been rummaging in the refrigerator, popped a couple of grapes in her mouth before she joined them at the table.

"He's outside tinkering with his toys," Jane said. "He brought a trailer heaping with rusty gold, as he calls it, from the auction yesterday."

Knox met Genevieve's gaze and he knew what she was thinking: When and how do we break the news? Jane was watching them closely, no doubt curious about this unusual morning visit.

"What do you think?" Genevieve asked him.

"No time like the present."

Jane clasped her hands on top of the table. "Is there something I should know before we get your father?"

"Ma'am, there really isn't any easy way to say this…"
Knox stopped to clear his throat.

"We eloped," Genevieve said plainly and held up her
hand so her mom could see her wedding ring.

There was silence at the table as Genevieve's mother
took a moment to digest the news she had just received.
Jane's expression changed from welcoming to confused
to happy in a span of moments. She jumped out of her
chair, embraced her daughter, kissed her once on the
cheek and then quickly came around the table to embrace him. Jane clasped her hands together happily in
front of her body, and Knox was shocked to see tears
of joy glistening in her eyes.

"Oh, ladybug! You're married?!"

Genevieve's jaw was still set as if she was ready to
deflect a bad reaction that wasn't coming. "I'm married. As of yesterday."

Jane rejoined them at the table, her face brightened
from the news. She reached for her daughter's hand.
"This means that you're going to stay in Rust Creek
Falls!"

That was the moment when Knox understood why
Jane had reacted so positively to the elopement. She
didn't care that she had missed the ceremony, she only
cared that her daughter wouldn't be moving away from
home. When he first made this wedding wager with
Genevieve, all he could think about was proving a point
to his own controlling father. The impact of the fake
marriage on someone as sweet and genuine as Jane
Lawrence hadn't occurred to him in the least. When
the marriage ended and Genevieve moved to California, Jane was going to be heartbroken. And, in part, it
would be his fault.

Jane spent the next several minutes asking expected questions. She knew how they met because Genevieve had told her about servicing the horses of the Ambling A, but she wanted all the other details—the romantic bits.

"I can honestly say," Knox said to Jane, "that I have never met anyone like your daughter before, Mrs. Lawrence."

Jane reached over and took his hand in hers and squeezed it tightly. "I always knew that my ladybug would find a man who truly loves her just as she is."

Genevieve was squirming uncomfortably in her chair in a way he'd never seen before. Like him, he had a feeling Genevieve was just starting to fully appreciate the impact that their ruse would have on everyone in their lives.

"And 'Mrs. Lawrence' is too formal for family." Jane's eyes started to glisten with happy tears again. "Shouldn't you call me *Mom*?"

"Let's not rush into anything," Genevieve interrupted.

"Do you mean like a marriage?" Jane countered with a sweet, motherly smile.

Knox had to appreciate how quickly his mother-in-law had turned the table on Genevieve. He had a feeling it didn't happen very often.

"I'm actually kind of shocked you aren't upset that you weren't at the ceremony." Genevieve ran her finger along a groove carved into the top of the table. "I thought you would be."

"I never expect you to have a typical anything, ladybug. Why would your marriage be any different?"

"Point taken."

"I can throw you a reception!" Jane said, as if the thought just occurred to her. "We can have it here and we can invite all of your friends and family. It will be the first time that the Crawfords and Lawrences come together. What do you say?"

Genevieve looked a little like a deer caught in the headlights. Knox was surprised too. Like Genevieve, he had never considered the idea that their families would want to celebrate their union. Still…

"I like the idea," Knox said, wanting to please Jane for some reason.

"You do?" Genevieve turned to him, her eyebrows raised in surprise.

"Sure." He nodded. "Why not?"

"Sure," she repeated slowly to her mom. "Why not?"

"Oh, that's so wonderful!" His mother-in-law's cheeks were flushed a happy shade of pink with excitement. "Now. I think it's time that we tell your father."

Genevieve started to get up but Knox stood up and held out his hand. "This is for me to do, Gen."

His wife resettled in her chair. "Hey, it's your funeral."

He winked at her. "Promise to take care of Silver if I don't make it back?"

Genevieve crossed her heart. "Girl Scouts honor."

Jane stood up and moved to the sink. "Genevieve was asked to leave the Girl Scouts for setting a tent on fire."

"A total accident!" his wife exclaimed.

Knox turned to his mother-in-law. "Mrs. Lawrence—"

Jane frowned at him for still using the formality.

He started again, this time correcting himself as he addressed her. "*Mom*…will you take care of Silver should I not make it back in one piece?"

"I would be honored to take care of my grandpuppy, yes." She nodded emphatically and gave him a smile.

"I find this whole conversation insulting," Genevieve said as she pointed to the back door. "You'll find Lionel out that'a way. God speed, young man."

Knox walked the short distance from the back porch to the shed in the backyard like a man walking the plank. He'd never met Lionel before and now he had to tell the man that he had eloped with his daughter? Not exactly starting off on the right foot.

"Hello, sir."

Lionel Lawrence was a man of average height, slender, with narrow shoulders and a ramrod straight back. He had deep-set blue eyes and about a day's worth of silver and brown whiskers on his long face. Lionel wore a faded green John Deere baseball cap and glasses with thick black frames.

"How do?" Lionel pulled a rag out of the back pocket of his jeans and wiped the sweat from the back of his neck.

Knox extended his hand. "I'm Knox Crawford."

Genevieve's father reached out his hand. "I've heard the name."

According to Genevieve, the Lawrences had been longtime friends of one of Rust Creek Falls's main families, the Traubs; even still, it wasn't a town secret that there had been a long-standing beef between the Traubs and the Crawfords. Knox was relieved that he didn't hear any carryover of that feud in Lionel's tone when he greeted him.

"What can I do for you, young man?"

Knox swallowed several times, finding that his tongue seemed to be stuck to the sides of his mouth.

"Well, sir…"

"While you're here, would you mind helping me move this aerator? Darn thing is too awkward for me to move myself."

Knox was grateful for the stay of execution. He grabbed one side of the piece of farm equipment while Lionel grabbed the other. Together, they moved the aerator out of the shed and into the yard. Lionel lifted up his hat, scratched the top of his head and then repositioned the ball cap so it shielded the sun from his eyes.

"That'll do for now," his father-in-law said. "I thank you."

"I was happy to help."

The two of them stood together for a moment, neither of them speaking until Lionel asked, "Your kin took up at the Ambling A, isn't that right?"

"Yes, sir." Knox nodded. "My father and my five brothers. By way of Dallas."

"It's a good piece of land."

"Yes, sir, it is."

"Good to have family all in one place."

Knox nodded his agreement.

"So…" Lionel rolled back on his heels a bit. "What brings you out to my neck of the woods?"

"Your daughter, sir."

Lionel's small eyes widened for a moment before they narrowed. "My daughter?"

"Yes, sir. Genevieve."

Genevieve's father didn't say anything, but the expression on his face said plenty. He was happy that a man might be coming to court his daughter.

"I don't know if you're aware that Genevieve has been coming out to the Ambling A for a while now. For the horses."

"I heard something 'bout it."

"Well, we've gotten to be pretty close."

Lionel's eyes were pinned on his face.

"And, well, sir…"

"Spit it out, son. I've only got so many good years left."

"…I married your daughter yesterday."

His father-in-law didn't blink for several seconds; he just stared at him, as if he were an old computer trying to process new information. Lionel stuck his finger in his ear and wiggled it around.

"I'm sorry, son. I don't think I heard you right. What did you say?"

"Genevieve and I got married yesterday."

For a moment, Knox actually thought that his father-in-law hadn't heard him because he just kept on staring at him. Then, Lionel put his hand over his heart, closed his eyes and pointed to the sky.

"Praise the lord," Lionel said. "My prayers have finally been answered."

Of all the responses Knox anticipated from Genevieve's father, this wasn't one of them.

Lionel opened his eyes and squinted up at him, "Do you love her?"

"I can honestly say that I've never met anyone like your daughter."

"She's as unique as they come." His father-in-law gave a big nod of agreement. "You can support a family should you be blessed with children."

It was a statement more than a question. Still, Knox felt compelled to answer.

"Yes, sir, I can." What else could he say?

"Do you want children?" Lionel pinned him with a pointed look.

They had already told so many lies, Knox couldn't bring himself to tell another. Instead, he told Lionel the truth. "Yes, sir, I do. When the time is right."

"Well, I hope your time is sooner rather than later." Lionel plopped his ball cap back onto his head. "I bet my Jane is tickled to pieces."

"Your wife's already planning the reception."

"That's my Jane! She never lets an opportunity to have a party pass her by." Lionel stuck out his hand, "Well, I suppose congratulations are in order. I don't know how you managed to get my daughter to that altar, but I'm mighty pleased you did. I've been worrying about her, I surely have."

Stunned, Knox shook his father-in-law's hand again. Neither of Genevieve's parents were upset about the elopement. In fact, they both seemed pretty pleased.

"Now, Knox, we Lawrences do have a strict no-return policy." Lionel looked at his face and then laughed loudly. "I'm just pulling your leg, son! Why would you want to give her back?"

Knox followed Lionel into the kitchen where Genevieve and Jane were awaiting their return with slightly anxious expressions on their faces. Lionel went straight over to his daughter and pulled her into a tight hug before he kissed her cheek.

"I've been waiting for years for you to find the right man to marry," Genevieve's father told her. "This is truly a blessing."

Knox caught Genevieve's eye and he could almost read her mind. *Lucky break.*

"Now, if only you can get her to quit that ridiculous job of hers and start working on some grandbabies, I could go gently into that good night a happy man."

"Dad..." Genevieve frowned at Lionel. Knox knew that the subject of her career was a sore spot for both daughter and father.

"Actually," Knox said, moving over to stand next to his wife, "Gen's career is what brought us together. I would never want her to give it up."

Chapter Eight

Genevieve felt a bit catatonic as they drove away from her parents' house. The reaction she had expected and prepared for had *not* been the reaction they received. Jane was planning a reception and Lionel was planning for her uterus to be occupied by a strong Crawford baby. Their reactions had caught her off guard, that was true, but what had also caught her off guard was how terrible she felt by the deception of it all. Perhaps if Lionel and Jane had been upset about the elopement, as Genevieve had anticipated, then the inevitable divorce wouldn't be such a big deal to them. Based on their reaction to the news of her nuptials, the divorce was going to crush them.

"Your mom is a total sweetheart."

Knox's comment broke through her reverie. She looked over at him as he pulled his truck into a parking spot at the Gold Rush Diner. She hadn't seen her own truck since the day before but it seemed like a lifetime ago that she had parked in the lot behind the diner. So much had happened in a little more than a twenty-four-hour period it seemed a bit surreal to see her truck, so grounded in what used to be her old life.

"She's always been my biggest fan." Genevieve unbuckled her seat belt. "She really liked you."

"I like her."

All her life she had been acting out, getting in trouble, pushing the boundaries. Her motto had always been, *Why blend in when we were born to stand out?* For all of the trouble and angst she had caused her parents, she had never really felt guilty about it. Honestly, she had always been having too much fun. But this time was different. This time, she felt horribly guilty. She didn't like the feeling.

"She was so happy," she said quietly, pensively, hugging Silver to her body for comfort. "I didn't expect that. Did you?"

"No."

Genevieve caught Knox's eye. "This is a whole lot heavier than I thought it would be."

He nodded.

"I just didn't think…" Her voice trailed off. Then, again, wasn't that the point her mother tried to make with her again and again? Think before you act? Look before you leap? "We are going to hurt a lot of people, Knox."

"I see that now."

She had canceled her morning clients but her afternoon was full. She didn't have time to dwell on the monumental mistake she had made by going through with the bet. Her mom was the sweetest, kindest soul she had ever met. Genevieve would never want to do anything to deliberately hurt her.

"I am a horrible person," she said aloud even though the self-recriminating comment was really meant for her own ears.

Her husband reached over and squeezed her hand, and somehow, the strength and warmth of his fingers on hers, however brief, gave her temporary relief.

"You're not a horrible person," Knox said.

"Yes, I am," she said firmly. "And so are you."

She could feel Knox examining her profile before he turned to stare out the windshield, seemingly in thought. Finally, he said, hesitantly, "We can call this whole thing off now."

She breathed in and let it out. "Trust me, I've thought of that already. We go to all of our family and say, hey, it was all a big joke."

"And?"

"I don't think we can, Knox. Not now. Max knows the marriage is real—he's seen the certificate. If we tell them it was all just a hoax, we'll end up looking like the biggest jerks on the planet. Do you want that?" She asked the question but she didn't wait for him to respond. "Maybe we are the biggest jerks on the planet, but I'd rather not broadcast that to the planet. No. We've gotten our families involved and my mom is so excited to plan the reception. I think our only course of action is to plow forward. I think that we just have to keep going."

She looked at her husband who didn't seem to have anything to say in the moment. "People get divorced all the time, after all. We'll just be another statistic. No one has to know how this started. No one has to know that this was never real."

* * *

After he dropped Genevieve off at her truck, Knox returned to the Ambling A. Before they'd left the Lawrence homestead, Genevieve had gone up to her garage apartment and packed a few suitcases full of clothes and necessities. Knox carried the suitcases inside his cabin, realizing that this was the first time he'd ever moved a woman in with him. He'd never had any desire to live with the women he'd dated previously. Now, though, he was moving Genevieve into his life and he hardly knew her.

After he dropped off the suitcases in the living room, he went to work. In his mind, work was the only thing that was going to get his mind off his marriage. But that proved to be a false notion because by the time he got back to the ranch, the news of his elopement had spread like a fire on a windy day. Everywhere he went, ranch hands congratulated him or teased him about having a "ball and chain." It seemed that no matter how hard he tried, he couldn't escape thoughts of his wife.

Genevieve returned to the Ambling A, well after dark. "Hey," she called out as she entered the cabin.

"Hey," Knox said from the kitchen. "You hungry?"

His wife looked weary and dirty from a day of work. Genevieve shut the front door behind her and leaned back against it, closing her eyes for the briefest of moments. "Starving."

She opened her eyes and smiled down at Silver, who was jumping up and barking to get her attention. She scooped him up, hugged him tightly and then kissed him on the head before putting him down.

This was the first time Knox had experienced Genevieve returning home from work and he recognized, in himself, an odd happiness at seeing her walk through the door. He'd never thought that sharing his life full-time with a woman was a particularly appealing idea, which was why he'd always kept his relationships quick, light and uncomplicated. But, so far, in the short term, he liked sharing his life with Genevieve.

"That smells good." She leaned her elbows on the counter, her eyes drooping down as if she could fall asleep standing upright.

"Why don't you take a bath? Dinner will be done by the time you get out."

Genevieve smiled at him wearily. "Where have you been all my life, Knox?"

"Texas."

She left her truck keys on the kitchen counter and walked slowly, with Silver trailing behind her, toward the bedroom. A few minutes later he heard the bathroom door shut and the water in the tub running. All his life he had imagined who his wife would be, what she would look like, how many kids they would have. Perhaps that was why he was so offended when his father had tried to marry him off like he was part of a game show. Knox wanted to find a wife on his own terms, in his own time. It was true that one day, sooner rather than later, this marriage would end. One day, Genevieve would leave Rust Creek Falls for California as they had agreed. But for now, she was his friend and his wife and he may as well enjoy her company while he had it.

"How's married life treating you?" Finn asked him on the way to the local feed store.

"Pretty good, actually," Knox was surprised to say. It hadn't taken them long to form a pattern in their marriage—a rhythm of sorts—of how to cohabitate. Knox, who had learned to cook over campfires when he was a kid, didn't mind whipping up what he liked to call "cowboy cuisine" because, as it turned out, Genevieve was barely able to boil water. His meals were stick-to-your-ribs, everything cooked in one pot kind of food, but his wife never complained. And, Genevieve didn't mind doing the dishes, which suited him just fine.

After they ate, they would go out onto the porch and sit out in the rocking chairs, drink a beer and watch the sun set. It was the time when they shared the details of their days; it was a time when the early bond they had developed as friends seemed to grow deeper. It was a time in his day that he was really beginning to look forward to—his evenings with Genevieve. It was a bonus that, regardless of the strange circumstances of their current living arrangement, their friendship was the glue that allowed them to navigate the new strange waters in which they found themselves.

Knox pulled up to the feed store and shut off the engine. "How's Viv Shuster's dating service?"

Everyone in the family knew that Finn was fickle— he fell in and out of love as a hobby, it seemed. Knox had a feeling that the more women Viv sent Finn's way, the more women he was going to want.

Finn grinned at him. "There's a lot of beautiful fish in that sea, brother. A *lot*."

"I believe the point is for you to settle on just one."

His brother matched his pace as they entered the store. "This from the man who used to make chasing women an Olympic sport."

Knox stepped up to the counter. "That's not my game anymore."

He heard the seriousness in his own voice when he said those words to Finn. The marriage wasn't real, but his commitment to it was. For now, he was officially off the market. It was strange, but the thought of dating someone else after his divorce didn't appeal to him. The only woman in his mind—the only woman he wanted to date—was his wife.

"What can I do for you?" a young man named Jace asked them from behind the counter.

"We're gonna need 1000 pounds of alfalfa seed and 500 pounds of fertilizer," Finn said.

"Can you put that on our account?" Knox asked. "The name is Crawford."

The lanky cowboy behind the counter looked up from his task. "Oh, I know who you are."

The way the guy was looking at him with narrowed eyes, and the unfriendly tone of his voice, caught Knox's attention.

"Is that right?" Knox asked.

"That's right."

"What's your problem?" Finn stepped up so he was shoulder to shoulder with him.

"I heard you married Genevieve."

Genevieve had mentioned to him that her father had set her up on dates with just about every cowboy in a fifty-mile radius. It stood to reason that he was going to run into a couple of them now and again.

"That's right," he said, his tone was steady, his face unsmiling. He didn't know where this was heading.

"I've known Genevieve since we were kids," Jace told him.

"You don't say."

"I do say," Jace snapped back at him. "There were

a lot of guys around these parts who wanted to marry Genevieve."

It stood to reason that Jace was one of the "guys" that had wanted a shot at lassoing the elusive Genevieve Lawrence.

"It don't make no sense that Gen would go for a foreigner."

Finn laughed. "We're from Texas. You know that, right?"

"Like I said." Jace scowled at them. "Foreigners."

"Jace," the owner of the Sawmill Feed and Seed interrupted the conversation. "Go on to the back and help Ben with the shipment."

With one last scowl in his direction, Jace tossed his pen on the counter and headed to the back of the shop.

"Sorry about that," the owner, a heavyset man wearing tan overalls, said. "The young men around here can get mighty passionate about our womenfolk."

"No worries," Knox said with a quick shake of his head, his expression neutral. "I'd be upset if I lost out on a woman like Genevieve."

"Truer words have never been spoken, sir. Our Gen is the cream of the crop."

Knox didn't know why he felt compelled to do it, but he lifted up his left hand so the owner could see his wedding ring. "I suppose she's my Gen now."

"I suppose she is," the owner agreed. "I'll put this seed and fertilizer on your tab."

"Thank you." Knox tipped his hat to the man. "You have yourself a nice day."

"My friends are *still* blowing up my phone." Genevieve was sitting in the rocking chair next to him,

Silver sitting in her lap and a half-drunk beer dangling in her fingertips. One leg was draped over the arm of the rocking chair, her cute bare toes within reaching distance of his hand.

Genevieve had decided the best way to announce their elopement to friends and extended family was en masse on social media. She had posted all of their wedding photos on her Instagram account and let the viral nature of social media do the rest of the work for them.

"Mine too." Knox had expected some interest in their elopement, but he couldn't go into town without someone stopping him to congratulate him or question him about his marriage to Genevieve. In the faces of some of the cowboys who approached him, he noted some downright jealousy that he, a Texas outsider, had managed to lasso the elusive Genevieve Lawrence.

"There are some pretty ticked-off people out there," Knox said before he took a swig of his own beer.

Genevieve sat upright, shifting a chubby, floppy Silver in her lap. "Tell me about it! I've gotten some pretty nasty looks out there. And the comments on my business Facebook page from anonymous women? Someone actually called me a gold digger. A *gold digger*! There are people I've known all my life who have actually convinced themselves that I must be pregnant. Pregnant! As if I would automatically race into a marriage just because I was pregnant. I mean what century are we living in?"

"I know," Knox agreed. "This whole thing has metastasized in a very strange direction."

"That's the truth. I didn't see any of this coming." She gave a little shake of her head. Their elopement had sent a shock wave through Rust Creek Falls. Genevieve nodded toward the wilderness that was their view. "Thank goodness for this."

Genevieve had shared with him that the only place she felt completely insulated from some of the negative reactions to their elopement was his cabin. It had become a sanctuary of sorts. There was no judgment—there was no suspicion or jealousy. It was just the three of them, the woods, cowboy chow and a rocking chair. It had made him feel good that she had called the cabin her little slice of heaven on Earth. He had noticed that Genevieve had begun to end her days a little earlier than was her norm just to get home in time to share a dinner with him. When they got divorced, Knox wondered if she would miss these moments with him. He had a feeling that he was going to miss it—perhaps even more than he even knew.

"I sure as heck hope that Viv can get one of your other brothers tied down soon so the spotlight can get off us," Genevieve said.

"Amen, Gen." Knox lifted up his bottle. "I'll drink to that."

"What are you doing?" Hunter's daughter, Wren, asked her.

Genevieve was standing on a step stool in the barn with an electric drill in her hand. "I'm getting these hooks into place so I can hang up my hammock."

"Why?"

She finished drilling the hole and turned slightly toward the little girl. "Do me a favor, will you? Hand me that silver hook right there by your foot."

Wren bent down and picked up the hook and held it out to her. "This one?"

Genevieve nodded. She slipped her drill into the tool belt on her waist and took the hook from Wren. "Thank you."

"Why are you putting a hammock up in the barn?" the young girl asked again.

"Because I can, for one." She leaned her body forward and twisted the hook into place. "And because I like to hang out with the horses and listen to them chew hay."

Once the hook was fully seated in the hole she had drilled, Genevieve climbed down off the step stool and grabbed one end of the hammock lying on the ground. She hooked one side to the hook she'd just drilled into the barn wall and then hooked the other side onto a hook on the opposite wall.

"This is perfect," she said, pleased. She now had a hammock that spanned the aisle of the barn. The Ambling A was her temporary home, she knew that even if the rest of the family didn't, and the only place that felt comfortable was the cabin. Genevieve wanted to change that. The only other place that made her happy on the Ambling A was the barn; when she wasn't at the cabin with Knox, she could spend some of her free time hanging out in the barn, relaxing in her hammock, listening to sound of the horses chewing their hay. That way, she would have two places on the Ambling A to call her own.

Wren watched her curiously as she leaned her hands on the hammock, testing to make sure that the hooks would hold.

"Seems stable enough." She removed her tool belt and put it off to the side.

With a happy smile on her face, Genevieve carefully sat down into the hammock, letting it slowly take her weight. When the whole thing didn't come crashing down, she leaned back, pushed her feet on the ground and then lifted her legs so the hammock would rock her back and forth.

"Oh, yes." She sighed. "This is the life right here."

"Can I get on?" Wren asked.

Genevieve sat up and stopped the hammock from rocking. "Sure."

Wren climbed onto the hammock and mirrored Genevieve's position. They both leaned back, legs dangling off the side of the hammock, their hands folded onto their stomachs. The hammock rocked gently back and forth and the only sound, other than the horses chewing their fresh pats of hay, was the creaking sound of the fabric rubbing against the metal hooks.

Genevieve sighed again, her eyes closed. She had always wanted to put a hammock up in a barn and this was her first real chance to do it.

"This is everything I ever thought it would be," she said to Wren. "What do you think?"

"I like it," her young companion said. "It's fun."

"It is fun."

The two of them swung together in silence, relaxing in the hammock and enjoying the company of the horses. Of course, all good things must come to an end and for Genevieve, that end came when Wren said, "My grandpa is coming."

Genevieve's eyes popped open and her head popped up; she saw Maximilian appear in the aisleway and the sight of him made her frown. She had made it her personal challenge to avoid her father-in-law and she had been pretty successful. As it always did when she saw Max, her stomach tightened like it was cramping and a rush of discomfort traveled through her body. He made her feel nauseated and nobody liked to feel that way.

"Do you like the hammock, Grandpa?" Wren asked Maximilian.

"No." There was that disapproving scowl Genevieve was accustomed to seeing. "I don't."

Her happy moment rudely interrupted by Knox's father, Genevieve helped Wren out of the hammock and then stood up as well.

"I'd like a moment of your time, young lady," Maximilian said to her as she took down the hammock.

The patriarch used the same tone as every school principal that had ever called her into their office, and every fiber of her being rebelled against that kind of tone.

"What can I do for you?" She stood with her hands on her hips, her eyes meeting his.

"Follow me."

Genevieve had to work to keep up the long-legged stride of her father-in-law as she followed him down the long aisleway. Max marched out of the barn to a nearby round pen where his newly acquired prized stallion was standing next to his trainer.

"Move him around a little, John," Max said to the trainer in a booming voice. "I want Miss Lawrence to see this."

No, the marriage wasn't actually *real*, but Max didn't know that. The fact that he insisted on referring to her as *Miss Lawrence* irked her but she kept her mouth shut about it. Her focus was on the stallion. She had been waiting—anticipating—the moment when Max tried to pin something on her with the horses. She knew that he doubted her ability as a farrier. Was this the moment she had been preparing for all along? Was this the moment he tried to blame her for an injury to one of his horses?

The trainer asked the stallion to move to the outside track of the round pen. The stallion, a tricolored tan, white-and-black paint with a black-and-white tail and blue eyes, was a magnificent horse—young and full of thick muscle and energy. But even though he had vet-checked sound, when he arrived at the Ambling A, he was lame. At the trot, the stallion was still exhibiting some telltale head bobbing that indicated that he still had some lameness problems.

"Just look at that," Maximilian said sternly. "John tells me you're responsible for this."

Genevieve bristled. "He was lame when he came off the trailer."

"I'm aware of that," her father-in-law was quick to retort.

"I didn't make him lame."

When Maximilian looked at her this time, Genevieve felt that he was seeing her for the first time. "I'm well aware of that, young lady."

"Then I'm afraid I'm missing your point."

Her father-in-law nodded toward the stallion. "He's better. He's not perfect, but he's better. How did you manage to do that?"

Genevieve wasn't often surprised, but this time she was caught completely off guard. She had been expecting, preparing for, an accusation. Not a compliment.

"His shoes were too tight, so I pulled them. He had

an infection in all four hooves and I've almost got that cleared up. If we keep on going in this direction, I think we can get him sound and keep him barefoot."

"You really think that you can get him sound?" Max asked her pointedly.

"Yes, sir. I do. It'll take time, but I've gotten a lot worse back to sound with some time, patience and some holistic approaches."

"Such as?"

"Acupuncture, for one."

"That's enough for now, John." Maximilian waved his hand to the trainer. Then he turned his attention back to her. "I've got a lot of money tied up in that horse. Can you get him sound or not?"

"I can get him back to sound," she told him.

"Then do whatever you need to do to get that done," Max said without an equivocation, and for the first time, she saw respect for her in his eyes. The man said his piece and then walked away without waiting for her response. A few feet away, he stopped and turned back to her.

"I expect you'll be at the family dinner tonight?"

Wren was listening, so Genevieve tempered her response. "I didn't get an invitation."

"Young lady, you don't need an invitation. You're family." Max looked her dead in the eye. "I'll expect you tonight. Come along, Wren."

Wren gave her a little wave before she trotted after her grandfather.

Genevieve was still rooted in her spot, a bit stunned by the interaction with her father-in-law. She was still standing there mulling over the interaction when Knox cantered up on Big Blue. The cowboy swung out of the saddle, ground tied his gelding and came to her side.

"What was that all about?" Her husband smelled of horse, and leather and sweat and she liked it.

"That was bizarre," she said. "Your father... He's given me carte blanche to do what I think is best to get the stallion sound."

Knox stared after his father, seeming as caught off guard as she felt.

"And he says he expects to see me at dinner tonight."

Knox adjusted his cowboy hat on his head. "Crap." They had both been happy to spend their dinners alone at the cabin in the woods—away from the spotlight— where they could be themselves and not pretend to be a crazy-in-love newlywed couple.

"My sentiments exactly," she agreed.

Chapter Nine

"How do I look?"

How did she look? Like a petite, blonde goddess.

"Beautiful." Knox and Silver had been waiting on the couch for Genevieve to emerge from the bedroom. Max liked to have family dinner served at 6:00 p.m. on the nose, so they both rushed to finish their work in order to get home, get cleaned up and get to the main house for dinner.

Genevieve looked down at her simple aqua-blue sundress with spaghetti straps. The skirt fell just above the knees, clinging to her shapely thighs which were muscular from years of horseback riding. "Are you sure? I can change."

"No." He loved how the aqua-blue fabric matched the intense blue of her wide-set eyes. "It's nearly perfect."

Her wispy long blond hair floating over her shoulders, his wife put her hands on her narrow hips with a curious frown. "*Nearly* perfect?"

Knox smiled. In a short amount of time he had managed to figure out how to push several of Genevieve's buttons. "It's a little plain."

"Thanks a lot, Knox." Genevieve spun around and headed back to the bedroom. "Now I *do* have to change."

He jogged forward, grabbed her hand and stopped her. "Hold up, cowgirl!"

"Don't try to fix it now, Knox. You tell a woman her dress is plain and you may as well tell her that she's wearing a *rag*."

He didn't let go of her hand, coaxing her to face him. The honeysuckle scent of her hair enveloped his senses and he wanted to pull her close, bury his face in her neck and breathe her in. What would she do, how would she react, if he acted on his impulses to hold her, to kiss her, to make love to her? Would she push him away or pull him close?

"I was just trying to set the mood."

"Oh, you set the mood perfectly, Knox. I was in a good mood and now I'm not."

"I was trying to set the mood so I could give you this." He pulled a small box out of his pocket and held it out for her to see.

Genevieve stared at the box for a moment before she looked up at him. "What's that?"

"Something for you."

When she didn't take the box from him, he took her hand and placed it in her palm. "It won't bite you, Gen."

"Why did you get me a present?" she asked, not moving to open the box.

His eyebrows lifted. Did his wife have to stray from

the norm on absolutely everything? Why couldn't she just be a typical woman for once and be happy with a gift?

"Are you going to open it?"

"Fine." She tugged the ribbon loose from the box. "But I don't understand why you would get a present for me."

Knox smiled at her; he truly liked his wife. He truly did. Gen handed him the ribbon as she carefully unwrapped the giftwrap. He would have expected her to rip the paper off but she was taking her time, slowly peeling off the tape a little at a time.

"If I had known you were going to take this long, I would have just put it in a gift bag."

"Hush up," she snapped, but there was playfulness in her tone that kept him right on smiling.

Finally, she handed him the paper and opened the box. Knox watched her face carefully; he wanted to remember the expression on her sweet, pretty face once she realized what was inside the box.

"Where did you get this?" She looked up at him with such surprise that he knew he had chosen well.

"I had it made for you."

Gen was speechless as she took the custom white gold necklace out of the box. On the chain was a cluster of three farrier tool charms made of gold—a file, nippers and a horseshoe hammer. His wife held the charms in the palm of her hand, the necklace dangling down from her fingers.

"Do you like it?"

Gen slowly touched each charm. "I've never seen anything like it."

"It's one of a kind," Knox said, pleased to see how

much she liked his gift. He hesitated before he added, "Just like you."

He helped her put the necklace on. He stood behind her, enjoying the warmth of her body so close to his, lifted the necklace over her head, and then joined the clasp. Gen went into the bathroom to look at her reflection in the mirror. When she returned, her eyes were shiny with emotion.

"Thank you, Knox. I love it." She stood in front of him. "But you didn't need to do this for me."

Knox reached out and turned one of the charms so it was lying flush on her smooth, tanned skin. "I wanted you to always remember how we met."

They stared at each other for several long seconds. There was a sincerity, and honesty, in Genevieve's eyes when she said, "I'll never forget how we met, Knox. Not ever."

There was that urge again—to take her in his arms and kiss her breathless. Instead, he crossed his arms in front of his chest and smiled at her. With a nod toward the necklace, he said, "Well, since you don't need a reminder, I suppose I *could* just send that necklace back?"

His wife laughed, a sound he had become accustomed to quickly, and her hand naturally moved back to the charms. "Just try it, cowboy, and you'll draw back a nub!"

"How's married life?" Sarah asked her after the family had moved from the dining room to the outside patio after dinner.

Genevieve couldn't stop playing with the charms on her new necklace. Each tool had a round, brilliant diamond embedded in the gold. It was such a thoughtful gift that it made her wonder if Knox was beginning to have feelings for her that went deeper than friendship. Was her husband beginning to fall for her?

How would she feel if he did?

"I'm enjoying it," she answered honestly. She had enjoyed being married to Knox so far. Yes, it had been a bit strange to move into his cabin, but she had adjusted more quickly than she would have thought. Every night, they both climbed into bed, exhausted from their long day of work, and with Silver curled up between them, Genevieve was lulled to sleep by the comforting sound of Knox's breathing. She had never *slept* with any man—Knox was her first. She had never lived with any of her previous boyfriends and she didn't do overnights. If she had known how wonderful it would be to have a man's presence, a man's heat, a man's scent in bed with her, perhaps she would have signed up for overnights years ago.

"You look really happy," Lily said from a nearby chair.

Genevieve smiled wordlessly. Xander's wife wasn't the first to mention that. She looked at her husband who was on the other side of the patio deep in conversation with Hunter and Logan and felt an odd rush of emotion. Knox was so handsome—he stood so straight and tall. She loved the way his shoulders filled out his customary button-down shirts and the way his jeans hugged his thick thighs. In truth, Knox Crawford had always set her heart to fluttering but she had been careful to guard her heart from him. But it was getting harder and harder to keep her defenses up. She knew herself well enough to know that, in spite of her best efforts, her feelings for Knox were beginning to grow and take on a life of their own.

The adorable baby was a great distraction and Genevieve smiled at Sophia, making the little girl laugh and gurgle. Genevieve reached out so Sophia could wrap a chubby hand around her finger.

"You're so good with her." Sarah shifted the baby on her lap. "Any plans for children in the near future, or do you want to hold off for a while?"

Genevieve had been watching Wren playing with Silver in the grass just off the patio. She had never really wanted children. She'd just never had that motherly urge that her sisters seemed to have from the time they were little girls. While they were playing with baby dolls, she was racing the boys bareback on her pony. But sometimes, when she watched Knox with Wren, or saw him helping an elderly woman carry her groceries out to the car, Genevieve wondered what it would be like to have a child with Knox's good looks and her blue eyes. With his good heart and her daring do.

"We're not in a hurry," she told Sarah, preferring to keep her thoughts secret.

"The two of you are going to make beautiful babies together," Lily, ever the romantic, said with a dreamy smile.

As if realizing that she needed to be rescued, Wilder, the youngest Crawford brother, sauntered over to her, his longish brown hair acting as the perfect frame for his mischievous dark eyes, and grabbed her hands. "Dance with me, sis!"

Wilder was always ready for a party. He had turned on the surround sound system and was piping music onto the patio. Wanting to escape from the baby conversation, Genevieve jumped out of the chair and followed her brother-in-law to the middle of the patio. Just like Knox, Wilder knew how to dance. He led her in a small circle, dipping her, twirling her, and spinning her around so fast that she started to get dizzy. Laughing, she held on to his shoulder to keep from tipping sideways.

"Go get your own woman, Wilder." Knox showed up at their side and tapped his brother on the shoulder.

The younger brother rolled his eyes at her, spun her around a couple more times, and then let her go. Wilder held up his hands and backed away, but the grin on his face let her know that he felt good about getting Knox all riled up with jealousy. And Genevieve could see plainly on her husband's face—he *was* jealous.

"He was just playing around," she said in Wilder's defense.

"I know," Knox agreed easily. "But I still didn't like it.

Knox took her in his arms. His body swayed with hers and he pulled her close so that her breasts were pressed against him. Even though they were already married, it seemed to her that Knox was laying claim to her—letting his bachelor brothers to keep a hands-off policy where she was concerned. Genevieve wasn't usually impressed with masculine displays or gestures born out of male irrational jealousy. In fact, it was a total turn-off for her. When Knox acted jealous, it had the opposite effect on her. For Genevieve, it meant that he actually cared for her—something beyond the scope of their bet.

The night air was balmy and there wasn't much of a breeze, but it didn't stop her from pressing her body more closely to her husband. She loved the feel of his arms around her waist and the way his warm, strong hands were splayed possessively on her back. They had danced together the day of their wedding; this moment was different. There was a tension in Knox's body, in his arms, in his eyes, that made every fiber of her body crackle. His head was dipped down toward her and she had the distinct feeling that Knox was resisting the urge to kiss her with all of his family as witnesses. But, this time, it felt to her as if it wouldn't just be to give them a show. This time, it felt as if his lips were being drawn to hers.

Knox lowered his head until his lips were hovering near her ear.

"You look so beautiful tonight, Gen."

The sensual undertone in his voice, the feel of his breath on her skin, made her sway into his body. She titled her head up as he looked down at her face. She wanted her husband to kiss her—right there, right then. She was asking for it, not for the show, but because Genevieve wanted to feel his lips on her lips. And, for a moment, a split second really, she actually thought Knox was going to kiss her, but the song ended and her husband let her go. Even though Logan and Xander had joined them on the makeshift dance floor sometime during the song, Genevieve hadn't noticed. All of her attention, all of her focus, had been on being cocooned in her husband's arms. When he let her go, Genevieve wrapped her arms around her body, suddenly feeling cold when the night was so warm.

"Are you okay?" Knox asked her, his hands in his pockets.

Genevieve nodded her head silently, afraid that there would be an emotional catch in her voice if she tried to say any words. No, she wasn't okay and she had no one to blame but herself for that.

Knox had watched all evening as his beautiful wife charmed his family without much effort at all. Even his father had begun to soften toward Genevieve, which was a miracle in its own right. His brothers—even Xander— seemed convinced that Genevieve was the best thing that had happened to him. All of them had said tonight that they'd never seen him so happy. But when he looked in the mirror, he looked exactly as he had a week ago. She fit in with Lily and Sarah and this had always been important to the brothers; they had always wanted their wives to be friends. So, everything was going according to plan. They were pulling off this fake marriage without much effort at all. He should feel triumphant. And yet, he didn't. In fact, he felt like he'd made a pretty big mess of things.

The one woman he had wanted to date in Rust Creek Falls was his wife—and he had promised not to touch her. Now, all he thought about was touching her. Morning, noon, night he thought about kissing Genevieve, he thought about holding Genevieve. He was exhausted from lack of sleep—while she seemed to easily fall asleep. She seemed completely unbothered by his presence in bed next to her, while he ached from wanting her. The scent of her hair, the warmth of her body, and the fact that he had only to reach over to touch her drove him wild with wanting. It seemed he spent every night with a mantra echoing in his head. *Forbidden. Forbidden.*

He found himself thinking it too when he'd held her in his arms as they danced tonight. And again when he'd put his hand on the small of her back when he ushered her inside their cabin after the evening was over.

"That was so much fun!" Genevieve said as she opened the back door to let Silver outside. "I can't believe I dreaded that for a second."

His wife was a bit tipsy, so her body movements were broad and languid as if she were moving through Jell-O.

"I'm glad you had a good time." Knox took his hat off and hung it on the rack just inside of the front door.

Silver came bolting back inside, his tail wagging and his fat paws slapping on the wooden floor. Laughing, Genevieve scooped up the growing puppy, hugged him tightly and kissed him on the head. Silver licked Gen on the face and lips.

"How is it that my dog gets more action around here than I do?" Those words sounded more bitter than he had intended. He had intended to make a joke but it didn't exactly come out that way.

His wife set Silver down, walked directly over to him, took his face in her hands and planted a kiss on his lips. Genevieve pulled away and looked at him with a surprised look as if she were shocked at her own behavior.

"Don't be such a grouch, Knox." She spun away from him and headed to the bedroom.

Knox followed her into the bedroom and found her lying flat on her back, her legs dangling off the side of the bed.

"Is the room spinning?" Genevieve pressed her hands over her eyes to block out the light.

"No." Knox tugged her cowgirl boots off and then pulled off her socks.

"Are you sure?" Genevieve giggled and wiggled her toes.

"Yes," he said. "I'm sure." Her dress had slipped up to the tops of her thighs and a hint of her panties could be seen where her thighs met.

Everything in his body ached to touch this woman who was his bride. Every night he had spent lying next to her, enveloped in the scent of her hair, her beautiful body not even an arm's length away, had been torture for him. How could he avoid being aroused when Genevieve was in his bed?

Knox grit his teeth as he pulled down the hem of her dress before he turned to walk away, but Genevieve reached out and grabbed his hand to stop him.

"Hey. Where are you going?"

"You need to get undressed so you can go to bed."

"You're such a killjoy." His wife pouted at him in a more playful way than he had seen from her before. "Really and truly you are."

"Get some sleep, Gen."

Knox forced himself to walk to the door and leave his wife. She was throwing off some pretty flirty vibes but she was also a few bottles of beer past her limit. As much as he wanted to stay and take her up on this sexy invitation, it wouldn't be right. Of course, he had thought about making love to Genevieve. She was his wife and she was nearly naked beside him in his bed every night. But, that wasn't the deal. He had promised to keep his hands off and he'd been a man of his word, a man of honor, on that front. But, it had been damn difficult. *Damn* difficult.

"Hey!" she said, catching his attention and getting

him to turn around. "Do you think that I have boy hips?"

Knox turned around to find that his wife had stripped off her sundress and was standing on the bed in pretty white lacy panties and a matching strapless bra. With her strong curvy thighs, flat stomach and pert breasts, she was his youthful fantasy come to life. If he could have designed his perfect woman, he would have created Genevieve.

"No." He heard the growl in his own voice. The growl of a man who wanted more than just to look at his wife—the growl of a man whose body was already growing and hardening just at the sight of Genevieve's nearly naked body. "You don't have boy hips."

She had the hips of a woman—the type of hips a man could hold on to when he was deep inside of her.

Gen ran her hands over her stomach and hips. "I've heard that complaint before, you know."

Knox took a step forward and then forced himself to stop in his tracks. He wouldn't break their agreement. Not like this—not when her mind was fuzzy from alcohol.

"They were idiots," he told her. He couldn't seem to take his eyes off her nipples pressing against the thin, silky material of her bra. The desire—the need—to take those nipples into his mouth made Knox clench his teeth until it actually hurt.

She beamed at him and put her hands on her hips. "They *were* idiots."

Genevieve looked down at her own body, lost her balance and fell backwards onto the pillows with a laugh. She was still giggling when Knox came over, tugged on the comforter so she could get under the

covers. Once he had his sexy wife tucked safely beneath the covers, he brushed her hair back away from
her forehead.

"You're the most beautiful woman I've ever seen,
Gen." Knox kissed her on the forehead. "Now go to
sleep."

"Hey!" She reached out for his hand but missed.
"Aren't you going to sleep in here with me tonight?"

Knox didn't trust himself to turn around when he
shut off the light and closed the door firmly behind him.
Without thought, Knox crossed the hall to the bathroom, turned on the cold water. This wasn't the first
cold shower he had taken with Genevieve in the cabin
and he knew it wouldn't be his last. With the icy water
pelting his skin like tiny needles, Knox hit the shower
wall in frustration.

Never in his life had he deprived himself of a woman's company—he'd never had to. If he wanted a woman,
she had always wanted him in return. If he wanted a
woman, he took her to bed. This hands-off policy with
Genevieve was making him feel a little bit nuts. He
wanted her—and maybe, just maybe, she wanted him.
But, this time, for him at least, it was more than just the
physical. He wanted to make love to her. He wanted to
show her, with his lips, with his hands, with his body,
what he was beginning to feel for her inside of his heart.
Knox stepped out of the shower and stared at his reflection in the mirror. What he was starting to feel for Genevieve was different than anything he'd felt before for
another woman. There was a deep, growing affection
for his wife and he was beginning to wonder…was this
what falling in love really felt like?

* * *

Genevieve awakened the next morning with a bad taste in her mouth and a roaring headache. She sat up, rubbed her hands over her face, yawned loudly and then flopped back onto the pillows. It was then that she noticed she was in her bra and panties and Knox's side of the bed hadn't been slept in. Even Silver was nowhere to be found.

"Silver!" she called out, only to realize that the sound of her own voice was making her head pound.

Silver came tearing around the corner, bounded onto the bed and then jumped into her lap, licking her face happily. Genevieve wrapped her arms around the puppy and kissed him on his head and face.

"Good morning, you stinky little puppy face."

Silver rolled over onto his back so she could pet his belly. She was in the middle of a very important belly rub when Knox appeared in the doorway of the bedroom holding a steaming cup of coffee in his hands.

"Mornin'." Knox looked crisp and clean and ready for his day of work. Not to mention handsome.

"Hi." Suddenly self-conscious of her lack of attire, she pulled the covers up and tucked them under her arms. She remembered every detail of the night before. Her inhibitions had been lowered and she had flirted shamelessly with her husband. And she had enjoyed it, every second. But for her trouble, it looked as if she had completely scared him away.

"Headache?" He handed her the coffee.

She nodded as she blew on the coffee. After taking a sip, she sighed. "Thank you."

"I've got to get on the road." Her husband seemed

to be avoiding her eyes. She clutched the covers tighter to her body, wishing she had managed to at least put on a T-shirt before passing out. "I'll see you tonight."

"Knox?" She wanted to ask him why he had slept on the couch the night before. She wanted to apologize for shamelessly kissing him and stripping off her dress in front of him.

He turned back toward her.

"Never mind," she said. All the words she wanted to say, all the questions she wanted to ask, got jammed up in her throat. She didn't want to sound desperate.

Knox waved his hand without meeting her eyes and headed out the door. She wasn't imagining it—something had changed between them. Knox usually lingered with her in the morning and shared a meal. Today, it seemed as if he couldn't get away from her fast enough. Genevieve slumped down onto the mattress, turned onto her side and grabbed Silver for a cuddle. She had come on to her husband and he was sprinting away from her.

"Great," she muttered. "Just great."

Then she remembered that they had both agreed to a platonic relationship. Knox had been the one to hold up his end of the bargain. What had she been doing going around kissing him and stripping in front of him? And why did it hurt her so much to awaken to an empty bed?

Before she could ponder those questions, the phone on the nightstand was chiming, signaling that she had several texts coming in. She stretched her arm back, grabbed her phone and looked at the messages. All of them were from her mother and sisters about the plans for the reception. Genevieve groaned and pushed her phone away. The last thing that she wanted to think about right now was the reception. How could she think about a wedding reception when she was in the midst of a very real emotional crisis?

Genevieve buried her head under her pillow with another mournful groan. "Of all the men in the world, you had to go and fall for your husband."

Chapter Ten

"Why don't you come with us to the picnic?" Hunter asked Knox as they walked toward the barn.

"I'm not much of a picnic kind of guy, brother."

"Neither am I," Hunter agreed. "But just wait until you have your own little girl one day. You'll find yourself doing all kinds of things you never thought you would do, just to put a smile on her face."

"I'll have to take your word for it," Knox said noncommittally. Not surprising, his brothers had all begun to ask him about when he was going to start a family with Genevieve. None of them could know that he had agreed to a platonic marriage with his sexy wife. None of them could know how frustrating it was to answer the baby question over and over again when he knew the truth—he hadn't consummated his marriage!

"It could happen sooner than you think," Hunter mused aloud.

They rounded the corner and spotted Wren with Genevieve. Knox had noticed how frequently he found Wren tagging along after Genevieve in the barn and he didn't like it. One day soon Genevieve was going to be gone and that little girl was going to get hurt. Wren didn't deserve that. And, deep down, he knew it would be his fault.

"I don't think it's such a good idea for Wren to be getting so attached to Genevieve." Knox spoke the words he had been thinking aloud.

Hunter's surprised expression made Knox regret having giving voice to his concern.

"Why not?" his brother asked. "She's your wife. I would think she's the perfect person for Wren to attach herself to. Why would you say that?"

It took Knox a split second to figure out what he could say to backtrack. "This thing with Genevieve and me is still new. Nothing is guaranteed in this life."

Hunter, who had always been the brother that seemed to have the best advice, clapped him on the shoulder. "You guys are going to make it, Knox. Everyone in the family can see that she's in love with you. A woman can't fake that."

A woman couldn't fake that? His wife had been faking it the whole time! Was Genevieve that good of an actress or was his family just that naive and blind? Genevieve didn't love him. In fact, hadn't she been the one who said she wouldn't have even dated him if he had asked?

"Are you ready, Wren?" Hunter asked his daughter who was watching Genevieve trim one of the horse's hooves.

Wren spun around at the sound of her father's voice, ran toward him and then leaped up into his arms for a hug.

"Can Genevieve come with us?"

Knox's throat tightened uncomfortably to stop himself from saying no. His attempt to keep Wren and Genevieve apart was failing miserably.

"If she wants." Hunter kept his arms around his daughter's shoulders. "Are you up for a back-to-school picnic, Genevieve?"

"Genevieve might have more horses to trim, Wren," Knox interjected quickly.

"Nope." His wife shook her head. "This was the last for today. Besides, I haven't eaten lunch and there's always really good food at picnics."

"I'm trying to convince Knox to go with us." Hunter looked at him. "Viv Shuster is still hard at work trying to get the last three Crawford bachelors married off. I'm telling you, a woman hurled herself at me at the feed store the other day."

"I was there and *hurled* is a pretty big exaggeration of the facts," Knox interjected.

"She *hurled* herself at me. She had the first button of my shirt undone before I knew what was happening! Thank goodness Wren wasn't with me." Hunter assured Genevieve. "I need a bodyguard."

Genevieve laughed. "A single father is pretty powerful catnip."

"See?" His brother nodded his head toward Genevieve. "She gets it. How can you abandon me in my time of need, Knox? I need someone I can trust to run interference for me."

"Come on, Uncle Knox." Wren turned that sweet smile on him. "It'll be fun."

* * *

"Why did you agree to go to this picnic?" Knox asked her as he opened the passenger door to his truck for her. "I thought we were trying to keep a low profile."

"It would be weird if we were reclusive all the time, right? If we want to silence our critics—of which there are many—trust me, just look at my social media! Then we've got to put on a show every now and again. Besides," Genevieve added as she swept her hair into a ponytail at the nape of her neck, "I'm hungry."

"You didn't have to rope me into going to this picnic just to get a hot dog on a stick, Gen."

Knox's tone caught her attention. She looked at his profile, his unsmiling lips, and tried to figure out what was going on with her husband. The first week of their marriage had gone more smoothly than either of them could have expected. But the second week had been a bit rocky, starting with Knox's reaction to his father's expectation that they would attend the weekly family dinners together at the main house. It seemed that whenever she did her part of convincing their friends and family that they were a real and legitimate couple, the more irritated Knox became. Genevieve would have thought that he would be excited that they were pulling off the impossible. Instead, he was getting grumpier by the day.

"You know what, Knox?" Genevieve said, her tone sugary sweet and laced heavily with sarcasm. "Maybe this picnic will be just the thing that will help you turn that frown upside down. We'll get you a balloon and have your face painted. And if you're a really good boy, we'll get you some cotton candy!"

He just *harrumphed.*

Realizing that Knox was determined to stay in a bad mood, Genevieve ignored her husband for the rest of the short ride to Rust Creek Falls Park. When they pulled up to the already-crowded picnic, her husband still had that ridiculous scowl on his handsome face.

"Hey," she said, a hint of irritation creeping into her tone. "Put your game face on, cowboy. It's showtime."

Knox looked over at her as he unclipped his seat belt and her words must have at least resonated a bit because his features softened. He wasn't smiling but at least he didn't look like a man who was itching to pick a fight.

Genevieve met him in front of the truck and slipped her hand into his. This would be their first official town event that they attended as a couple and she was determined to give the whole town a show they wouldn't soon forget. By the time they left the picnic, the doubters and the haters would be silenced. But only if Knox cooperated!

"Lean down and kiss me," she said with a sunny smile plastered on her face.

Knox obliged but the kiss was flat and felt more like a platonic peck from a distant relative. She wanted to kick him—really kick him hard—but instead, she tossed her head back and laughed as if he had said something amazingly funny and held on to his arm like a woman who wanted to let every other female within fifty paces know that Knox was *hers*.

"Aunt Gen! Uncle Knox!" Wren raced toward them through the throng of people.

Was it her imagination or had Knox stiffened next to her when his niece had called her *aunt*?

"Hi, sweet pea." Her husband always had warmth in

his eyes and a smile on his lips for his slight, fair-haired niece. "What do you want to do first?"

"I want to get my face painted." Wren began to count on her fingers. "I want to go on the Ferris wheel, ride on the bumper cars and go in the bouncy house."

"And consume copious amounts of sugar," Hunter added as he joined them. "I can't thank you guys enough for coming. Walking through that crowd was like navigating my way through a deadly gauntlet."

Hunter lowered his voice so Wren wouldn't hear his next words. "Remember the woman from the feed store I was just telling you about? She's here selling cotton candy. I'm terrified she's going to spot me!"

"We'll protect you, Hunter." Genevieve smiled at her brother-in-law. She liked Hunter; he was a nice man and a wonderful, doting father. In fact, she was beginning to warm up to all of Knox's brothers. She had never thought about what it was going to feel like to walk away from the Crawford family once this sham marriage ended. In her heart, she knew now that it was going to hurt. When she went to California, a piece of her was going to be left behind at the Ambling A.

Holding on to Knox's arm, Genevieve could feel so many eyes on them as they wound their way through the picnic crowd toward the face-painting booth. By the time they made it there, they had been inundated with congratulations, kisses and hugs from the townsfolk. There were also some people who greeted them with sour expressions and their congratulations rang hollow; some of them were no doubt the anonymous people on social media who had accused her of being a gold digger or pregnant. Genevieve's head spinning from all of the attention and, when she finally had a chance to look up at Knox's face, she saw that he was scowling again.

"Smile." She squeezed his arm. "You look miserable."

Knox forced a smile while she waited in line with Wren to get their faces painted. Her husband's demeanor and attitude at the picnic was really starting to get under her skin. As far as she could tell, she was working overtime trying to convince everyone that their marriage was legit, while he was busy undermining all of her effort.

"What are you going to get?" Wren asked her excitedly while they waited for their turn.

"Hmm," she mused aloud. "I think I'll get a unicorn."

"Me too! I'll get a unicorn too!"

When they returned to Hunter and Knox, Genevieve and Wren had matching unicorns on the right cheeks of their faces. Hunter swept his daughter up into his arms and admired her face. "That's a mighty pretty unicorn for a mighty pretty little girl."

Wren giggled happily in her father's arms while Knox examined Genevieve in a strange way that made her neck suddenly feel hot. But before she could ask him why he was looking at her in such an odd way, schoolteachers Paige Traub and Marina Dalton, and Josselyn Strickland, the school librarian, joined their small group.

"Genevieve!" Paige hugged her tightly. "We're so happy to see you here! We've been meaning to get in touch with you to say congratulations, haven't we, Marina?"

Marina was the next to hug her. "We have! But you

know how the beginning of school year is for us. We've been so swamped."

After congratulating them on their marriage, Marina and Josselyn were quick to make a big fuss over Wren. It could be tough for a child to go to a new school, but Wren seemed to have taken a liking to her teacher and she was beginning to make some friends.

"Oh, Hunter," Josselyn said. "I've been meaning to ask you. Is it true that your family found an old diary in the floorboards at the Ambling A?"

"It's true," Hunter said. "Found it when we were refurbishing the wood floors."

"I just love Rust Creek Falls history and folklore." Josselyn's eyes lit up with the news. "I would love to see it."

"What's this about?" Genevieve hadn't heard anything about a diary.

"We found this jewel-encrusted diary in the floorboards of the main house," Knox explained. "It's got to be at least sixty or seventy years old."

"Fantastic." Josselyn clasped her hands together. "Is there a name?"

"We're assuming it was written by one of the Abernathys, the previous owners of the Ambling A. We searched on the internet for information on the family, but that was a dry well. Xander did manage to open the diary with a screwdriver and found some love letters written by someone with the initial W. Other than that, we've still got a lot of missing holes in that story."

"An unsolved mystery." Genevieve rubbed the palms of her hands together with a smile. "How can we figure this out, Josselyn?"

"Well," the librarian drawled, her brow wrinkled in

thought, "if I were the one looking, I would go straight to the *Rust Creek Falls Gazette*. The town newspaper will have a cache of historical records that can't be found on the internet."

"We'll have to try that, Josselyn." Hunter smiled his gratitude. "Thank you for the tip."

"Oh, you are so welcome. Please, please, *please* keep me in the loop. I am just dying to know more about this diary!"

After the face painting, Genevieve insisted on heading straight for the area where the food vendors were selling their wares. Three corn dogs and a large cola later, she was beginning to feel full. But she left a small amount of room for some homemade pie. What would a picnic be without a piece of pie?

"Are you sure three corn dogs were enough? Why not go for four?" Knox was sitting across from her with a genuine smile in his eyes. It was the first she had seen during their time at the picnic.

"I thought you liked a woman with a healthy appetite?" she teased him.

"I do." He leaned forward and rested his elbows on the table. "I never cottoned to women who picked at their food like chickens pecking at seed on the ground."

It was moments like these that made Genevieve glad that she had agreed to Knox's crazy scheme—when her husband, so handsome and rugged, was smiling at her in a way that made her feel like she was truly appreciated for who she was. Instinctively, she reached across the table and squeezed his hand.

"I like it when you smile at me, Knox."

This entire fake marriage had blurred so many lines that it was difficult to know when they were being real with each other and when they were just putting on a show. This time, her words weren't for anyone other than Knox and she hoped he knew that.

"Welcome, everyone, to the Back to School Picnic!"

Genevieve's attention was drawn away from her husband to Mayor Collin Traub who had just stepped behind the microphone on the main stage.

"That man dearly loves a microphone." She laughed. The Traubs and the Lawrences had been friends for years and years. In fact, she kept her horse, Spartacus, out at the Traubs' Triple T Ranch.

The mayor made several announcements, including some raffle ticket winners. Then Collin seemed to be scanning the crowd for something, or someone, and when his eyes landed on her, Genevieve realized that *she* was the someone the mayor had been looking for.

"Ladies and gentlemen, we have some newlyweds with us today!" Collin said loudly into the microphone. "Come on up here, Knox and Genevieve!"

"Damn it!" Knox cursed under his breath but loudly enough for people sitting around them at the other picnic tables to overhear. "If I have to hear one more person tell me congratulations!"

With a smile plastered on her face, Genevieve kicked her husband under the table. She stood up quickly, acutely aware of the stares they were drawing, and grabbed Knox's hand. She was relieved when he stood up, held on to her hand and led her through the crowd toward the stage. Once on stage, Knox stood stiff as petrified wood next to her with an equally stiff, unconvincing smile on his face. He looked like a hostage and she couldn't do anything about it. Instead, she kept right on smiling and waving to the crowd. She leaned her head on Knox's shoulder several times for effect and gazed up at him adoringly.

"Congratulations to Mr. and Mrs. Knox Crawford!" the mayor announced and led the crowd in loud clapping.

"Kiss her, man!" someone in the crowd called out and others followed.

Without a moment's notice, Knox hooked his arm around her, drew her into his body, bent her back over his arm and kissed her like he'd never kissed her before. The kiss was deep, and long, and as his tongue danced across hers, the sound of catcalls from the crowd faded into the background and the only sound she could hear was the sound of her own beating heart.

Genevieve wasn't speaking to him and he couldn't muster the strength to care. Soon after being forced up on stage in front of the entire town, Knox insisted that they leave the picnic. All the way home, his wife was giving him the silent treatment and it was for the best. Yes, this whole scheme had been his idea, but now he was convinced it was the worst idea he'd ever had in his life. And for that, he had no one else to blame other than himself. This was *his* fault.

When they got home, Knox couldn't help it. His eyes touched on every pile of paper, every shoe left near the door, everything that was out of place, because he had brought Genevieve into his home. "Why do you have to leave your bra on the couch, Gen?"

"Really?" Genevieve looked at him like she was looking at a misbehaving toddler in a grocery store. "That's your big problem? Your sensibilities are offended by my bra on your couch?"

"No." He took off his cowboy hat and slammed it down on the kitchen counter. "My sensibilities are offended when you walk around here without your bra on!"

Genevieve stared at him for a second and then laughed. "I live here, Knox. Every now and then you're going to accidentally see me crossing the hall to the bathroom in, *God forbid*, my underwear."

He leaned back against the counter, his eyes stormy, his arms crossed in front of his body. "You prance around here in your underwear and your tank top and what, I'm not supposed to notice?"

Genevieve rolled her eyes. "Get over it! I'm not going to wear a muumuu to go to the bathroom. Besides," she said, waving her hands at his chest, "you walk around here without your shirt on all the time. You don't see me having a cow about it, do you?"

"That's not the same thing," Knox said, rubbing his neck which was sore from restless nights spent out on the couch.

"So says you," she retorted.

There was a moment of silence between them and then Knox said quietly, seriously, "This isn't working for me anymore."

He hated to see the flash of hurt and confusion that he saw on Genevieve's pretty face. "If that's how you feel, then let's get an annulment."

That very thought had crossed his mind but when the words came out of Genevieve's mouth Knox knew it wasn't what he really wanted. He didn't want an annulment; he wanted more of his wife, not less.

"I don't want an annulment," he said, honestly.

"Then *what* do you want, Knox? Are you so much like

your father that you can't be happy when you actually get what you want? The whole town thinks we're really and truly married!" And then she added, "No thanks to you."

Knox pushed his hands into his jeans pockets to keep from hauling Genevieve into his arms. What would she say when he told her the truth? What would she do when she found out that he couldn't go on wanting her, needing her, dreaming of making love to her? He was completely eaten up with desire for his wife—a woman he had promised not to touch. Knox knew, one way or another, something had to change between them.

"Tell me, Knox." Genevieve walked over to stand in front of him. "What do you want?"

Knox's eyes focused on the softness of Gen's lips and the honeysuckle scent of her wispy blond hair. He didn't have any words for her; he could only show her.

He pulled her into his arms and kissed her. Not a kiss for show—this was a kiss that was all about them. His arms tightened around her slender body as he deepened the kiss, encouraged by the fact that his wife had melted in his arms. Knox kissed a trail from his lips to her neck.

"I want you," he whispered harshly. "I want *this*."

"I want you too, Knox."

Surprise mixed with relief registered on his handsome face. "Are you sure, Gen?"

She locked gazes with him so he could see how serious she was. "I'm sure." She slowly unbuttoned one button on his shirt. "Now…in keeping with our tradition, I dare you to take me, Knox."

"You dare me?" A playful glint flashed in his dark eyes.

"I dare you."

"Be careful who you're daring, Gen," Knox echoed

her own words that seemed so far in their past. "You'll be my wife in every way a woman can be a wife before the sun goes down."

Genevieve unbuttoned a second button. "That doesn't scare me, Knox. Does it scare you?"

"Nothing scares me, Mrs. Crawford." Knox swung her up into his arms as he had on their wedding day and carried her across the threshold of his bedroom. "You should know that by now."

Knox carried his bride into the bedroom and kicked the door shut behind them. She was light in his arms; the sweet smell of his hair intoxicating to his senses, and the curve of her breast pressed into his body, were tantalizing reminders of all good things to come. Genevieve dropped little, butterfly kisses on his neck as he lowered her down to the mattress. He loved the feel of her lips on his skin and could only imagine what it would feel like to have her kiss him in other, more private parts of his body.

His wife smiled up at him welcomingly, letting him know that this moment was what they both wanted. Knox shut the blinds, darkening the room, before he quickly unbuttoned and shrugged out of his shirt. Genevieve knelt on the edge of the bed, hooked her finger into his bell loop, and pulled him toward her.

"I think this moment was inevitable." She unsnapped his pants.

He knew that he was looking at her like a hungry lion looks at its prey as her hand lingered at his groin.

"Don't you?" she asked, her fingers sliding the zipper down.

Genevieve slipped her hand inside of his underwear

and wrapped her fingers around him. Knox closed his eyes, his head tilted back, and groaned at the feel of his wife's cool fingers touching his hot skin. This moment, played out so many times in his head, was so much better than his imagination had conjured.

Knox opened his eyes and looked down at his wife's lovely face; there was an impish, teasing expression in her cornflower blue eyes. He quickly disrobed. He wanted her to see all of him, to touch all of him.

The expression on her face told him all he wanted to know—she wasn't disappointed. His wife ran her hands over his chest, down his stomach and back to his hard shaft.

"Hmm," she said with a sexy smile in her voice. "You are handsome, cowboy."

Unable to wait a moment longer to see her naked, Knox lifted Genevieve so she was standing on the bed in front of him. He rid her of her shirt and her bra, a routine he had perfected over the years. But, this time it was different. This time it was his lovely Genevieve.

Those nipples, so taut and rosy, were too tempting to ignore. Knox took one into his mouth, suckled it lightly, while his large hand covered the other breast, massaging it gently. He was rewarded with a sensual gasp as Genevieve raked her fingers through his hair.

"My beautiful wife," Knox murmured against her body.

Her fingers still buried in his hair, Knox quickly unzipped her jeans and pushed them down over her hips. He couldn't wait to slip his hand inside of her simple white cotton panties to cup her. Genevieve arched her back and pressed herself down into his hand begging him to slide his fingers into her slick, tight warmth.

"Don't wait." Genevieve's fingernails were digging into his shoulders as she held on to him. "Please, don't wait."

It was clear that she wanted him to be inside of her as much as he did. Knox stripped her jeans and panties from her body and tossed them on the floor. Genevieve was waiting for him, her hair spread out on the pillows, her arms open to welcome him. Knox grabbed a condom from the nightstand, rolled it on, and then rolled into her arms.

"Yes, my beauty," Knox said, watching the expression of pure pleasure on her face as he joined their bodies together.

Knox buried his face into her neck and he buried himself more deeply into her body. Theirs was a rhythm of two like-minded souls—two pieces from the same puzzle—working in natural harmony. They didn't need to "figure each other out." They just knew how to move together.

Genevieve clung to him, her fingers flexing on his biceps, her breathing shallow and quick. He could feel her tightening around him and it made him thrust deeper and harder. He wanted her to come apart in his arms.

"Oh, Knox." Gen lifted her hips to meet him.

"Yes, baby." He kissed her lips. "Come for me."

One hard thrust and he broke the dam; Genevieve cried out as she bucked up against him, demanding more—taking more. She was slicker now and so hot that Knox couldn't wait another minute. Bracing his arms on either side of her body, Knox drove into her one last time and exploded. Shocked by his own body's reaction to this woman, Knox lowered himself down and wrapped Genevieve tightly in his arms. He kissed her lips, her cheeks, and her forehead, wanting to savor the aftermath in a way he'd never desired before. Knox had taken countless women to bed, but he was certain that this was the first time he'd ever made love

Chapter Eleven

Genevieve awakened after dark. She blinked her eyes and yawned, taking a minute to realize that she had become the middle of the sandwich—she was spooning Silver and Knox was spooning her. By the sound of her husband's breathing, he was still asleep after they had made love for the third time. Not wanting to awaken them, Genevieve tried to readjust her body ever so slightly so the moment wouldn't end. Usually the first time making love was a bit awkward for her—not with Knox. Making love with Knox had been like coming home; he seemed to know her body in a way that didn't make sense. The way he held her, the way her touched her, the way he kissed her—it was everything she had always wanted and thought impossible to have. When he made love to her, with such gentle intensity, Knox gave her everything she had ever needed. And then he gave it to her again and again.

Genevieve closed her eyes and reveled in the feeling of her husband's warm skin and his hard chest muscles pressed against her back. She reveled in the feel of his arms holding on to her so tightly and the feel of his breath on the back of her neck. There was part of her that wanted to dwell on the negative side—the impending, inevitable divorce—yet the part of her that wanted to bask in the afterglow of their lovemaking won out when Knox tightened his arm around her body and kissed the nape of her neck.

"Are you awake?" he asked groggily.

"Yes."

Knox's large hand moved down to her bare stomach and pulled her back into his body. "Any regrets?"

"No." There were no regrets. Maybe one day there would be, but for now, she was happy they had consummated their marriage.

"Good," her husband murmured behind her.

Genevieve threaded her fingers with his and kissed his hand. "Well, maybe one regret."

She felt Knox lift his head up off the pillow and it made her smile as she continued. "I do regret that we missed dinner."

Her husband dropped his head back onto the pillow with a groan. "I've never known another woman to be so driven by her stomach."

She spun around in his arms so she was lying on her back. Silver sprang upright, barked and then used both of their bodies as a springboard to jump off the bed.

"Feed us," Genevieve demanded playfully.

Knox yawned again and rubbed his hand over his face and eyes. "Fine. I'm getting up."

Like two teenagers left alone in their parents' house,

Genevieve and Knox raided the refrigerator. Genevieve pulled on a T-shirt and her underwear while Knox opted to wear only his boxer briefs. They gathered their snacks and headed for the couch. After Silver gobbled up the food in his bowl, he jumped up onto the couch, and sat down on a bag of chips.

"Silver!" Genevieve scolded him. "You have no manners!"

Knox pulled the bag of chips out from underneath the puppy.

"I'm serious, Knox. Your puppy needs some training."

"*Our* puppy," he corrected, dipping a chip into the salsa. "Don't try to shirk your responsibility to the family."

"Fine. *Our* puppy needs to be trained. We can't just keep on carrying him around. He needs to learn to walk on a leash, heel and sit."

"He's sitting now," Knox said before he popped the chip into his mouth. "Aren't you, boy?"

Silver wagged his tail at Knox happily, looking between the both of them, hoping that someone would take mercy on him and pass a treat his way.

"I'm going to enroll him in a puppy class." Genevieve took a swig of her beer. She couldn't imagine a better post-lovemaking snack than chips, salsa and a cold bottle of beer.

"I will leave the education of our puppy to you." Her husband raised his bottle up to her.

"Talk about shirking your duties." She smiled at him.

They finished eating their snack and then headed back to the bedroom. It was unspoken, but they both wanted to get back into each other's arms. It felt as if they were truly newlyweds on their honeymoon—they couldn't get enough of each other. Genevieve stripped out of her scant clothing and slipped under the covers into Knox's awaiting arms. She curled her body into his, draping her leg over his thickly muscled thigh. Her hand on his chest, Genevieve sighed happily. Knox rested his chin on the top of her head, his free hand petting her hair.

"An annulment is off the table now." She felt his voice as much as she heard it in the dark.

Genevieve tried not to stiffen her body when his words registered. She felt his words like a cut on her skin. Why would he bring up the end of their relationship at a moment like this? She pushed away from him and turned over.

"Hey, what's wrong?" Knox tried to bring her back into his arms.

She didn't answer him. If she needed to explain it to him, then he wasn't as smart as she had originally given him credit for. She heard him sigh.

"That was a stupid thing to say," he acknowledged.

She didn't respond because she was fighting to keep tears at bay. She so rarely cried that, much like these new feelings for Knox, this well of emotion caught her completely off guard. Genevieve bit her lip hard to keep the tears in her eyes from falling.

"Gen." He said her name again. "I'm sorry. I just…" He paused for a second and then restarted. "I broke a promise to you. I told you this was going to be a marriage in name only and I let us both down.

"Please," he added. "Don't turn away from me."

When she felt that she could speak again, Genevieve turned back to her husband. "I wanted this to happen."

Knox tucked wayward strands of hair behind her ear and then put his hand gently on her face. "I don't want you to have any regrets, Genevieve."

"My regrets are mine. If I have them, I own them." She reached out to put her hand over his heart. "Besides, this was bound to happen, Knox. You've been walking around without your shirt on, bare chested. A red-blooded American woman can only be expected to have so much willpower."

That made her husband laugh and it broke the tension between. He took her hand and kissed it.

"If memory serves, *you* were the one teasing *me*." He tugged her closer to his body.

"Oh, trust me." She tucked her head into the crook of his neck so she could listen to his beating heart. "I was."

Knox put his finger beneath her chin and brought her lips up to his for a sweet, lingering kiss.

"Hmm." She ran her hand over his tensed, bulging biceps. "I love the way you kiss."

As if on cue, Silver climbed on top of them like he was climbing a hill, flopped down in between their bodies and began to lick their faces.

"See?" Genevieve laughed. "No manners!"

Silver started to scratch an itch on his neck, smacking Genevieve in the face with his foot.

"Okay, brat." Knox scooped up Silver. "Out of the bedroom with you."

In the sparse light coming in the bedroom window, Genevieve admired the sheer beauty of her husband's naked body as he walked back toward her. The man was a leaner version of Michelangelo's David and for the time being at least, he was all hers. Knox returned to her and wordlessly began to love her with his mouth and his hands. Genevieve closed her eyes and clung to her husband, giving him control, knowing that he would take care of her, knowing that he was about to take her on another glorious ride.

Making love to his wife had become Knox's new favorite pastime. What he had truly grown to love about Genevieve was her sense of adventure, which, as it turned out, was just as present when it came to the physical side of their marriage. Their desire for each other made them act like two horny teenagers and when they could sneak away to make love, they did. When they weren't making love, they were finding excuses to touch each other, to hold hands, as if they were afraid that the other one would suddenly disappear. And there was a part of him, like a little warning bell ringing in the back of his mind, that reminded him that, like it or not, Genevieve was going to leave him. That was the deal. Yet, that knowledge didn't stop him from wanting his wife in every way he could possibly want her. As a companion, as a friend, and now, as his lover.

He simply couldn't stop thinking about her.

As if his thoughts conjured her up, she appeared on the ladder to the hayloft where he was working.

"What are you doing up here?" Genevieve asked as she climbed up into the hayloft. "Aren't you supposed to be fixing fences with Logan and Xander?"

He put his finger to his lips and winked at her as he took her hand in his. He led her through a maze of hay bales stacked to the roof until he reached a small clearing tucked away from prying eyes. On a small bed of loose hay, Knox had put down a soft flannel blanket. Knox studied his wife's pretty face to see her reaction to his secret hideaway in the hayloft. Without a word, Genevieve nodded her head in agreement. She was game to make love in the hay loft with him. Knox was eager to join his body to hers; it was all he had been thinking about since he'd had the idea to make love to her in the loft. There was going to be something so sexy about being seated between his wife's thighs, his lips on hers, his world standing still in a moment of ecstasy while the work of the ranch continued all around them.

When her husband sent her a text asking her to meet him in the hayloft, she had assumed that he wanted to discuss some sort of change in the hay they were feeding some of the higher-end horses. A sexy afternoon rendezvous hadn't even been on the radar! But, she couldn't deny that she loved the idea. She had always wanted to make love in a hayloft and this was her chance. What better person than the man who had turned out to be her most incredible lover?

"You can't be noisy," she warned him with a lover's smile as she shimmied out of her jeans.

"Me?" he asked in a loud whisper. "You!"

"Shhhh." She put her fingers to her lips. "Someone will hear you."

Knox had his jeans unzipped and she was immediately drawn to the outline of his erection pressed against his boxer briefs. She tugged his briefs down and wrapped her lips around his hard shaft.

"Oh, God." If Knox had tried to speak those words in a lowered tone, it hadn't worked.

Laughing quietly, Genevieve lay back on the blanket and opened her arms to him. Instead of taking her invitation, Knox knelt down between her thighs and kissed her on that most sensitive spot. Biting her lip hard to stop herself from crying, Genevieve slipped her fingers into Knox's hair and arched her back. Turnabout was fair play and he was making it nearly impossible for her to keep their location a secret.

"Knox." She whispered his name over and over again while his tongue slipped in and out of her body.

She was panting and aching when he sat up so he could look at her with a Cheshire cat smile. She reached out her arms to him.

"Please," she said under her breath. "Hurry."

With his smile in place, Knox searched his pocket and then the look on his face changed.

"What's wrong?"

"The condom." Her husband checked his other pockets. "It must have fallen out of my pocket."

Genevieve covered her face and groaned in frustration. *"No."*

Her body was so revved up that she ached with wanting. She *needed* to feel Knox inside of her now—she needed him to relieve this gnawing ache he had created in her.

"I need you." She grabbed the blanket in her fists and squeezed tightly.

"I need you," he said, the expression on his face pained—they were both so ready for each other that it seemed impossible to stop now. She held out her arms to him and he covered her body with his, but he was careful not to enter her.

Knowing it was a risk, and not caring in the moment, Genevieve reached between them and guided him to her slick opening.

"Are you sure?" Knox asked through gritted teeth.

"I mean it, Knox," she demanded, her body demanding relief.

He slid his thick shaft inside of her, so deep, so hard, making her forget about everything except for Knox. He moved inside of her, slow and steady, knowing what she liked—giving her exactly what she needed.

"Yes, my beauty." Knox nibbled on her ear, cupping her bottom and seating himself so deeply inside of her that it brought her to climax.

Gasping and shuddering in his arms, Genevieve clung to Knox tightly, her breath mingling with his as buried his face in her neck to stifle the sounds that he just couldn't contain.

"God, I love you." The words seemed to be wrenched out of his throat, unplanned and unexpected.

Not trusting her own ears, Genevieve held her husband tightly, kissing his chest, and admiring his pure masculine appeal at the moment of his release. The muscles of his biceps bulging and sweat dripping down his chest, Knox threw back his head, his eyes closed with a stifled growl on his lips.

Both of them spent and satiated, Knox rolled over onto his back, taking her with him. Genevieve draped her leg over thighs and rested her head on his chest, listening to his beating heart. Many times during their lovemaking, Knox had said that he *loved to be with her*, but this was the first time it had been boiled down to just "I love you." Had he been too overcome with passion to get the rest of the words out or had this been a true declaration? Nestled in her husband's arms, the scent of sweet alfalfa hay in the air, Genevieve genuinely wished she knew the answer to that question. It was clear in her mind that she had fallen for her husband, but it was not at all clear to her if Knox had, indeed, fallen for her.

"What do you think of the menu?" Jane Lawrence was bustling around her cheerful yellow kitchen.

"If you're happy, I'm happy," Genevieve said non-committally. Her mother and sisters had all been driving her nuts with the plans for the wedding reception shindig. Party planning was not her activity of choice and she wished that her family would just make all the arrangements and leave her out of it.

"What do you think, Knox?" Jane turned her attention to her son-in-law, who was busy stuffing his face with a bowlful of Jane's homemade beef stew.

Seemingly perfectly at home in her parents' house, Knox took a quick break from the stew. "I think you have a really good variety, Mom. Something for everyone."

"Thank you, Knox." Her mom hugged him and sent her daughter a disapproving glance. "At least one of you is involved in the planning."

"Seriously? Mom, he hasn't even looked at the menu and somehow he's the good one?"

"I've looked at the menu," Knox told her. "Margo emailed it to me."

"How did *Margo* get your email?"

"Ella gave it to her," her husband said.

Genevieve lifted up her hands in the air. "Since when are you in contact with Ella? What the heck is going on around here?"

Before he could reply, her mother said, "Since you wouldn't respond to any of my emails about the reception, I got in touch with Knox…"

"And we've been texting ever since," Knox finished as he smiled at Jane fondly.

Genevieve turned to Knox. "You're texting with my mom and emailing with my sisters? I feel like there's a whole lot of stuff going on behind my back."

"Going on right in front of your face." Her husband scooped up the last spoonful of beef stew.

Genevieve sat back in her chair and watched her mother interact like a giddy schoolgirl with Knox. There was no doubt that the two of them had hit it off. It pained Genevieve to think about how hurt her mom was going to be when the marriage ended. She had asked Knox to not call Jane "Mom" but whenever he tried to call her by her given name, her mom corrected him. What a tangled mess they had created.

"Did you see the beautiful picture Knox had framed for us?" Jane asked, picking up Knox's empty bowl.

"No."

"Oh! It's so lovely." Her mom disappeared into the formal living room and came back with a framed picture of them in Lawrence Park on their wedding day.

Knox did look a bit sheepish when he said to her, "I was over here helping your father with the tractor."

"Honestly!" Genevieve crossed her arms in front of her body. "Am I literally the last person to know anything that's going on in my own family?"

"Ladybug." Her mom hugged her tightly around the neck and planted rapid-fire kisses on her cheek. "I know it's difficult to discover that the world doesn't actually revolve around you."

Genevieve just groaned.

She knew it would get only worse when her sisters arrived for dinner.

Dinner at the Lawrence house was a less formal affair than at the Ambling A, but it was just as loud and raucous when the entire family was present. And minutes later, they were.

Ella, the youngest of the three Lawrence daughters, arrived first with her twin boy toddlers, her husband, Jason, and a very pregnant belly. Once Margo arrived with her brood of four children, the noise volume in the house doubled.

"Outside! Outside! Outside!" Margo shuttled her four children through the kitchen and out into the backyard with their grandfather. Her sister shut the door with a happy sigh. "Thank goodness it's not raining so they can run off all that energy."

The Lawrence sisters all looked very similar, with blond hair and blue eyes. Both of her sisters were taller and leaner, and out of the three of them, Margo had always had the curves.

Her youngest sister put her hands low on her back and leaned backward with a wince. "Take the boys outside will you, honey? It'll be good for them to play with their cousins."

Once her husband and the twins were on their way outside, Ella joined them at the table. "Phew. I am ready for this girl to come on out."

Margo lifted up the paper towel covering the fried chicken their mom had made earlier and snitched a small piece of the skin before she took the last seat at the round kitchen table.

"I really appreciated your feedback on the decorations, Knox."

"Yes," Ella agreed. "You've been so helpful. Unlike some people who shall remain nameless."

Genevieve caught Knox's eye. "I can't believe you're so interested in the reception."

"Of course I'm interested." Her husband said it so convincingly that she would have believed it if she didn't know the truth. "I only intend to get married once."

Chapter Twelve

Three weeks into the marriage and it felt to Knox like Genevieve had always been an integral part of his life. They had developed a rhythm; they had developed a way of moving in each other's lives that made sense. Not only did he have a lover now, his friendship had deepened. Between their busy work schedules, they had found time to play together. Genevieve, as it turned out, was a skilled fisherwoman and one of their first afternoon getaways was to his newfound favorite fishing spot. That night, they served their freshly caught bounty to the family. When it was his wife's turn to pick their next outing, she chose rock climbing. Everything Genevieve liked to do for fun involved some sort of risk to life and limb. In spite of the fact that he was not the biggest fan of heights, Knox had allowed her to strap him into the safety gear and he managed to climb his way up the sheer face of a mountain. Once he got to the top, he was rewarded with a kiss from his beautiful wife, but the family jewels were still sore from the safety straps and there wasn't a snowball's chance in hades that Genevieve was going to convince him to rock climb again.

They were on their way to another outing this afternoon, albeit a tamer, less risky one.

"I can't wait for you to meet Spartacus!" his wife said excitedly from the passenger seat. They had both finished their work early because Genevieve wanted to take him out to the Triple T Ranch, the sprawling Traub family cattle spread.

Knox found that when it came to Genevieve, he could muster enthusiasm for just about anything. The wedding reception was a perfect example. He wouldn't typically be interested in menus and decorations, but it was Gen's family and he wanted to make a good impression on them. He wanted them to like him; he wanted them to accept him.

"Look!" She pointed out of the window as they turned onto Triple T land. "There he is!"

"Holy monster horse," Knox exclaimed. "What the heck is he?"

"Stop here." She was already opening the door and he hadn't stopped the truck. "He's a Percheron, of course."

With a halter and an apple in her hands, Genevieve climbed up to the top of the fence and straddled it. She whistled at Spartacus, who lifted his large black head, snorted and then began to gallop at full speed toward the fence. Gen laughed, her cheeks flushed with happiness, her blue eyes shining in the most enchanting way. Spartacus bucked several times, his muscular black body glistening in the sun and his thick black mane and tail dancing in the wind.

"You're gorgeous!" Genevieve called out to her horse.

Spartacus was so big and so powerful that Knox worried that he might try to jump the fence. Gen stood up on the fence, her boots balanced precariously on the planks, to greet the Percheron. Spartacus slid to a halt in front of her, snorting and tossing his head and pawing at the ground.

"Yes, my beautiful boy." Gen offered him the apple before putting the halter on his head. "I'm happy to see you too."

"What are you doing?" Knox leaned over so his voice would reach her through the open truck window.

"I'll meet you at the barn." Genevieve climbed on the horse's back. Spartacus kicked up his hind leg in protest, but Gen just gently chided him. "Knock that off, grump."

Without any warning to him, his wife squeezed her legs on the horse's side and Spartacus took off at a full gallop.

"Darn it, Gen." Knox fumbled to get the truck out of Park. He stepped on the gas and tried to keep his eyes on his wife as she galloped bareback on the giant Percheron. With her blond hair loose around her shoulders, Genevieve reminded him of a warrior goddess racing into battle. Had he ever seen anything more incredible than his wife, his lover, riding bareback on this magnificent black horse?

Knox quickly found a place to park his truck near the barn, grabbed his keys, jumped out and ran to the fence. He had lost sight of Gen as she rode into the woods and he was anxious to see her emerge in one piece.

"Howdy, Knox." Collin Traub walked out of the barn and headed toward him.

Knox gave the town mayor a quick nod but his eyes were laser focused on the spot where Genevieve should appear any moment.

"She's riding Spartacus bareback again, I take it?" Collin asked.

"No bit, no bridle," Knox said.

"That's about right," the mayor said. "I'd better open that gate for her or she'll try to jump it."

Collin walked quickly over to the gate that led from the field to a riding arena adjacent to the barn. Knox didn't realize that he was holding his breath until he let it out when Genevieve appeared. Still galloping, his wife headed straight for the open gate.

"Watch this." Collin rejoined him at the fence.

One hand holding on to Spartacus's thick mane, once she guided the gelding into the arena, Genevieve leaned her weight back and the draft horse halted. Laughing, his wife patted the horse on his neck and then smiled at Knox.

"Has she always been like this?" Knox heard himself asking the question aloud.

"Yes, sir." Collin chuckled. "You've got a tiger by the tail, my friend."

All Knox wanted Genevieve to do was get off of the horse. Yes, she was an accomplished horsewoman but for some reason this horse seemed riskier than the quarter horses he was used to riding at the ranch. Spartacus was nearly eighteen hands tall; Big Blue was only sixteen hands.

"Now what's she doing?" Knox muttered.

"What she always does," Collin responded with another chuckle.

Genevieve pulled off her boots and socks and tossed them toward the fence. Now barefoot, she slowly stood up on Spartacus's broad back. The horse stood stock still for his mistress while Knox's heart started to beat faster in his chest. The thought of Genevieve getting hurt made his stomach knot. And yet, she wasn't the type of woman who would ever be hemmed in. He was just going to have to get used to watching his wife take risks with her life and limb.

Once she was balanced on Spartacus's back, she leaned forward, pressed her palms on the horse's rump and then lifted her legs into the air.

"Have you ever seen anything like that before?" Collin asked him.

"No," he said. "I can honestly say I haven't."

No one in his or her right mind would think to do a handstand on the back of a horse—at least no one he knew in Texas. This was a first.

Genevieve executed a perfect handstand on Spartacus's back before she carefully lowered her legs and carefully slid into a seated position. Once seated, his wife clucked her tongue and asked the horse to move over to the fence where Knox and Collin were waiting for her.

"Hi, Collin." Genevieve held out her hand to high-five the mayor.

"Howdy, Genevieve."

Knox's wife smiled and held out her hand to him. "Get on."

The last thing Knox wanted to do was get on Spartacus bareback. Honestly, he wasn't too sure he'd be all that jazzed to ride the draft horse with a saddle and bridle. Collin was staring at him with an amused look on his face, as if he knew that Genevieve had him between a rock and a hard place. Not wanting to look like a coward in front of the mayor or Genevieve, Knox climbed up the fence and onto Spartacus's back.

"Wrap your arms around me," Genevieve said. "You're about to go on the ride of your life."

That was exactly what he was afraid of.

"Have fun, you two." Collin gave a wave of his hand.

"Have you done this before?" Knox asked the mayor.

"Oh, yes." Collin grinned at him. "I have. All I can say is hold on tight, my friend. Hold on *real* tight."

As it turned out, that was the best advice anyone had given him in a long time.

Genevieve turned the Percheron toward the open field and the next thing he knew, he was working overtime to stay on the back of the draft horse. His wife was laughing like she was having the time of her life while his legs were on fire from gripping the horse. Genevieve had only one speed and that was full-steam ahead. She pointed the gelding toward the woods and all Knox could see was a maze of tree limbs just ripe for taking off their heads.

"This is the best part," Genevieve said as she leaned forward.

Knox instinctively tightened his hold on his wife's waist. If she thought something was the "best part" he had a feeling he wasn't going to like what was about to happen next. Over the top of Genevieve's head, he spotted a creek without a bridge.

"No, Gen!"

"Yes, Knox!"

The next thing he knew, his body was lifting off the back of the horse as Spartacus jumped over the creek. When the horse's hooves touched the ground, Knox landed hard and he felt his private parts get smashed in the process. All the way back to the riding arena, he was gritting his teeth against the pain he was feeling between his legs. He'd never been so happy to get off a horse in his life.

"Wasn't that the best time ever?" Gen slid off her horse, gave him a kiss on his nose, took off the halter and let the horse run back through the gate and into the field.

Knox took a step and winced in pain. He would be walking a bit more bowlegged for a while, thanks to that ride. And not for nothing, there might be a question of his ability to procreate. Once his brothers saw him limping around and riding tender in the saddle, they were never going to let him hear the end of it.

His wife, oblivious to his distress, linked her arm with his. "I'm so glad I got to share that with you."

"Oh, yeah." He shook his leg to reposition himself. "Me too."

After their amazing ride on Spartacus, Knox had insisted that they go straight home. Disappointed, Genevieve couldn't figure out why they had to cut their afternoon short until Knox made a beeline for the kitchen, stuffed some ice into a Ziploc bag and stripped down to his boxer briefs.

Sitting on the couch with a bag of ice on his private area, a clearer picture began to form in her mind.

"I thought you might've landed a bit hard on the other side of the creek," Genevieve said contritely.

Knox frowned at her. "Why does every activity you pick for us to do end with me needing an ice pack?"

She sat cross-legged on the couch next to him and called Silver up to sit beside her. "Not *everything*."

"Rock climbing," he recounted. "I couldn't sit in the saddle for two days after that little episode."

"Sorry." She giggled. She couldn't help it. Knox was as masculine a man as they made and it was cute to see him show some vulnerability.

"Now this." He held up two fingers. "And what? Next week you want us to go bungee jumping?"

Her face lit up. "Yes! Let's do it. You'll love it."

"No." He shook his head. "I won't *love* it. You'll love it and I'll end up sitting on the couch with another ice pack. No. Thank. You."

She frowned at him playfully. "Spoilsport."

"Look, woman." Knox repositioned his ice pack. "If you want to have children one day, you're gonna have to pick activities that don't involve crushing the family jewels."

Genevieve stopped smiling. It wasn't the first time Knox had talked about their marriage as if it didn't have an expiration date. Now that they had been intimate, all of the lines had been blurred and it was difficult to know what was real and what was fantasy. Sometimes she felt that Knox was in her same boat—that he was falling for her in the same way she couldn't help but be falling for him. But nothing tangible had been said. And no promises—other than a promise of a divorce—had been made.

"You know what?" She reached out and patted him affectionately on the arm. "I'm going to make you dinner."

"Do you know how to cook?"

She sprang up off the couch. "I know enough to get by. You're always making dinner for me, so now it's my turn to spoil you."

A short while later Genevieve had to admit that she had oversold her ability in the kitchen. They ended up eating turkey sandwiches with a side of potato chips on the front porch. But one of the many things that she liked about Knox was his willingness to appreciate her smallest effort. Like the day she'd done their laundry. Knox had acted like she had done something really special for him. Out of every man she'd ever known, Genevieve was beginning to believe that Knox understood her in a way that no one else ever had.

"It's so beautiful here, Knox," she said, looking out at the setting sun. "I'm really going to miss it."

Knox turned his head and she could feel him staring at her profile. She found herself giving him opportunities to talk her into staying, but no matter how many times she opened that door, Knox never walked through it. He never said, "I don't want you to go."

"I saw that you got some literature in the mail from some stables in California."

She nodded. "It's not easy to find a place suitable for a horse like Spartacus."

"That's an understatement."

"His size can be intimidating and he does have food aggression in the stall, so I have to be careful where I stable him."

"Did you find any good prospects?"

"No. Not yet."

For a minute or two, they sat in silence, each in their own thoughts.

"So, California is still the dream?" Knox asked.

California had been her dream for so long it was hard to imagine her life without that goal in mind. And yet, the time she had spent with Knox had begun to make her imagine a different kind of life. A life with a family, a husband and a dog—not in California, but right here in Rust Creek Falls.

When she didn't respond, Knox filled in his own blanks. "California is the right place for you, Gen. I want you to be happy."

Maybe California was right for her. Maybe she would be happy there. But would she be happier than she was right now, sitting on the front porch of Knox's cabin in the woods?

No. That was the answer that floated into her mind. No. She wouldn't be happier. Being Knox Crawford's wife had brought a new level of happiness into her life. But she couldn't be so sure that Knox shared her desire to stay married. Yes, he was an eager and passionate lover—the best she'd ever had—but physical chemistry didn't automatically translate to happily-ever-after. She had never been a chicken before in her life until now. She just couldn't bring herself to build up the nerve to tell her husband that she had fallen in love with him.

That night, Knox made love to Genevieve slow and long. He didn't want the moment to end. Perhaps he was afraid of what it was going to feel like when she was gone from his life. The day he had found information from California in their PO Box, he had actually been contemplating asking Genevieve to give their marriage a chance. There had been moments when he was sure that Gen returned his feelings. It certainly felt that way when they made love. And it was more than just the physical. It was all of the little things she did for him that made him believe she cared—like doing his laundry or picking up his favorite barbecue sandwich on her way home. She noticed every little thing about him and tried to make his life more comfortable. What she didn't realize was that just her being in his life, being his friend, had made his life so much better.

Knox curled his body around Genevieve's body, holding her tightly as they both were drifting off to sleep.

"Knox?"

"Hmm?"

"I had a wonderful time with you today."

He smiled, his eyes still closed. He pulled her just a little bit closer. "I'm glad."

"Knox?"

"Hmm?"

"Do you want to have children?"

Knox's eyes opened in the dark. When he had mentioned giving Genevieve children earlier in the day, he had regretted those words the second they came out of his mouth. Sometimes it was difficult for him to remember that this thing between them wasn't the real deal. It felt like the real deal to him.

"Yes." He stared at her flaxen hair that was spread out across the pillow. He had imagined a little girl with Genevieve's blond hair, blue eyes and tomboy fearlessness. "I do."

Several seconds passed before she responded. "I've seen you with Wren and my nieces and nephews. I think you are going to be an amazing father one day, Knox. I really mean it."

He hadn't ever voiced it aloud, but he had often imagined Genevieve in the role of mother. Yes, she was tough and fiercely independent, but she had a nurturing side. He had seen it particularly in her kindness to Wren. Genevieve saw that Wren needed extra attention and she gave her exactly that.

"I think you'll be a wonderful mother."

He felt her hand tighten in his at the compliment. "I never thought that I wanted to be a mother."

He heard an unspoken "but" dangling off the end of that sentence.

"Has that changed?"

His wife snuggled more deeply into his arms. "Yes. I think it has."

Chapter Thirteen

"Happy one month anniversary."

After a long day of work, Genevieve had put up her barn hammock and was swinging gently, listening to the horses chewing their early evening hay. At the sound of her husband's voice, she opened her eyes. Knox was holding out a small bouquet of wildflowers.

Genevieve took the flowers and held them up to her nose. "Thank you. Happy anniversary."

"I can't believe that Dad has let you get away with this hammock idea."

She held up her pinky. "I told you. Totally wrapped. Care to join me?"

Knox didn't move to get in the hammock, but she could tell that he was tempted. She scooted over just a bit, not enough to tip the hammock over. "Come on. Live a little, cowboy."

"Why do I let you talk me into all kinds of odd things?"

"I don't know." She held on to the edge of the hammock while Knox sat down. "But I'm glad I do."

Knox took his hat off, leaned back slowly until his head was next to hers. She leaned forward so he could put his arm under her head. Resting her head on his shoulder, Genevieve curled into his body. She rocked the hammock back and forth a bit to make it swing them gently. Knox placed his cowboy hat on his stomach and at first the muscles in his arms and legs were stiff.

"Relax," she whispered.

"I feel ridiculous."

"Relax," she repeated. "Just listen to the horses and ignore everything else."

It took him a minute or two, but she felt Knox's body begin to relax next to her. She glanced up and he had closed his eyes. She loved to be in this hammock, listening to the horses. It had never occurred to her that she would be able to lure Knox into the hammock with her.

"Hmm," she murmured. "This is nice."

"Only for you," Knox said, but this time his voice had a languid quality that let her know that the magic of the hammock was working on him too.

"You have to admit—this is relaxing."

Instead of answering, Genevieve heard Knox's breathing change. Her husband could fall asleep faster than any other person she knew. Five short minutes in the hammock and Knox had drifted off. With a happy smile, Genevieve wrapped her arm around Knox's body, nuzzled her head down into his shoulder, and closed her eyes. In her mind, this was heaven on Earth.

"Why aren't you moving the herd with Finn and Wilder?"

Crap. The sound of Maximilian's stern, distinctive

voice made her eyes pop wide open. It was like being caught skipping class by the principal. It was her fault that Knox was sleeping on the job in a hammock.

Her husband surprised her. Instead of sitting up at the sound of his father's voice, Knox stayed where he was in the hammock, his arm still tightly around her.

"They've got it handled," he said. "I wanted to wish my wife a happy anniversary. One month today."

Genevieve was very curious about Maximilian's re-action to the news of their one-month anniversary. Her father-in-law didn't have any response, which in her opinion was an improvement.

Maximilian pointed at her. "I'd like a moment of your time, Genevieve."

Huh. She had graduated from "young lady" to "Genevieve." Nice.

It took some doing, and some laughing, but they both managed to roll out of the hammock while Max looked on. Genevieve had never seen Knox allow himself to be so silly in front of his father, nor had she ever seen her father-in-law so silent in the face of so much silliness.

"Did you receive your invitation for the reception?" she asked her father-in-law as she worked double time to keep up with his long stride.

"I'll be there."

It would be strange to have Maximilian in their farm-house—it didn't seem natural to encounter him any-where other than the Ambling A. But Jane was giddy with excitement about the party and because of the guilt she felt over the fact that the whole marriage was based on a wager, Genevieve wouldn't deny her mother any-thing. She tried to not dwell on how her mother would react once she knew the truth.

Knox walked out to the corral with them. He caught her hand as they walked beside Max. Genevieve looked over at him, once again surprised. Her husband was growing into being his own man, unafraid to be who he was in front of his father. That was the whole reason why he wanted to elope in the first place and now she was seeing that unfold right before her eyes. Knox Crawford was his own man, full stop. And it was plain to see that, however grudgingly, Maximilian was beginning to respect his son's autonomy.

As they rounded the corner, Genevieve saw her father-in-law's prized paint stallion in the round pen. Per Maximilian's instructions, she had contacted a veterinarian trained in advanced acupuncture and laser therapy. It had cost a pretty penny to fly the vet in from out of state, but Maximilian had said he wanted no expense spared to improve the Stallion's health. The three of them stopped outside of the round pen.

"Make him move a bit, John," Max said.

The trainer asked the stallion to move to the outside track and trot. Genevieve had been working hard to get this stallion sound. She cared about all of her clients, but this stallion in particular was her way of proving herself to her father-in-law. His opinion of her mattered. After all, he was Knox's father.

"Look at that," Max said in a quieter voice than she'd ever heard him use. "Will you look at that?"

Knox put his arm around her shoulder and kissed her on the top of the head. "You've got a gift, Gen. A real gift."

"I didn't do that by myself."

"No," Max agreed. "You didn't. But you knew what to do."

It was moments like this when Genevieve thought that maybe, just maybe, she could make a life as a farrier in Montana. If she could change the mind of a man like Maximilian, there was hope for others to follow.

Her father-in-law turned to her. "I thought Knox was damn crazy hiring you."

Knox kept his hand on her shoulder as if to lend her extra support.

"I thought he was doing some hippy-dippy millennial equality-of-the-sexes garbage."

Genevieve had to bite her lip to stop herself from arguing that equality of the sexes was not *garbage*, but decided to let these baby steps for Maximilian play out.

"But I wasn't exactly right about that."

An odd way to admit that he was wrong, Genevieve had to admit.

Finished with what he had to say, Maximilian simply turned on his heel and left.

"That's the closest I've ever heard him come to admitting that he was wrong," Knox said to her and she heard the amazement in his voice.

Genevieve looked after her towering father-in-law. "Your father is a very odd man."

Her husband laughed in that hearty way she had come to love. "I can't really argue with that."

"Happy anniversary." Genevieve surprised him with a plate of homemade cookies when they arrived back at their cabin.

"Did you make these?" He took a bite of one of the cookies which was chock-full of white chocolate chips—his favorite.

"I stopped by mom's yesterday and baked them. I

don't bake for just anyone." She smiled. "Okay—let me rephrase that. I've never baked for *anyone* before. I hope you like them."

He leaned over and kissed her on the lips. "They're delicious."

"I'm glad." She smiled at him. "And that's not your only surprise."

Genevieve put her anniversary wildflowers in a small vase by the sink and then hooked a leash onto Silver's collar. Knox grabbed two more cookies before he followed her out back.

"Watch this."

His wife proceeded to take Silver through some basic training sequences, asking him to heel, sit and stay. The puppy performed on command.

"Did you see that?" she asked excitedly. "He's so smart!"

"When did you have time to do this?"

"I worked with him a little here and there." She leaned down and took the leash off and gave Silver a big rub on his head. "Didn't I, handsome?"

Silver pranced around her legs, wagging his tail and barking loudly. It never failed to amaze him how talented his wife was. If a man didn't feel confident in himself, a woman like Genevieve could be too intimidating for him.

"Thank you." He wrapped his arms around her shoulders and kissed her again.

"You're welcome."

"We should do something for our anniversary. Don't you think?"

"What did you have in mind?"

"I'm up for suggestions."

They all went inside and Genevieve curled up next to him on the couch in a way he enjoyed. Silver, who was growing like a weed, sprawled out on the other end of the couch.

"How about we go to the Ace in the Hole?" she suggested.

"Heck no."

"Why not?"

"Because it's my anniversary and I don't want to share my wife with a bunch of sweaty, dirty, drunk cowpokes, that's why."

Genevieve wrinkled her nose at him. "Fine."

"Don't sound so disappointed."

"I like the Ace in the Hole."

Knox ran his fingers through his wife's hair, loving how silky it felt in his fingers. "How about we go camping? We could find a romantic spot to pitch a tent in the Flathead National Forest."

Genevieve spun around so she was facing him more fully. "I love that idea! We could cook by campfire..."

"Sleep under the stars..."

She wiggled her eyebrows at him suggestively. "Make love in a sleeping bag."

He put his hand on her face, tipping her head up gently so he could kiss her again. Those lips, so soft and willing, made him want to forget camping and just move into the bedroom. But this was a special night—an anniversary night—and they both seemed to want to celebrate it.

"Have I told you lately how much I love spending time with you?" he asked.

It was rare to see her blush and he felt pleased that

he had managed to pull that feminine side of Genevieve out into the open.

"I love spending time with you too, Knox."

He gave her another quick kiss before he got up. "I'll throw the camping gear in the truck if you want to grab some supplies in here."

She nodded. "We'll probably have to stop by the general store on the way out of town."

"Good idea," he agreed before he went out the front door to prep for their impromptu overnight anniversary camping trip.

Genevieve made quick work of packing some essentials for them. She had camped all of her life, so it was second nature to gather up things that they would need. In the bathroom, she threw some toiletries they could share into a bag. When she was rummaging for a small bottle of mouthwash under the sink, she noticed a box of tampons, unopened, in the back corner. For some reason, that unopened box struck her as odd. Sitting on the side of the tub, Genevieve looked at the calendar on her phone and tried to remember when she had her last period. She had been married to Knox for a month today and she hadn't had a period. This meant that her last period was *before* the wedding.

"Oh." She stared at the calendar on her phone. "No."

She wasn't irregular. Never had been. And she and Knox had not always been careful during some of their more adventurous, passionate moments. The roll in the hay was just one of many careless moments they had shared.

Genevieve dropped her head into her hands and sat on the edge of that tub for several minutes. It was a biological fact that she could be pregnant. She lifted up her head and stared at the wall. If she were pregnant, what in the world would she say to Knox? No promises had been made other than the promise of a quickie divorce. Yes, Knox had said he wanted to be a father, but not *this* way. And this wasn't how she wanted to become a mother either. She wanted much better for herself and any child she brought into the world.

"Gen?" Knox knocked on the door. "You okay in there?"

She cleared her throat. "Yes! I'll be out in just a minute."

Genevieve stood up and looked at her reflection in the mirror. In a whisper, she told herself, "Remain calm and carry on."

She put a smile on her face and swung the door open.

"Ready?" Knox was waiting for her at the front door.

"Let me just grab something in the bedroom and I'll be ready to go." She ran into the bedroom, opened the top drawer of the nightstand, took a handful of condoms out and stuffed them into her overnight bag.

"Okay. I've got a change of clothes for both of us, supplies for Silver and for us. We definitely need to stop by the general store and get some food for dinner and breakfast."

They made a quick stop at Crawford's General Store for food and some other staples before they headed out of town toward Kalispell.

"The last time we were on this road, we were heading toward our wedding," Genevieve reminisced.

"It seems like a lifetime ago."

She looked out the window, her hand on her stomach. "It was a lifetime ago."

As much as she tried to put the missed period out

of her mind, she couldn't. It seemed unfair not to tell Knox what was going on, but then again, she could get him upset for absolutely no reason. He was so excited about their anniversary, as was she—why ruin it for them both? After the wedding reception tomorrow she would find a way to get her hands on a pregnancy test. Of course, the last thing she was going to do was buy a pregnancy test in Rust Creek Falls. The whole town would know she missed her period before she even had a chance to get the pregnancy test out of the box.

"Are you okay?" Knox looked over at her.

"Yes," she said with a small smile. "I'm just a little tired, I suppose."

He reached for her hand. "We'll go to bed early tonight. Tomorrow is a big day."

"I know. My mom has been driving me nuts!"

Knox found them the perfect place to make camp. Flathead National Forest was right outside of Kalispell and it felt fitting that they should return to the place where they had been wed. For Genevieve, every moment of the marriage had been filled with so many mixed emotions. She was certain now that she was deeply in love with her husband—and there was a part of her that sincerely felt that Knox returned her feelings. But he had said that he loved her only once, when they were making love. Any other time he mentioned the word *love*, it was framed more in friendship than romance. It had always been push me/pull me with Knox. He would celebrate their one-month anniversary today and then bring up her moving to California tomorrow. Perhaps it was time that she confronted him. Was he just enjoying the ride while it lasted—enjoying their physical chemistry and friendship—while not caring that it would end? Or did he, like her, want something more?

"Come here." Knox opened his arms to her. They had just finished cleaning up after their meal and the campfire was dying down.

Genevieve sat between his legs, careful to keep a hold of Silver's leash, and let Knox wrap her up in his arms.

"I've never had a friend like you, Gen."

She cringed at the word *friend*. Yes, she wanted to be Knox's friend—of course she did. But was that all she really was for him? A friend with benefits?

"I'm tired," she said with a sigh. "Would you mind if we went to bed?"

They doused the fire and went inside the tent. Silver curled up in a bed of blankets they created for him while they slipped inside a sleeping bag designed for two. She turned her back to Knox and let him put his arms around her as he liked to do. He started to kiss her neck but she couldn't concentrate on lovemaking. Her brain was too filled with worries about being pregnant.

"I'm sorry, Knox," she said in the dark. "I'm so tired."

He was quiet for a moment. This was the first time she had ever begged off lovemaking with him. Knox kissed her again, this time more platonically.

"You don't need to apologize," he told her. "I'm just happy we're here together, Gen."

"Me too."

She said the words but she wasn't so sure she meant them. She had been happy until she got the scare of her life. An unplanned pregnancy would be a disaster for them now. Knox would be tied to her for the rest of his life when all he'd ever really said out loud was that he wanted things to end in divorce when the time was right.

The whole marriage was a careless decision made by two impulsive people. They'd done something serious based on a frivolous wedding wager. And to make matters worse, they had involved their families, innocent bystanders who would be collateral damage. Genevieve couldn't stomach the idea of bringing an innocent baby into the bargain and she prayed over and over again for it not to be true until she finally fell into a fitful sleep.

Chapter Fourteen

Genevieve drove herself to her parents' house ahead of the wedding reception. When she arrived at the farmhouse, she slowed down to admire the decorations. Her mom had outdone herself. The large oak trees lining the drive were decorated with lace and ribbon and flowers. The house was also decorated in that same white-and-silver theme, including the porch railing, which was wrapped with garlands of flowers.

"Oh, Mom." Genevieve sat in the truck with the engine off, just staring at the house. "I am so sorry."

Before she could get to the top of the porch stairs, her mom threw open the door and rushed out to greet her.

"What do you think?" Jane was aflutter. Her pretty blue eyes were shining and her fleshy cheeks were flushed pink. Her mom always died her hair at home, but for the party, she had gone into Kalispell for a new hairstyle and a professional coloring.

"Mom." She felt her eyes well up with tears—tears because she was touched by the work her family had put into this party on her behalf and because this whole party was based on a lie. "It's more beautiful than I could have ever imagined."

Her mom took Genevieve's face in her hands and kissed her on the cheek. "We love you so much, lady-bug. We just want you to be happy."

The moment she entered the house the sweet and spicy aroma of barbecue coming from the kitchen made her stomach growl. Her mom, dad and sisters had invited nearly the entire town and there would be food enough for people to take home leftovers. That was the Rust Creek Falls way.

"I'm going to change my clothes." Genevieve carried her dress over her arm as she went upstairs to her old bedroom.

"Take your time, sweetheart. This is your special day with Knox."

Knox. He had been texting her for the last hour and she hadn't responded. He had thought that they would come to the party together, but she had grabbed her dress and makeup and had come alone.

Genevieve peeked outside of her bedroom window, remembering how many times she had climbed out of that window when she was a kid. Watching her father setting up the long tables for the buffet-style service, Genevieve wondered why she was still causing her family so much heartache. Why hadn't she learned more from her childhood mistakes?

Her phone rang and it was Knox. "Hello?"

"Gen! Where are you?"

"I'm at Mom and Dad's."

There was a pause on the other end of the line. "I thought we'd go together."

"I know. But I wanted to get here early just in case Mom needed help."

Another pause.

"Okay," Knox said slowly as if he didn't fully believe her. "Are you sure everything's all right?"

It was strange. Knox knew her better than she realized. He had picked up on a change in her behavior even when she had tried to hide the fact that something was wrong. Now that it had occurred to her that she had missed a period, it was all she could think about.

"I'm good." It was a lie, but it was a necessity. More than anything, she did not want to ruin this day for their families. They deserved to have this day after what Knox and she had put them through needlessly and thoughtlessly.

"Okay." He was still speaking in that slow, unconvinced voice. "Then I'll see you later."

"Of course. It's our wedding reception."

Genevieve took her time getting ready. She left her hair long and loose, just like the day she married Knox. Her wedding dress had been dry-cleaned for this party and when she put it back on, all of the feelings she had when she had married Knox—fear, excitement and exhilaration—came flooding back. Once she was dressed, Genevieve lay down on top of the covers of her bed and hugged her pillows. She stayed there even when she heard guests beginning to arrive. She stayed there even when she knew that she should go down to greet the people who had come to celebrate her union to Knox Crawford.

A rapid banging on the wall next to the stairs let her know that her time sequestering herself in her bedroom was over. "Ladybug! Your husband is here."

With a heavy sigh, she pushed herself upright, swung her legs off the bed and walked slowly to her door. The moment she left this bedroom she was going to have to play a part—the part of the happy, carefree bride. She had done it before and she had played her part well. But her heart wasn't in it anymore. The fun—the thrill—was gone. And the only thing she had left now was regret and a pain in the pit of her stomach.

At the top of the stairs, Genevieve paused. At the bottom of the stairs, Knox awaited. Her heart, as it always did when she saw him, gave a little jump. He was dressed in a suit—not the ill-fitting suit in which he was married—but a dapper dark gray suit that fit his broad shoulders and long legs.

"Gen." He said her name with awe, with reverence, and it made her breath catch. He did have feelings for her. He must. He couldn't possibly look at her that way if he didn't feel something for her.

As she descended the stairs, their eyes remained locked. Guests milled past Knox, but they faded into the background the closer she came to her husband. Those dark, enigmatic eyes drank her in as she landed on the last step.

"You're wearing your wedding dress." His eyes swept down the full length of her.

"My mom wanted to see me in it."

"You look…" He paused with a shake of his head. "More beautiful now than the day I married you."

He held out his hand for her and she took it. How easily her hand slipped into his larger, stronger one. Hand in hand, they greeted their guests. It was a whirlwind of hugs and congratulations and well wishes for a long and happy marriage. Even though her mother specified "no gifts," there was a growing cache of prettily wrapped presents in the formal living room. They would all have to be returned.

"I need some fresh air." Genevieve felt hot all over her body and beads of sweat were rolling down the back of her neck.

Together, they went outside to the backyard where her father was holding an impromptu revival, preaching the word of God to anyone who would listen.

"Are you hungry?"

Oddly, she wasn't. She had been starving earlier but somewhere along the way, she had lost her appetite.

"I think I'll wait." Genevieve begged off the food. "But you go."

"I'm not leaving your side."

"It's okay, Knox. Truly. I just need to sit down and cool off."

It took some convincing, but she finally got Knox to head off to the food tables. Genevieve moved into the shadows and watched the townsfolk laughing and talking. Everyone seemed to be having a wonderful time. Even Maximilian who seemed to have difficulty enjoying life in general had cracked a smile or two.

"Hey, sis!" Finn popped up out of nowhere, making her jump. He sat down next to her and bumped her with his shoulder. She punched him on the arm in retaliation.

"Don't sneak up on me like that, Finn!"

"What are you doing over here moping in the dark? Isn't this your party?"

"I'm just taking a breather."

"Your mom throws a great party." Finn stretched out his long legs in front of him. "So many pretty girls."

"I've heard Viv is keeping you busy."

Finn laughed. His laugh was so similar to Knox's that she couldn't help but smile. "I've been dating a new girl every week. One gets off the carousel and another one gets on. I don't ever want this ride to stop."

"The point is for you to get married, Finn, not date for the rest of your life."

Finn stood up, distracted by another pretty girl. "Life's too short to settle down, sis."

Her brother-in-law disappeared into the crowd and then Knox appeared at her side. He handed her a plate. "I brought you some food just in case you changed your mind."

The man could be so thoughtful. Not wanting to give him a reason to be suspicious, Genevieve decided just to acquiesce and eat a bit. Once she got started eating the barbecue and potato salad and coleslaw, she couldn't stop until she was completely stuffed.

"Now that's the Genevieve I know." Knox was watching her clean her plate. "I was beginning to wonder where she went."

"She's still here."

Together they milled through the crowd and Knox reached out to grab ahold of her hand.

"I want to dance with you." He said it loud enough for her to hear over the din of the crowd. "Like we did the night we were married."

If she were honest with herself, she would admit that

she wanted to dance with Knox too. "Let me just go check on Mom. When I get back, I promise you we'll dance."

Knox held on to her fingers until the very last second as if he were afraid to let her go. She walked away, but glanced back over her shoulder to find him still watching her. Genevieve found her mom in the kitchen checking on her pies.

"Mom."

"Yes, ladybug?" Jane untied her apron and hung it on a hook on the wall. "Are you having the time of your life?"

"It's your best party yet." It was the truth, so Genevieve didn't hesitate to say it.

"Mom?"

"Yes, sweetheart?"

"Why is there a goat in the kitchen?"

In the corner of the kitchen, a baby pygmy goat, the color of ginger and cream, was curled up in one of her mother's good comforters.

Jane ran her hand gently over her hair to smooth it down. "Oh! Well, that's Old Gene and Melba's goat."

"Why do they have a goat?"

"I can't say that I know," her mother said with a quick shrug.

"You didn't think to ask why they brought a goat to a wedding reception?"

"No. I didn't want to be rude about it. Besides, I figure if they wanted to tell me why they had a goat they would tell me. Otherwise, I don't think it's any of my business really."

"Except that it's in your kitchen."

"You go tend to your husband and let me tend to the goat."

Her mom shooed her out of the kitchen and Genevieve decided to take her mom's advice. After all, this was her wedding reception. Why not push any thoughts of pregnancy out of her mind and focus on having some fun?

"Do you want to dance, cowboy?" Genevieve asked as she walked up to Knox and put her hand on his arm.

"Just don't tell my wife." Knox winked at her as he took her hand in his.

He led her onto the makeshift dance floor and, just like the first night, they danced as a married couple, Genevieve relaxed into his strong, capable arms and let herself get totally lost in the silky, dark depths of his soulful eyes.

The Lawrence family had organized one heck of a wedding reception. Knox had eaten his way through the buffet table, danced with his wife until they were both too tired for one more dance and he had laughed with friends and family for hours. It was one of the best nights he had had in recent memory. When he had watched Genevieve descend the stairs in her wedding dress, all thoughts had vanished from his mind and it felt as if he had been frozen in his spot. For him, she was the most beautiful woman. He loved her bright blue eyes, the way she threw her head back when she laughed and her sharp intelligence. Perhaps more than any other moment since he had married her on a bet, Knox realized that he loved Genevieve. He loved her as a friend. He loved her as a partner and a lover. He loved her as the woman he wanted to spend the rest of his life with.

The party was winding down and many of the guests had already left. Knox had been standing alone watching Genevieve talking with her sisters and holding one of her twin nephews in her arms.

"She's been good for you."

At the sound of his father's voice, Knox turned toward him. "I love her."

It was strange to admit it out loud to his father, the man who had begun this entire chain of events because of his bargain with Viv Shuster. Knox's plan to marry Genevieve had begun out of a desire to prove something to his father and in the end, it had taken on a life of its own. His feelings for Genevieve—his relationship with his wife—had absolutely nothing to do with his father and everything to do with falling in love. Now all he had to do was convince Genevieve that her life was here with him and not in California. She loved him—he could feel it. But did she love him enough to give their marriage an honest try? Did she love him enough to give up on her lifelong dream of making a life in California?

It was difficult to admit that he didn't know the answers to those questions. Every day that he left things unsaid between himself and Genevieve was a day closer to losing the woman he loved. It was time to propose real marriage to his wife. It was past time.

"Congratulations, son." Max held out his hand to him.

It was a moment that Knox never thought to have with his father. Yes, they loved each other. They were family. But the two of them had always butted heads, beginning when he was a teenager. Perhaps it would always be a complicated relationship, but his father's acceptance of his marriage to Genevieve went a long way to heal some old wounds.

"Thank you, Dad." Knox shook his father's hand. In truth, Max had brought him Genevieve and he needed to be grateful to him for that.

After his family took their leave, Knox ran into Collin Traub as the mayor was heading out of the front door.

"Hey, Collin, let me bend your ear for a minute."

The mayor paused just outside of the front door of the Lawrence home.

"I'd like to arrange to move Spartacus to the Ambling A," he told Collin. "As a surprise."

The mayor raised his eyebrows and the look on his face wasn't encouraging. "Genevieve isn't all that keen on surprises. I'm sure you know that."

"I'm aware." Knox felt his jaw tense. "But she lives at the Ambling A now and I want her to have access to her horse. It makes sense that Spartacus should be with us."

Collin gave a quick nod of his head. "I get that it makes sense, Knox. The question is, will it make sense to Genevieve."

Knox didn't like the fact that the mayor was debating this idea with him. There had been a long-standing family feud between the Crawford and the Traub families going back generations. But because the two families had marriages between them, the feud had been squashed. Despite the fact that most of the new generation couldn't remember what started the feud, perhaps there was some lingering animosity bubbling up in this conversation.

"This is a wedding gift from me to my wife," Knox said in a tone that brooked no argument. "I've got to find a trailer big enough to haul him and once I do, I'll be in touch with the details."

Gen joined them then, interrupting the conversation. "Collin, I just wanted to thank you so much for coming."

The mayor hugged Genevieve, gave Knox a little salute and then headed down the porch stairs. Genevieve had pulled her hair back into a ponytail and her cheeks were still flushed from all the dancing they had done.

"Did I interrupt something?" His wife had a keen eye.

Knox had a bad feeling in his gut that Collin was going to tell Genevieve about his plan to move Spartacus. The Traub and Lawrence families went way back and his loyalty would be to Genevieve.

"I was talking to Collin about moving Spartacus to the Ambling A," Knox told her, deciding maybe a total surprise wasn't the way to go. "As a wedding gift to you."

The expression on Genevieve's face changed. She stood stock still while she stared up at him, then came the unexpected flash of anger in her eyes. His wife spun on her heel, marched down the steps and then waved her hand for him to follow her. They walked along the driveway and away from the house. When they were far enough away from prying eyes and listening ears, Genevieve said, "Why would you *do* that? Why would you talk to Collin about my horse? *My* horse?"

"I wanted to do it for you," Knox said. "Why are you getting so upset, Gen?"

"Why am I so upset? Because Spartacus is off-limits, that's why. He's the only thing in this world that's truly mine. *I* make the decisions about his life. No one but me."

They stopped walking and he turned to face his wife. This wasn't at all how he expected their night to end.

He was hoping to continue the celebration at home, take her to bed, make love to her and propose real marriage. A fight hadn't been in the plan.

"Okay, I get it. I wasn't trying to make you upset, Gen. I was just trying to surprise my wife."

"I don't like surprises." Her words echoed Collin's and it only served to irritate him.

"I know," Knox acknowledged. "But now that we're talking about it, it makes sense that Spartacus move to the Ambling A. We're just going to have to find a trailer big enough for a giant, is all."

Gen shook her head. "It doesn't make a bit of sense to move him."

Perhaps in his own way he was giving his wife a test. He knew how much she loved Spartacus and if she agreed to move him to the Ambling A, it would be a signal to him that she thought of his family's ranch as home.

"It doesn't make a bit of sense to move him," she reiterated.

"Ambling A is your home," he reminded her.

"For now," she snapped. "But for how much longer? Until Viv finds wives for the rest of your brothers? Why would I go through the trouble of moving him, upsetting his routine, only to have to move him again when this whole thing between us falls apart?"

Chapter Fifteen

Knox was blindsided but maybe he shouldn't have been. Nothing between them had been solidified and that was his fault. Their relationship had been such a whirlwind, he hadn't been able to figure out his own feelings fast enough. But the fact that Gen didn't want to move her horse to the Ambling A spoke volumes. In her mind, the Ambling A wasn't her home. Now it was his job to convince her otherwise.

"Why do things between us have to fall apart, Gen?"

Hurt, pure hurt, entered her eyes. It was an emotion he'd never seen there before and hoped to never see again.

"That's a cruel thing to say, Knox." His wife crossed her arms tightly in front of her body. "Divorce was always in the cards for us. That was the deal, right?"

"Gen." He tried to reach for her hand but she turned

away from him. "What I'm trying to say to you—clumsily I admit—is that I—"

His wife interrupted him and pointed back at the house. "Look at what we've done, Knox! Just look at what we've done! We've involved the whole blasted town in this ridiculous lie!"

"I thought we were having a good time tonight, Gen. Was that part of the lie?"

"Of course we were having a good time. That's all you and I do. We do what feels good and damn the consequences! We're so…irresponsible. And selfish."

Suddenly, Knox felt in his gut that Genevieve was saying one thing but talking about something entirely different. There was something deeper going on and he was certain he didn't know what it was.

"Tell me what's going on, Genevieve. What's wrong?"

Her arms still crossed tightly in front of her body and her expression grim, Gen said, "I'm done with this game."

Knox's hands tightened reflexively into fists at his side. He wanted to grab her, hold her and stop her from leaving him. And she was leaving him—he could feel it in his gut. And yet, all he could ask was, "What do you mean?"

"I mean I'm not going home with you tonight."

"Gen, please."

"No." She shook her head. "I'm serious, Knox. I'm staying here tonight and I'm telling my mom everything—the whole truth. After all of this—" she nodded her head back toward the house "—she deserves the truth."

There was a long silence between them before he asked his next question. "And then what?"

"Then we get a divorce. Sooner or later, that was always going to happen. Now I want it to happen sooner rather than later."

The morning after the wedding reception, Genevieve awakened in her garage apartment with Oscar the cat sleeping half on her pillow and half on her face. For some reason, Knox speaking to Collin about moving Spartacus had been the proverbial straw that had broken the camel's back. Had she meant to end her marriage behind an oak tree on her parents' driveway? No. But it had happened and now she needed to go forward. She still had to confess to her mom and then she needed to find a pregnancy test ASAP so she could find out if this fake marriage was going to be with her for the rest of her life in the form of a child.

"I love you." She hugged the round fluffy feline tightly and kissed him on the head. Oscar, as he always did, began to purr loudly for her.

Genevieve slowly extracted herself from beneath the weight of the cat and sat upright on the edge of the bed. Her mom was well aware that she hadn't gone home with Knox after the party, but she didn't know why. Now it was time for Genevieve to pay the piper. Knox had been calling and texting regularly; she had ignored all of his attempts to talk. What was there to say? At this point, she wasn't so sure of her own feelings anymore and she certainly wasn't convinced of his. Either way, the two of them had made a royal mess of things.

Genevieve pulled her hair back into a quick ponytail, threw on some old jeans and a T-shirt and walked barefoot down the stairs, across the yard and up to the front door. Inside the house, the remnants of the party lingered—half-inflated balloons hanging from the stair-well railing and the large pile of unsolicited gifts in the formal living room that she was going to have to return. From the kitchen, she could hear her mother humming. As it always did, the thought of her mother in that cheerful yellow kitchen gave her a sense of security, of well-being—even when there wasn't any reason to feel those things. Her mother had always been her comfort.

"Good morning." Genevieve walked into the kitchen and was greeted by the scent of coffee brewing.

Jane turned toward the sound of her voice and there was such kindness and care in her mother's eyes that Genevieve had to stop herself from immediately bursting into tears.

"You don't look like you had a good night, ladybug." Jane enveloped her in a hug. "Sit down and I'll get you a cup of coffee."

Genevieve rested her head in her hands, dreading the conversation to come. Her poor mother had been put through the ringer while Genevieve was in high school. This table had seen more than its fair share of "what has Genevieve gotten into now" conversations. Now that she was in her early thirties, it was getting through her thick skull that she needed to grow up and start taking her adult responsibilities more seriously. Not everything in life needed to be approached like a death-defying, adrenaline-producing adventure. And she didn't have to win every time.

Jane set the cup of coffee down in front of her and then joined her at the table. Her mother's cool hand felt good on her arm. She lifted up her head out of her hands and looked into her mother's kind eyes.

"What's wrong, ladybug? Why didn't you go home with your husband last night?"

"Does Dad know I'm here?"

"No." Jane shook her head. "He left before dawn to go to that farm supply auction. He won't be back until late this evening."

That was a lucky break. She knew that everyone in town would soon know that her marriage to Knox was over, but it was going to be particularly difficult to tell her father. The man was beside himself with happiness that she was finally married to someone he considered to be a "good, solid, God-fearing man." For all she knew, that grandchild he had always wanted from her might very well be on the way. Then she would be a single, divorced mother.

"I've really screwed up, Mom."

"Nothing is so bad that it can't be fixed."

Genevieve wrapped her hands around the warm coffee cup, her eyes focused on a scratch on the table.

"Holding it in only makes it worse," her mother said in a gentle tone. "Light is the best disinfectant. Speak it and heal it, sweetheart."

"I don't even know where to begin." She sighed. "I never meant to hurt anybody, especially you."

"Genevieve." Her mother said her name in a way that made her lift her eyes up. "You are my daughter, my firstborn. You have given me a run for my money, that is the God's honest truth. But I love you more than any person has a right to love another. No matter what, that is never going to change."

Genevieve took in a deep, calming breath and then let it out very slowly. "My marriage to Knox isn't real."

Saying those words aloud to her mother—speaking

that truth—hurt. For the first time, tears of sadness and anguish formed in her eyes and she didn't try to stop them. She had wanted to cry over Knox for weeks, but she hadn't allowed herself to acknowledge—truly acknowledge—that this relationship wasn't going to work out for her. If he loved her, he would have told her.

Jane stared at her, stunned. Of all the things her mother might have imagined to be wrong, this obviously wasn't on her radar. Her mother stood up, grabbed a box of tissues and brought them over to the table. She pulled a couple of tissues free from the box and handed them to her.

Genevieve wiped the tears from her face before she blew her nose. The tissues crumpled up into a ball on the table as she waited for the questions from her mother that were bound to come.

"Your marriage isn't real?" Jane's words came out very slowly. "What do you mean? You aren't really married to Knox?"

"No." She frowned. "I'm really married."

"Then, I don't understand, Genevieve. You need to spell this out for me."

Once she started talking, recounting the whole story, from the initial wager to the elopement to the layers of lies they had told in order to make the whole plan work, she couldn't seem to stop. She told her mother everything, including that they had consummated the marriage and that she feared she was pregnant. It took her a long while to finish confessing, and when she did, her mom didn't say a word. She just sat at the table, her round face unsmiling, her finger tapping on the tabletop while she mulled over what her daughter had just told her.

"Oh, Genevieve," Jane finally said with deep sadness laced in her voice. "When are you ever going to learn to look before you leap?"

"Hopefully I've learned that lesson now. I'm so sorry, Mom. I'm sorry I hurt you. I'm sorry I had you go through all of this planning and expense for the wedding reception."

"Don't you be sorry for a thing. I'm not. I had the time of my life and don't have a bit of regret."

"But the money—"

"Ladybug, when you were born, your father and I started a college fund and a wedding fund. I spent your wedding fund to throw this party."

"Well, at least I don't have to feel guilty about the money anymore."

"No. And there's no sense feeling guilty about anything. It's a complete waste of energy." Her mother reached for her hand and squeezed it. "And do you know what else I think? I think your husband is crazy about you. I think he's head over heels for you, I really do. Everyone sees it. Everyone. Even your father sees it and that man is blind as a bat when it comes to just about everything. As a matter of fact, even Maximilian Crawford sees it. He told me so himself last night. So maybe this marriage isn't as fake as you believe."

"I don't see it," Genevieve muttered. "He's never said it to me."

With the exception of that one time in the loft when they were making love. In her mind, coming as it did in a moment of passion, that didn't count.

"Some men are just slow to come to their senses," Jane said. "Your father loved me for months before it occurred to him to speak the words aloud. I remember he actually thought he told me that he loved me and he hadn't. He'd thought it in his mind and didn't bother to get the words out of his mouth. If Knox loves you, he'll break down the door looking for you and then you'll know."

"Maybe. But that's not my biggest problem right now. A baby wasn't part of our bargain, Mom."

"Life is what happens when you're busy making other plans, ladybug. I think it's time we find out if there's even anything to worry about."

"I'm not going to buy a pregnancy test at the general store."

"Oh, no," Jane agreed. "Absolutely not."

Her mother got up and walked over to the phone on the wall and dialed a number. "Darling, do you happen to have any pregnancy tests in your medicine cabinet?"

Of course. As often as her sisters got pregnant, no doubt they had a stockpile of pregnancy tests in their bathrooms.

"Thank you, love," Jane said into the phone. "We'll see you in a minute."

Her mother hung up the phone.

"There. Problem solved. Ella is coming over and we'll have our answer right quick. Better to know than sit around worrying and wondering."

As usual, her mom was right. If she *was* pregnant, she needed to know. And if she did have a Crawford bun in the oven, then that was going to take the next conversation she had with her husband in a whole different direction. In fact, it was going to take her whole *life* in a different direction.

Knox took his hammer and smashed into the hinge, banging it again and again even though it didn't budge.

"Are you trying to fix that or break it more, Knox?" Hunter was holding the gate up so he could try to unseat the rusted hinge.

Knox gave the stuck hinge a few more hard whacks before he cursed and threw his hammer on the ground. Frustrated, he kicked the gate several times. With a concerned look on his face, Hunter let go of the gate and focused his attention on Knox.

"What's going on? You've been off all day."

If it had been any other brother than Hunter asking, Knox would have made an excuse, any excuse, just to end the conversation. But Hunter was different. He had been married, and he had a daughter for whom he was responsible. It made Hunter more grounded and Knox trusted his counsel.

Knox wiped the sweat off his brow with his sleeve. "Genevieve left me."

He hadn't spoken those words aloud. It felt like a punch in the gut to give them a voice.

Hunter stared at him for a second or two and then waved his hand with a smile. "If that's a joke, brother, it ain't funny."

"It's not a joke. She left me. She didn't come home with me last night. As far as I know, she's planning on moving back into that garage apartment at her parents' house."

Now he had Hunter's full attention.

"I don't understand," Hunter said. "The party…"

Knox kicked the gate again. "It was a lie. All of it was a damn lie."

Perhaps he shouldn't have begun to tell Hunter the truth, but once he told him one part of the problem with Genevieve, his brother wasn't satisfied until he knew the whole truth of the matter. When he was done explaining his elopement scheme, the disbelieving, disappointed look on his brother's face spoke volumes.

"You and Dad are cut from the same bolt of cloth, Knox," Hunter said with a shake of his head. "The same darn bolt of cloth."

Knox hated to hear that, yet there was a ring of truth in his brother's words. Both he and his father would go to any lengths to get their way, to be in control—to be right.

"You need to go and fight for her," Hunter said plainly. "If you love her, then don't let her go."

"I tried to tell her how I felt last night."

"You tried," his brother scoffed. "Please."

"I did," Knox said. "Now she won't answer my calls. My texts."

"I know you can't possibly be as dense as you're sounding right now, Knox. A woman wants her man to fight for her. Genevieve is begging for you to step up and be a man and *claim* her, to prove to her that this marriage might have started out as a wager but it ended up as the real deal. Instead of going over there and fighting for her, you're standing here and kicking a fence! That woman is the best darn thing that has ever happened to you. We all see it. And you're a better man for having married her, no matter the circumstances. If you let her go, then all I can say is that I love you but you're not the man that I believed you were."

Genevieve sat on the side of her garage apartment bed and stared at the pregnancy test. Never in her life had she experienced such mixed emotions. One minute she was happy and the next she was incredibly sad, like a giant grandfather clock pendulum swinging back and forth. With a heavy sigh, she slid the pregnancy test back into the box, walked into the bathroom and put it on the edge of the sink. All she wanted to do with the rest of her day was hide under her covers. The confession to her mother and then her sister had exhausted her. It was going to take a full day of sleeping just to prepare her for the next round—dealing with her father and then with Knox.

With a heavy heart, Genevieve climbed under the covers and rested her head on the pillow next to Oscar, who had easily slept right through her traumatic morning. Genevieve rubbed Oscar's fat belly, causing the cat to roll on his back and purr loudly. Why couldn't her life be a simple as Oscar's life? She pulled the covers over her head to block out the light and wished for sleep. She had deliberately turned off her phone because she didn't want to be disturbed. For now, she wanted her life and everyone in it to just go away.

Sleep had thankfully come and Genevieve had no idea how long she had slept when a loud knock on the door jolted her awake.

"Go away!" she grumbled, turning over and burying her head back under the covers.

"Gen!" Knox's strong, determined voice penetrated the door. "Open up, please. We need to talk."

"Go away!" she yelled. She wasn't ready to speak to him.

When he didn't respond, didn't fight her on it, it only confirmed her suspicions that her feelings for Knox were one-sided. It really had been just a game to that Crawford cowboy.

A sound like a key in the door made her pop her head

out from underneath the covers. The door opened and suddenly Knox, as handsome and put together as always, was standing inside of her sanctuary.

"Mom gave you a key."

Knox shut the door behind him. "She did."

"I'm not in the mood to talk to you." Genevieve pushed her mussed hair out of her eyes.

Her husband sat on the edge of the bed, his eyes steady, his face more somber than she had ever seen.

"You don't have to talk if you don't want to, Genevieve. I just need you to hear me out. I just need you to listen."

Chapter Sixteen

Knox had never truly been in love before. Perhaps that was why he hadn't been able to pinpoint the exact moment he had fallen in love with Genevieve. But he certainly knew it when she walked away from him. That moment was burned into his brain and his heart. The night of the wedding reception, he had returned home to Silver and an empty bed. Yes, he had known that Genevieve had quickly become an integral part of his life, but it wasn't until she was no longer filling the cabin with her laughter and her sweet smile that he realized how important she had become to the very fabric of his happiness. He had never been so happy as he was when he opened the door to the garage apartment to find a groggy, grumpy Genevieve scowling at him. Even a disgruntled Gen was better than no Gen at all.

"This is all my fault," he said for openers.

Gen looked up at him with narrowed eyes. "You know, I've been thinking about that a lot. And, you're absolutely right. This *is* all your fault. If you hadn't bet me to marry you, we wouldn't be in this mess."

"I know." Knox turned his body so he was able to look her in the eye. "But if I hadn't convinced you to elope with me, would we have ever fallen in love?"

His wife's eyes widened for a moment before they narrowed. "Who says we did?"

Knox reached for her hand; he was encouraged that she didn't pull her hand away from him.

"You know we did, Gen." He looked at her with an open and steady gaze. He wanted her to see what was inside of his heart. "Do you remember when I told you that I wasn't afraid of anything?"

His wife nodded.

"That wasn't true. I am afraid of something. I'm afraid of losing the best thing that's ever happened to me. I'm afraid of losing you."

A single tear slipped onto her cheek and the sight of that tear crushed him. He reached out and wiped it away with his thumb. "I'm so sorry I didn't tell you this before, Gen. I love you. I *love* you. With everything that I am, and with everything I have, I love you. I believe I've loved you from the first moment I saw your picture on your website."

"Why didn't you tell me?" she asked with an emotional crack in her voice.

He couldn't wait a moment longer—he gathered his wife up in his arms and hugged her so tightly. "I don't know. I'm a man. I'm an idiot. I'm a slow learner."

Through her freshly shed tears, Genevieve laughed: "You are all of those things."

He leaned back so he could see her face. "Yes. I am all of those things. But I'm also the man who loves you, Genevieve. I'm the man who wants to spend the rest of his life with you."

Knox kissed his wife, tasting the salt from her tears on his lips. He kissed her tears from her cheeks and then took both of her hands in his.

"Tell me that you love me."

"I love you, Knox."

Knox noticed the engagement ring made of hay he had given her sitting on the nightstand. He reached for it and held it out for her to see. "I want you to be my wife, Genevieve."

With a little laugh she took the ring and held it gently in her hand, as if it were made of precious metal. "I am your wife, Knox."

"Then promise to be my wife for the rest of my life, Gen. Promise me."

"I promise you."

"Thank God." Knox pulled her back into his arms.

During the hug, Knox felt Genevieve rub her face on his shoulder. He sat back with a suspicious smile. "Did you just dry your face on my shirt?"

His wife grinned at him guiltily. "Maybe just a little."

Knox stood up and looked around for a box of tissues. Genevieve pointed to the bathroom. "Toilet paper in there."

He walked over to the bathroom and when he was bending over to pull some toilet paper off the roll, something caught his attention on the bathroom sink. Squares of toilet paper crumpled in his hand, he reached out to pick up the pregnancy test. He stared at the box and then, with legs that didn't seem to want to move, he looked in the direction of his wife.

Genevieve was still reeling from the sudden appearance of Knox in her garage apartment and his profession of love. It took a minute for it to register that he was in the bathroom with the pregnancy test. Careful not to disturb Oscar, who had managed to keep on sleeping, Genevieve got out of bed. She was heading toward the bathroom when Knox emerged holding the box.

"Are you?" he asked quietly.

Feeling sadder than she could express in words, she shook her head. Genevieve took the box from his hand and threw it in the trash. When she turned around, she turned into Knox's waiting arms.

"Are you okay?"

She buried her head into his chest and nodded. He kissed the top of her head so sweetly that it almost made her start crying all over again. It was the strangest feeling. She was actually mourning a baby that never was. When she'd seen that the pregnancy test was negative, it had driven home how much she had begun to like the idea of being a mom. No, it wouldn't have been easy to be a single mother, and no, she wouldn't have wanted to trap Knox with an unplanned pregnancy. But in the end, she had *wanted* to be pregnant and now she knew she wasn't.

"Why didn't you tell me?" He rested his chin on her head.

"I didn't know for sure." She put her hand over his heart. "I missed my period but I wasn't sure."

He handed her the balled-up toilet paper so she could blow her nose and then they sat down on the end of the bed together.

"Are you sad that you aren't pregnant? Is that it?" He held her hands in his.

"Actually," she admitted, "I am sad. I don't even know why."

Knox put his arm tightly around her. "Maybe because you're ready to be a mom now."

"Are you ready to be a dad?"

Her husband looked down at her and met her eyes. "With you? Absolutely."

"A woman's fertility drops off a cliff after thirty-five," she told him after she blew her nose again. "That's only a couple of years away."

Knox got off the bed, kneeled down on one knee before her, and held her hands in his. "Why don't we go on a honeymoon, Genevieve? I'll take you anywhere in the world you want to go."

"Anywhere?"

"Anywhere."

The one place in the whole entire world that popped into her mind was the one place she had always wanted to go.

"Paris," she told him. "I want to go to Paris."

"Paris?"

She nodded.

"A cowgirl in Paris? I didn't expect that."

"You said that you would take me anywhere in the world I wanted to go."

"I did. And I meant it." Knox stood up and coaxed her up as well. "If you want to go to Paris for our honeymoon, then that's where we'll go."

Genevieve had never felt more safe or loved as she did when she was being held in Knox's arms. Knox kissed her again—a kiss filled with the promise of so much love to come.

"Maybe we could try for a baby on our honeymoon?"

"My beautiful wife, I'll give you as many babies as you want." Knox pulled her into his body. "And we don't have to wait until Paris. We can start trying for that baby right now."

As good as his word, Knox made all the arrangements for their honeymoon. The first leg of the trip was made by private jet to Paris and they couldn't resist making love over the Atlantic Ocean. After a quick shower, Genevieve slipped back into bed while Knox went to talk to the stewardess about a late-night snack.

"How does chocolate and champagne sound?" Knox opened the door carrying a silver tray.

"Amazing." She smiled at him warmly. "I would say we worked up an appetite."

Knox put the tray on the small table just inside of the bedroom door.

"Would you grab my robe out of the suitcase?" Genevieve climbed out of bed, her arms wrapped around her body. "I'm cold for some reason."

Her husband unzipped the suitcase while she sat at the table and took a bite out of juicy, chocolate-covered strawberry.

"Hmm. This is delicious."

Knox joined her at the table, kissed some strawberry juice from her chin and handed her the robe.

"Look what Xander put in our suitcase." Knox put the old Abernathy diary on the table.

Genevieve slipped her arms into the robe quickly so she could get her hands on the antique diary.

"Why would he do that?" She sat down, holding on to the diary as if it were precious.

"Here's the note he put with it."

Gen took the note and read it. According to Xander, the romantic passages in the diary acted as an aphrodisiac.

With a laugh, she said, "Xander thinks that we help in the lovemaking department."

"Do we?" Knox asked teasingly.

"Not hardly," she reassured him, even though she knew he was teasing. Genevieve carefully ran her fingers over the yellowed and tattered pages of the diary. Holding this diary was like reaching back into the past and touching someone's heart. These were someone's private thoughts—their most heartfelt desires.

"Find anything interesting?" Knox put a glass of champagne on the table near her.

"Yes! As a matter of fact." Genevieve looked up from the pages. "It says here that W's girlfriend was pregnant! That's a huge clue if I've ever seen one, don't you think?"

Knox drained his glass, stood up and took her hand. "I think that I'd rather worry about getting you pregnant."

With a happy laugh, Genevieve abandoned the diary and let her husband take her back to bed.

Knox was a very enthusiastic partner in their attempt to conceive. Genevieve didn't care if they conceived in a private jet or a hotel in Paris or under the stars in a national park. All she cared about was having a healthy baby with the man she loved.

"Have you ever seen anything so beautiful?" Genevieve was sitting on a window seat in their hotel room.

Knox had found them the perfect room with a view of the Eiffel Tower. At night, with the Eiffel Tower lit brightly, Genevieve would sit in the window seat and gaze at that amazing iconic structure.

Her husband sat behind her and pulled her back so she was leaning against his chest. "As a matter of fact, I have seen something that beautiful."

She hugged his arms into her body, so happy to be with this man in the most romantic city in the world.

"I think we should come back here every year," Genevieve mused aloud. "Every year on our anniversary."

"Whatever you want, my love."

She had everything she wanted. It was everything she hadn't even known that she wanted. Genevieve had been so focused on her career that she hadn't considered how fulfilling finding true love with a man could be. Yes, she would always have her career—that was a given— but now she had so much more. She had this man who adored her—and hopefully, someday very soon, she would have a child—a child created from so much love.

Genevieve snuggled more deeply into Knox's arms, her eyes drinking in the lights from the Eiffel Tower. "You've made my dream come true."

"It's only fair that I return the favor."

Knox moved to stand up and she shifted her weight toward the window, wanting to burn the image of the Paris skyline in her brain. Her husband returned and put a small box on the window seat next to her.

"What is this?" She looked up at him in surprise.

"I know you don't like surprises." He smiled at her. "But maybe you'll let me have just this one."

"You didn't have to get me anything, Knox. You've already given me so much."

Carefully, Genevieve unwrapped the paper from the box. Her heart was pounding in the most ridiculous way when she opened the lid. Inside of the box, nestled in black velvet, was a sparkling diamond ring.

"Oh, Knox. It's beautiful."

Her husband took the ring out of the box, bent down on one knee with the lights from the Eiffel Tower in the background.

"Genevieve Lawrence Crawford, would you do me the honor of being my wife?"

She took his handsome face in her hands and kissed him. "Yes, Knox. It would be my honor to continue to be your wife."

Knox slipped the ring onto her finger and they stood up together to embrace. "I wanted you to have a real proposal and a real engagement ring. You deserve that."

"I never expected to have a Paris proposal." She twisted her hand back and forth to make her ring sparkle.

"Now you have."

In their elegant hotel room in the heart of Paris, they danced together. Knox played his country music playlist so they could have a touch of home with them.

"Do you think they've ever had anyone dance the Texas Two-Step in this room?" Knox moved her across the carpet.

She laughed the laugh of a woman who was happy and in love. "I don't think so, cowboy."

They danced until they were both tired and thirsty for more champagne. Knox poured her a glass and they toasted each other. Once her glass was empty, her husband went back to kissing her. He couldn't seem to get enough of her lips and she had no complaints. Knox slipped his hands beneath her blouse, his hands so warm on her skin. He kissed her neck, his breath sending chills of anticipation down her spine. She knew where this was leading. Knox wanted her again and she wanted him. It didn't take him much effort to undress her, and soon she was standing in the middle of their hotel room wearing nothing but her new engagement ring.

He lifted her into his arms and carried her to the bed, kissing her all along the way. She lay back in a mountain of soft overstuffed pillows, feeling languid and decadent while Knox disrobed. It was her pleasure to watch her husband, so lean and muscular, in the sparse light.

"You are so handsome." She held out her arms to him.

The moment his hot skin pressed against hers, she moaned with delight. His biceps tightened as he wrapped her up so snuggly into his arms. With his lips on her neck, his hands on her body, it was easy to lose herself in the feeling of this man. Knox pressed her back into the mattress, the weight of his body such an odd relief. She wanted to be joined with him, no waiting, no fanfare—just two bodies becoming one.

He captured her face in his hands. "I love you, Genevieve."

"Oh, Knox," she gasped. "I love you."

Their bodies joined so tightly, their breath mingled, their hands clasped together, it was as if they were making love for the very first time. Every movement, every touch, every whisper of love took Genevieve to a whole new level of joy. Knox took them on a delicious ride, so slow, so sweet, until they were both crying out each other's names. Trying to catch her breath, Genevieve curled her body into her husband's, her head resting atop his rapidly beating heart. They looked at each other and began to laugh at their own incredible luck to have found each other.

"We are so very good at that." She kissed his chest affectionately.

"Yes. We are." Knox rubbed his hand over her arm, his eyes closed contentedly. "I might have just given you a child, Mrs. Crawford."

"Hmmm," she murmured sleepily. "That would be the most wonderful souvenir."

They fell asleep in each other's arms then, both of them spent from a night of eating and dancing and lovemaking. In the early morning light, Knox awakened her with butterfly kisses on her neck. After they made love, they ordered room service and began to plan their day of sightseeing.

"When we get back to Rust Creek Falls, we're going to have to move the rest of my things from the garage apartment to the cabin."

Barefoot and shirtless, Knox joined her on the window seat wearing faded jeans. Her husband had to be the sexiest cowboy to ever visit France.

"And you need to move Spartacus to the Ambling A," he reminded her as he pulled her pajama top down her arm so he could kiss her shoulder.

"Yes." She admired his persistence. For him, if her horse was at the Ambling A, that meant she was officially at the Ambling A to stay. "I will move Spartacus. As soon as we get back."

"Good."

Sitting wrapped up in Knox Crawford's arms, Genevieve realized that for the first time she had managed to win big by losing a wager.

"What do you want to do today?" she asked her husband. "Paris awaits."

"First, I'm going to take you back to bed," Knox whispered lovingly in her ear.

"And then?"

"I'm going to keep you there for the rest of the day."

With a delighted laugh, Genevieve decided it was time to make another wager with her husband. "I bet you can't get me pregnant before we leave Paris."

Always up for a friendly wager, Knox picked her up in his arms and carried her back to bed. "Oh, my lovely wife, I'll just bet you I can."

* * * * *

MILLS & BOON

Coming next month

CINDERELLA'S PRINCE UNDER
THE MISTLETOE
Cara Colter

Imogen could tell Luca's experience with snowballs was limited. The ball was misshapen and did not look like it would survive a flight through the air.

"Yes, Your Highness," she said with pretended meekness, "please remember I'm injured." Then she swatted his snowball out of his hand. Before he could recover himself, ignoring the pain in her foot, she plowed through a drift of heavy, wet snow. She snatched up a handful of it, shaped a missile, turned back and let fly.

It hit him smack dab in the middle of his face.

She chortled with glee at his stunned expression. He reached up and brushed the snow away. But her laughter only lasted a moment. His scowl was ferocious. And he was coming after her!

She tried to run, but her foot hurt, and her legs were so much shorter than his in the deep snow. He caught her with incredible swiftness, spun her around into his chest.

"Oh, dear," she breathed.

"What would an ordinary guy do?" he growled.

Kiss me. She stared up at him. The tension hissed between them.

"Cat got your tongue?"

She stuck it out at him. "Apparently not." Then she wriggled free of his grasp, turned and ran again. And she suspected her heart beating so hard had very little to do with the exertion of running through the snow and what felt like it was a near miss of a kiss!

With the carefree hearts of children, the air was soon filled with flying snowballs – most of which missed their targets by wide margins – and their laughter. They played until they were both breathless. Imogen finally had to stop as her foot could not take another second of this. Though with her hands on knees, breathing heavily, she decided it was well worth a little pain.

He took advantage of her vulnerability, pelting her with snowballs, until she collapsed in the snow, laughing so hard her legs would not hold her anymore.

"I surrender," she gasped. "You win."

He collapsed in the snow beside her and a comfortable silence drifted over them as the huge snowflakes fluttered down and landed on their upturned faces.

Finally, he found his feet, and held out his hand to her.

"We're both wet, we better get at that snowman."

She took his hand. "Before the dreaded hypothermia sets in."

He tugged and she found her feet and stumbled into him. His hand went around her waist to steady her, and he pulled her closer. She could feel a lovely warmth radiating through the wetness of his jacket. She could feel the strong, sure beat of his heart. His scent filled her nostrils, as heady as the mountain sweet crispness of the air around them.

She looked up at him: the whisker-roughness of his chin and cheeks, the perfection of his features, the steadiness in the velvet-brown warmth of his eyes.

They were back at that question: what would an ordinary guy do?

But despite his clothing, he was not an ordinary guy. A prince! She was chasing through this mountain meadow with a prince.

Would kissing him enhance the sense of enchantment or destroy it

Continue reading
CINDERELLA'S PRINCE UNDER THE MISTLETOE
Cara Colter

Available next month
www.millsandboon.co.uk

LET'S TALK

Romance

For exclusive extracts, competitions
and special offers, find us online:

 facebook.com/millsandboon

@MillsandBoon

@MillsandBoonUK

Get in touch on 01413 063232

For all the latest titles coming soon, visit

millsandboon.co.uk/nextmonth

MILLS & BOON
MEDICAL
Pulse-Racing Passion

Set your pulse racing with dedicated, delectable doctors in the high-pressure world of medicine, where emotions run high and passion, comfort and love are the best medicine.

Eight Medical stories published every month, find them all

millsandboon.co.uk

MILLS & BOON

HISTORICAL

Awaken the romance of the past

Escape with historical heroes from time gone by. Whether your passion is for wicked Regency Rakes, muscled Viking warriors or rugged Highlanders, indulge your fantasies and awaken the romance of the past.

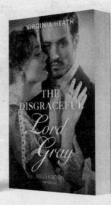

MILLS & BOON

Desire

Indulge in secrets and scandal, intense drama and plenty of sizzling hot action with powerful and passionate heroes who have it all: wealth, status, good looks... everything but the right woman.

JOIN US ON SOCIAL MEDIA!

Stay up to date with our latest releases, author news and gossip, special offers and discounts, and all the behind-the-scenes action from Mills & Boon...

 millsandboon

 millsandboonuk

 millsandboon

might just be true love...